The Lion of Wales: The Complete Series (Books 1-5)

Sarah Woodbury

Published by The Morgan-Stanwood Publishing Group, 2017.

This is a work of fiction. Similarities to real people, places, or events are entirely coincidental.

THE LION OF WALES: THE COMPLETE SERIES (BOOKS 1-5)

First edition. January 14, 2017.

Copyright © 2017 Sarah Woodbury.

ISBN: 978-1393393344

Written by Sarah Woodbury.

To Everyone Who Believes

Book One: Cold My Heart

Cold My Heart

BY THE AUTUMN OF 537 AD, all who are loyal to King Arthur have retreated to a small parcel of land in north Wales. They are surrounded on all sides, heavily outnumbered, and facing near certain defeat.

But Myrddin and Nell, two of the king's companions, have a secret that neither has ever been able to face: each has seen that on a cold and snowy day in December, Saxon soldiers sent by Modred will ambush and kill King Arthur.

And together, they must decide what they are willing to do, and to sacrifice, to avert that fate.

Cold My Heart is the first book in *The Lion of Wales* series.

Chapter One

TO ARCHBISHOP DAFYDD:

We must speak of the evils wrought upon us by my nephew Modred and his Saxon allies, how the peace formerly made has been violated in all the clauses of the treaty, how churches have been fired and devastated, and ecclesiastical persons, priests, monks and nuns slaughtered, women slain with children at their breast, hospitals and other houses of religion burned, the Welsh murdered in their homes, in churches, yes at the very altar, with other sacrilegious offences horrible to hear...

We fight because we are forced to fight and are left without any remedy ... I do not ask for your blessing in these last endeavors, only your understanding.

Arthur ap Uther,
King of Wales and Lord of Eryri
November, 537 A.D.

"GET OVER HERE, MYRDDIN!"

I urged my horse across the clearing, through the ankle-deep snow and towards Gawain, the captain of my lord's guard. He resembled a greyhound, whip-thin but muscled, his grey-streaked hair held away from his face by a leather tie at the nape of his neck.

"Sir," I said.

Gawain pointed to a stand of pine trees some hundred yards away on the other side of the Cam River. "What do you see?"

At thirty-six, after a lifetime of soldiering, my eyes weren't what they used to be. I stared anyway, trying to glimpse what Gawain had noticed. *Christ! It can't be!* Cold settled into my belly. "The branches are moving." I glanced at Gawain. "Didn't our scouts check those trees?"

"Yes." The word hissed through Gawain's teeth. "They did. I saw to it myself."

"The company must move now. It isn't safe here." I forced myself to remain calm instead of shouting the words at Gawain as I wanted to.

"No, it isn't," Gawain said. "I said as much to the king before we began this journey."

"Maybe he'll listen now."

"I'll speak to him. For your part, take four men—Ifan, Dai, two others. Clear out those trees. I don't care how you do it." He clapped a hand on my shoulder, punctuating the command.

"Yes, sir."

I directed my horse towards the north, riding past the church, St. Cannen's, that squatted in the middle of the clearing. An up-and-coming half-Saxon lord, Edgar, son of King Arthur's youngest sister, had sent a letter asking to discuss the transfer of his allegiance from Modred to Arthur. That his overture was genuine had always seemed unlikely, yet Modred's war had gone on so long that Arthur felt he had to grab any chance that came his way, on the hope that he could shift the balance of power in his favor. Recent victories had given us real hope that we might prevail, but if those trees held Saxon soldiers, then the king was going to die, along with all of his men. Including me. He'd walked into a trap from which none of us would escape.

"Ifan!" I waved my friend closer.

He spurred his horse to intersect mine. "What is it?"

"Mercians," I said. "Possibly."

Ifan, as pale as I was dark such that a man could mistake him for a Saxon, had campaigned beside King Arthur even longer than I. He didn't ask for details. Once I'd collected several more men, we circled behind the church, heading for the ford of the River Cam on the northwestern edge of the church property. The trees along the river shielded us from the field beyond. Once across the Cam, however, we left their cover.

"Shields up," I said—and just in time. An arrow slammed into Ifan's shield and then, a moment later, into mine.

"Back, back!" Ifan wheeled his horse to retreat down the riverbank. "We'll have to go around!"

But before we'd ridden halfway across the river, a company of Saxon cavalry burst from the woods to the west of the church. A quick glance revealed their considerable numbers—more than the eighteen men the king had brought to the rendezvous. Along with a few of our compatriots, who reacted at the same instant, we raced to intercept them, splashing through the water and back into the clearing. Our numbers wouldn't be enough to turn them aside, but as I met the first Saxon sword with my own, I put our chances from my mind.

I slashed my sword—once, twice, three times—before my horse stumbled, a tendon severed by a man on the ground. I pulled my feet from the stirrups, leaping free in time to meet the advancing sword of yet another Saxon. He glared through his visored helmet, a thick, red beard the only part of his face I could see.

"Retreat!"

The call came from behind me. I almost laughed. *Retreat where?* The church had little advantage in defense over the clearing. Admittedly, I'd last seen Arthur standing alongside the priest in the nave near the altar. In the back of my mind, I'd held onto the hope that if he made his last stand inside, even a heathen Saxon would be loath to kill my king before the cross.

I ducked under the Saxon's guard and then burst upwards, one hand on the hilt of my sword and my gauntleted left hand on the blade. I thrust my weapon at his mid-section, forcing it through his mail armor. I pulled the sword from his body, and he fell. Then I turned and ran full out for the front of the church, hurtling past the small knots of men battling between me and the front door.

But the king had already left the safety of the nave. A pace from the church steps, Arthur faced two men at the same time. The king had twenty years on me yet fought like a much younger man. He slashed his sword at one Saxon soldier and then snapped an elbow into the face of the other. Blood cascaded from the man's nose.

I launched myself at the second Saxon soldier, driving my shoulder into his ribs and sending both of us sprawling. Hardly pausing for breath, I pushed up on one knee and shoved the tip of my sword beneath his chin. Helmet askew and blood coating my surcoat, I stood, spinning on one heel, determined to defend my king to my last breath.

Except King Arthur had already fallen, overcome by a third knight coming late to the fight.

6

Aghast, I drove my sword into the man's back just as he raised his arms for a final strike at the king. As the Saxon died, I knocked him aside and turned to stand astride the body of my lord. Even if it meant my death, I would gainsay anyone who dared come against me. But as my sword met that of the next Saxon warrior, the back of my head exploded in sudden pain from a blow I hadn't seen coming. Barely conscious, I fell across the failing body of King Arthur.

Chapter Two

2 November 537 AD

NELL SURGED UPWARDS from her pallet, disturbed far more by the shouts echoing through the stone corridors of the convent than by the abrupt ending to the dream. It felt real every time she dreamt it, but once awake, she acknowledged it for what it was: a dream, a *seeing*, if such a thing were possible, and a weight around her neck since she was a girl. Arthur ap Uther was going to die a little more than a month from now at the hands of the Saxons. A man she knew only as Myrddin—a man she'd *lived* for more nights than she could count—would die with him. And Nell had no way to stop it.

The shouts came clearer now. Thrusting her heavy braid over her shoulder, Nell pulled on her habit to cover her night shift, adjusted the thick wool around her waist more comfortably, and slipped into her boots. She slid through the cloth doorway that separated her room from the hall. As the infirmarer and a senior member of the convent, she had her own cell, separate from the dormitory where the novices and younger nuns slept.

"What is it?" Nell reached out a hand to stop Bronwen, a blond-haired, blue-eyed initiate who was far too beautiful to have chosen this life at such a young age.

Unfortunately for her, she was heiress to extensive estates, and her uncle had seen to her speedy incarceration in the convent after her father died. The old abbess wouldn't have allowed it, but all discipline had broken down since the Saxon invasion of Anglesey, which had followed hard on the heels of the abbess' death.

"Soldiers!" Bronwen said. "They came to the door, and the watchman let them in. The Saxons are coming!"

Dear God. They'd been foolish to think their lone convent could escape the Mercian barbarism that had become so common in recent months. Lord Modred's soldiers had pushed King Arthur's forces out of every haven but his last stronghold in Eryri, or Snowdonia as the Saxons called it. They would overrun all Wales if Arthur died as her dream promised. Once upon a time, that moment had resided in the impossibly distant future. Not anymore.

Bronwen made to run, but Nell still held her arm. "Not that way. Did you see Sister Mari?"

"Yes. In the dormitory."

Nell nodded. "Good. Tell her I said to gather as many of the girls as she can. If we can get to the chapel, we can bar the doors from the inside. Bring them quick as you can. Remember—the chapel, not the church. From the shouts outside, the Saxon soldiers are already there."

"Yes, sister," the girl said, Nell's evident calm easing her fears.

Nell released her, and Bronwen ran back the way she'd come. The Saxons hadn't penetrated the convent this far as yet. Sister Mari was not only a good friend, but she was reliable. She would come. Meanwhile, Nell needed to discover what had happened to the abbess, who had left her room. Nell hiked up her skirts and trotted down the stairs towards the common areas of the convent. As Nell arrived in the dining hall from a back entrance, having already searched the warming room and the scriptorium, two sisters spoke to one another, alone and in quiet voices, near the main door a dozen yards away. Her abbess' posture was as if nothing untoward was happening in the courtyard beyond.

"What are you doing here?" Nell ran up to them, heedless of decorum or her dignity. "We must flee!"

"Lord Wulfere told me to wait here for him, and he would explain everything." Abbess Annis' eyes were wide and guileless.

"And you believed him?"

"Of course," she said. "He told me that his soldiers merely needed to commission a quantity of our foodstuffs."

"Commissio—" Nell broke off the word as a man flung open the door to the dining hall. Tall and dark, with a bushy black beard that obscured his face, Wulfere, the commander of the Saxon forces on Anglesey, strode towards them. He towered over Nell, who was slightly less than middle height for a woman. His heavy boots left a muddy track across the floor, evidence of the unrelenting rain that had fallen over the island during the last week.

Wulfere had set up his camp to the southwest of the convent, in preparation for the moment Modred allowed him to cross the Menai Strait and attack King Arthur's seat at Garth Celyn. The *Traeth Lafan*, the Lavan Sands, had served as a crossing point of the Menai Strait for millennia, but the waters in the Strait were unpredictable and treacherous, even to those long accustomed to their moods. To counter that unpredictability, the Saxons had built a bridge of boats, a hundred of them lashed together and anchored at both ends. Wulfere was waiting for Modred's signal to cross.

Meanwhile, he amused himself the best he could. *Apparently, now, with us.*

"Madame Abbess." Wulfere spoke in butchered Welsh and Saxon and gave Annis a slight tip of his head. "Thank you for your hospitality."

Annis simpered back, the loose flesh around her mouth giving way to a vacant smile. "It is our honor to serve Lord Modred, our rightful king, in whatever way we can."

Nell bit her lip. King Arthur had no heir, and whispers had begun already that when Arthur died, stability under Modred and his Saxon allies was preferable to the chaos that would inevitably ensue as Welsh stakeholders fought among themselves for Arthur's crown.

"Are you mad?" Nell kept her voice low and even, so Wulfere wouldn't react to the tone, if not the words themselves.

"It isn't just foodstuffs they want!" Sister Ilar chimed in, for once supporting Nell's position. "They've turned Queen Gwenhwyfar's coffin into a horse trough!"

"It is our duty to bring peace to Anglesey," Annis said.

"Do you object, sister, to assisting those in need?" Wulfere asked Nell. "Are not my soldiers as much God's children as any other men?" He gazed at the three women, amusement in his face, and although Nell wanted to stare him down, she didn't dare defy him. Annis might be blind to what was happening in her convent, but Nell was not. It was time to leave. Annis wouldn't act, so it was up to Nell to stand in her stead.

"Excuse me." Nell curtseyed to both Wulfere and Annis and backed away. Just as she turned towards the side door that led to the cloisters, a number of Saxon soldiers came through the door behind Wulfere. Nell didn't wait to see what they wanted.

I can't believe she just opened the convent to them! How could she betray us so? But Nell knew how it was possible. In an effort to quell what the Church viewed as a convent of too-independent women, Archbishop Dafydd had appointed an un-ambitious innocent to lead them. For all that Annis was approaching her fiftieth year, she knew nothing of men, the world, or anything in it. Nell was not so naïve.

She closed the door to the dining hall. It had no lock, but since the cloister could be accessed by four other entrances, it would have been futile to try to stop the men from reaching it. They hadn't found it yet, but perhaps that was because the church and food stores were keeping them occupied. They would ransack them and then turn their attention to the women. The Welsh were hardly more than animals to the Saxons, and they treated them as such.

11

Nell was relieved to see Bronwen and Mari, a cluster of sisters in their wake, hustling towards the chapel from the dormitory entrance. Nell intercepted them at the chapel door. "Thank the Lord you've come!" She grasped Mari's hand and squeezed it, trying to convey her relief and reassurance.

Mari leaned forward and spoke low, so as not to alarm the other women. "What's happening, Nell?"

Nell let the rest of her sisters file inside the chapel before replying. "The worst. I must see to those in the infirmary. Some might be well enough to travel with us. Perhaps I can hide the rest."

"I'll come with you," Mari said.

Nell shook her head. Mari's eyes were too wide, and her hair had come loose around her shoulders, a match in color to Nell's, although Mari's red-tinged strands were shot with grey. "No. Stay inside the chapel. Without you, the younger sisters will fall to pieces. Bar the door until I get back. If I don't return within a count of one hundred, you must go with our sisters into the tunnel beneath the crypt."

"I can't leave you!"

"You can and you will." Nell's heart pounded in her ears but she fought the rushing sound and the panic, determined to hide her feelings so as not to upset Mari further. Mari was soft-hearted, which is why she mothered the younger novices, but not one to take charge. There was no one else to lead if Nell didn't. "But I hope you won't need to."

Without waiting to see if Mari obeyed her, Nell dashed towards the entrance to the infirmary, situated at the very rear of the complex and isolated from the rest of the living quarters by a narrow passage, in case a quarantine was ever necessary. The sisters could access the room from the herb garden beyond, and Nell had a secondary thought that her sisters could flee that way, if the tunnel proved impassable.

Nell pushed at the thick oak door to the infirmary and froze on the threshold. Hell on earth stared her in the face. Blood ran from the beds to the floor, soaking the undyed wool blankets a deep red. The half dozen sisters who'd lain under her care, along with the elderly sister who watched over them at night, had been murdered as they slept. The far door that led to the outside world bumped against the inner wall, moving in the gusting wind. Beyond, darkness showed. She couldn't risk escaping with her sisters that way, not with the men who'd done this so close. Nell stared at the carnage, then spun on her heel and fled back to the chapel.

Mari had disobeyed, hovering in the doorway to wait for Nell's return. "What is it?" Mari asked when Nell reached her.

"They're dead." Nell pushed Mari into the chapel, even as she looked over her shoulder at the first Saxon soldiers spilling into the cloister, torches blazing in their hands.

"You there!" A soldier said, in Saxon.

"Hurry!" Mari's voice went high.

Nell slammed the door shut and dropped the bar across it. As more shouts filled the cloister, she faced the other women. Mari stood three paces away, taking in huge gulps of air, her hand to her heart. Nell's lungs refused to properly fill with air either.

A young voice piped up from the rear of the group. "What about the rest of our sisters?"

Someone thudded a fist on the door. "Open up!"

Nell set her jaw and grabbed a candle from a shrine to St. Tomos before pushing through the small group of women and girls. "We can't help them." She led the way down the steps into the crypt, trotting past the ancient tombs, the voices of the soldiers fading behind them the deeper they went.

King Arthur had commissioned Llanfaes Abbey upon the death of his beloved wife, Gwenhwyfar. Her grave lay in the church, which the Saxons were sacking even now. The chapel was older, far smaller, and had served the people of Anglesey since Christianity came to the island, back when the Romans ruled it. Rather than pull the chapel down, King Arthur had constructed his abbey around it—and refurbished the Roman tunnel that ran beneath it, and which matched the one underneath Garth Celyn.

Some might have said that the king was overly cautious to have expended so much effort on the chance that a hidden escape route might one day be needed. As far as Nell knew, none ever had, either here or at Garth Celyn—at least, not until today. Given the actions of the Saxons over the last month, King Arthur was proving not only cautious, but prescient.

Maybe he *saw* too.

The convent itself sat a hundred yards from the edge of the Menai Strait, so that King Arthur could look across the water to the spot where he'd buried his wife. A current of air bringing the smell of damp and mold wafted over Nell as she approached the entrance to the tunnel. The near constant autumn rain on Anglesey, coupled with having built so close to the sea, meant they couldn't stop the water from seeping between the stones.

"Here it is." Nell came to a halt in front of a blank wall.

"Here what is?" Mari peered over Nell's shoulder at the unadorned stones.

"The entrance," Nell said. "I need more light."

Someone raised a torch so it shone at the wall. Nell handed her candle to Mari and then pressed both hands on a rounded stone at waist height. With a scraping sound, the door swung open on its central pin, revealing darkness beyond. The tunnel that led from the crypt stretched north, under the protective wall of the convent and beyond.

"We have to go inside?" Bronwen said. "What if there's no way out! We'll die in there!"

14

"The dark can't hurt you," Nell said. "Saxon soldiers most definitely can."

"But how do we know—"

Nell grabbed Bronwen's arm. She'd never thought of Bronwen as one of the more outspoken novices, but that was proving the case tonight. "Because all the sisters in the infirmary are dead, slaughtered as they slept. I don't want that to happen to you!"

"But Lord Modred wouldn't—"

Nell cut her off again. "It's time to grow up, Bronwen. All of you." Nell gazed at the face of each girl in turn. "It doesn't matter if you support Lord Modred's claim to the throne, or King Arthur's resistance. Both sides have committed atrocities in this war. Do you want me to list all the religious houses the men out there—and others like them—have sacked? The villages they've destroyed? The women they've raped?"

Bronwen shook her head uncertainly.

"If you don't want to be one of them," Mari broke in, "I suggest you do as Sister Nell asks."

"Yes, sister." Bronwen kept her eyes downcast.

Nell turned away; she didn't think it was her imagination that her sisters gave her more space now than before. It wasn't their fault they didn't know what went on beyond the walls. Many of them had lived at the convent their whole lives. At fifteen and newly married, she'd been as ignorant and innocent as Bronwen. But Nell had come to Llanfaes as an adult, ten years ago at the death of her husband and her two little boys, four year old Llelo and infant Ieuan.

She'd seen—and she'd *seen*—what men could do.

Once inside the narrow passage, Nell let the others file past her, Mari in the lead still carrying the candle. Nell then pulled at the door and allowed it to close with a gentle *click*. Her shoulders sagged in relief that they were safe, at least for now. At worst, she was wrong about Wulfere's men, and Annis could administer to Nell whatever penance she chose for leading her sisters astray and into the wild in the middle of the night. As unpleasant as that might be, Nell wished for it.

But she wasn't wrong. The scent of smoke, from a source not as far off as she might like, drifted from the chapel through a crack underneath the door, pulled into the tunnel by the open air at the far end. Without further hesitation, Nell hefted her skirts and trotted after Mari.

"Are we almost there?" Mari asked when Nell reached the front of the line of women.

"It isn't much farther," Nell said. "Before her death, Abbess Alis entrusted me with the secret of the tunnel. As soon as the Saxons landed on Anglesey, I came here to make sure the tunnel hadn't collapsed. That was some months ago, of course."

Mari nodded, and then said, her voice so low Nell could barely make out the words, "Do I smell smoke?"

"I fear they are firing the chapel," Nell said.

"Why would they do that?" Mari said, and then answered her own question before Nell could, her voice flat and accepting. "Because they couldn't open the door. They think we're still inside."

Nell canted her head, agreeing, though not wanting to give more emphasis to Mari's guess than that.

But Mari wasn't finished. "Without this tunnel, our choice would have been to die, or to surrender to the soldiers."

"Llanfaes is an abbey patronized by King Arthur," Nell said. "Wulfere sees nothing wrong with leaving no one alive to remember it."

A hundred steps later, they turned a corner, and the tunnel began to slope upwards. Mari's torch reflected off the wooden beams that supported the roof and then finally shone on the trap door that led to one of the Abbey's outlying barns.

"This is it?" Mari said.

"Yes." The height of the tunnel had shrunk to just above Nell's head. With the flat of her hand, she pushed up on the square of wood, three feet on a side, which loosened and then popped free with a snap.

Nell froze, but after a count of ten, she couldn't see or hear anything amiss. She shoved the cover to one side and grasped the edges of the opening. With a boost from Mari and another sister, she pulled herself out of the tunnel and into a sitting position on the floor of the barn.

Hay lay scattered about in the stall in which she found herself. While the hay loft above her head was full, the horse stalls were empty. They used this barn only at harvest time and when the overflow from the Abbey's visitors was such that there was no more room for equine guests in the Abbey's stables. Nell got to her feet and walked to the far wall. Hidden in plain sight among the tools and farming implements was a short ladder. She removed it and brought it back to the hole.

"I hope we'll be safe here for the rest of the night." Nell looked down on Mari's upturned face. "Let's get them into the loft."

IT WASN'T QUITE LIGHT when Nell slipped through the barn door. It creaked, and the wind banged it back against the jam, stilling Nell at the noise. Then she reminded herself that the entire barn was a half century old and patched here and there with scraps of wood or wattle and daub, when using wood seemed a waste of resources. A little creaking and banging was a given.

She'd left Mari in charge of their sleeping sisters, every one exhausted from the events of the night. As the sky lightened, Nell had noted smoke rising from the convent a half-mile away and had felt obliged to discover what had passed there in their absence: to see if the soldiers had left, and if any of her sisters had survived.

Mari had begged her to stay, fearing for her life if she went out, but Nell thought that daylight might bring some measure of security—that the soldiers wouldn't risk attacking a woman on the open road. To be safer, she'd removed her habit and traded it for a patched-together dress and cloak from one of the younger nuns-to-be who hadn't yet committed to her vocation.

Nell hadn't wanted to sleep anyway, although she hadn't told Mari why. She was afraid that the dream of King Arthur's death would come again, and she couldn't cope with seeing it—not with what had happened to her sisters—not with the power of the Saxons so evident. Admittedly, it took far less strength to overpower a convent than to kill a king, but to live through one horror only to dream another immediately after was more than Nell could bear just now. At least with her sisters, she'd taken action. That she could find a way to help King Arthur seemed as out of reach now as it ever had.

A bird chirped to Nell's left, a cheery counterpoint to the staccato of her heart. She gazed across the brown fields, harvested this autumn to the advantage of the Saxons instead of the Welsh, since the soldiers had captured the island in early September, intending to deprive the mainland of food. The convent continued to smoke, wisps spiraling skyward in the murky dawn. Nell braced herself for the effort—more emotional than physical—and set out towards what had been her home.

A short time later, she circled around to the east of the convent and crouched in the grass, screened from the entrance by a fence and blackberry bramble. The front gate of the convent sat wide open, revealing churned earth and grey stone beyond. From the looks, the Saxons hadn't fired the church itself, just the inner chapel which Nell couldn't see from her present position.

What she could see were several bodies sprawled in the dirt, two inside the gatehouse and a third ten paces from Nell's hiding place. That body lay face down in the mud. Nell assumed this sister was dead along with the others until the woman moved a hand. Nell sprang to her feet, sprinted the distance between them, and fell to her knees beside the woman. She turned her over to reveal Ilar's battered face.

Ilar opened her eyes. "Nell." She raised her hand to touch Nell's chin and then dropped it.

"What—?" Nell stopped. It was pointless to ask what had happened. Any fool could see it.

"Annis is dead. All the others," Ilar said. "I thought you died in the chapel."

"We used the tunnel. Mari and some of the novices are safe in the barn this side of Coed Mawr."

"Coed Mawr?" Ilar lifted her head as if she wanted to stand and come with Nell; as if she hadn't bled out through the long gash along her right side. "No—" She fell back and moaned, rocking her head from side to side.

"What's wrong? 'No'—what?" Nell grabbed Ilar's shoulders, wanting to shake her, but her hands came away bloody. She stared at her fingers, and then at Ilar's face. Ilar had closed her eyes again.

"They know of it." Ilar just managed to get out the words. "Annis told Wulfere about the tunnel—" Her head sagged to one side, spent.

Nell put a hand to Ilar's neck. Her pulse faltered and then stopped. Nell sat back on her heels, straightened Ilar's dress, and wiped her hands on the damp cloth of the skirt. Her stomach rebelled to know that even though no trace of blood remained, she could still feel it on her fingers.

Swallowing hard, she pushed the thought away. She had no time for a more proper remembrance and rose to her feet, searching the landscape for any sign of Wulfere's solders. *Why did I leave the barn? They'll have no chance without me!*

No movement caught her eye, either at the convent or in the distance, but then—*There! Along the road!* A company of Wulfere's men rode northeast, away from their camp and towards the spot where Nell had hidden her companions.

"No!"

Nell screamed the word. Knowing it was useless, that she'd never reach the barn in time, but unable to stop the cry or her tears from tumbling down her cheeks, Nell ran back the way she'd come. She stumbled and sobbed through the muddy fields and stands of trees, only staying on her feet over the rough terrain because she couldn't bear not to—until reason reasserted itself.

She pulled up, having run two-thirds of the distance back to the barn. Breathing hard, as much from horror as from the exertion, she rested her cheek against the smooth bark of a willow tree, cool against her flushed face. She tightened her arms around the slender trunk, holding on for dear life, and gazed across the last two hundred yards to the entrance to the barn.

She had led her sisters to safety, only to abandon them to their fate. The completeness of her failure overwhelmed her as Wulfere's soldiers hauled the helpless girls and women out of the barn, arms wrenched behind their backs. When Wulfere's men had pillaged and burned the convent the night before, the majority of the women they'd encountered had been older or weakened like those in the infirmary. These were more to their liking.

Her sisters' screams echoed across the fields and into her ears; Nell sank to her knees in the long grass, her arms around her waist and her head bowed. She couldn't help them nor watch any longer. She leaned forward and sobbed.

Chapter Three
4 November 537 AD

"GET OVER HERE, MYRDDIN!"

I urged my horse across the clearing, through the ankle-deep snow and towards Gawain, the captain of my lord's guard. He resembled a greyhound, whip-thin but muscled ...

"I FEAR THE WEATHER will turn worse this evening." Lord Aelric tucked his fine, grey cloak closer around himself. "You'll have a cold ride home."

Myrddin blinked at the man, his breath choking him, trying to recover from the sudden shift in perspective. He gritted his teeth, stunned by the dramatic transition from dream state to consciousness. The vision of his defeat at the church had come so clearly to him, passing in front of his eyes with such intensity that he'd forgotten where he was. That had never happened to him before.

"Rain in the lowlands; snow in the hills," Myrddin said, in Saxon, thankful that Aelric hadn't noticed his inattention.

The battle had occurred only in his mind—in a flash of understanding—and hardly ten heartbeats had passed in the real world in the time it took for him to fight and die inside his head. Myrddin took in a deep breath to ease his pounding heart. The vision had been clearer and more *real* than any he'd experienced before. Myrddin knew, even if he was loath to admit it, that his dreams pressed on him more every day. They were getting worse—not to mention more demanding in their urgency that he *do* something. Yet as little more than a journeyman knight in the king's company, he didn't know what that something might be.

He maintained his seat on his horse, Cadfarch, and rode between the two grey standing stones that marked the pass of Bwlch y Ddeufaen. This was the highest point on the road that led from Garth Celyn, King Arthur's seat on the northern coast of Eryri, east to Caerhun and then across the Conwy River into the part of Gwynedd controlled by Modred. They'd reached the high moor, long since denuded of trees, but the windswept countryside provided a magnificent contrast to the mountains behind them and the sea in the distance. Rain was normal for Wales this time of year, and every time of year for that matter, but it had abated today.

Myrddin's answer satisfied Lord Aelric, who continued to saunter down the road with Myrddin, their horses at a steady walk. Three other knights followed. Myrddin hadn't spoken to them since he'd led them out of Garth Celyn, and they'd been content for him to entertain their master.

"I've never liked passing among the pagan stones," Lord Aelric said, once the stones lay behind them and the company had headed down the hill towards the Conwy River valley, still green in places despite the imminent winter weather. "I'll suggest that Lord Modred pull them down in due course, once your king has bowed to the inevitable."

He shot a glance at Myrddin, a sneer on his lips. Lord Aelric was baiting Myrddin and waited to see if Myrddin would respond to his arrogance. Aelric had no qualms about speaking his mind and keeping any Welshman in his place, one far below his. Myrddin kept his face expressionless.

As he'd just reminded himself, Lord Aelric was counselor to Modred, and Myrddin was a middle-aged warrior, worn around the edges from a lifetime of warfare and rough living. From an impoverished, if noble, beginning, he'd risen among the ranks of

Arthur's company. Thanks to his reckless courage as a young man, King Arthur had knighted him after a battle in his twenty-fourth year. At the time, it had served to increase Myrddin's devotion to him. Since then, that devotion had been tempered by a certain, frank realism. Twenty years of war—and dreams of death—did that to a man.

"The populace will object, my lord," Myrddin said, his voice mild.

Aelric sniffed, indicating what he thought of the populace. Myrddin smoothed the mustache that grew along each cheek, less flamboyantly than many a Welshman's but still of considerable size. Then it struck him that in his dream, he no longer wore it. *Had that always been the case?* Myrddin had dreamt the fight so many times he'd memorized it. Or thought he had.

Twenty miles later and after hours of stilted conversation—such that Myrddin feared he'd bitten right through his tongue in his attempts to contain what was in his mind—the road connected to another one running north/south, which would take Aelric the remaining miles to Denbigh. By the time they reached the crossroads, the sun had nearly set. Although Aelric urged Myrddin to continue on to Denbigh Castle, he declined. His king had given him his orders and they didn't include dinner in Modred's hall—in a castle that a few weeks ago had belonged to Arthur's brother, Cai. That Cai had been more treasonous than not over the years was beside the point, since he again fought at King Arthur's side. Myrddin didn't think he could have stomached any more of Aelric's company anyway.

The troop of men flowed around Myrddin without a second look. As they disappeared around a bend, he gazed after them, unseeing. The first time he'd had the dream of the king's death—and his own—he'd been no more than twelve. At the time, he'd come awake shocked and alert, with his heart racing, although part of him had thrilled at the vision of the future, of battle, and that he'd fought for Arthur.

He'd had the dream perhaps a dozen times between twelve and twenty. Fifteen years ago, however, the dreams had begun to change, becoming darker in intent, richer in color, and yet more stark, the white snow standing out against the blackness of the forest. They'd also grown more detailed, more urgent and, unfortunately, more common.

Lost in thought, Myrddin drifted to the edge of the road and into the trees that lined it. Cadfarch willingly cropped the grass that crept between the stones, unconcerned when Myrddin dismounted to leave the reins trailing. The war horses in Wales were bred smaller and more versatile than their Saxon counterparts so as to more easily navigate the rocky and uneven ground on which the Welsh lived and fought. Many a night Cadfarch had slept outside rather than in a stable.

At first, Myrddin sat on the edge the road, his knees drawn up. Then, as darkness descended, nearly complete since clouds covered the sky from horizon to horizon, he lay on his back and stared upwards into the nothingness.

Over the years, Myrddin had learned to push the dream away, denying it, even as it dogged his steps. Yet, because it had come so much more frequently in the past year, every week certainly, sometimes every day, he could no longer ignore it or take it as casually as he wished. Just two days ago, Myrddin had downed enough wine and mead to blind a giant in hopes of heading off the vision, only to awaken halfway through the night in a cold sweat.

Even as he pushed the events of December 11th aside, going about his business as if that day wasn't fast approaching—as if the dream was just a dream—he'd finally begun to admit the truth.

It wasn't just a dream.

Myrddin focused on the leaves above his head. Who was he to *see* like this? He was a nobody. His mother, the orphaned daughter of a landless knight, had lived as a lady-in-waiting in the household of a minor Welsh lordling. She'd birthed him out of wedlock. The Welsh ignored illegitimacy provided a father acknowledged his offspring, but Myrddin's mother had died at his birth before she revealed his father's identity. Consequently, he grew up an orphan in the lord's house, living off the scraps of the high table and grateful to have received even that.

At the same time, Myrddin was Welsh. It was in his blood to *see*. Didn't the priests speak often of the native saints, whose visions had led them on despite the death and despair that surrounded them? Myrddin snorted under his breath at that thought. He might be many things, but a saint wasn't one of them.

Myrddin could have lain beside the road the whole night, his limbs growing stiff from the cold ground despite the warmth of his wool cloak, if a woman's scream hadn't split the air and forced him back to life. The depth of fear in her cry carried her panic through the trees to where he lay. Myrddin was on his feet in an instant. He threw himself onto Cadfarch's back, turned him in the direction from which the sound had come, and urged him forward.

Myrddin couldn't see a damned thing in the dark, but Cadfarch's eyes were more capable than his at night. The horse raced unerringly along the road at a gallop, his head pushed forward and his tail streaming behind him, while Myrddin pressed his cheek against the horse's neck.

Ahead, off the road in a cleared, grassy patch, a torch flickered, revealing the shapes of three people hovering over a fourth. The woman hadn't screamed again, but she writhed on the ground before them and even managed to lash out with her foot at one of the men, who cursed aloud. "St. Dewy's arse! I'll teach y—"

But the man didn't finish his sentence. As Cadfarch's hooves pounded on the stones of the road, the three men rose to their feet and turned to look at Myrddin. One reached for his sword, but the other two men were unarmed, having strapped their weapons to their saddlebags in preparation for molesting the woman.

Myrddin raised his sword and swung it at the armed man, who stupidly chose to stand his ground and catch Myrddin's sword against his. The force of Myrddin's blow threw him backwards and, before he could recover, Myrddin flung himself off Cadfarch to land hard in the grass.

Without pausing for breath, Myrddin slipped his sword under the knight's ribs. The blade slid in easily since, while the man may have worn a sword, indicating his high status, he'd neglected his armor this evening. Perhaps, like his companions, he thought he'd have little need of it, and it would only hinder him in his carousing.

Myrddin pulled the sword from the man's midsection and looked around for more men to fight, but the other two were already away. Well-horsed, and in train with a third horse, now masterless, they raced north along the road to Rhuddlan, preferring an ignominious departure to facing down an armed and angry knight.

The woman crouched in a ditch where she'd come to rest, her hands in front of her mouth and her eyes wide and staring. The dress she wore might once have been fine but the men had ripped the fabric from neck to waist, revealing her shift. At least no blood marred the front. Her eyes were shadowed but Myrddin didn't know if the cause of that was the torchlight or men's fists.

"It's all right." He spoke in Welsh, guessing at her nationality. "You're safe."

"I never thought—" she began in the same language, and then stopped, swallowing hard. "I didn't think anyone would come."

"I heard you scream." Myrddin took a step nearer and though the woman shrank from him, she didn't run away.

Moving slowly, as if she were a wild animal rather than human, Myrddin put a hand under her elbow and urged her to stand. Once upright, the top of her head didn't even reach his chin. Then he stepped back, thinking to keep his distance so as not to frighten her.

"Let me take you home." Myrddin checked the road. No sign remained of the men who'd run but that didn't mean they weren't close by, waiting for a second chance. It made sense to hurry.

The woman didn't respond, so he grasped her left arm and urged her towards Cadfarch. Her feet, thankfully still shod in well worn-boots, stuck to the earth at first, but he got her moving and was glad that she wasn't in such shock that she ran away screaming. Myrddin had lived a long and varied life, but even for him that would have been a first.

Myrddin bent to wipe the blade of his sword on the tail of the dead man's cloak and then sheathed the weapon. The torch the men had carried sputtered in the grass beside the man's body, so Myrddin picked it up in order to hold it close enough to illumine both the woman's face and his. The light had almost burned out, but he still needed it. He wanted her to see that he wouldn't hurt her, and he needed her to talk.

"Tell me your name." He lifted the torch high. "And where you're from."

The woman pulled the ends of her torn dress together and then crossed her arms across her chest, shivering in the night air. Myrddin loosened the ties that held his cloak closed at the neck, removed it, and swung it around her shoulders so that the fabric enveloped her. She clutched at it while Myrddin lifted the hood to hide her hair which had come loose from the chignon at the back of her head. He didn't bother trying to find her linen coif.

Myrddin gazed at her and then swept his eyes up and down to take in her appearance from head to foot. It was only then that the woman finally raised her eyes from the ground. They were a deep green that complemented her hair, and Myrddin acknowledged that he was correct in his initial assessment: she was beautiful.

He guessed that she was close in age to him, although she could have been younger. The events of the night had hollowed her cheeks and eyes but time and warmth could reveal her youth. Her diction, given the few words she'd spoken, was that of an educated woman.

"My name is Nell ferch Morgan. And I have no home."

"But you must have once," he said. "Did the Saxons turn you out of it?"

That, of all things he could have asked, garnered a real response. To Myrddin's relief, it wasn't tears she expressed, but anger.

"I come from the convent at Llanfaes, on the Island of Anglesey. The Saxons burned the Abbey to the ground and defiled the grave of Queen Gwenhwyfar." Nell spit out the words, her biting tone compressing all her hatred of the Saxons into one sentence.

"You've come far." Myrddin didn't even blink at the Saxon sacrilege. Their barbarity was well-practiced and well known among his people. "Where is your father? Your family?"

"Dead," she said.

"And the rest of your sisters?"

"I don't even want to say." Nell looked away from Myrddin now, her sadness conquering her anger. "They're dead too. I knew of what the Saxons were capable, but we were too vulnerable—too unprepared for when they came. I managed to hide a few of my sisters at first, but—"

"But what?"

Nell gazed down at her shoes again, and a tear dropped onto the rough, brown leather covering her left foot. "I left them. I thought they would be safe in a nearby barn, so I went to see what had become of the convent after we escaped. To find other survivors. In my absence, the Saxons found them. And—and—" Nell stuttered, swallowed hard, and finished, even if Myrddin already knew what she was going say, "—took them."

Myrddin studied Nell's down-turned head, going over her tale in his mind. The garrison at Garth Celyn had smelled smoke blowing across the Strait, but the fog and rain had been so unrelenting, they'd not known what was happening. Perhaps, in Myrddin's absence, the king had received word of this atrocity today. "You must come to Garth Celyn."

Although she'd expressed no fear of him up until now, Nell paled. She shook her head and took a step back. "I don't think so."

"I saved you," Myrddin said, nonplussed at this sudden reversal. "I won't harm you."

Finding Nell here might be fate—might be one more nail in his coffin—but as the wind whipped the dead leaves from the trees, bringing the strong scent of the sea and the smell of winter, Myrddin felt a change in the air. By lying on the road for longer than he should have, he'd been given the chance to save one life out of all those that might be lost between now and December 11th. Whether by her choice or his, Nell was riding home with him, even if he had to tie her up and throw her across Cadfarch's withers.

Nell must have heard his thoughts. Without warning, she turned on her heel, dropping his cloak in order to hike her skirts above her knees. She headed for the trees that lined the road, running flat out along a trail that only she could see.

"Stop!" *Goddamn it!* Cursing, Myrddin started after her. Where she thought she was going to go in the middle of the night, in Saxon territory, with a torn dress, was beyond him.

29

In the end, it was an unseen root that undid her. She tripped and fell forward onto her hands. When it happened, Myrddin was only a few paces behind, unhindered by skirts and with longer legs. He came down on her back, pressed her to the earth, and grasped each of her wrists in order to hold her arms out to either side and contain her struggles.

"Get. Off. Me!" Nell rocked her hips back and forth.

As Myrddin was half again as large as she and had twenty years of fighting under his belt, Nell hadn't a chance. "I won't hurt you." Myrddin repeated the words again and again until her movements calmed and she breathed heavily into the musty leaves. "My name is Myrddin. I serve Arthur ap Uther."

Silence. Nell put her forehead into the dirt, arching her neck as she did so.

Myrddin could practically hear her thinking, although he couldn't discern her thoughts. "If you were at Llanfaes Abbey, the king must hear of its burning. He would have my head for setting you loose east of the Conwy River."

"Then don't tell him."

Now it was Myrddin who had no answer. Finally, he said, "That I cannot do."

Nell mumbled something into the muddy leaves, something Myrddin didn't catch, other than the word 'men', which she spat into the earth. He eased off of her and then stood, taking a step away from her to leave her free. She twisted onto her back and gazed up at him for a long count of ten.

He held out his hand. After another pause, she grasped his fingers, and he pulled her upright. Then he released her hand before she threw it from her.

"Will you come with me, or do I have to tie you up?"

It was dark under the trees so Myrddin couldn't read her expression, but the words came grudgingly, subdued at last—at least on the surface. "I'll come."

They walked back to Cadfarch, who was waiting where Myrddin had left him. Myrddin swathed Nell in his cloak once again, swung into the saddle, and pulled her up after him. Nell had to rest on the saddlebags. It wasn't the most comfortable seat but would provide her a better cushion than the horn at the front of the saddle.

Her hem rode up her legs, revealing the undyed leggings she wore underneath her dress. She tugged the skirt down before spreading his cloak wide for modesty. Myrddin waited for her to wrap her arms around his waist, which she eventually did, resting her small hands on his belt.

Cadfarch, of course, had no dreams of the future, good or ill, or any thought but when he might rest or next find his feed bag full. Uncomplaining, he pointed his nose west, in the direction of home.

Chapter Four
5 November 537 AD

PAST MIDNIGHT—IN NOVEMBER—IN the rain—was not the best time for riding, even on a road as well made as the one that ran from St. Asaph to Garth Celyn. Nell was grateful for Myrddin's cloak, which protected her from the deluge that fell from the sky. The cloak she'd borrowed from that poor almost-nun had become trampled in the mud and muck beside the road, so Myrddin had left it where it lay. In his generosity, however, Myrddin had left himself open to the elements.

Although Nell wasn't happy to be heading back towards Eryri, she was content for the moment to ride behind Myrddin. He'd driven her attackers away and knew enough not to touch her unless he had to. It was she who was touching him, her arms cinched around his waist, keeping both of them warm and her fears at bay. *How can this be anything other than my fate? Perhaps God isn't done with me yet.*

She'd run from Myrddin before she knew who he was. Because of the dark and that enormous mustache masking his face, it wasn't until she lay under him in the dirt and he'd said his name that she'd recognized him. Once she knew him, the dream of King Arthur's death had come into vivid relief. It felt for a moment as if going with Myrddin would tie her to a future she didn't want to be true. But the truth remained inescapable. He was here, and real, and had saved her. It occurred to her that few girls ever got to meet the man of their dreams.

Myrddin had decided that they shouldn't seek shelter before they reached the garrison at Caerhun, an old Roman fort that King Arthur had resurrected to watch the Conwy River. Even then, Nell wasn't sure how she felt about sleeping in a fort among a dozen unfamiliar soldiers. Fear—of men, of the future—had hounded her all the way from Anglesey to St. Asaph. If anything, mile after mile her terror had grown as she replayed in her head the events at the convent—as if she were living them and dreaming them both at the same time.

But despite what she knew of men, she'd been unprepared for the attack on the road. Without Myrddin, those Saxons would have taken her and killed her. Nell knew it, and her heart caught in her throat every time she allowed her mind to focus on it.

"Tell me again who you are," she said, after they'd ridden five miles, retracing both her steps and his. It had taken her that many miles to steady herself and to be able to speak without a hitch in her voice.

"My name is Myrddin. I serve King Arthur. I escorted the Lord Aelric to St. Asaph and was preparing to return when I came upon you."

That sounded reasonable to Nell. Despite her fears about this journey and the notion of having anything to do with any man, she gave in to relief. At last, some of the horror of the attack drained away, and she rested her forehead between Myrddin's shoulder blades. "Thank you. I haven't thanked you yet."

"Are you much hurt?"

"I was terrified of the men, panicked beyond all measure, but they didn't rape me if that's what you're asking."

The word *rape* twisted on her lips, and she shuddered into Myrddin's back, but she was glad she'd said it. They didn't need to dance around the question now.

"Praise God," Myrddin said. "Why were you traveling that road? Alone?"

"I had a family, once, and sons, although they're all dead now. I've not spent my life behind stone walls. I have no one who depends on me, no husband, and no desire ever to have one again.

With nothing to tie me to Anglesey, I saw no reason why I shouldn't travel where I wished to go."

"In the middle of a war," Myrddin said.

Nell's hackles rose at the distrust in his voice. "What do you mean?"

"What could have possessed you to come so far on your own, unless it was for some nefarious purpose? I saved you from genuine peril, but even spies can find themselves in over their heads when they meet men more devious than they."

"What? You can't mean that." Nell found laughter mingling with a mixture of incredulity and hysteria. Then again, she too could imagine a scenario in which a woman such as she imparted information about King Arthur's movements to the men who attacked her, only to have them decide she'd outlived her usefulness.

"Convince me otherwise," Myrddin said.

Nell thought for a moment, sure she couldn't tell him the whole truth—not about the dreams or that she knew him from them—but she could tell him something. "Our abbess died during the summer, just before the Saxons came. The new one the Archbishop appointed was—" she paused, searching for a word that would convey the truth but wasn't as stark as 'an idiot', "—ineffective."

"What was your role?" Myrddin said. "Were you the prioress?"

"I was the infirmarer."

"So you left. All by yourself."

"I did," she said. "And nearly paid for my stupidity with my life."

"But why were you at St. Asaph after dark?"

"That close to so many fortified towns, I thought I'd be safe."

"You were safe—from masterless men—but not from Modred's men."

"I intended to seek shelter at the convent at Rhuddlan," Nell said. "I had another hour to walk, no more."

"An hour that proved your undoing," Myrddin said. "You should have sheltered instead at the convent at Conwy, south of Caerhun."

"I couldn't—" Nell paused, trying to explain what she'd come to understand, though she'd never articulated it to herself. "You misunderstand. I wasn't going to stay at the convent at Rhuddlan. I can't go back to that life."

"What do you mean?"

"I took vows, I know, but I chose the convent when I was so angry at God I couldn't bear to live with myself anywhere else."

Myrddin barked a laugh. "That doesn't make sense."

"It did to me; it does to me." She paused again. "It wasn't God who burned Llanfaes and killed my sisters."

"Some would say God allowed it to happ—"

Nell cut him off. "Don't be a child. With Llanfaes burned, my sisters dead or worse, not just the Abbey, but my life lies in ashes around my feet. I've come to realize that I will not rebuild it again as a nun."

"The entire world has turned upside down these last months." Myrddin nodded. "A clear path is hard for anyone to see."

Nell could only agree with that. She lowered her voice, less because she was afraid it would carry than because of the force of the emotion behind it. "I hate the Saxons, so much that I fear I'll be consumed by it. Yet I'm afraid of them also, and of the future they represent."

Myrddin's hand found hers at his waist, and he squeezed. "It burns through me too."

The pair rode through the night, the downpour turning into a gentle rain in the early hours of the morning. Still, the rain had soaked them through, and Nell was glad when, in the murky light that preceded sunrise, Myrddin turned into the entrance of the fort.

She checked the sky, thinking that if they left Caerhun shortly after noon, they could travel the ten miles to Garth Celyn before darkness fell. Desperation rose within her at the thought of journeying all the way back to a point just shy of the one from which she'd started. And yet, it allowed her a moment of stark clarity: she would never leave Gwynedd now. She would have to ride this war out in Eryri, in the very castle from which King Arthur governed.

Myrddin brought Cadfarch to a halt. "There'll be provisions and dry cloaks to borrow here."

Nell accepted Myrddin's help dismounting. Once on the ground, however, she hesitated as she looked toward the central hall, some thirty paces away, and then back at Myrddin.

"You can wait for me inside." Myrddin started to lead Cadfarch away.

"No. No, I can't." She strode past him, heading towards the stables.

"Nell—"

She ignored him.

Once inside, Myrddin, still shaking his head at her, unbuckled the saddle bags and lifted Cadfarch's saddle from the horse's back. Nell picked up a brush and began to work at the mane. The motion felt good after the long ride, since her muscles were stiffened and sore.

As she worked, she sensed Myrddin watching her out of the corner of his eye. She could tell he wasn't sure what to say to her, or if he should say anything at all. Nell decided that since she already knew everything a woman needed to know about what kind of man he was—even without the clarity of her dreams—he knew nothing of her, and she would save him from his perplexity.

"My mother died at my birth." She moved the brush to Cadfarch's legs. The horse whickered, absorbing the treatment Nell was giving him. "My father didn't marry again nor have other children." She glanced up at Myrddin, a half-smile on her lips. "He saw no reason why I shouldn't become familiar with horses."

"Where was this?" Myrddin rested his forearm along Cadfarch's back and leaned on it, watching her face.

"In Powys," she said. "My father had a small holding along the Irfon River. We were never wealthy, but lived well for all that."

"And your husband? You said you had one."

"I married at fifteen. My two sons were born and died before I was twenty. Then my husband was killed in a minor skirmish ten years ago."

"So you went into a convent," Myrddin said.

"I did."

"A common enough decision," Myrddin said, "but why so far from Powys?"

"My father had died, and the Saxons had confiscated his lands. I'd lived among them for most of my life, but my father supported King Arthur and had taught me to support him too."

Myrddin tipped his head, acknowledging her admission of allegiance even if he didn't necessarily believe it, especially since she'd now confessed that she'd grown up among the Saxons. They finished grooming Cadfarch, still not in accord, and crossed the courtyard to enter the main building through a side door. It led to a hall, forty feet on a side, with long tables for dining or congregating. The smell of cooking wafted through a far doorway, indicating an adjacent cookhouse.

"Myrddin! You look well!" A stocky man dressed in mail armor much like Myrddin's appeared and strolled towards them. Also like Myrddin, his broad shoulders told her he'd worn that armor for his entire adult life.

"I disbelieve you, Rhodri, since I haven't slept in far too long," Myrddin replied, by way of a greeting.

Rhodri laughed.

Myrddin placed a hand at the small of Nell's back, pushing her forward with him as he walked towards Rhodri. "We need food and rest and a place to dry our cloaks, if we may. We must return to Garth Celyn before the sun sets."

"Done." Rhodri grinned. "As long as you tell me one piece of news."

"That I can do," Myrddin said.

Rhodri seated himself at the end of one of the long tables. Nell pushed back the hood of Myrddin's cloak and went to stand by the fire, her back to the heat. She met Myrddin's eyes across the distance that separated them and realized he'd been observing her, his lips pursed.

"And we need dry clothes," Myrddin said.

"We'll start there." Rhodri looked Myrddin up and down. Myrddin's surcoat was damp, and the water glistened on the links of the mail he wore beneath it. Rhodri jerked his head in the direction of a side doorway. "Help yourself."

Myrddin tipped his head to Nell, and she followed him to a supply room, reached by a narrow hallway. Once inside, she stopped, uncertain, but Myrddin had everything in hand.

"I've been here before." He lifted up the lid of a trunk, which held a variety of garments. "And been in need before."

"I wouldn't mind hearing that story some day," Nell said.

Myrddin shot her a grin and then turned back to the trunk. "This will have to do." He tossed her an ugly, grey dress.

Nell caught it, gazing first at it and then at him. He turned to face away from her to give her a measure of privacy, and tears pricked at her eyes at his understanding. Hastily, she wiped them away before stripping off his cloak and the torn dress she'd worn continually since she'd borrowed it from the young novice whose fate Nell couldn't bear to think on.

When she'd finished, Myrddin swung around to look at her. He grunted. "I don't like it. The color doesn't suit you, and it's too big. We'll find you better at Garth Celyn."

Nell had regained control over herself by then, and she tipped her head in what she hoped was calm acceptance. "At least it's in one piece."

Then, not entirely sure of herself, Nell moved forward to help him remove his armor. Myrddin accepted her touch with equanimity, even as he studied her with his calm, hazel eyes that revealed nothing of the thoughts behind them. When Nell traced with one finger the long scar that ran the length of his lower left rib, Myrddin shrugged. "An errant knife. A small matter, considering what it could have been."

Up close and without his armor, Myrddin proved to be less squat and taller than her first impression, with long rangy limbs, albeit thick shoulders and neck from years of swordplay. For lack of a satchel, Nell wrapped Myrddin's armor in his wet surcoat. A squire at Garth Celyn would polish the links so they wouldn't rust. Then, while Myrddin dressed, Nell busied herself in returning the contents of the chest that Myrddin had upended to their place so that she needn't look at him.

"Ready?" Myrddin adjusted his sword at his waist.

Nell looked up and nodded. Myrddin took his armor from her, tucked it under one arm, and led the way back to the dining hall.

In their absence, the daughter of the garrison captain, a girl just entering womanhood, had put together a meal. Once they were seated, she laid a trencher in front of Nell and Myrddin and set a cup beside it. She assumed they'd share, which was not out of the ordinary, but the action revealed to Nell that both the girl and Rhodri believed that Nell belonged to Myrddin.

Nell gave Myrddin a quick glance, wondering if he knew it too. He was focused on Rhodri, so he didn't see her look, and then Nell decided that an explanation to the contrary was not in order. They could think what they liked. She could stand to ride pillion a while longer.

"I brought Lord Aelric as far as St. Asaph last night," Myrddin said, oblivious to Nell and her concerns. "The discussions between Modred and King Arthur continue."

"So we have a few days' breathing space." Rhodri nodded. To Nell, he added, "Modred, when he attacks Eryri, will come through here."

Nell had known that. Modred's intent was to open two fronts in Eryri, splitting King Arthur's forces and attention. Wulfere would attack from Anglesey, and Modred himself from the east, along the very road on which Nell and Myrddin had traveled. But while the army on Anglesey had been in position for months, Modred had faced resistance all along the border between Mercia and Gwynedd, which had delayed the combined assault.

And then, at the very moment Modred had been ready to advance across the Conwy River, Archbishop Dafydd had intervened. Loath to have uncle and nephew fighting each other and despoiling Wales between them, he suggested the possibility of a peace settlement. King Arthur and Modred had agreed to try, and they'd been working on it since the middle of October. Lord Aelric had merely delivered the latest missive.

"Indeed," Myrddin said. "Archbishop Dafydd has not given up, but I have no news beyond that. We met no Saxons on the road, once we headed west from St. Asaph."

"I'll tell the captain." Rhodri stood and departed, leaving Nell and Myrddin alone with their simple meal of bread, cheese, boiled onions, and sweet mead. Myrddin ate the fresh food with gusto. Nell, in contrast, picked at hers.

"Are you all right?" Myrddin asked between mouthfuls.

Nell pushed the trencher more towards him, having eaten only three or four bites. Over the last two days, it seemed the nervous pit in her stomach had become permanent. It wasn't going to go away just because she was behind stone walls and ostensibly safe. "I'm more tired than hungry."

Myrddin nodded and hurried through the rest of the meal. Rhodri hadn't returned by the time he finished so, once again, Nell followed Myrddin out of the hall. This time, he led her up a staircase to the sleeping rooms set aside for guests. On the floor of one room lay six pallets, each with a folded blanket on its end.

"You may sleep here," Myrddin said.

Nell took a few hesitant steps into the room and then looked to where Myrddin lounged in the doorway, one shoulder braced against the frame. "What about you?"

"I'll bunk in the barracks across the courtyard." He tipped his head to indicate their general direction.

"No!" The word burst from Nell, and once said, she didn't want to take it back.

Myrddin dropped his hands to his sides and straightened. "What?"

"I can't stay here without you. Please don't leave me alone."

Myrddin gaped at her. "You ask the impossible, Nell. I can't sleep in the same room as you!"

"Please, Myrddin. I can't—" Nell choked on the words. Once again, the terrors of the last three days which she'd been holding at bay threatened to overwhelm her, and she buried her face in her hands.

"All right; all right." Myrddin held one hand out to her. "I don't mind. I can sleep anywhere, but you must be certain. Last week you were a nun, and today—" He stopped.

Nell let the silence stretch between them while she took several deep breaths to calm herself. "Today I'm not." She walked to one of the pallets which was set against a far wall and sat down on it, before pointing to a second pallet near where Myrddin stood. "Could you shut the door and move the pallet to block it? If you sleep across it ...?" Her voice trailed off.

After a final, long look, Myrddin nodded. "I can sleep here," he said, although his expression told her otherwise. It was as if he was concerned, curious, and amused all at the same time.

Comforted that he would stay, regardless of what he really thought, Nell lay down, turned her back on Myrddin, and pulled the blanket to her chin.

MYRDDIN BREATHED IN the high moorland air, pungent with the smell of dried grass, juniper, and agrimony, patches of which grew all along the road. They'd reached a point where they were well above the farmlands of the Aber river valley and could see all the way to the Irish Sea. The water showed grey-blue and reflected the clouds that had begun to blow in from the west.

"It's so peaceful up here. Not like down below." Nell removed a hand from Myrddin's waist and gestured towards the island of Anglesey, which squatted in the distance. "The Saxons plan to conquer Eryri next, and we can't let them. They will move soon."

Myrddin squinted, but to him the island wasn't anything more than a grey smudge on the horizon. "Do you know that for a fact?"

"The ferryman at Bangor took me across the Menai Strait on the evening of November 2nd, not long after Wulfere's men—" Nell swallowed and then continued as if the words weren't poisoning her heart, "—found my sisters. But he only helped me because he was ferrying himself across. He felt an ill wind blowing and didn't want to be caught in the middle of it. He didn't intend to return to the island until it was over."

"You speak of Wulfere. Does he still head the Saxon forces?" Myrddin said.

"Yes," Nell said. "The people of Anglesey call him 'the pig.'"

As before when Nell had spoken of the atrocities at the convent, Myrddin sensed that if she were less well-bred, she would have spat on the ground rather than speak Wulfere's name.

"If anyone deserves it, Wulfere does," Myrddin said. "He once chopped off a man's hand for failing to give him his carafe of wine as quickly as he liked."

"May he burn in hell for what he did to my sisters," Nell said.

"I will see to it if I can," Myrddin said. "Before I left yesterday morning, King Arthur's scouts were reporting unusual activity on and near the bridge of boats. When they come, we'll be ready."

In fact, one of Arthur's many spies had told him that Wulfere, frustrated by the delay, had openly commented that Modred lacked sufficient courage to fight King Arthur when it came to it and sought a way to force Modred's hand. Arthur believed that soon Wulfere would order his men across the Strait, hoping for a surprise attack and a swift victory. Instead, he would find himself facing an army of Welshmen.

Myrddin could already hear the screams of dying men, blood coating them and him, taste salt and sand on his lips as the wind spit surf into his face, and feel again the slick thrust of his sword through an enemy's flesh.

Nell and Myrddin made their way out of the mountains and into the forests and fields that surrounded Garth Celyn, following the Roman road. An hour later, they approached the gates to the castle. Arthur's banner—the red dragon of Wales on a white background—flew from the flagpole. A shiver went through Myrddin at the knowledge that if he couldn't stop Arthur from going to the church by the Cam River, that flag might never fly in Wales again. While Myrddin never had any intention of allowing that to happen, it was dawning on him only now—so late he was embarrassed to admit it—that it was *he* who would have to see to it.

The certainty of Myrddin's new knowledge grew in him—along with his fear. All his life, he'd lived as other men had directed and been content with that. His lord pointed, and he went. How was he going to change course so late in life? How was he to face the oncoming storm when he couldn't tell anyone his thoughts, his fears, his *dreams*? How was he to stand his ground against this fate?

A head popped over the battlements. It was Ifan, Myrddin's old compatriot. Myrddin waved a hand.

"You've returned." Ifan rested his forearms on the wooden rail at the top of the wall so he could see Myrddin better. He raised his eyebrows at the sight of Nell but didn't comment, for which Myrddin was grateful. Through the arrow slits, the shadows of other men paced along the wall-walk.

"You expected something different?" Myrddin said.

Ifan laughed. "When one rides among the Saxons, one can never be too sure of one's safety." He lifted his chin. "The garrison at Caerhun is secure?"

"It is," Myrddin said, "and the mead excellent."

Ifan snorted laughter and waved them in as the guards below pushed open the gate.

Two torches in sconces lit the front of the gatehouse. Garth Celyn was much more a fort or manor house than a castle, for all that a high palisade surrounded it. It perched on a slight hill overlooking the farmland and sea to the north and had a line of sight in all directions so the defenders could see the Saxons coming before they reached the castle—in order to give them time to flee.

Which they would need to do since Garth Celyn wasn't defensible. It lacked both the height of most of King Arthur's bastions and the elaborate ditch and rampart construction that were mandatory for flatland castles. It did contain many buildings, including a great hall and kitchen, behind which sat a two story house with many rooms for guests. A barracks lay near the gatehouse, along with the armory, chapel, and craft halls.

At Nell's convent, the tunnel which King Arthur had repaired had been intended as an escape route for early Christians who'd worshipped under an edict of death when the Romans ruled Wales. Garth Celyn, in turn, had two tunnels. One headed north, leading to the sea, and the other emptied into a meadow near Aber Falls. A grown man could walk easily along the underground passages.

Myrddin's stomach clenched at the thought of Nell navigating the tunnel underneath Llanfaes Abbey, leading her sisters to what she hoped was safety, only to find that her Abbess had compromised her safe haven. Such courage was rare, even in a soldier. He would not have expected to find it in a nun. *Or rather, former nun.* That she'd asked to share a room with him at Caerhun still stunned him. They'd slept apart, but nobody else knew that. He still couldn't believe she'd wanted it.

Nell's arms clenched Myrddin's waist.

"What is it?" He hoped his thoughts hadn't influenced hers. When she didn't answer, he added, "There's nothing to fear."

"I—" Nell stopped. "I am not at home here."

"You worry needlessly," he said. "The king will not hold the news of the Saxon depredations against you."

Once inside the walls, Myrddin dismounted onto packed earth, dryer than at Caerhun thanks to today's limited sunshine. Looking around, Myrddin was pleased to be a part of the bustle and activity of the castle. Nell caught him smiling.

"I see soldiers." She pulled her cloak close around her and put up the hood. "I see war. Death. You must see something different."

Myrddin surveyed the courtyard. Three men-at-arms slouched near the smithy, waiting for their horses to be reshod. A handful of men watched two others wrestle by the stables, and a host of peasants—servants in the kitchen and the hall—moved in and out of the huts that sat hard against the palisade. A boy holding a stick urged a pig towards its stall while another ran towards Myrddin and reached for Cadfarch's reins.

"My lord!" he said. "All is well?"

"It is, Adda." Myrddin tousled his hair. "I'll be in to see Cadfarch later."

"Yes, sir."

Nell watched the exchange through narrowed eyes. "You are a knight," she said, as if there had been some doubt on that score.

"I am." Myrddin turned to look at her, surprised she hadn't known it.

She wrinkled her nose at him. "I should have guessed it since you were charged with the welfare of Lord Aelric. But you traveled alone ..." Her words tapered off.

"And my cloth is poor, for all that I wear mail armor. I know. I have the look of a man-at-arms but, in truth—" he spread his arms wide like a bard preparing to sing a paean to Arthur, "—I'm an impoverished knight." Myrddin laughed and tossed a small coin to Adda. "We do what we can with what we are given."

Nell didn't respond, still embarrassed perhaps, so Myrddin grasped her elbow and steered her towards the great hall. Despite her fears, she would have to speak to the king about the events at Llanfaes and the desecration of his wife's grave, as well as confirm that the populace on Anglesey believed the Saxons would move across the Strait soon in hopes of striking here, at Garth Celyn.

The guards who watched the entrance to the great hall pulled open the eight-foot doors at the top of the steps to allow Myrddin and Nell to enter. A wave of warmth enveloped them, along with that familiar musky smell of damp wool, herbs, and humanity. Nell relaxed beside him. Often in winter, it was cold enough to see one's breath in the hall, but darkness had fallen and it was dinner time, so men—eating, drinking, and talking—filled the room. The fire in the hearth blazed.

King Arthur sat at the high table at the far end of the hall, as was his custom, and it was so warm next to the fire that he'd shed his cloak. Two senior advisors flanked him: Geraint, one of his foremost commanders, and Bedwyr, his seneschal. Bedwyr was a grizzled, thick-set man of Arthur's generation who had supported Arthur since the early days of his reign. It was Bedwyr who kept order in Eryri when Arthur was away. More often than not, the two of them could communicate without speaking.

Myrddin stared at the king, feeling the familiar punch to the gut that seeing him alive after having dreamed of his death always gave him. Myrddin was sick of the dreams, terrified of the waking vision he'd had the day before, but there was no denying that King Arthur had acted as the beacon of Myrddin's existence in a world gone mad for his entire adult life. Myrddin may have long denied the future that stared him in the face; he might not know what it was going to take to change that future; he didn't know how he was going to become other than he was. But he knew, somehow, that he had to find a way. *By God, there has to be an answer here.*

As Myrddin urged Nell forward, pushing through her hesitation, Arthur noted their appearance and beckoned them to him.

"You'll do fine," Myrddin said. "Come."

And then before his eyes, Nell transformed herself from an insecure girl to the confident nun who'd taken charge of her sisters when nobody else would. She straightened her shoulders and raised her chin, as aware as Myrddin that if everyone in the room hadn't noticed them at first, they watched them now. They threaded their way between the closer tables, many of which had been added because of the increased number of men in the garrison, and then walked up the aisle to King Arthur's seat. They stopped before him. Myrddin bowed while Nell curtseyed.

"Myrddin," Arthur said, with that particular, dry tone he often used when addressing him.

"My lord."

"Lord Aelric reached home safely?" King Arthur's eyes tracked from Myrddin to Nell.

"He did," Myrddin said. "Neither he nor Lord Modred can have any cause for complaint."

"And yet, you come back in one piece." A smile twitched at the corner of King Arthur's mouth.

"As you say, my lord," Myrddin said. "For all Modred's perfidy, the Archbishop would countenance nothing less."

"Good." The king turned to Nell. "Welcome to Garth Celyn, madam. I remember your attention to the details of my wife's funeral." Somehow it didn't surprise Myrddin that Arthur recognized her. She was certainly memorable, and he was the King of Wales. It was his job to remember faces. "I confess I'm concerned to see you here, however, dressed as you are."

"The convent is dissolved, my lord," Nell said.

At Nell's words, the air in the room turned icy cold as Arthur's face darkened. When the king became angry, he rarely shouted or overtly lost his temper. Instead, he grew still, and his voice became lower and deceptively gentler.

"Tell me," he said.

Nell enumerated the Saxon crimes while King Arthur sat, still and silent, his jaw clenched and bulging. Once she finished,

Myrddin took the liberty of stepping into the conversation before King Arthur's heart gave out.

"My lord," Myrddin said. "Nell has heard that the Saxons intend to cross the Strait soon."

"So my scouts at Penryhn tell me," Arthur said. "Modred attacks me despite the peace."

"Or rather, Wulfere does." Myrddin swallowed hard at his impertinence in correcting his king. Still, he didn't take it back. The man he needed to be wasn't going to come without taking risks.

"Certainly." Arthur looked amused rather than angry at Myrddin's interjection. "But we aren't supposed to know that, are we?"

"Modred isn't interested in peace, regardless of what Archbishop Dafydd hopes," Geraint added, from Arthur's left.

Nell shifted from one foot to another beside Myrddin, and he glanced at her. Her clear skin had gone paler than its usual white. Concerned, he slipped an arm around her waist to support her.

Also noting her distress, Arthur waved a hand to one of the ladies of the court who came forward. He looked into Nell's eyes. "You have a home here as long as you want it. If there is anything you need, ask Myrddin, here, or Bedwyr."

"Yes, my lord," Nell said. "Thank you."

To the lady, the king said, "See to our guest's comfort."

Meanwhile, Myrddin murmured under his breath to Nell, "Will you be all right?"

"I'm fine." Nell looked up at him, placed a hand on his chest, and patted once. Myrddin released her, and Nell followed the girl without wavering on her feet. When she reached the door to the stairs, she looked back at Myrddin, her face expressionless. Myrddin liked that even less than her show of weakness. He nodded his encouragement, and she disappeared.

Myrddin focused again on King Arthur.

"I hope you weren't planning to sleep tonight," the king said.

"No, sire. I slept at Caerhun."

All the way down the road from the standing stones, Myrddin had been thinking of the battle that was to come. He'd drawn his sword yesterday in defense of Nell, his muscles moving in their remembered patterns, but it wasn't the same as a real battle. Myrddin hadn't fought in formation since the brutal defeats of the previous year after which King Arthur was forced to surrender far too much to Modred and confine himself to his lands in Eryri. Myrddin wasn't glad to have killed a man yesterday, but it gave him confidence that he still knew how to fight, even at thirty-six. He needed to get his head in the right place if he was going to be the knight upon whom his companions depended. Myrddin touched his sword at his waist, reassured at its comforting weight.

The king had turned to speak to Bedwyr. Because King Arthur had not yet dismissed him, Myrddin remained standing on the opposite side of the table from the king's seat, trying not to shift from one foot to another in awkwardness and impatience. Geraint, who'd remained on Arthur's left throughout the conversation, winked at Myrddin in a rare moment of camaraderie, his eyes alight with amusement. Myrddin bowed gravely back.

Arthur spoke another few words, so low Myrddin didn't catch them due to the hubbub in the room, and then turned to face front again. He sat, slouched a bit in his chair, an elbow on the armrest and a finger to his lips, and studied Myrddin. "There is something different about you today."

Myrddin straightened his shoulders. "Is there?"

"How many years have you served me?"

"Since I became a man." In Wales, legally, that was at the age of fourteen, although Myrddin was sixteen when he'd come to Garth Celyn and marked his transition from boy to man by that event.

"Perhaps it's time you found yourself a wife," he said. "Or I did."

Myrddin blinked. Nothing could have been further from his mind than that. Wives brought complications that were of no interest to him, both because of the commitment involved and the logistics.

"A wife, my lord?" Myrddin said. "I have no means to support a wife."

"You should," Arthur said. "In the new year, I will see to it that you are rewarded for your long service."

Myrddin's mouth fell open, just managing not to choke on his astonishment. "Thank you my lord."

Arthur smiled and waved his hand, dismissing him.

Myrddin bowed, still stuttering his thanks, but King Arthur's attention was again directed elsewhere.

Geraint grinned at Myrddin and raised his cup in a salute. Myrddin shook his head, simultaneously bemused and appalled. Ever since the dreams had started to come more often, he'd felt himself haunted. He'd kept himself aloof and behind walls no woman could penetrate. He'd long since tallied the cost of letting anyone get inside them and found it too high.

But now here he stood, among friends he would trust with his life, in the hall of a king for whom he'd willingly die—and had died in his dreams more times than he could count—surrounded by people he knew so well he could recite their conversations for them. Whether he liked it or not, the walls were down. He was going to save them all or die in the attempt.

With nothing left to say, Myrddin turned away, heading towards a vacant spot at one of the long tables next to where Ifan sat. Ifan moved over to give Myrddin room and handed him a trencher for his food.

"What was that about?" Ifan said.

Myrddin poured a cup of wine, studied it, and slaked his thirst, while reminding himself not to drink too much. He wasn't interested in drinking himself into a stupor. Perhaps if he paid closer attention to his dreams, and dreamed more often, he could identify the necessary details that might give him an edge in saving Arthur. "The king plans to find me a wife. Or, rather, he told me that he would choose one for me if I don't do the deed myself."

Ifan had been taking a drink as Myrddin spoke, and now he choked and laughed at the same time, spraying wine across the table. Coughing, he used the tail of his cloak to dab at his mustache. "A wife?"

"That's what he said."

Shaking his head, Ifan set to his food once more, laughing between bites. "Myrddin with a wife."

Myrddin shook his head too and laughed into his cup. Unless he could find a way for Arthur to live into the new year, the entire discussion was moot. It was comical to even think about.

A wife. Instead, how about a life that lasts beyond the next thirty-six days?

Chapter Five
6 November 537 AD

NELL STOOD ON THE RAMPART above the gatehouse to watch Myrddin, Lord Geraint, and all but a handful of the men-at-arms from the garrison ride away from Garth Celyn in the pre-dawn hush. Myrddin rode among the leaders, just to the left of Gareth, younger brother to Gawain and a commander in his own right. It was a promotion of a sort, apparently, which hadn't gone unremarked among those left behind.

Anything that distinguished one man from another—any time a man found favor in the sight of King Arthur—invited comment. The soldiers rode without torches, relying on the moon, which at present was playing hide and seek with the clouds, to guide them.

Damn all men for their love of battle! Even as Nell thought the words, she knew they weren't fair. This war had been forced on King Arthur by his brother, Cai, who'd attacked one of Modred's strongholds without consulting Arthur. Modred had used the ill-advised assault as an excuse to restart the war. The son of one of Arthur's many sisters, Modred had set his sights on Wales from the moment he realized that he was the eldest nephew and that Arthur wouldn't produce a son of his own.

Modred's Mercian allies, on the other hand, had never forgiven Arthur for defeating them at Mt. Badon on his way to controlling all but the most southern regions of Wales. For thirty-seven years, they'd carried that grudge. By now, even the most die-hard apologists didn't doubt that Arthur's choices were few: to fight, to die, or to give up his patrimony entirely.

Nell braved the wind until the hoof beats faded, and in the end was the last silent watcher left on the battlement. The men had long since disappeared into the mist when she turned away. It was

53

strange to be so alone, with no responsibilities, no young novice to reassure or put to work depending on the hour, no religious office to keep. Even odder was the preponderance of men around her. Few women with whom she might associate lived in the castle—and should she even try, with hardly more than a month to live?

At the entrance to the hall, King Arthur himself greeted her and gestured that she should sit with him while he ate his meal. He'd watched his men ride away and, contrary to her expectations, didn't retire to his office rather than allow his people the opportunity to observe how he handled the next few painful hours as they waited to hear the results of the battle.

Arthur took a sip from his goblet and put it down. "Anxious?" he said, once she'd seated herself on his left.

"Yes," she said, opting for the truth. She felt confident that Myrddin himself, if he was to fight for the king in a month's time, would live through this battle. The king had few enough men, however, that the loss of even one was a tragedy.

"Myrddin is one of my best men," Arthur said. "There is less need to worry for him than for most. He was a stripling when he came to me and I took him on despite the reservations of some of my counselors. I have not regretted it."

"He isn't as young as he once was," Nell said.

"Nor are any of us." King Arthur laughed. "But there will be little enough fighting today, by my reckoning."

"How's that, my lord?" Nell said.

"The Saxons don't know the Strait like we do," Arthur said. "We take its temperamental nature for granted, but Wulfere has been here only a few months. He's arrogant. His bridge won't hold."

"I admit it's an odd construction," Nell said. The Saxons had hammered boards over the top of their bridge of boats to make a makeshift road from Anglesey to the Eryri shore. Even at low tide, the bridge wouldn't provide an easy crossing.

"It isn't so much the bridge as the tides," King Arthur said. "Slack water occurs four times a day: an hour before high or low tide. Geraint has a boy severing the ropes and pins that hold the bridge together. Either the Saxons will discover the damage, it will delay them past the optimum time to cross, and they'll have to wait six hours for the next slack water—or they won't, and the bridge will break and dump them into the Strait."

"And you think that Wulfere plans to cross this morning?"

"Yes. That's what the girl said."

Nell had been shredding the remains of a biscuit that a servant had set in front of her, but now she glanced at the king. "Girl?"

The king gazed at her over his goblet and then set it down. "Wulfere's new doxy wasted no time in finding a way to reach one of my men. The Saxon camp is full of followers and hangers on. I have at least a half-dozen men and boys among them who confirm her information."

Nell's heart was in her throat, and she could barely speak around the lump. "Do you know her name?"

King Arthur's forehead wrinkled in thought, and then he turned in his seat. Bedwyr was just entering the hall from the corridor beyond, and Arthur called to him. "Do you know the name of the new girl in Wulfere's bed?"

Nell clamped her teeth together, trying to keep them from chattering at the casual way he asked the question. The girl meant nothing to him other than a source of information.

"Bronwen, I think." Bedwyr didn't even break stride as he headed towards the front of the hall.

"That's it." Arthur snapped his fingers. "Bronwen."

Nell placed her palms together and her fingers to her lips, but instead of prayer, she was trying to force back the tears that threatened to spill from her eyes. All she could think of was the sweet-faced, sharp-tongued girl Bronwen had been in the convent. Now she was Wulfere's whore, but she had enough courage behind that pretty face, despite everything she'd endured, to defy him and spy for Arthur. "That poor child."

"Bronwen is a common enough name," Arthur said. "You don't know that she was one of your sisters."

"Perhaps," Nell said, pretending for Arthur that she wasn't certain, although inside she was certain that she knew the truth.

"And what about you?" Arthur said. "You're welcome to stay at Garth Celyn as long as you choose. Your knowledge of herbs and healing is a most welcome addition to the castle, but surely you would prefer a different haven? Perhaps the convent in Gwytherin?"

"No, my lord," Nell said. "Thank you, but I can't go back to that life."

"Can't," Arthur said. "Or won't?"

Nell tipped her head in acknowledgement of the king's distinction. "Won't."

"As you wish." Arthur kept his voice level, but she could tell he was curious as to her reasons. Fortunately, he was too polite to ask.

Just then, Bedwyr reentered the hall, leaving the front door wide. The sun had risen, and the grey dawn filtered through the scattered clouds, revealing an unusually clear day that would give the watchers a fine view of the Menai Strait and Anglesey beyond.

"My king!" Bedwyr strode towards Arthur. "The Saxons are delayed, but there is no doubt they intend to come today!"

Arthur's eyes lit, and he stood. Nell stood with him.

"Excellent," King Arthur said.

"Will you go to see it, my lord?" she said.

"No," Arthur said. "I will not undermine the authority of Geraint and Gareth. My faith in my men is not misplaced."

That showed remarkable patience. Nell, for her part, couldn't keep still. Instead of trying to tame her emotions, she curtseyed to Arthur and left the hall for the battlements. Nell told herself she was going outside again so she could see what had become of Llanfaes. It wasn't necessarily that she was going to spend the day watching for Myrddin.

The sun shone and the wind was calmer than in the pre-dawn hours, so it was warmer than before. Nell paced along the wall-walk, stopping every few feet to look over the rail at the sea sparkling in the sunshine less than a half-mile away. Penrhyn Castle, Gareth's hereditary estate, lay between Garth Celyn and the bridge of boats, but she could see it in her mind's eye.

Sweet Mary, mother of God, keep him safe! She sent another prayer to Saint Jude, patron saint of fools and desperate causes. And then she laughed because she didn't know if she was praying for Myrddin, or for herself.

WULFERE'S MEN DID DISCOVER the break in the ropes that bound the bridge together. Repairing it delayed them past their intended, early starting time, so it was exactly noon when Wulfere ordered his men to march. It was the perfect opportunity. The Strait was as calm as it ever got.

"Here they come." Ifan broke the expectant silence that had seeped among the men during the long hours of waiting.

"Nervous, are you?" Myrddin said to his friend as they watched the horsed Saxon knights navigate their engineering marvel.

"They'd better make it quick, is all I can say," Ifan said. "I'm tired of sitting doing nothing."

"And your back aches," Myrddin said.

"Worse this week than ever," Ifan said. "Must be this rotten weather."

Although from Myrddin's perspective, the weather wasn't that bad for November. It was just that Ifan was nearing forty and so many years of fighting had given him aches and pains no remedy could ease. Myrddin counted himself lucky that, while his eyes were failing him, his body so far hadn't.

As Myrddin watched, the lead riders cleared the mainland end of the bridge and rode across the sand. Wulfere, one of the foremost knights, was recognizable by his black beard and the matching black plume on his helmet. Nell had shuddered at the mention of his name. Given his composure and presence, Myrddin couldn't blame her.

Myrddin's fellow knights and men-at-arms stayed in the trees on the edge of the beach, waiting for the fifty archers on the hill above them to loose their arrows. Geraint held their fire until the cavalry were almost to the woods and the entire company of Saxon foot soldiers marched on the bridge. Then he gave the signal.

"Fire at the horses!" Geraint's voice carried all the way down to Myrddin's position.

Arrows flew from bows in a hail of metal and wood, turning the beach into chaos in a matter of a few heartbeats. Six of the Saxon horses went down in the first volley. Saxon knights knew about archers, having encountered them in battle with the Welsh many a time (to their loss), even if they hadn't employed any of their own in this venture.

Therefore, instead of retreating, they did the smart thing, which was to charge. Holding their shields high to protect their chests, they urged their horses to close the distance to the woods. Perhaps they thought they'd find safety there. If nothing else, their action ensured that the tops of the trees restricted the archers' angle of fire.

Gareth commanded the cavalry in this battle and took Geraint's words as a signal to move. "Charge!"

The Welsh cavalry came out of the woods in a phalanx, fifty feet wide, Myrddin among them. His heart pounded in his ears, drowning all sound but the relentless beat and making him oblivious to anything but the Saxon soldiers in front of him. *Christ, I'd forgotten!* Directing Cadfarch with his knees because he needed his left arm to hold his shield while his right hand held his sword, Myrddin plowed through the front rank of the opposing force.

His momentum carried him past a knight sporting an ostentatious, red feather on his helmet. When the man swung around to face Myrddin, his horse's hooves sank into the soft sand and threw him off balance. Myrddin slid the tip of his sword along the man's blade and, with a flick of his wrist, disarmed him. Myrddin then shifted the other way. Using his left arm, he hit the Saxon soldier full in the face with the flat surface of his shield.

The man fell, no longer a threat, and the noise of battle broke over Myrddin like an unexpected wave, assaulting his senses. He froze for a moment, adjusting to the cacophony. Above him, Geraint's archers rained their arrows down on the Saxon soldiers on the bridge.

To the east, the Welsh foot soldiers, who'd come out of the trees at the same time as the cavalry, roared, starting their run towards the Saxon lines. Their axes and pikes were raised high and their mouths were open in the universal cry that gives men courage in the face of death. Fewer than half the Saxon foot soldiers had reached the beach. Thus, the Welshmen outnumbered the initial Saxon ranks, and the invaders went down under the onslaught.

Myrddin turned his attention back to the Saxon cavalry and found himself face to face with Wulfere himself. Myrddin clenched his teeth and almost bit off the end of his tongue. This was the one man he'd most wanted to meet—and the one of whom he was also the most afraid.

Wulfere's black beard covered his face from chin to eyes and was split by an unholy sneer. Blood coated Wulfere's sword, and he met Myrddin's blade with enormous force—enough to make Myrddin fear he'd lose his grip on the hilt. They struggled together, neither finding the upper hand but hacking away at each other, all elegance or restraint lost in the desperation of battle.

"Back! Back! Back!" The words came in both Saxon and Welsh as one of Wulfere's captains tried to reach everyone who fought with him. Wulfere might have been doing well, but that wasn't true of many of his companions.

"No!" Wulfere's refusal carried across the whole of the battlefield.

Myrddin took that instant of distraction to launch himself at the Saxon lord and wrestle Wulfere from his horse. Their brief sword play had shown Myrddin what he'd feared—that he would have trouble defeating this man in a straight fight. At one time in his life, he'd relished the fear and power of exchanging blows, but he was no longer interested in trying. Thirty-six wasn't twenty-four.

The two men fell to the ground, Wulfere beneath Myrddin. While the force of the fall had knocked the breath from Myrddin's lungs, the jolt had dazed Wulfere even more, and his confusion allowed Myrddin to rise and straddle him. He stared into Wulfere's eyes. They were fogged and unfocused. The big Saxon moaned, undone by the fall and suddenly human. Myrddin swallowed hard—and with a mighty thrust, forced his sword through Wulfere's armor and into his heart. Wulfere would never rise again.

Myrddin rose unsteadily to his feet. The killing left an acid taste in Myrddin's mouth, but he swallowed it down too. Of all the men who'd died by his hand, this was one he wouldn't regret.

Overall, the battle had been short and brutal. By the time Myrddin looked up, a dozen dead Saxons lay on the sand. The rest had begun the retreat. The Saxon foot soldiers had the numbers to push back at the Welshmen but, at the sight of their horsed superiors passing behind them to the bridge, they turned as one and ran back the way they'd come.

It seemed the entire Saxon army had taken to its heels and was fighting each other to be the first to reach Anglesey. They appeared oblivious to the fact that the Welsh were less dangerous to them now than the water. Following Geraint's orders, the Welsh let them go. They didn't want to get stuck on the Saxon bridge, and they didn't have the manpower to fight them on Anglesey, or King Arthur would have tried it already.

Unfortunately for Wulfere's men, it was by now almost one in the afternoon—high tide—and the most dangerous time to cross the Strait. The bridge of boats bucked and bent from the strain of so many men and horses.

Then, with only an ominous creak as warning, the bridge snapped. The two ends of the break swung apart, moving away from each other at a speed of two and a half knots. The separation occurred so suddenly, few men were able to stay upright. Within a count of five, the Saxon army had fallen into the treacherous waters of the Strait, with just a few men hanging onto the wooden planks, face down and gripping the wood as if their lives depended on it. Which they did.

"By all that is holy, I've never seen the like." Geraint came to stand beside Myrddin, his sword pointed down and blood dripping off it into the sand.

"We could retake Anglesey." Gareth halted on Myrddin's other side. Blood stained his sword too, and he'd lost his helmet at some point in the battle, but he appeared otherwise undamaged. He was a twenty-five-year-old, bachelor knight and a child of a long and powerful lineage. It wouldn't have done for him to die just yet.

"We don't need the lands they hold until the spring planting." Geraint looked past Myrddin to Gareth, his gaze piercing. "And I say that, even with the knowledge that your lands languish in the hands of your cousin."

"He's down." Gareth's voice carried no emotion. One glance showed an iron set to his jaw. It occurred to Myrddin that Gareth might have taken on his traitorous cousin himself. Both men were grandsons of a great warlord who'd been steward to Arthur's uncle, Ambrosius. That family had been torn in pieces by this war, half fighting for Modred and half for Arthur. And this cousin had come down on Modred's side. To his loss.

Geraint nodded. "I will give the order to kill any Saxons who wash ashore." He slapped his hand on Myrddin's shoulder. "You are the king's favorite messenger. Ride to him and tell him of the victory."

"Today is your reward for all those times you've brought bad news." A smile hovered around Gareth's lips despite the grimness of the carnage before them.

Geraint shot Myrddin a grin. "And once again, you've shown yourself in possession of the Devil's own luck. I saw you vanquish Wulfere. It was well done."

"Thank you, my lord," Myrddin said.

His legs moving stiffly in the aftermath of the fight, Myrddin returned to Cadfarch. When he'd leapt from the horse's back to bring down Wulfere, Cadfarch had stayed close by in case Myrddin needed him, unafraid of the smell of blood or the clash of weapons.

Myrddin was glad to see Ifan on his feet not far away, his head resting against his horse's neck.

Ifan waved a hand half-heartedly in Myrddin's direction. "You're off to see the king, then?"

"As I am bid," Myrddin said.

"Better you than me, friend," Ifan said. "I've a mind to lay down right here in the sand."

"You do that," Myrddin said, more glad than he could say that Ifan still lived.

Myrddin mounted Cadfarch and directed him towards the road from Bangor to Garth Celyn, skirting the manor house at Penrhyn to which they'd bring the wounded. They'd lost no more than two or three men-at-arms and a dozen foot soldiers, but many more had surface wounds that could suppurate if they weren't treated. Over the years, more out of chance than design, the doctoring of the company's wounds had fallen to Myrddin, who'd found himself more adept at it than he might have expected. Gareth and Geraint would need every healer of whatever skill today. Myrddin intended to aid the men as soon as Arthur gave him leave to return.

The north coast of Wales was endlessly green, even in the middle of winter. The beauty of it drew Myrddin forward, easing the tension of the battle and draining away the adrenaline that had allowed him to fight it. By Myrddin's calculation, at least a dozen Saxon knights and an equal number of squires had died, in addition to the hundreds of Saxon foot soldiers. It wasn't a staggering total, but would be devastating to Modred, if only because of the knights he'd lost. Many were of his own household, his and Arthur's close kin.

From some distance away, Myrddin spied the towers of Garth Celyn and noted the great number of people atop the battlements. They were watching for him. He raised a hand, knowing they would understand what it meant. If they'd lost, he would have been moving faster—if he'd been able to come at all. As it was, the gates opened while Myrddin was still fifty yards away. He rode inside and was instantly besieged by questions. Myrddin glanced up from his inquisitors to see King Arthur standing on the top step to the hall, Nell beside him.

Myrddin dismounted, trotted to where King Arthur stood, and didn't make him wait for the news. "It is a great victory, my lord. The bridge is broken."

"What are our casualties?" Arthur said.

"Slight," Myrddin said. "Geraint has their names. I do know there were few, mostly among those who were unhorsed or came to the battle on foot."

"Well done," King Arthur said. "That is good news indeed."

Arthur gestured for Myrddin to enter the hall, but Myrddin hesitated to obey. "I must return to Penrhyn, my lord." Myrddin bowed to indicate his continued respect. "Nell and I can help with the wounded."

The king studied Myrddin, eyebrows raised. In the silence that followed, Myrddin realized his error. The man he'd been before St. Asaph would have forsaken the hall for the wounded only when he'd had no choice. He certainly would have taken a drink or two as his reward for surviving another battle, and thought that the following morning was soon enough to take up his duties once more.

"Of course," the king said.

Nell broke in. "I looking through your infirmary earlier, my lord, and made a satchel of herbs and linens in preparation for tending those wounded in the fighting."

"Very well," Arthur said, his puzzlement turning to amusement that Myrddin and Nell had taken matters into their own hands. "You have leave to go. However, I will come as well."

While they waited for the king, Myrddin pulled Nell behind him on Cadfarch again. She didn't resist, and even seemed to take for granted what she'd resisted only yesterday.

"Are you well?" Without apology, Nell had already inspected Myrddin's armor, surcoat, and head for damage, and now she patted down his arms and sides, checking for wounds.

"I took a hard fall with Wulfere beneath me. Otherwise, I am uninjured," Myrddin said. "Although, I find that I am too old for this."

For the first time since they'd met, she gave him a genuine laugh. Myrddin was glad. She'd had little reason for amusement these last two days and there wasn't going to be much smiling in the coming hours. Regardless of the victory, they had injured men, and dead ones, and loved ones to inform of the loss.

Arriving at Penrhyn, Arthur strode up the steps to the hall while his company—with the exception of Nell and Myrddin—stayed with their horses. Gareth met him at the entryway. Wounded men lay spread across the floor of the hall in the same chaos that followed every battle. Myrddin swallowed hard at the sight of so much blood. He never got used to it, and it was probably better that he didn't.

"I have something to show you," Gareth said to the king, minus his customary formal greeting.

Arthur didn't blink at the impertinence but gestured as if to say *lead on!* Gareth turned on his heel and led the way to the back of the hall and then through a doorway on the right. Nell stayed behind, but Myrddin followed, unsure if he should come too but as he wasn't stopped, came anyway.

They entered a corridor that had several small rooms leading off of it. Gareth turned into the first doorway on the left, striding straight through it, but Arthur came to an abrupt halt on the threshold. Myrddin, for his part, just managed to stop before he ran into the king's back. After a few moments of contemplation, King Arthur continued forward, leaving Myrddin hovering in the doorway.

Gareth's cousin, Hywel, lay on a pallet on the floor. He wasn't dead, but didn't appear to have long to live.

King Arthur directed his attention at the wounded man who stared up at him. "I loved your father and grandfather."

"Sir." Hywel's voice was stronger than it should have been given the enormous hole in his midsection. Even if the king gave them the opportunity, neither Myrddin nor Nell would be able to do anything for him.

"I couldn't leave him on the beach."

Myrddin sensed defensiveness in Gareth rather than anger or sadness in his clipped words, but King Arthur didn't remark on the reasons Gareth had brought his cousin to Penrhyn, despite the order to leave no survivors. Given the difficulties among the members of Arthur's own family over the years, he undoubtedly understood them.

"Why?" Arthur aimed his patrician nose at the man on the floor.

Hywel, along with his two brothers, Rhys and Llywelyn, both churchmen, had swung over to Modred's side five years before when Modred had consolidated his alliance with the Mercians and begun pressing his claim to the Welsh throne even though Arthur still lived. That war had ended badly for King Arthur, but not so much that he'd lost his lands entirely. He'd been forced to agree to a treaty with Modred, and subsequently, the brothers had returned to Eryri as if they'd never betrayed Wales. Since then, as one could imagine, their interactions with the king had been stilted, taking place in formal situations where they all avoided speaking to each other.

Hywel attempted a shrug. "My father was the youngest son. Our inheritance wasn't enough for the three of us to share. My brothers and I agreed that if one of us joined Modred, we all would." That didn't explain everything, of course, as Gareth had many brothers too, and he still stood with Arthur.

"How noble of you." Gareth looked down his nose at Hywel, in imitation of the king.

"I can't say it was my first choice," Hywel said, "but Rhys and Llywelyn insisted on it."

"Rhys is a supercilious, avaricious snake and a disgrace to the Church and the cloth he wears," Gareth said, "and Llywelyn is no better. Were they also at Llanfaes?"

"Yes," Hywel said, selling out his brothers without compunction.

King Arthur's face grew even more rigid. Gareth pursed his lips. Gareth's family had entangled themselves into a mare's nest of shifting allegiances, but it looked as if at least one of them was about to be released from his burden.

"Modred bought you with the promise of land?" King Arthur said. "That was enough to sell out your country? To take up arms against your companions and loved ones? Against me?"

"I have a family," Hywel said. "I have to think of them. It is a choice any man would make."

Arthur snorted his disbelief. "Inform me when he's dead." He turned on his heel and strode out of the room before anyone else could speak.

Myrddin had ducked through the doorway and into the room before the king reached him, and now he stayed leaning against the wall in case Gareth had need of him. Myrddin shared the king's loathing for Gareth's cousin. But he'd been a soldier long enough to turn physician, and it was the latter role that prevented him from leaving the room.

Hywel tipped up his chin to look at the exposed rafters that formed the frame of the ceiling. "I don't need your forgiveness," he told Gareth.

"Good, because you don't have it." Gareth had been gazing out the window into the courtyard of his manor, and now glanced over at Myrddin. "You can go."

Myrddin had noted Hywel's glazed eyes, so didn't yet obey Gareth, taking a step towards the wounded man. "I can fetch some wine. He doesn't have to suffer this much."

Gareth swung around to face Myrddin full on. In contrast to the anger in his voice, his eyes showed tears he'd so far refused to shed. "Doesn't he?"

It was strange to see Gareth in this light. He rarely revealed anything of himself. He'd brushed off the betrayal of his cousins like a man would flick a crumb from his shirt. Gareth appeared different to Myrddin today, more emotional and passionately Welsh. *Perhaps I'm not the only one among the king's men who's had an epiphany in the last few days.*

Myrddin countered Gareth's obstinate glare with a calm face and nodded his acceptance of his wishes. "As you say, my lord." Myrddin left the room, although once he passed through the doorway and was out of sight, he froze in mid-stride at a sudden sound emitting from the open door behind him. Myrddin made to return, and then thought better of it. It wasn't Hywel in his death throes that he'd heard, but Gareth, choking back a sob.

"Hold my hand." Gareth's boots scraped on the wooden floor as he crouched beside his cousin.

Myrddin turned away. He could do nothing for either of them.

Chapter Six
7 November 537 AD

"DON'T TURN AROUND, but we are no longer alone," Myrddin said.

He and Nell had worked through day and night but, despite her exhaustion, Nell still had enough wit to glance up from the man she was tending with a smile twitching at the corner of her mouth. "You mean we were alone before? There's two dozen wounded men in front of you."

"Lord Cai is here."

"And you don't like him," she said.

"I grew up under the roof of one of his men, a man named Madoc. My foster brother, Deiniol, still serves Cai," Myrddin said.

"And from the venom in your voice, those are days you'd prefer to forget," Nell said.

Myrddin didn't answer, instead blanking his expression as Cai came to a halt at the feet of the man they were tending. Cai held his helmet under one arm and appeared to have traveled through the night in order to reach Penrhyn at this early hour. Myrddin stood, more comfortable in this lord's presence on his feet, and moved to a spot that half-blocked Nell from Cai's view. He couldn't help it; he wanted to protect her, even if reason told him that for all Cai's perfidy—he'd once conspired to murder Arthur after all—the notion that he presented any kind of threat today was more than ridiculous.

"Will he die?" Cai said.

They all looked down at the man. Myrddin hadn't recognized the soldier as a member of Arthur's company. Cai's presence revealed that he might be part of his household, much as Myrddin's foster father had been and Deiniol still was. "I cannot say as yet, my lord." The title stuck in Myrddin's throat. "It's likely."

The door to the hall swung open, and King Arthur strode across the floor towards his brother. As he approached the group, he gestured to the soldier on the floor. "Your man fought well, I understand."

"So Gareth said." Cai didn't clasp his brother's forearm as would have been customary, and their eyes met for less than a heartbeat before they flicked away. Disconcertingly, Myrddin found Arthur observing him. He hastily half-turned, so as to impose less on the brothers' conversation.

"Why are you here, Cai?" Arthur's voice remained mild, but the question was abrupt.

"I understand that Modred sits at Denbigh," Cai said.

"That is true," Arthur said.

"Those are *my* lands," Cai said. "My castle."

"I've said that we will get it back," Arthur said. "Our recent victory puts Modred in a difficult position, unable to force either the Strait or the Conwy River. When we are ready, we will push him and his Saxon allies out of Gwynedd."

"When?"

"Soon."

"You promised me this weeks ago."

"It was you who lost control of those lands," Arthur said. "From my castle at Dolwyddelan, you have the power to prevent Modred from advancing on us through the mountains. Our southern allies will see that the winds blow our way, and together we will force Modred out of Wales, once and for all."

"You know the solution to our problems." Cai pushed closer to King Arthur, who stood his ground.

"We've discussed this before. Now is not the time."

"Modred must die."

Arthur made an impatient movement with his hand, which Cai ignored, pressing on undeterred. He put his face into Arthur's, so close their noses were a hand span apart. As Arthur was four inches taller, it had the effect of forcing Cai to look upwards, like a boy facing down a man. Myrddin couldn't help listening, although Nell had the modesty to look away so neither man would see her staring. Again, Arthur caught Myrddin's eye for a heartbeat and then answered his brother.

"He is our nephew, Cai. I will countenance no further discussion of the matter."

"Then perhaps you don't have the balls to be the King of Wales," Cai said. "But then we knew that already, didn't we?"

Cai shot these last words at King Arthur in a loud hiss that had the unfortunate effect of carrying throughout the hall. His words sucked all the air from the room. Cai didn't appear to care—and remarkably, was still breathing himself since Arthur had the restraint to keep his sword sheathed and his brother in one piece. Cai shoved past Arthur, knocking into his shoulder as he strode towards the door of the hall.

The offensive—and unfair—comment referred to the fact that, in his long life, Arthur had fathered one child, a daughter, and no sons. As a result, it was either Cai or Modred who remained Arthur's heir, both with two legitimate sons to follow them. Myrddin could understand Arthur's pain. Myrddin himself had bedded many women, but never fathered a child either—or at least none whose mother had named him. In Wales, a bastard was accounted as legitimate if his father acknowledged him. Therefore, nothing could be gained from hiding his identity. No mother would choose it.

Well, except mine.

Arthur didn't turn to watch his brother go, standing as Cai had left him, hands clasped behind his back, legs spread, and staring at the far wall of the hall. An enormous boar's head hung above the fireplace; rumor had it that Gareth and his brother Gawain together had brought it down. Myrddin didn't doubt it.

"You two," Arthur pointed at Nell and Myrddin with his chin, "will return to Garth Celyn." Myrddin turned towards him, surprised, and King Arthur moved closer. "Have either of you slept?"

Myrddin glanced at Nell before shaking his head. That King Arthur could brush off his brother's insults in favor of concern for his own people was one of the reasons he was a great king. It was also one of the many contradictions about him. Depending on whom one talked to, Arthur was worth dying for because of *who* he was and the position he held, or he was an arrogant son-of-a bitch whose regard for his own power was paramount.

He wore his status and dignity with kingly bearing, while at the same time was obnoxiously protective of them. He carried a vision of a united Wales, but had fought and schemed for nearly forty years to hold onto what was his. And yet, despite his faults, there was nobody more suited to ruling Wales than he—and his people knew it. Myrddin knew it.

"You're no use to me exhausted. I want your full report this time, Myrddin." Arthur turned away and began walking towards the front doors. "I understand you were the one who brought down Wulfere."

"Yes, my lord," Myrddin said.

Arthur waved a hand, gesturing to Gareth who'd just come into the hall from the rooms beyond it. "Myrddin is with me."

Gareth nodded.

Arthur marched toward the entry doors, expecting Nell and Myrddin to follow. Myrddin took a long step after him before he noticed that Nell hadn't moved.

Myrddin looked back at her. "He meant you as well."

His comment shook Nell out of her reverie, and she hurried to walk beside him. "I know. But why?"

"I don't even know why he wants me to come," Myrddin said.

"You are a most trusted companion." Nell stated this as a truth.

"Three days ago, I wouldn't have said that was the case."

And that, when he examined the facts, was his own fault. He'd lived no differently from every other man in his position: he fought battles and drank himself to sleep afterwards; he caroused with the other warriors and made love to any woman who'd consent to share his bed. He'd been an oft-chosen messenger for the king, and perhaps Arthur's sudden confidence in him was a natural outgrowth of Myrddin's ability to perform his duties as he asked. Still, Myrddin found it odd that just at the point he was ready to step forward, to take on more of a leadership role than he ever had before, and had practically forced himself upon his betters, Arthur had decided to accept him.

It had been dark in the hall, the few windows letting in glimmers of light. He and Nell had doctored the men by torchlight, so it wasn't until they exited the hall for the courtyard of the manor house that Myrddin realized that the sun had risen and moved well up in the sky. Nell bent her head to inspect her blood-spattered skirt and made an unhappy face. Arthur had already mounted his horse and was surrounded by his escorts. Perhaps he'd been astride when Cai had arrived and taken the opportunity to speak to him while he'd had the chance.

"There will be clothes for you at Garth Celyn," Myrddin said to Nell, mounting when the boy brought Cadfarch to him and hauling her up behind. It was a short ride to the castle from Penrhyn, and as before, they would take the road along the coast, riding down from the heights into the valley and then back up again to the hill on which Garth Celyn perched.

73

Nell wrapped her arms around Myrddin's waist and pressed her face into the back of his cloak. "So much death. How do you live with it?"

"Do I?" Myrddin said. "Is it any wonder that most men drink themselves into a stupor every night, rather than see the faces of the men who've fallen by their hands, or the faces of their friends who died instead of them?"

"You killed Wulfere," she said.

"I did."

Nell sat silent for a heartbeat. "And that man at St. Asaph too. In defense of me."

"Yes," he said. "I've killed more men then I can count and will kill many more."

"How do you live with it?"

"My thinking has changed over the years, Nell. That first man—him I killed with an arrow. We were screened from the Saxons by trees, trying to pick them off one-by-one. It was dangerous work because with an ambush, there is always the fear that the enemy will charge into the wood to find you. Late in the day, I hit a man right through the neck, and he toppled off his horse. I was not alone in that. We killed a dozen more before we retreated."

"And what did you feel?"

"*Nothing*," Myrddin said, "at least not at first, not for hours. It came as a shock to me that killing could be the easiest thing in the world to do. One moment the man was alive, laughing among his fellows, and then he was on the ground, felled by my arrow. At the time, when it first happened, I was so surprised all I could think was, *I did it! That wasn't so hard!* It was the difference between taking a breath and letting it out."

Nell's arms were around his waist, holding on. "And then?" It warmed him that she knew him well enough already to know there had to be an 'and then'.

"And then I woke in the night and couldn't get the man out of my head: watching the arrow hit, watching him fall. One of the men allowed me to sob in his arms. It was only then I realized they all knew, even as they congratulated me, that this was coming."

"How old were you?"

Myrddin's chest rose and fell as he breathed in more of the cold air. "I'd just turned seventeen."

Nell made a sympathetic noise, which Myrddin brushed off.

"And after that?" she said.

"I have killed so many times, Nell, with bow and with sword. At first, even in the midst of battle, I wouldn't expect to actually kill anyone. After that—" Myrddin paused. "After that, I learned to expect it, to admit my regrets, and to understand that I would owe penance for every soul I took. It remains a dreadful necessity."

"That's how you come to terms with the killing?" Nell said. "By telling yourself it's necessary?"

"Yes," Myrddin said.

"You can ask for absolution ..." Her voice trailed off, perhaps because she realized how ridiculous that sounded.

"Absolution is for those who regret their offense and swear they will refrain from committing it in the future. Much of the time, neither is possible for me."

"That's partly why I can't be a nun," Nell said. "I no longer have either the certainty or the grace."

Myrddin pondered that, unspeaking, for another half-mile, at which point, he could no longer tolerate his own uncertainty. If he'd brought a snake into Garth Celyn, he needed to know. "What were you really doing at St. Asaph?" He kept his voice low and deceptively gentle.

75

"I-I told you," Nell said.

"You told me you traveled on your own, but to what end? What haven did you ultimately hope to reach?"

"I—" She stopped. "You wouldn't understand."

"Try me."

"Scotland," Nell said. "I fear King Arthur is going to lose this war, and I will not watch it happen. I will not live in a Gwynedd ruled by Modred."

Those were strong words, forcefully spoken. He'd never heard anyone give voice to his own fears as clearly as this. "And if I were to accuse you again of spying for the man himself?"

Nell took in a sharp breath. And then, unaccountably, she began to laugh. "You really believe that? You still doubt me enough to ask such a question?"

Myrddin didn't reply, and she laughed all the harder, burying her face in Myrddin's back and clutching at his cloak with both fists to keep her seat on the saddle bags.

They'd garnered some curious glances as their conversation had progressed, but with Nell's laughter, the looks turned to open smirks. Myrddin slowed Cadfarch and smiled back at his friends, covering for Nell. In truth, they were both well beyond their prime. Whatever was going on between them—whatever it was—had little import, other than the oddity of Myrddin's interest in any woman beyond a single night. Myrddin's companions turned away, all except Ifan who gave him a knowing smirk before straightening in his seat. Myrddin made a mental note to cuff him upside the head later.

"It isn't funny," Myrddin said.

Nell sobered enough to speak. "Yes, it is."

"You haven't answered my question."

Nell swallowed hard, the laughter gone. "I'm not a spy, Myrddin. Whatever else I may have been or might become, never think that."

Myrddin nodded, somewhat mollified and yet more curious than ever.

When they reached Garth Celyn, men and horses filled the bailey, and they jostled against one another as Myrddin dismounted from Cadfarch. Just as his feet hit the ground, Ifan bumped into his back, unbalancing both Nell and him such that he clutched her to his chest.

"Whoops." Ifan shot Myrddin a wicked grin. "Looks like you don't need the king's help finding yourself a wife after all."

Myrddin froze, even as Nell stiffened too. Myrddin had his arm around her waist to hold her upright, and she turned in the circle of it and poked him in the chest. Her laughter had turned into a more manageable anger. "Wife? What's he talking about?"

Her eyes snapped in her upturned face. Myrddin hastened to appease her. "It has nothing to do with you."

"Then tell me what it has to do with," she said. "You're avoiding the question."

"When we arrived at Garth Celyn—could that only be two nights ago?—King Arthur told me that I appeared different to him. He has begun to trust me more since the war was renewed, and I've earned some honor in his eyes. I'm penniless, as I told you, and he said that he will give me land to support a wife in the new year."

"Myrddin!" Nell's anger melted. "That's quite an offer, especially when he's besieged on every side." Together they observed Arthur's retreating back as he entered the castle's great hall.

"But perhaps a hollow one, too," Myrddin said. "Many battles stand between this moment and that promise. As you yourself said, there is reason to fear for his life and for the future of Wales."

Nell's eyes narrowed, surveying the bailey and the activity around them. "I've lived shut away from the world too long. I should have realized after Caerhun that I couldn't ride or dine or spend any time in your company—any man's company—without causing talk."

Given the trauma of the last few days, as well as her wish (that she'd expressed) and Myrddin's (that he hadn't) never to marry, Myrddin took her comment as his signal to apologize. "I'm sorry, Nell—"

She cut him off. "Leave it. It isn't your fault. Besides, if everyone thinks I belong to you, so much the better. It will give me the freedom to come and go as I please, unremarked. I would prefer to avoid attention from any other man."

"Are you sure—?"

She cut him off again. "I'm long past having any interest in sitting in the solar amongst the other women, Myrddin." Then she looked up into his face. "You helped me before. You protected me before. Will you help me again?"

Oh, yes, I think so. Myrddin nodded.

"Good. I'll find us a place to sleep." She set off for the great hall. Myrddin, leaving Cadfarch once again in Adda's care, followed in her wake, more bemused than surprised. Nell might not be a spy, but she was *something*, knew something, that was out of the ordinary.

Myrddin had a mind to find out what that was.

Book Two: The Oaken Door

The Oaken Door

THE ONSLAUGHT OF MODRED'S forces may have been temporarily halted, but danger lurks around every corner for Myrddin and Nell. Not only do they face treachery on the part of their enemies, but allies—and even family—cannot be trusted. Only by joining forces can they succeed in averting the terrible fate that threatens their king, their country, and their own lives.

The Oaken Door is book two in *The Lion of Wales* series.

Chapter One
8 November 537 AD

"MYRDDIN! GET OVER HERE!"

I obeyed, riding toward Gawain, my captain. At his grim look, I pulled up beside him and reached for my sword—not to fight him, but because he already held his.

"The Saxons are here!" he said.

I squinted in the direction he pointed, but could see nothing beyond movement in the branches opposite. "I'll root them out, my lord."

I gathered my men together and we crossed the creek to the north of the church where King Arthur waited even now to meet with Lord Edgar. I knew it was a trap. It was always a trap. I struggled to turn aside but we rode relentlessly on, across the creek, up the bank, and through the trees. Once we left the protection of the woods, the arrows flew, and Ifan shouted that we must turn back.

"Myrddin! No!" As I charged the Saxon line, a woman screamed. The screaming grew louder, but I ignored it, instead spurring my horse forward, my heart racing. "Myrddin!"

NELL SAT UP WITH A start and her breath came in gasps. She could still see the dream hanging before her eyes like a veil, even as Myrddin sprang from his pallet and moved towards her through the lingering image.

"What is it?"

"Just a dream." Nell put a hand to her chest in hopes that it would ease her racing heart.

"Of St. Asaph?" Myrddin crouched before her.

Nell took in a breath and let it out. "No." She lifted a hand to him, and he took it, warming it in his two larger ones. "Not that. It was one I often have. It's nothing."

"Is it?" Myrddin said.

Nell froze, hearing the change of tone in his voice, and looked into his face. She'd asked that he leave a candle burning in its dish and it still guttered, within moments of going out but still giving off enough light to show his expression. "Yes. Why?"

"You called my name," he said. "Or rather, cried it."

"Oh."

"I'm curious that if it was a dream you've often had, that you would have dreamt of me before you met me."

Nell twitched her shoulders. For so many years she'd longed to tell someone of the dream, but now that it came to it, she couldn't. He would think her—no, know her—crazed. She gazed into Myrddin's face, warring with herself, unable to answer. "It—" She stopped. "I didn't—"

Myrddin sat back on his heels. "It's all right. You don't have to tell me now if you don't want to."

Nell didn't know if that was really better or not. If not for the screaming, he probably would have thought she was dreaming of him in a romantic way but was too embarrassed to admit it. It irked her how wrong that was, but she had no way to fix it. Under his gaze, she forced herself to relax and lie down. But she didn't turn her back to him as she had earlier. Instead, she studied him as he was studying her.

He'd made sure, once she'd found space for them in one of the small, closet-like sleeping rooms in the manor house, that this was truly what she wanted. The room had been empty as they'd entered. He'd closed the door to lean against it while she shifted one of the pallets so it no longer abutted any of the others.

"After this, there's no going back, Nell," he'd said.

Nell had laughed, the sound coming more harshly than she'd intended. "It isn't very nun-like is it?" She arrested her movements to focus on him. "It's better this way, Myrddin. I slept that first night amongst the other women, ten of us strewn across the floor. My dreaming woke them three times. They don't want me there, and I don't want to lie among them."

"I'm not saying it's uncommon," Myrddin said. "It's done all the time. Most of the men here haven't married their women, but none of those women spent the last ten years in a convent. This is going to ruin your reputation."

"Or yours?" She looked up at him, truly worried about the arrangement for the first time. "The king—"

"Cares not a whit," he said. "His concern, like mine, would be for you."

"This is my choice."

"If you say so." He'd gestured to a spot against the opposite wall from where she sat. "I gather my pallet is over there."

"You gather correctly." She shot him a grin. "If another woman catches your eye, just tell me, and I'll make myself scarce."

"Damn it, Nell." He'd turned on her, his hands on his hips. "This isn't funny."

"Isn't it? I have to look at it this way. Otherwise, the only other choice is despair."

Now, Myrddin invoked that earlier conversation. "I know about despair, Nell." He eased backwards onto his pallet. "I didn't realize it at the time, but last night when you spoke to me of it, you weren't speaking just about what happened at St. Asaph, or even Llanfaes, were you?"

"No," Nell said. "Despair is a companion with whom I'm long acquainted."

Myrddin matched her, lying on his side with the blankets pulled to his chin. "I have dreams too, Nell."

Nell nodded, but she still wasn't ready to reveal her true thoughts: *Not like mine, you don't.*

MYRDDIN SLEPT PAST the dawn and awoke, his brain churning, thinking about Nell, knowing that she'd dreamt of him even if she wouldn't admit it. He hoped the dream was a good one, but he somehow doubted it.

Nell's auburn hair cascaded off the edge of the pallet, having come loose from her braid in the restless night. She turned her head, met his eyes, looked away, and then looked back. "Thank you for understanding."

Myrddin sat up. "I didn't say I understood. I just decided not to press you right away. At some point soon, I'm going to ask you to tell me what is going on behind that sweet smile."

"Oh, is that it?" she said, giving him the smile he wanted. "Well, not this moment anyway." She got to her feet. "While you wait, you can help me dress."

Myrddin took that for what it was—a chaste invitation. Well-bred women wore elaborate skirts that scraped the ground, got in the way, and forced women to walk in a mincing fashion. At Arthur's insistence, Nell had given away both the homespun dress which the men had ripped at St. Asaph before Myrddin had rescued her and the coarse dress from Caerhun that blood-stains had irreparably damaged. In exchange, she now wore the fashionable gown of a lady, which was a bit harder to get into.

By the time they arrived in the great hall, it was full of people and rumors. A rider from Modred had arrived, and the inhabitants of Garth Celyn were abuzz with what the letter he carried contained. Myrddin pulled Nell to a seat near Ifan, who (after a knowing look that encompassed them both and what he assumed had gone on between them in the night) shrugged when Myrddin queried him.

"Your guess is as good as mine," Ifan said. "Lord Aelric carried a letter from King Arthur to Modred. I assume this is Modred's response. It won't change anything."

"But with the battle at the Strait—" Nell said.

Myrddin shook his head. "Modred won't even mention it. He believes he has the better of King Arthur. Such is his arrogance that he believes it is our king who is in rebellion and in danger of excommunication. By his lights, our only recourse is to beg for mercy."

"Bollocks to that," Ifan said.

Nell caught Myrddin's eye. "What do you think Archbishop Dafydd has told him?"

"It's what Modred has promised the Church, more like," Ifan said, the same sour expression on his face.

Before they'd finished their breakfast, Gareth appeared at the end of the table. He leaned heavily on his hands, the weight of the world on his back, and looked directly at Myrddin. "The king wants you."

Nell, who wasn't invited, wrinkled her nose in annoyance. Myrddin shrugged back at her and got to his feet. He followed Gareth to the rear of the hall and down the corridor to Arthur's receiving room near one of the towers. When they arrived, King Arthur, Geraint, and Bedwyr were already in the room, along with Lord Cai, whose face was a thundercloud.

Myrddin's eyes narrowed to see him there. He hated the man—all the more after the exchange the day before. Nell, in her former life as a nun, would have told him that it was wrong to hate at all, but when speaking of Cai, anything less than hatred would have been doing him a disservice. The man begged for retribution, but to his regret, Myrddin would never be the one to give it.

Over the years, Cai had betrayed his brother in many ways and by diverse means, even to the point of conspiring with Modred to wage war against Arthur (twice), and an assassination attempt. Whenever Myrddin was in Cai's presence, he avoided looking at him at all and worked very hard not to show his disdain. King Arthur's face didn't reveal what he thought of Cai either, but then, he'd spent a lifetime masking his feelings towards his brother. Most of the time, it was best not to think on it, especially since Cai stood beside Arthur once again.

Myrddin had arrived in the middle of a conversation between Cai and Arthur, and this time they were in agreement, even if both were angry. Arthur stood, his back to the other men in the room, staring out at the heavily falling rain which was making muddy puddles in the courtyard.

Cai, for his part, snorted his derision, disgust in every line of his body. "At least he offers you a plot of land in Mercia in exchange for Eryri. Modred's letter to me states that 'peace' means I must take the cross, travel to the Holy Land, and never return to Wales. I'll give him peace! He is a fool."

Arthur turned to his brother, his expression mild. "If we deny his requests, he will see to it that the Archbishop excommunicates us. He states his intention boldly."

"Archbishops have not always spoken for God to our kings." Cai spat out his response. "If we are excommunicate for protecting our country and our people, then so be it."

The stance was a brave one and, for the first time in his life, Myrddin found himself agreeing with Cai. He had more fire behind his words since he'd started this war. It almost made Myrddin think that he had concern for something or someone besides himself.

"And these messengers bother me," King Arthur said. "They bear a white flag of truce, but they wear Agravaine's colors, not Modred's."

At the mention of Agravaine, every man in the room hissed under his breath. Everywhere Arthur had turned of late, there Agravaine had been. He was the key coordinator of military activity in Wales for Modred. He'd gained this position over the heads of all the other barons who supported him, including Lord Edgar of Powys and Lord Cedric of Brecon, Modred's cousins.

"These riders will do what they can to spy on us," Bedwyr said. "We don't want them running around Eryri unobserved."

"That's what I need you for, Myrddin." King Arthur had finally noted him in his corner. "Follow them as far as the Conwy River and then return to me this evening. Take Ifan. When I'm ready, you will then carry my answer to Modred."

"Yes, my lord," Myrddin said.

"Take Deiniol with you as well." Cai halted Myrddin's progress towards the door. "He's your brother, I believe."

His stomach roiling, Myrddin inwardly corrected him: *foster brother*. "Yes, my lord," he said instead, and turned away.

Did he know how much Myrddin hated him? *He* being Cai, and *him* being Deiniol, who knew damn well that Myrddin despised him down to his ugly boots.

"What's wrong?" Nell caught Myrddin as he walked stiff-legged across the hall, heading towards the front doors, which opened, exposing the hall to the elements as another soldier left the room.

It was cold, even for November. A dozen men were preparing to ride their horses on similar missions—to other lords and barons whose estates were within a few days' ride of Garth Celyn. Modred had sent a letter to the Council of Wales as well as one each to Cai and Arthur. The Council, made up of the highest ranking barons and lords in Wales, needed to see it, discuss it, and respond, just as Arthur and Cai did. Raindrops reflected off the links of the men's mail, which were just visible beneath the thick wool of their cloaks. Myrddin didn't envy them even as he acknowledged that he would soon be one of them.

"I am sent to follow the Saxon riders who brought the messages to the king," Myrddin said. "To make sure they return to their side of the Conwy."

"And that makes you angry?"

Myrddin halted and turned to her, forcing down the anger and the memories that had formed a film over his eyes.

THE RAIN DRIPS DOWN my neck into the collar of my linen shirt. Ripped and torn after my struggles in the woods over the last hour, it provides little protection anyway. If I ever reach the safety of the castle, I will leave it in the rag pile on my way in.

I shiver. "Come on, Myrddin, you spineless bastard. Move!"

But I cannot. I bend aside a branch of the bush in which I'm cowering and peer through the murk, looking for my pursuer. I see nothing but the rain and the muddy track separating me from the gatehouse of the castle.

Bracing myself, I leave the safety of my bush. In ten quick steps, I'm through the gatehouse and across the bailey at a run, heading for the stables. I reach it and then press my back against the wall beside the open doorway. I listen for movement, to calm myself and become one with my surrounding as I've been taught, but my beating heart and the pounding rain overwhelm my senses.

At last, I risk entry. I slip through the doorway and head for the shadow of the horse stalls. A horse whickers a gentle greeting, and I touch his nose to quiet him. From the door at the far end of the stables, it's a dozen yards to a side door of the keep. Once there, I'll be safe.

For now. I reach the last stall and quicken my pace, sensing freedom. Instead, the door swings open and I'm face to face with Deiniol.

He grins.

I back away.

A single lantern lights the expansive space between the doorway and the horses. The light glints off a knife Deiniol holds. As I watch, he shifts it from one hand to the other. Deiniol is a seasoned fighter, full grown and strong. Even though I'm already sixteen, I'm still a scrawny half-child, speaking in a voice that breaks instead of the low voice of a man.

Deiniol has always been bigger than I, possessing a cruel streak I'd discovered before I could talk. There are more ways to hurt than through physical pain and Deiniol has tried them all on me at one time or another. He's hounded me all afternoon, and it's as if this moment is the culmination of a lifetime of animosity. I'll have one chance to escape him, if I have any chance at all.

Between one heartbeat and the next, Deiniol moves forward, and I spring to my right, only to find myself caught between two large hands that grip my arms and twist them behind my back. A booted foot comes around my legs and pinions them. I twist and jerk my body, but cannot break free.

"Aeden," I spit out, recognizing this new foe as Deiniol's cousin on his mother's side. "Why do you help him?"

Aeden laughs. "Drop the weapon, Deiniol. I'll hold the rat while you hit him."

Deiniol's eyes glint alarmingly. They're almost more frightening than the knife he carries. Deiniol takes a step forward, knife outstretched. Then he tosses it aside into one of the stalls.

I smirk.

Instantly, I know I've made a mistake and try to tame my expression, but it's too late.

Deiniol's face twists in hatred. He rushes forward and drives his shoulder into me. Aeden has already backed away and Deiniol and I go down: me underneath and Deiniol straddling my abdomen. I rock my hips trying to throw him off and then scrabble my hands on either side for a fistful of hay to throw into his face, but the stable floor is unaccountably clean and smooth.

I can feel the restlessness in the horses, as they, in turn, sense my distress. They cannot help me, however, and Deiniol ignores both them and my struggles. He grasps my wrists so tightly my hands go numb and pulls them above my head.

We glare at each other. There's blood on my lip where I bit it, and my belly aches from Deiniol's pummels. Still, I don't look away and, at long last, Deiniol sees something in me that gives him pause. His eyes narrow, and we still.

I can't breathe. Suddenly, Deiniol tips back his head and screams his frustration to the sky. Only then does help come, in the form of Deiniol's mother.

"Boys!" she says, insulting all three of us without thought. "We leave for Mercia tomorrow, and yet all you can think to do is scuffle in the dust!"

"So it's true," Aeden says. "Cai has defected to Modred."

"And we with him," my foster mother says.

Deiniol rolls off me.

I get to my feet and meet his gaze.

"I will remember this, mochyn," he says. It is the word for 'pig', but means bastard. "This is only the beginning."

"Don't be ridiculous." His mother brushes straw from Deiniol's shoulders. "Myrddin, I expected better of you."

Her casual unfairness leaves me speechless and unable to defend myself. Deiniol smirks at me from behind his mother's back. He tips his head to Aeden and prances after his mother, leaving me alone in the stables.

What Deiniol doesn't realize is that this time, the lesson I've learned is the opposite of the one he intended. When we meet next, four years later, Arthur is in the ascendancy, and it is Deiniol, not me, who stands downcast on the losing side.

"I FIND THAT I MUST travel to Caerhun in the company of my foster father's son. I spoke to you of him yesterday."

Nell's look was sympathetic. "I wish I could come with you instead. I'm useless here."

"That isn't true." Myrddin reached out and smoothed the hair near her forehead. "Besides. It's impossible. You know that."

"This is all new to me," she said. "I'm at loose ends."

"There's an herb garden behind the kitchen," Myrddin said, "and a drying shed beyond. Perhaps you can be of some assistance there."

"Don't—" Nell broke off and swallowed the rest of her sentence. Myrddin watched her carefully as she looked away, took a deep breath, and turned back to him. "I've already found it. You're right. They have need of me here."

Unsure what her cut-short comment would have been but glad that Nell would make an attempt to be content, at least for today, Myrddin inspected the mustering men in the courtyard. The clouds hung low, and the rain fell so hard it was like they were standing in a waterfall.

He sighed and set out into it. It would be a hideously cold ride to Caerhun.

"You," Deiniol said, as his initial greeting.

They stood beneath the gatehouse archway while a stable boy used a cloth to dry Myrddin's saddle. Deiniol had already mounted and wore his hood pulled tight around his head to counter the rain.

Regardless, even wearing wool cloaks, it wouldn't take long for rain this heavy to soak everyone through.

"Deiniol," Myrddin said.

"I see you haven't changed," he said. "Still a sniveling child with a snotty nose and a craven look about you."

"Sweet Mary." Having pulled up her hood and come to see what kind of man Myrddin despised, Nell spoke sincerely.

"Is that your woman?" Deiniol lifted his chin and pointed it at Nell. "I heard men speak of her in the hall."

Myrddin had an overwhelming urge to drive his fist into Deiniol's face. Nell, perhaps sensing this, moved closer.

"I hear she used to be a nun," Deiniol continued. "You'll have a cold bed to come home to, won't you?"

Now, Nell caught Myrddin's elbow and held on. "I'm a grown woman. I've heard worse, and experienced worse, as you well know. Don't get in trouble on my behalf."

Ifan muttered under his breath, turning towards Myrddin and pretending to inspect the length of his stirrups. "Does he rehearse these insults? A man could take lessons from him."

"It's been many years since I was forced into his company," Myrddin said.

"No doubt this was far too soon for a reunion," Ifan said.

"Twenty miles we have to go today," Myrddin said, "and each one will seem like an eternity."

"He hates you," Nell said.

Myrddin looked into her concerned face as her eyes flicked from Deiniol to him. Fortunately, Deiniol had turned his horse's head and urged him out from under the gatehouse into the rain. Myrddin had a vision of the tower coming loose and crushing him as he rode beneath it.

"He does," Myrddin said. "I have never known why."

"Some men don't need a reason." Ifan straightened his saddle bags. "Did you say that he's your brother?"

"Foster brother. Don't remind me," Myrddin said.

"No wonder you rabbited about so much all those years ago, jumping at every shadow." Two years older than Myrddin, Ifan had been a squire in Lord Bedwyr's retinue when Myrddin had come to Garth Celyn. "I gather it was he who gave you those bruises that were just fading when you came to the king?"

"You never said anything about them. I hoped nobody had noticed. It wouldn't do for a future knight to reveal so clearly how unable he was to defend himself."

Ifan shrugged, embarrassed perhaps to have brought them up. "You survived, didn't you? Sometimes a man wears bruises because he's the last one standing."

That made Myrddin smile. It was odd to think that he'd spent nearly twenty years in Ifan's company and this was the first Ifan had mentioned the day he'd arrived. It had been a cold day in March, with snow in the mountains. Myrddin had come down the road to Garth Celyn all on his own, with little more than a broken down horse he'd taken from Madoc's stables and his sword, a not-insignificant inheritance from his mother.

The news of Cai's stunning defection had just hit, and Garth Celyn had been in upheaval. Arthur had barely glanced at Myrddin, just informed his captain to find him a place to sleep in the barracks, a better horse, and decent armor if he was to be of any use to him at all. King Arthur had needed men, and Myrddin had found being treated like a man to his liking.

"By the balls of St. Mari!" Deiniol swore as the rain turned to sleet, and then the first flakes of snow began to coat his shoulders.

Even Ifan blinked twice at that bit of blasphemy and reluctantly mounted his horse. "Would King Arthur be upset if

I killed him? We could run him through and throw him into a chasm. No one would be the wiser."

"We'll do it on the way back if we're truly desperate," Myrddin said.

"I'll watch his back, miss." Ifan nodded at Nell, and then turned his horse's head towards the sea to follow Deiniol.

Myrddin lifted Nell's hand from his coat. "I'm five years younger than Deiniol, and the last time we spent any time in each other's company was the evening I ran away. He wanted to kill me. It was only the sudden arrival of his mother that stopped him."

"At least Ifan is with you," she said.

Myrddin laughed. "An hour ago, I would have thought he would act as a barrier to me killing Deiniol. But now I'm pretty sure I'll have to get in line."

Nell wrinkled her nose at him. If they hadn't had that conversation the day before about him sleeping across the room from her, Myrddin would have called it coquettish. "You be careful."

"Let's go, *mochyn!*" Deiniol had stopped some forty feet away to wait for Ifan to catch up, and they both twisted in their seats to look for Myrddin. "The Saxons ride away."

Because it was urgent and he was right, Myrddin did as he was asked, telling himself that he was doing the king's will. Myrddin gave a final nod to Nell and then spurred Cadfarch. The three men rode out of Garth Celyn, heading towards the southern pass.

Chapter Two

11 November 537 AD

NELL PERCHED ON HER stool, leaning over the narrow wooden table in front of her. Dried plants hung from the ceiling while herbs and spices crowded the shelves. In short order, she'd made the gardener's shed that lay across the herb garden from the kitchen a haven, installing a warming brazier and cushioned stool, taking Myrddin's advice and making the idea her own. The only light, other than from the brazier, shone from a pewter candelabra in front of her which held three glowing candles.

A hole in the roof let out the smoke, but other than that, the room allowed no exterior light. Admittedly, a window would have done her little good, as it was late afternoon and already dark.

"How are you?"

Nell looked up as Myrddin entered the hut. She'd been writing on a scrap of vellum, detailing the dream she'd had the previous night. If she closed her eyes, she could see it running in an endless loop behind her eyelids. It came so often now, night after night, that she sometimes felt she was more awake when she was dreaming than the other way around.

"Fine." She straightened, hoping she hadn't given anything away. She wasn't fine, of course. It was hard to see how she was ever going to be fine again.

Myrddin, for his part, watched her warily, as if he knew she was lying to him. She hated feeling so vulnerable. She missed those high convent walls, keeping out the world.

"How long have you been standing there?"

"Long enough to watch you fill the page. I heard a few phrases that could have been curses, too." Myrddin smiled. "You haven't been spending time among the garrison in my absence, have you? At least Deiniol isn't here to bother you."

She found that she couldn't smile back. It was no laughing matter that Deiniol had ridden with Myrddin and Ifan only as far as the pagan stones before taking a track south into the mountains. They'd let him go alone into the wilderness, rather than lose the Saxon messengers they'd been sent to follow.

Myrddin walked to her and peered over her shoulder, resting one hand on the table beside the inkpot. Nell hunched her shoulders and covered the page with one hand so he couldn't read her words. It was just like him to be able to read too: he pretended to be a bachelor, journeyman knight, but every now and then he would evidence some new, unexpected skill that belied his claim. He couldn't fool her anymore.

He stood at her shoulder, refusing to take the hint. After another count of ten, he sighed and eased away from her. But he didn't leave her alone as she wanted—or part of her wanted, and the rest didn't.

"What is it, Nell? Tell me what's bothering you. You can trust me."

She glanced up at him. "It isn't that I don't trust you."

"Isn't it?" he said. "I would like to think that you're telling me the truth this time, but it's hard to tell. I share a room with you, and meals, but you never talk of anything more momentous than the weather. The world is falling in around us. We're in the middle of a war. Why won't you speak of it?"

Nell bowed her head.

Endlessly patient as always, Myrddin leaned against the counter on which she prepared her herbs and ointments.

Finally, she pushed away the paper and turned in her seat to face him. "I'm tired, Myrddin. I'm thirty years old, and I feel a hundred."

"You don't look it." He tried to coax a smile. This time, she obliged, although it quickly faded.

"Why did you come to find me, Myrddin?"

"We have news from Powys," Myrddin said. "Lord Edgar has sent word that he might be persuaded to change sides, given the proper incentives."

Nell stared at him, her stomach sinking into her boots while a vision of the church by the Cam River rose unbidden before her eyes. "That couldn't possibly be true. His family has ever been faithful to the kings of Mercia—and now Modred. Does King Arthur believe it?"

"King Arthur has said nothing to me, but just this morning he sent a captain south to prepare to open a second front against the Saxons—on our terms this time, not Modred's. Geraint told me that given this new approach from Edgar, the king will want to lead his men himself."

Nell shook her head, an iciness taking over her limbs. Ten heartbeats ago she was alone with her dreams and her fears, and now the dream was a reality. "I don't think this is a good idea. Surely the king must see that?"

"The king needs to change the balance of power, and perhaps making Edgar an ally is the way to do it."

"What about—" Nell thought desperately for anything—any idea—that could divert this folly. Twenty years of dreaming, and she'd never been this close to the king—or to complete failure. "You have the king's confidence. What if you suggested to the king that he look to someone else to turn aside from Modred. Someone like Lord Cedric of Brecon. He hates Modred."

In 521, Cedric's father had fought against Modred and Icel, the King of Mercia at that time, in a war over the border territory between Mercia and Wessex. Cedric's family had allied with Arthur, who had some stake in the outcome, though not a large one. But Cedric's father had died of the wounds he received at Shrewsbury, and Cedric himself, only sixteen at the time, had witnessed his father's wounding and subsequent death while in Modred's custody.

Myrddin laughed. "He's none too fond of Arthur either. And he's as mercenary as Cai."

"True," she said. "But he's more open about it. You never have to wonder at his motives. You just need to make sure your goals align with his. And from what I know of the man, he's always been up-front with his allegiances. If he walked away from an alliance with Modred, he'd probably tell him about it in advance, rather than stab him in the back."

"Yes," Myrddin agreed. "But it isn't he who has sent a message to King Arthur."

"But— " Nell stopped. A curious look had passed across Myrddin's face. *Could I have said something right?* "It was his family who sided with King Arthur sixteen years ago. They might do it again."

"Modred forgave Cedric's family their treason." Myrddin nodded as he thought it through. "But the death of a father due to the mercilessness of one's lord is not something any man can easily forget, or forgive, especially one arising from as ancient a lineage as Cedric's."

"Arthur wants to unite Wales as its king," Nell said. "Cedric wants his bit of land secure and to stop having to fight either Arthur or his own supposed allies for the right to it. He wants more land too, but it's unlikely that Modred is going to award him any more—not any time soon."

"The land would be at the expense of Agravaine, Aelric, or Edgar," Myrddin said, "staunch allies of Modred."

"Well, except possibly for Edgar," Nell said, "which is, of course, why King Arthur can believe he might change sides."

"And you say that, why?"

"Because Edgar is—" Nell paused and pursed her lips, uncertain as to whether or not she should say more.

"Edgar is what?"

"Edgar does not prefer women," Nell said, as delicately as she could. "To my mind, this is why Modred has withheld Edgar's inheritance since his father died. None of the Mercian barons think Edgar is a fit heir, but it *is* his right."

"And how do you know all this?"

Nell stared at the floor, biting her bottom lip. She had so many things to tell him, so many things he might not forgive or understand.

Myrddin waited through the silence.

Finally, Nell waved a hand, apologetically, unable to avoid revealing to him this bit of the truth. "My husband served as a man-at-arms at Wigmore Castle."

Myrddin gaped at her. "He was part of the garrison? For Edgar's family?"

Nell couldn't mistake the anger and distrust that rose in his face—the same distrust he'd felt that first night on the road from St. Asaph. "Yes."

"Why didn't you tell me this before?"

"Because you're a staunch supporter of Arthur!" Nell's voice went high and tears pricked at her eyes in her anxiety. "You thought I was a spy! How could I tell you my husband served a Saxon lord?" A lone tear fell across her cheek, and she angrily brushed it away with the back of her hand.

"I already suspected the worst," Myrddin said. "It would have confirmed my suspicions."

Her heart sank. "And you still have them now."

"No man can ever truly know what is in another's soul." Myrddin was unrelenting. "Was your husband Saxon?"

"No." Nell crossed her arms and stared at the floor. "Many of the men-at-arms who serve the Saxons are Welsh."

"So who was he?"

Nell closed her eyes. "His name was Rhys. He was ten years older than I, the younger son of a landowner who held lands to the south of my father's." She'd been such a child when she married him. Not so much foolish, but innocent, in love with the handsome soldier she barely knew, even if she'd known him from infancy, but sure of her future with him. "Fifteen years ago there was peace between Wales and Mercia and my father didn't object to the marriage."

"But you didn't want to stay?" Myrddin said. "Once your husband and children died?"

"No," Nell said. "I didn't. I told you that before, and it was nothing but the truth. It was Edgar, in fact, who helped me return to Wales."

"And you haven't been back since?" Myrddin said.

"No."

"And Edgar?" Myrddin said. "Have you a further thought, then, about his message to King Arthur?"

"I don't know about that," Nell said. "It's Agravaine who has the real power. Modred put him in charge of all his forces, including Edgar's, for a reason. I wouldn't be surprised if the letter to the king was Agravaine's idea, and Edgar was only going along with the deception because he wanted to prove to Modred his loyalty—to force him to acknowledge that he is his father's rightful heir."

"That is my thought too," Myrddin said. "If Arthur goes to meet Edgar, I fear he goes to his death."

Nell had been studying her toes, not looking at Myrddin as he interrogated her. Now she glanced up, surprised that he would say such a thing so openly and surely. "I feel that too. Can you think of a way to stop him? I will help you if I can!"

Myrddin kept his gaze on her face, and she didn't look away. His lips twisted. "We'll see." With a last nod, he spun on one heel and left the hut.

Nell stared after him. When his footsteps had faded, she leaned her head back against wall and closed her eyes. In twenty years of dreaming, nothing she'd tried had turned out right. This was obviously not working either. Perhaps she shouldn't have allowed Myrddin to bring her to Garth Celyn after all.

Chapter Three

12 November 537 AD

AS HE STARED UP AT the battlements of Rhuddlan Castle, Myrddin felt for the letter from King Arthur to Modred—as reassurance—one last time. As he'd promised, Arthur had selected him to bring it. In the end, Myrddin had come alone because the king had determined that it was better to lose one man to an early grave or Modred's dungeon than a company of them.

"I'm not too happy about this either, Nell," Myrddin had said as they stood in Garth Celyn's courtyard that morning. Nell had held Cadfarch's bridle and fed him carrots while Myrddin adjusted his saddlebags. "Nor is the king."

"Take me with you," she said. "Nobody will know or care if I leave here, or what happens to me."

"I will care." Myrddin wouldn't soon forget her tears from yesterday and their effect on his heart. "The road I'm taking passes right through St. Asaph. You don't need to ride through there again."

"Maybe I do need to," Nell said.

"Nell—"

"I wouldn't be alone this time," Nell said. "I'd be with you, and I'd pretend to be your little brother. Nobody would give me a second look."

"In boy's clothes?" Myrddin said.

"Of course."

"No," he said, more firmly than before. "You're a nun."

"Not anymore," she said, "and I have no intention of ever being one again."

"The law—"

"*The woman shall not wear that which pertaineth unto a man, neither shall a man put on a woman's garment: for all that do so are abomination unto the Lord thy God,*" Nell quoted. "Give me credit for knowing at least that. But with Eryri about to fall to Modred, wearing a boy's discarded breeches is surely a small matter."

She gazed at him, disconcerting him because a vision of her lifeless and abused body had risen before his eyes. He blinked to clear them before she realized he'd seen it. That she'd experienced attempted rape and murder even once was unconscionable. She was crazed to think Myrddin would let her near the scene of the crime again.

"It wouldn't work." Regardless of his opinion, the request was ludicrous, and she had to know it. Still, Myrddin understood what she was feeling, too. She was a vibrant and competent woman, adrift in the middle of a war. Little wonder that she was struggling with it. But riding with him wasn't the answer.

"It isn't because you don't trust me, is it?" she said. "It isn't because you still believe that I spy for Modred?"

"That's not it," Myrddin said, acknowledging at last, albeit grudgingly, that the idea had always been unlikely.

"Besides." Nell changed tack. "Masterless men didn't attack me. Those men were knights. I just happened to get in their way."

Myrddin snorted under his breath. "Don't you think I know that? Modred would never allow marauders so close to Rhuddlan. His men are disciplined and he would have taken care of any such men who'd dared roam his territory. But who's going to *be* at Rhuddlan? Those very same men! The thought of you left to your own devices at Rhuddlan Castle sends chills down my spine."

Nell studied his face and then sighed, backing down. "Yes, my lord."

Myrddin's eyes narrowed at her uncharacteristic use of his title.

Her shoulders had fallen, but then she poked him in the chest. "But I'm holding it against you."

"I can accept that," Myrddin had said. He'd glanced back once as he left the castle to see Nell and Ifan standing on the battlements, watching him ride away. Nell had tucked herself into her cloak, with the hood up, but Ifan stood bareheaded, his crop of short, blonde hair unmistakable. Each had lifted a hand to wave him down the road. Myrddin had responded with a salute.

Now, at sunset, he followed the western side of the Clwyd River, past the drawbridge and its lesser gate, to the ford. Cadfarch splashed through the river, came up the bank, and stopped in front of the main defensive tower in the outer palisade. Myrddin waited, hoping that the archers who peered at him from the battlements would remain patient. He was Welsh but that didn't mean that he was an enemy. Sad, but true.

A guard called to him from the walkway above the gatehouse. "Give me your name and your purpose." The man, tall and helmetless, spoke in heavily accented Welsh.

"I come at the request of Arthur ap Uther, King of Wales," Myrddin said, answering him in Saxon, the language in which the guard was sure to be most comfortable. "I have a letter for Lord Modred."

The man studied Myrddin and then nodded. "You may enter provided you surrender your weapons."

The words came this time in flawless Saxon, confirming Myrddin's assessment, and Myrddin agreed with reluctance to what the soldier asked.

Men wore weapons as a matter of course, and for a man *not* to wear his sword was unusual—and insulting to the unarmed man, which is of course why the soldier intended to strip Myrddin of his. It wasn't that he feared Myrddin would use his sword against

Modred, but because he sought to humiliate him, and by association, King Arthur.

Myrddin urged Cadfarch under the gatehouse and into the outer bailey. Once inside the curtain wall, a cobbled path led to the massive double towers of the second gatehouse which protected the great hall behind it. Modred's fort was impregnable. No one had ever taken it by force, although not for lack of trying. Cai had attacked it after taking down one of Modred's more eastern castles the previous spring, but other than causing some damage from fire, he'd gone away unsatisfied.

It might be possible to starve the defenders out, but Myrddin wouldn't have been surprised to learn that Modred had built an escape tunnel under his castle, just like at Garth Celyn. Then again, he had less experience in losing wars and so perhaps hadn't thought he needed one.

Torches flared in sconces—dozens of them—lighting the bailey almost as if it were day. Like everything else about Rhuddlan, the expansive light was a display of wealth and power that the local populace would surely notice. Compared to any of King Arthur's castles, which tended to be coldly utilitarian, even if their castellans did everything they could to make them comfortable, Rhuddlan was a palace. Modred's image of himself had grown ever more resplendent as his victories had increased in number.

Myrddin dismounted and instantly three men were upon him, two gripping his upper arms while a third disarmed him. He patted Myrddin down, finding one knife in his boot and a second tucked into the bracer on his forearm. Myrddin had hoped they'd miss that one and kicked himself for not having a maid sew a smaller knife into the lining of his cloak. A true spy, he wasn't. Perhaps it was time he learned.

Just as they finished, another man of obvious rank, given his clothing and the artistry in the hilt of his sword, came out from under the secondary gatehouse. Even his walk was purposeful and distinctive. The men sitting outside the stables with doxies on their laps hastily put them aside to stand at his approach. The man didn't indicate that he noticed—although, if he was a captain worth his salt, he would confront them later.

When the man reached Myrddin, he gave Myrddin a curt nod and said, "Lord Modred will see you now."

Myrddin hadn't expected anything different in terms of courtesy, although it would have been nice to brush the dust from his clothes and polish himself up so as to represent Arthur better. With no help for it, he allowed a stable boy to lead Cadfarch away, and then he trailed after the man, followed by one of the men-at-arms carrying his weapons. Even Modred knew he couldn't have his men toss them in a corner. Myrddin couldn't countenance it. They were his livelihood and the value of the sword alone was that of an entire village.

Rhuddlan's walls and towers loomed even larger from the ground than on horseback. As Myrddin followed the knight through the second gatehouse, the second bailey, and into the great hall, he had to shake his head over the amount of time and treasure it had taken to build it. Modred's people must be suffering greatly to have given him so much in such a short time.

The hall was full of men at their evening meal. Myrddin and his escort by-passed them, however, and headed down a corridor to Modred's receiving room. The metal fittings of Myrddin's boots clacked loudly on the stones as he paced along the corridor, a match to the pounding of his heart. His stomach seemed to rise farther into his throat with every step.

Then he told himself that if he was to turn aside the fate set for Wales in the dream, if he was to become the man Arthur needed him to be, he'd have to do better.

When facing down an enemy, whether Deiniol as a boy or a hated upstart nobleman, confidence was everything. Much as Nell had done when she'd first spoken to King Arthur back at Garth Celyn, Myrddin replaced uncertainty with pride. Straightening his shoulders, Myrddin nodded at the man who'd brought him. The man's eyes crinkled at the corners, acknowledging the transition Myrddin had affected, and nodded back.

The man threw open the door to Modred's receiving room. It was the same size as the great hall at Garth Celyn, but as it was only a third as large as the hall Myrddin had just come through, Modred used it for his private meetings. Not that this was going to be private. Myrddin had walked into a room full of people and had their immediate attention. Deliberately ignoring everyone but the man in charge, Myrddin strode towards Modred. He no longer had a sword at his waist but he held a missive of defiance close to his heart, which was almost the same thing, and perhaps better.

His heart caught in his throat, however, at the sight of Archbishop Dafydd standing to Modred's right. Myrddin hadn't realized, even with all the discussion of peace lately, that the two men were so close—and that Modred had this level of support from the Church. For his part, the Archbishop observed Myrddin as he came to a halt five paces from Modred's throne, with its gilt frame, raised dais, and thick rug. Myrddin bowed, straightened, his hands at his sides, and looked straight at Modred.

"Come," Modred said. "Let's see what my beloved uncle has to say to me today."

Modred appeared exactly as he should, which was to say, like a king. He was forty years old, into middle-age, but he didn't look it. He had a full head of dark hair, broad shoulders, and eyes that Myrddin would have avoided if he could. It was hard not to think that they saw right through him.

Christ, I hate him.

Still upright, refusing to allow his thoughts to show, Myrddin advanced towards Modred's throne. He removed the letter from his breast pocket and with a second, short bow, held it out to Modred.

"My lord," Myrddin said. "King Arthur greets you and hopes that his royal nephew is well."

"How kind of him to inquire." Modred took the letter, watching Myrddin out of the corner of his eye as he did so, and broke the seal. He unrolled it and read for no more than a count of ten. Without re-rolling it, Modred handed the letter to the Archbishop, who took it. Myrddin kept his hands relaxed at his sides, wondering what would happen next. He didn't like the feeling he was getting from Modred or his lackeys, many of whom were watching him like he was a rare beast in a cage. Or a chicken intended for slaughter.

While the Archbishop read Arthur's letter, Modred sat still, his only movement the tapping of his forefinger on the arm of his chair as he waited. He didn't appear disturbed or angered by King Arthur's words, just impatient. The letter seemed no more or less than what he had expected.

"And Cai's response?" Modred said.

Myrddin had that letter too. He didn't know precisely what it said, but he suspected it was far less polite than Arthur's. "Here, my lord." Myrddin pulled it from his pocket and handed it to Modred.

Modred took it, split the seal, and passed it off to the Archbishop so quickly he couldn't have read more than three words. Instead, he revealed that he had other things on his mind. "And what was your role in the battle at the Strait?"

Myrddin blinked, nonplussed. And then he decided that the question wasn't so surprising. Very few of Modred's men had survived the battle, and perhaps he hadn't yet had a good first-hand account.

"I am one of the knights in my king's household guard," Myrddin said, deciding there was no harm in telling him this bit of truth. Eventually he'd hear it from someone else. "I was at the forefront of the initial charge."

"Tell me what you remember," Modred said.

Myrddin took in a breath. Modred would hate what he had to say, but then, it was unlikely Myrddin's explanation could make it worse for him. "The Saxon forces crossed the Strait at noon on November 6th. Once the cavalry reached the beach and the foot soldiers were marching on the bridge, we unleashed our arrows." Myrddin stopped.

"And then?" Modred watched Myrddin's face. The silence in the hall was complete.

"And then we charged," Myrddin said.

"Who killed Wulfere?" Modred said.

Myrddin hesitated. "I did."

A pause. Unaccountably, Modred smiled. Then he began to laugh. He continued, tears spilling out of his eyes and rolling down his cheeks. After a moment of stunned silence, the rest of the people in the room began to laugh too, even if they, as Myrddin, had no idea what their lord thought was so funny.

Myrddin remained standing in front of Modred. He shared a quick look with the Archbishop, who was the only other person not in hysterics. Then he glanced at the stars beginning to show through the glass in the window to his left. As in the courtyard, the wealth on display in the hall was palpable, from the glass in the windows, to the dual fireplaces, one on each side of the hall, to the tapestries that adorned the walls.

Myrddin wished he was gone already but until the king dismissed him, he had to stay.

Finally, Modred calmed enough to explain himself. "Your king has quite a sense of humor. He sends his letter with the one man he knows I won't touch. He probably thinks I should thank you for doing to Wulfere what I would have done myself, except that you robbed me of my pleasure."

"My lord, my apologies if I displeased you, but Wulfere attacked me." Myrddin bowed again, for lack of anything better to do or say. Wulfere had disobeyed a direct order. If he hadn't lost his life at the Strait, if Modred was angry enough, he might have hanged him from the tallest tower at Rhuddlan and afterwards stuck his head on a pike for display. On the whole, given Modred's cruel streak, Myrddin had done Wulfere a favor.

Modred barked another laugh. "No regrets, eh?" He fingered his lip. "To repay the loss of my prize, you can render me a small service while you're here, especially as you appear so adept at delivering messages."

"If I can, my lord," Myrddin said.

"Lord Cedric of Brecon awaits my pleasure," he said. "I think I've kept him waiting long enough. Bring him to me."

"Certainly, sir," Myrddin said.

He turned on his heel, his mind racing. *What a gift! The very man he'd wanted to meet*! Nell would have his head if he didn't take advantage of the opportunity—he almost wished he'd brought her with him to help him think of what to say. Myrddin marched towards the door, the space between his shoulder blades tingling with the force of the glare that he felt Modred was directing at him. He would have run from the room if he could, but as it was, the instant Myrddin cleared the doorway, he heaved a sigh of relief.

Myrddin had no idea where Modred was keeping Cedric, whether in the dungeon, a tower, or a private suite. It was a simple matter, however, to ask a servant, who gave him directions and informed him, as a by-the-way, that Cedric had arrived just after dawn and had been cooling his heels in his rooms ever since, waiting for Modred to send for him.

To give Modred credit, he *was* treating Cedric as an honored guest, which was somewhat surprising given the disaster at the Strait and the fact that the two men hated each other. Still, Cedric had remained overtly loyal to Modred and was a high ranking nobleman—and Modred's cousin—even if every task he performed for Modred was accomplished with great loathing.

As Myrddin approached Cedric's rooms, a disturbing amount of mumbling and shouting began leaking through the half-open door into the passage. He fought his instinct to run into the room to quiet the man. Didn't Cedric realize he was in enemy territory? Didn't he see the need to bury his emotions and keep his thoughts more private?

"Fools!" Cedric's voice echoed down the corridor. "The indignity of being forced to wait in my rooms! To have my honor called into question!"

Myrddin arrived in Cedric's doorway, knocked, and then took a step back so as not to crowd the threshold. Booted feet echoed on the floor and Cedric himself opened the door. Beyond, the room was empty.

"Lord Cedric." Myrddin bowed and pretended he hadn't overheard him. "Lord Modred requests your presence."

At the sight of Myrddin, Cedric's face transformed from rage to a blank and expressionless façade—all except for his eyes, which glinted, the sole indication of the fire behind them. He glared at Myrddin and then slid the sword he'd been brandishing at his unseen listeners into the sheath at his waist.

"Finally," he said. "Is the Archbishop beside him?"

"Yes, my lord," Myrddin said.

"And who are you?" He pointed his chin at Myrddin. "By your features, you are a Welshmen, yet your Saxon is perfect."

"Myrddin. A knight in the retinue of King Arthur ap Uther."

That got Cedric's attention. He examined Myrddin through narrowed eyes. Then he tipped his face to study the rafters above him and spoke in a low voice. "Why does Modred send you to me? What is it that I don't know?"

"I came to Rhuddlan because I bore a message from my king to Modred." Myrddin answered him even if the question had been rhetorical—and then decided that he would take advantage of the opportunity Modred had given him. Maybe there really was a way to prevent Arthur from meeting Lord Edgar at that damned church a month from now. "But it is well that Lord Modred sent me here, for I have a query for you on behalf of my king."

Cedric's head came down at that, and he looked at Myrddin warily. He pushed past Myrddin to look both ways down the hall, and then gave Myrddin a curt nod. "Tell me quickly."

"You and King Arthur have been at odds," Myrddin said. "He would rather you were allies."

Cedric pursed his lips and looked away. He contemplated the hilt of his sword, on which he rested his left hand, and tapped a staccato with one finger at its end, in a thinking pose similar to Modred's. Then, without looking at Myrddin, he strode into the corridor.

Unable to read Cedric and wondering how big a mistake he'd made, Myrddin followed. He assumed that Cedric expected him to walk behind him, given Myrddin's nationality and as befitting Cedric's rank, which was so much higher than Myrddin's, but Cedric motioned impatiently for Myrddin to come abreast. Myrddin did as he asked and the two men walked together down the passage. Or rather, Myrddin walked, and Cedric stalked.

"What is his mood?" Cedric didn't need to explain whose mood he meant. Apparently they were going to ignore King Arthur's supposed message.

"I have no idea," Myrddin said. "The Archbishop stood beside him and said nothing either. I can't imagine Modred was happy with Archbishop Dafydd's attempts to mediate a peace settlement, but he would never reveal what he is thinking—to anyone perhaps, but certainly not to one of King Arthur's men."

Cedric grunted, but whether that meant agreement or disapproval, Myrddin didn't know. Then, as they approached Modred's receiving room, Cedric slowed. "You have served King Arthur for many years?"

"Yes."

"Does he strike you as a man with a temper?"

Myrddin glanced warily at him, not sure where this was leading. "No. He has one, of course, but when it rises he turns cold, not hot."

Cedric nodded. "Lord Modred is not one to cross. For me to do so would have ramifications for generations to come. You tell that to your lord."

Uncertain, Myrddin stood frozen to the floor for an indrawn breath—as long as it took Cedric to push open the door leading to Modred's rooms. Then, galvanized by Cedric's retreating back, Myrddin hurried after him as Cedric crossed the twenty feet to where Modred sat, no longer on his throne but behind a desk that was set under one of the windows to the left of the central fireplace.

Modred had emptied the hall in Myrddin's absence. Now, Archbishop Dafydd was the only other man present. Both Archbishop and Lord Modred had been bent over a piece of paper, which the Archbishop now folded and slid into a hidden pocket beneath his robes.

It was warmer in the room than before, despite the fewer bodies to heat it. The fires had been stoked and blazed brightly. Like Arthur, Modred had the best of everything. The remains of dinner lay on the corner of his table. The Archbishop held a goblet of wine and a hint of spice wafted from it.

Cedric reached Modred and bowed at the precisely correct angle that was required. In contrast, Myrddin's feet stuck to the floor just inside the doorway, near the bench where his untended weapons lay. For a heartbeat, Myrddin considered grabbing his sword and making a run for it. One glance at the guards by the open door who had shifted to more ready stances had him biding his time a while longer.

The exit was a long way away, through the great hall and two well-guarded gatehouses. If Myrddin was going to reach it, it wasn't going to be at a flat-out run. Stealth would have to be the order of the day.

"You summoned me, sire?" Cedric said.

Modred leaned back in his chair and for a count of ten sat unmoving, elbows resting on the arms, seemingly relaxed. Cedric's words hung in the air as Modred left his question unanswered. Cedric waited with what appeared to be patience for his lord's response.

"Tell me of the defeat at the Menai Strait," Modred said, finally, as if discussing the dreadful weather, and as if he hadn't just asked Myrddin the same question half an hour before.

"My lord—" Cedric began.

Modred cut him off, leaning forward to punctuate his next words with a pointing finger. "Explain to me why so many of my men are dead: Wulfere, Golm, Halfric, Dane, not to mention the equipment and horses that are now at the bottom of the sea! Do you understand the huge expenses I am incurring in this business? Of the criminal waste that this defeat has entailed?" By the end of his query, Modred's voice had risen to the point where the sound buffeted Cedric like waves.

"Wulfere refused to listen to me." Cedric lifted his chin, aiming to withstand the onslaught. "He, not I, was the commander in the field. He, not I, is to blame for the loss of so many of our men."

"And he, not you, paid for his error with his life." Modred sat back in his chair as if he'd never raised his voice. "By the sword of our friend, here." He gestured with one hand towards Myrddin. Cedric's eyes met Myrddin's. The corner of Cedric's mouth twitched before his face blanked, and he turned back to his lord.

"As you say, my lord." Cedric bowed his head and then raised it to meet Modred's eyes. "I tried to convince Wulfere and the others that you would not countenance an attack on that day, not with the Archbishop in the middle of negotiations and hoping for a settlement between you and King Arthur. Wulfere thought he could ensure that a settlement was unnecessary. He supposed that a great victory could convince Arthur to submit to you, or at best, he could capture the king by driving down the coast to Garth Celyn, once he'd navigated the bridge. Regardless, he refused to listen to my cautions."

From what Myrddin knew of both Cedric and Wulfere, he believed Cedric's story. Myrddin had to wonder, however, how hard Cedric had tried to get Wulfere to change course. He must have despised Wulfere—everyone did. Even Modred couldn't have admired the man as a person. He had put Wulfere in charge of his troops because he could be trusted to get the job done.

That alone had to have been a huge sore point for Cedric, whom Modred had overlooked from the start of the war in favor of Agravaine in particular. To have put Wulfere in charge of the men on Anglesey added insult to injury. To Cedric's mind, if Wulfere had won the battle, Cedric could have gone along with it; if Wulfere made a fool of himself, Cedric wouldn't have been at fault. Nobody but King Arthur himself had foreseen the total disaster the battle had become for the Saxons.

"On the day of the attack, a fault in the bridge of boats delayed us," Cedric said, continuing his story. "Wulfere had intended to cross at dawn but ended up crossing at noon. It was the optimal time, with the water high, but as we traversed the bridge, we failed to surprise the Welsh forces. They caught us on the beach, low ground, between the trees and the water. When we retreated, the swift waters of the Strait and the weight of the horses and equipment on the bridge ensured our near total defeat."

"And gave Arthur new reason to resist me." Modred surged to his feet. Myrddin would have said he was furious, but as always, his eyes remained cold, revealing nothing of the man inside. "He sits in his eyrie in Snowdonia, mocking me, as if I haven't the power to root him out! I will accept nothing less from that bastard king than complete submission!"

If the back of Myrddin's knees had not been resting on the edge of the bench, he would have taken a step back at the king's vehemence. Even Cedric, for all his confidence, thought better of any reply. Myrddin decided not to mention that Arthur, of all the Welsh lords, appeared to have been born legitimate.

For Modred's part, he wasn't done. "Arthur is arrogant! Impossible! Look at the letter he sends me!" Modred leaned over the desk and shoved one of the pieces of parchment towards Cedric who just managed to catch it before it fell from the table. Unrolling the paper, he studied the words in silence, but Myrddin knew well what they said:

... WE ARE READY TO COME to the Archbishop's grace, if it is offered in a form safe and honourable for us. But the form contained in the articles which were sent to us, is in no particular either safe or honourable ... indeed, so far from it that all who hear it are astonished, since it tends rather to the destruction and ruin of our people and our

person than to our honour and safety ... for never would our nobles and subjects consent in the inevitable destruction and dissipation that would surely derive from it ...

CEDRIC HANDED THE LETTER back to Modred who tossed it into a wooden box on the floor behind him and sat heavily in his chair once again.

"My spies inform me that Arthur has sent men south to open a new front against me in Powys," Modred said.

Myrddin started at that, the pit forming in his stomach and the chills running down his spine telling him that Modred's attitude towards him had changed in the time he'd been gone. Myrddin gritted his teeth, fighting back the cold certainty. Despite what Modred had said earlier about not harming him because he'd killed Wulfere, he must have decided Myrddin would never leave Rhuddlan or he would not have spoken openly of this.

Myrddin was a walking dead man.

"I've heard that Lord Gawain is marshalling a force to threaten Brecon," Cedric said.

"You wish to be relieved of your duties in the north, then?" Modred said. "To deal with this new threat?"

Myrddin couldn't tell if he was mocking Cedric or asking a serious question. Cedric treated it as genuine.

"If it please you, my lord. A strong hand is needed at Brecon or my lands might fall to Arthur's army. That would serve neither me nor you."

Modred contemplated Cedric's face. Cedric, for his part, kept his back straight, looking forward, even if it might cost him Modred's favor. Modred tapped one finger to his lips, as was his habit, and spoke.

"I will not have a repeat of the Anglesey disaster. I had ordered Wulfere to delay his attack. It is fortunate for him that our friend, here, killed him before I could myself."

"I understand completely, my lord," Cedric said. "If I offended you in any way, it was not my intent."

"Is that so?" If anything, Modred grew more still. No doubt he was thinking, as Myrddin was, of that long ago war. "It is I, and I alone, who will determine that."

"Yes, my lord." Cedric's jaw was set, and he spoke through gritted teeth. "I have further news, sire, that might interest you. Lord Edgar has sent a letter to Arthur, inviting him south. If the king wasn't already resolved to lead his men himself, this will confirm his intent."

Was there anything the Saxons didn't know?

Modred leaned forward, apparently truly interested for the first time. "The king has agreed to this meeting?"

"I know not, my lord."

Modred sat back, sneering. "Arthur will agree. I am sure of it. He is that desperate—and naïve. The notion that Edgar would side with a rebel such as he is laughable."

Cedric didn't respond to Modred's assertion any more than Myrddin did, even if Cedric's mind had to be revolving with the same calculations as Myrddin's. Did Modred know that Edgar's resentments were as great as Cedric's own, for all he was younger and less experienced? Did Modred know of Edgar's anger at being denied his inheritance?

"May I go, my lord?" Cedric said.

"Go." Modred waved his hand dismissively. "When we meet next, Arthur will be dead, and I will have all Wales in the palm of my hand."

Cedric bowed one more time and turned for the door. He held Myrddin's gaze as he walked the thirty feet between them.

Myrddin couldn't read his expression but felt he was trying to tell him something. Cedric's eyes flicked to the door and then back to Myrddin.

Flee now?

If Arthur died, Wales would be left rudderless. Arthur had no sons to come after him, and his death would solidify Edgar's station with Modred. The thought could not have been comforting to Cedric. He had to despise Modred's vision of the future of Wales. For Myrddin's part, he didn't like Modred's confident power. He didn't like it at all.

Chapter Four

13 November 537 AD

THE HOURS AFTER MIDNIGHT can be bleak. Certainly, the dungeon under the southwest tower of Rhuddlan Castle was not an enjoyable location in which to spend them. The castle was new, true, but the walls seeped water, which came from either the moat or the river—it hardly mattered which one, but given Myrddin's location, he suspected the river—and mold had formed in the corners of his cell. From his fixed position on the wall, he could smell it, although not see it, since darkness shrouded his cell. The sole light came from the torch in a sconce on the wall in the guardroom on the other side of the door.

A hole, bifurcated by a single bar, had been cut in the door. Beyond, shadows and the occasional figures of Myrddin's guard, passed. Representing almost a greater threat than the guards were the three rats that had found their way to a far corner. Those, Myrddin could see as well as hear, and they ensured that any notion of dropping off to sleep in such an uncomfortable position was squashed before he took it seriously.

He was still cursing himself as to how in the hell he'd ended up here in the first place.

AFTER MODRED HAD DISMISSED Cedric, Myrddin had snatched up his weapons and followed Cedric out the door. With a confidence he didn't really feel, Myrddin moved along the hallway, buckling on his sword and intending to make a quick getaway. Cedric heard his steps behind him, however, and pulled Myrddin aside.

"Modred won't let you leave."

"I fear you are correct," Myrddin said, "but I must try."

"Wait a while," he said. "Dine with me. After the meal, I'll see what I can do for you."

Myrddin doubted he could trust him, but believed the guards would prevent him from walking out the front gate. So Myrddin went to the great hall with Cedric. Full darkness had descended shortly after he'd arrived at Rhuddlan, and by now they'd missed the bulk of the meal. But like Modred, Cedric got to eat whenever he wanted.

The hall was still full of men, all of whom would have been hostile to Myrddin if they'd known who he was. But since he entered as Cedric's new-found companion, if not friend, nobody approached them. Cedric was known for standing on ceremony and insisting on the comforts and accolades of his office—much like King Arthur.

A servant appeared with trenchers for their food and goblets for wine, which she laid before them. She wore the garb of a Saxon girl and was perhaps one of the villagers whom Modred had brought to Rhuddlan for this purpose. Although she was young and lovely, in a blonde, Saxon way, Cedric didn't spare her a glance. It supported the rumors Myrddin had heard that Cedric was faithful to his wife—an unusual trait among noble men. And something else he didn't share with Modred, although Modred apparently did love his wife to distraction.

Myrddin shifted in his seat to see past Cedric to the rest of the room. "Is Agravaine here?" He'd never met the man and wanted to know what he looked like.

"No," Cedric said, without looking around. He ate with small, dainty bites, as if he wasn't quite sure as to the safety or spicing of the food. "He'd sleep in a barn rather than stay at Rhuddlan."

"Why is that?" Myrddin said.

"The man's a ghost; flitting in and out among Modred's possessions, never stopping anywhere for more than a day if the castle belongs to someone other than himself. Agravaine trusts no one. Modred puts up with it because he wins battles and does as he's told. Half the time it seems he can see the future before it happens."

Myrddin didn't like the sound of that and would have inquired further, but Cedric was done with the subject, taking a sip of wine and then gesturing to the servant for more turnips. Myrddin went back to surveying the hall. Plenty of Welshmen were scattered among the diners—both men who'd sided with Modred from the first and recent defectors. Beyond Cedric's left shoulder, two monks whom Myrddin thought he recognized sat at a far table.

A quick inspection of their undyed robes and cloaks confirmed his suspicions: they were the brothers Llywelyn and Rhys, cousins to Gareth, and brothers to the Hywel who'd died at Penrhyn after the battle at the Strait. Brother Llywelyn was the prior of the monastery at Bangor, and Rhys was the friar of St. Deiniol, the cathedral church, also in Bangor.

As Hywel had explained, it was Llywelyn who'd talked his brothers into betraying King Arthur. Myrddin's disgust for him and that loathsome act hadn't abated in the intervening years. Perhaps feeling the intensity of Myrddin's stare, Llywelyn glanced up, caught Myrddin's eye, and glowered. Once Rhys noted Llywelyn's attention, he turned to look at him as well. Myrddin didn't glance away, but returned their glares. It was childish of him but he refused to back down.

"What are you looking at?" Cedric said, noting Myrddin's odd behavior. He twisted in his seat to glance behind him.

"I know those two monks over there." Myrddin pointed at them with his chin.

Cedric pursed his lips, turning back to his food. "I don't like traitors. Not even ones on my side."

"I suppose it's a matter of perspective," Myrddin said. "One man's traitor is another man's loyal subject."

"Edgar won't betray Lord Modred." Cedric spoke as if they'd had a conversation about Edgar already which had been interrupted, even though they hadn't. "If Modred keeps Agravaine on a tight leash, Agravaine keeps an even tighter one on Edgar. He will do nothing of his own accord."

"Would that be true for you as well?" Myrddin said.

Cedric pointed his knife at Myrddin. "Don't let King Arthur come south."

Myrddin canted his head to the side. "And leave your lands alone?"

Cedric chuckled deep in his throat, but then cut it off. "I'd prefer it."

"What would Modred think of your warning?"

Cedric gave Myrddin a hard look. "He's the one who allowed you to hear of the danger that awaits your king in Powys. Weren't you paying attention earlier? I've not said anything that he hasn't already made clear."

Myrddin shook his head at the complexity of it all. His visions were incomplete and by now, nearly useless. He'd accepted that he had to take action, but while the dreams told him that Arthur shouldn't come south to meet with Edgar, they didn't tell him what needed to happen instead. To have Cedric informing him of what he already knew—even though it hadn't yet happened—was disconcerting.

Cedric pushed away his plate, the food on it half-eaten. He was gathering himself to get to his feet when Modred strode into the room, trailed by the Archbishop. He, in turn, was flanked by two more churchmen whom Myrddin didn't recognize, and said as much to Cedric.

"Bishop Anian of St. Asaph." Cedric rose to his feet as they always did in the presence of Modred. "The other is the Archdeacon of Anglesey."

Myrddin's heart sank into his boots, for he knew what was coming, just as King Arthur had predicted to his brother. At Modred's raised hand, the room quieted. Modred lifted his voice so that it carried to the far corners of the hall.

"I present to you Archbishop Dafydd. Listen well and take heed of his words."

The Archbishop stepped forward, a piece of paper in his shaking hands. Maybe it was because he suffered from palsy, even though he couldn't have been much older than Myrddin. Myrddin was willing to believe the archbishop understood the significance of what he was about to do and half-regretted it. Myrddin briefly felt sorry for him.

Dafydd spoke in Latin, and then again in Saxon so everyone in the room would understand:

ARTHUR AP UTHER, ALONG with his brother, Cai, notwithstanding the formal canonical warning of 17 June last and the repeated appeals to desist from their intentions, have performed a schismatical act of disobedience and have therefore incurred the penalty of excommunication latae sententiae. The priests and faithful are warned not to support the schism of Arthur and Cai, otherwise they shall incur ipso facto a similar punishment.

THERE IT WAS. ARTHUR was a devout believer, and would care—fearing for his soul—but this pronouncement would change nothing. The churches in Gwynedd—as opposed to those Archbishop Dafydd oversaw in the south of Wales—would continue to administer to the faithful: marrying, baptizing, and seeing to their spiritual needs, in defiance of the injustice of this act.

"This will make it easier for those who are so inclined to betray King Arthur." Cedric sat down again as Modred left the hall and the priests found seats at the high table.

Myrddin shrugged. "Or the opposite. The excommunication of their leader at the behest of a despised usurper might only confirm the rightness of their choice in their eyes."

"Did you say *despised usurper*?" Cedric said. "You are too bold."

"A man must live by his conscience," Myrddin said. "When men say that they speak for God, in pursuit of their own power, it calls their words into doubt."

Cedric's hard look was back. Myrddin thought better of further conversation, but even if he'd wanted to speak, he wasn't given a chance. Two men-at-arms appeared, one on either side of Myrddin, grasped him under the arms, and lifted him bodily over his bench. Before Myrddin had a chance to do more than sputter, they had him up against the wall, his back braced and his legs spread.

"What's this?" Cedric gestured with his knife. "We were eating."

The man on Myrddin's right spoke. "Our apologies, my lord. Lord Modred has given orders."

IN THOSE FIRST MOMENTS of his captivity, his face already bruised from the guard's fists, Myrddin had hoped he could withstand their treatment and not submit. It was clear fairly quickly, however, that they didn't want any information from him.

Perhaps they beat prisoners—and King Arthur's men—as a matter of course.

Five hours later, Myrddin's body was stiff from the cold, his wrists and ankles chained, and he had an almighty headache. The one positive note was that the blood along Myrddin's upper lip had dried and was no longer dripping onto his clothing and the floor. He didn't want to attract those rats to his toes, which, absent his boots, were too easily accessible. Myrddin wiggled them, trying to increase their circulation.

A light flickered through the small window in the wooden door that blocked the entrance to Myrddin's cell. Myrddin shifted, awkward, the shackles digging into his wrists. A rime of blood seeped around the metal band every time he moved, the edge cutting farther into his skin. Then the door opened to reveal Modred himself and two guards, one of whom carried an upright, wooden chair. He set it in the middle of the cell. Modred turned it around and sat facing Myrddin, his arms resting along the top rail.

"So," he said. "Now that we both are situated more comfortably, perhaps you'll answer some of my questions."

It was a jest, but Myrddin wasn't laughing. "I answered truthfully before. I would have answered whatever other questions you chose to put to me in your hall."

"Perhaps." Modred flicked a crumb off his sleeve with one finger towards the rats in the corner. The rats scurried to where the crumb had fallen and, after a brief scuffle, the dominant one ate it. Myrddin watched, horrified, thinking of how easily one could take a bite out of him. "But not as quickly or completely."

Myrddin moved his eyes back to Modred's face. "Why would I be any more likely to do as you ask now, since you're going to kill me anyway?"

"Ah," Modred said. "But the manner of your death remains a mystery. It is something to be negotiated."

126

Myrddin had known all along that Modred was a murderous son-of-a-bitch. What Welshman didn't know that? But, naïvely, Myrddin hadn't expected him to direct this level of villainy at him. Then again, this was the man who hanged a hundred of his own merchants so he could confiscate their possessions—and pay for his war against Arthur. Nothing was beyond this man. Worse, Modred knew that Myrddin knew it.

When Myrddin didn't reply, Modred nodded at one of the guards, who fisted his hand and shot it into Myrddin's midsection. If Myrddin's bonds hadn't held him tightly, he would have gone down and stayed down. As it was, he couldn't even bend forward to better absorb the blow.

"Now," Modred said. "I want the truth. What happened at the Menai Strait?"

"I told you already." Myrddin said. "Cedric did too. It was just as he said."

The guard backhanded Myrddin across the face, and his head clunked against the stones behind him. Blood formed at the corner of his mouth and dripped down his chin. Myrddin turned his head and hunched his shoulders, trying to staunch it on his shirt. He couldn't reach, however, and fell back, moaning more from frustration at his helplessness than the pain.

"I want the rest." Modred said. "There's more. What haven't you told me?"

Myrddin was at a loss, both for something else to give and for what Arthur would think was acceptable for him to say. Myrddin took a stab at a new piece of information. "We sabotaged the boats."

"Better," Modred said. "Whose idea was that?"

"Mine."

Another blow to the kidneys.

"I want the traitor's name," Modred said.

127

Myrddin must have looked as blank as he felt because he received another shot to the face. "Traitor? You mean Lord Cai?"

Modred's face purpled, revealing a passion that was likely to give him heart failure. In his youth, Modred had been Cai's squire. They'd remained close companions for many years afterwards, even after Modred began to assert his own claim to the throne over Cai's. Whatever bond had survived the years had been severed with Cai's latest actions. Perhaps in Modred—as in Cai—love and hatred were two sides of the same coin.

Modred and Myrddin stared at each other and, slowly, Modred's color subsided. He barked a laugh. "I'll give you that. He betrays both sides as it pleases him. No, I want the traitor in my ranks. The one who informed you that Wulfere would cross the Strait that day. I want to know why you were ready for him."

Myrddin opted for a shrug. "We knew. I don't know all the people who told us, but there were many sources. Wulfere was too open about his plans, at least on the Anglesey side. Not all the people there support the Saxon cause."

Another slap, which Myrddin should have known was coming for being cheeky.

"Names," Modred said.

"I have none to give you." Before Myrddin could elaborate on that lack of knowledge, he received another thrust to his abdomen. The pain was intense. His ears still rang from the previous blow, and his eyes no longer saw straight. A black mist rose across his vision. Myrddin fought it, blinking and struggling to stay conscious, even though the blackness would have been a relief. "A doxy. A fisherman. A ferryman. A nun. They all told us."

Modred eased backwards. Myrddin had a brief hope that he'd leave, but Modred got to his feet and came around the chair to stand in front of Myrddin. "You can do better than that."

Myrddin tried to focus on his face, but there appeared to be several of him now. "You have two noses." He found the idea amusing, but the words came out slurred and his eyes blurred from tears he couldn't stop from falling. They hadn't even left him the dignity of wiping at them with the back of his hand.

Modred snorted his disgust. "He's done. For now." He turned away, followed by the guards who pulled the door closed behind them and left the cell in darkness.

Chapter Five
14 November 537 AD

"YOU ARE WELL AND TRULY out of your mind!" Ifan followed Nell down the hall towards Lord Cedric of Brecon's quarters, a stack of logs in his arms for stoking the fire in Cedric's room.

Nell glanced back at him, careful not to tip her tray of food and drink. "Am I? And what was your plan for getting Myrddin out of prison? A straight assault?"

They'd arrived at Rhuddlan in time to see Myrddin hauled away from Cedric's table—and the protest, albeit slight, that engendered from Cedric—and then spent the rest of that night and the next day mingling among the lowlier members of the castle. They both spoke Saxon, Nell better than Ifan, but only Welsh had been required so far, which was engendering a quiet rage in Nell. Her people had done far more to betray Arthur than the Saxons ever could. Well, except for his looming death at the church by the Cam River.

"Better than all this sneaking around," Ifan mumbled, not so low that she couldn't hear him.

At the same time, he hadn't protested more than that, and so far had not objected to her taking charge of this aspect of the endeavor. Clearly, she'd spent far too many years in the company of women, and her confidence was out of place in a castle run by men.

"You got us safely to Rhuddlan," she said. "Trust me to manage this."

Ifan had caught her coming out of her room back at Garth Celyn, dressed as a boy. At first, Ifan hadn't recognized her, which was all to the good as far as she was concerned. Then he'd grabbed her arm and hissed, "What are you doing?"

"Going after Myrddin," she said.

"Alone? Are you mad? Myrddin told me what happened at St. Asaph; what he'd arrived almost too late to stop. You'd risk that again?"

"Better than staying here and allowing him to go into danger alone," Nell had said. "To die at Modred's hands. I don't—I don't have a good feeling about this."

That had brought Ifan up short. He'd looked at her, suspicious. Nell gazed back. Unfortunately, it was no less than the truth, although as always, not all of it. Myrddin went off on his own all the time. The difference today had been her dream last night. Frighteningly, instead of dreaming as Myrddin as she always had, she'd watched the battle from above, looking down on the king's death. Myrddin wasn't even there. Nell's breath had caught in her throat at what that might mean.

And yet, she'd told Ifan more of the truth than she liked to admit. Her visions of Arthur's death took her only so far. Sometimes she simply had a *feeling* that she should do something, or that something wasn't right—as if she could sense the currents and emotions of the people around her and they all added up to a conclusion that she couldn't explain. She'd felt that way in the first moments of Wulfere's attack on her convent. To her regret, she *hadn't* felt it when she'd left her sisters alone in the barn. But she'd learned not to ignore her sense of wrongness when it came.

Ifan nodded. "Neither do I. But this is not a task for a woman. I'll go."

"No!" Nell had said. "You're not going anywhere without me."

"I'll tell the king—"

Nell cut Ifan off with a finger to his lips. "Don't you dare. Besides, I'm a free woman, with no husband or obligations to anyone but myself."

"Except to Myrddin?"

"That is my choice," Nell said.

Ifan had stared into her face for a long moment, and then nodded. "I'll talk to Geraint."

So here they were, thirty miles from Garth Celyn, in the very belly of the Saxon beast. Nell raised a hand to knock at Cedric's door.

"Come in."

Nell pushed the door open and entered the room, followed by Ifan. The room was less rich than some she'd seen in the castle. She'd flitted in and out of many over the last hours, always accompanied by Ifan and his logs. Nobody had to know that those were the same three pieces of wood he'd carried all day. They'd simply moved from room to room, purposeful and diligent, determining the lay of the land.

Nobody ever questioned them or wondered at their actions. Far more than at Garth Celyn, servants here were invisible—even to other servants, provided she and Ifan kept their heads down. Rhuddlan was so huge that it was impossible for any one person to keep track of all the comings and goings.

"My lord," Nell said in Saxon, curtseying, "I've brought you a meal."

Cedric glanced up. "I didn't ask for—" He cut off the sentence when Nell met his gaze with a sharp look she couldn't help. It had been far sharper than he'd probably received from anyone since he was in his nurse's care. "I see," he said, after a quick scan of her face and clothes. "Put it there."

"My name is Nell ferch Morgan," Nell said, abandoning the pretense that she was a boy. She gestured to Ifan, "And this is Ifan, from Garth Celyn."

"You're Myrddin's rescue party, are you?" Cedric's mind discerned the truth faster than Nell could have hoped. "Are there more of you?"

"No." Nell paused. "Unless you're willing to help us?"

"Now why would I want to do that?"

Nell gazed at him, her expression calm while she thought furiously for an answer.

But it was Ifan who spoke. "Because you've got bigger *ceilliau* than Modred."

Cedric smiled.

"WE'RE GETTING YOU OUT of here," Nell said.

Myrddin swam upwards towards the faint light in his cell, coming to himself with his arms around Nell and his head on her shoulder.

"You." He felt marvelous all of a sudden.

Ifan crouched at Myrddin's feet, working at the chains that bound his ankles. Myrddin imagined they too were blood-rimmed, but his lower extremities were so numb from the cold and being forced to stay in one position for so long, he couldn't feel them.

A voice growled from behind Nell. "*I'm* getting you out of here."

Myrddin lifted his head to squint towards the form in the doorway.

Cedric lounged against the frame, his arms folded across his chest. "Hurry up. We haven't much time."

"Not like his lordship couldn't help," Ifan muttered in Welsh, under his breath.

"I grew up in Wales." Cedric's tone was mild. "I learned Welsh in my nurse's arms."

Nell lifted a hand to Myrddin's face. With shaking fingers, she touched his eyebrow. "It's the only part of you that isn't wounded." She was trying to jest, but her voice wavered.

At last Ifan fitted the key into the final lock and opened it. "We need to move."

"I'm fine." Myrddin took a step. "Let's get out of here."

Just because the manacles were loose, however, didn't mean he could walk. If Nell hadn't still been holding him, he would have fallen. Seeing Myrddin's peril, Ifan came up on his other side, his arm around Myrddin's waist. Together, they hobbled towards the door, Myrddin's feet tingling as the blood rushed into them.

Myrddin feared for guards, but Cedric kept a smirk on his face, unconcerned about the treasonous act in which he was openly participating. He turned at their approach, led the way across the stones of the foyer where Myrddin had seen guards earlier, and up the stairs.

They came out of the stairwell into a larger room containing three soldiers, all unconscious. One sprawled across the table at which he'd been sitting at dice, while his companion's head lolled against the right hand wall. The third guard had fallen off his bench onto the floor. He lay on his side, legs splayed in front of him. Like the others, his eyes were closed.

"Drunk." Cedric strode past the table at which they sat, not looking at them but at the same time not even attempting to be quiet.

"The poppy juice I brought helped," Nell said.

Myrddin swiveled his head, searching for his weapons, but Ifan had taken care of the problem. "Your sword's right here." He patted his waist. "We recovered it first, in case we had to leave in a hurry. I left mine outside the castle with the horses."

"Thank you." The sound came out more as a grunt than a word.

A moment later, they were through the far doorway and into the outer bailey. The dungeon—or at least Myrddin's dungeon—was situated in the basement of the southwest, square guard tower that overlooked the Clwyd River. The guardroom door sat at the base of the tower wall, effectively in a ditch, looking up to the inner wall, over two hundred feet away. If Modred had held Myrddin in one of the six towers that defended the inner bailey, he'd never have escaped.

Myrddin had known where Modred had put him, of course, and now that he was being rescued, it seemed more suspicious than lucky to be so far from the central workings of the castle. Then again, maybe Modred didn't like to disturb the castle inhabitants, including his beloved wife, with screaming.

Cedric led them along the curtain wall that fronted the river to the river gate. The drawbridge was up, as it had been when Myrddin had arrived, but the postern door was unguarded. As Cedric drew it open, a moan sounded from farther along the wall in the shadow of the tower.

"He sent him a whore." Nell whispered to Myrddin as she and Ifan dragged Myrddin through the opening.

Cedric halted in the doorway. "I leave you here. You may retrieve your horse at Brecon Castle, my home, should you care to do so."

Myrddin dropped his right arm from Nell's shoulder and held it out to Cedric. "Thank you."

Cedric grasped Myrddin's forearm, nodded stiffly, and shut the door in Myrddin's face. He'd gone before Myrddin realized he'd never responded to Arthur's message.

But then, on second thought, perhaps he had.

Nell, Ifan, and Myrddin staggered down the sharp bank that descended from the gate to the river. They could have crossed at a low spot a half-mile upstream, but it wouldn't do to walk under the walls and expose themselves on the castle side of the Clywd, even at this hour of the night. The sooner they left the vicinity of Rhuddlan the better.

"Can you swim?" Nell said.

"He's a fish when his arms work," Ifan said.

"I'm here," Myrddin said. "I can speak."

"In," Nell said.

Obediently, Myrddin plunged into the water and struck out for the opposite bank. At worst, if he couldn't have made it, he could have let the current carry him north to the ford that he'd ridden across on Cadfarch. Determined to succeed and not put Ifan or Nell into any further danger, Myrddin forced himself to stroke and kick long enough to reach the muddy bank.

He crawled up it, bedraggled and soaking wet, although the cold water made his wounds feel a bit better. Myrddin could even sense his feet and, for the first time, was happy not to have worn boots. Nell and Ifan had kept theirs on and would have to stop once they were clear of the castle to empty them of water.

"How far?" Myrddin said, once they'd clawed their way out of the brush, onto the road, and then across it into the ditch on the other side.

"We left the horses close by." Nell grasped Myrddin's arm and lifted him out of the scrub. "You can make it."

"I'm not sure that I can do anything anymore without you." The words were out before he could censor them. Nell had her head up, watching the road, and didn't respond, for which Myrddin was grateful. Perhaps she hadn't heard him.

Close by wasn't quite as close as he'd hoped. More time passed, Myrddin hobbling on tender feet, before they reached the copse of beech trees in which Ifan had tied the horses. They'd brought only two so, once again, Nell and Myrddin would share. Ifan passed Myrddin his water flask, but Myrddin's hands were so cold, and he was so tired, that he couldn't remove the stopper.

Nell pulled it out, but even then his hands shook so much that the water spilled out the top. In the end, Nell placed both of her hands on either side of his and helped Myrddin tip it up. Then she had to help him out of his wet clothes and into loose breeches and shirt.

"From Caerhun again?" he said as she fastened the cloak around his neck.

"Rhodri laughed when I asked for them," she said, "but he gave way. It was better to be safe than sorry."

Finally, when they were all dressed in dry clothing, Myrddin had to face the notion of climbing on the horse. The saddle looked miles away.

"Come on, lad," Ifan said.

Myrddin rested a hand on Nell's shoulder while Ifan steadied him. With Myrddin's foot in a stirrup, they shoved him hard upwards, shooting him towards the saddle. He sprawled across the horse's withers, exhausted. With some more pushing from Ifan, Myrddin managed to swing his leg over the horse's back and straighten. His forearm was one of the few limbs that didn't hurt, so Myrddin offered it to Nell. She grasped it, clambering into place behind him.

Every bone, muscle, and nerve in Myrddin's body screamed at him. The only reason he was even upright was because Nell held him on the horse. It had been a long time since he'd felt this terrible. If it wouldn't end up hurting him more, Myrddin would have rubbed his face to hide the tears—of pain and the frustration that he couldn't control—that threatened to spill from his eyes.

Myrddin swallowed hard, fighting for control. "Talk," he said, once they urged the horses out of the brush and had given them their heads.

"We followed you," Ifan said, giving Myrddin a chance to gather his wits. "I received permission from Lord Geraint—more or less—and we were gone within an hour of your own departure. As we knew where you were going, we hardly needed to trail you closely."

"Where'd you get the boys' clothes?" Myrddin asked Nell.

"From a stable boy," she said. "He'd outgrown them and his mother'd been saving them for his younger brother."

"And then?" Myrddin said, when neither wanted to continue.

"We followed you all the way here." Ifan shrugged.

"There was a chance you'd rest with the garrison at Caerhun," Nell said, "but Rhodri said they hadn't seen you."

"Or rather," Ifan added, "they'd seen you but you'd crossed the ford instead of turning in at the fort."

"Because we took time at Caerhun and had to hide the horses, we reached Rhuddlan a few hours behind you. It was full dark, but the villagers were still up and about."

"We entered the castle in the back of a hay wagon," Ifan said.

The tag-team story telling was giving Myrddin a headache, but they were in full spate, and Myrddin chose not to stop them. "Go on."

"Hundreds of people work in that castle," Ifan said. "As I left my weapons and armor with the horses on the other side of the Clywd, it was a simple matter to pretend to be other than what we are."

"What I want to know, more than anything, is about Cedric," Myrddin said. "How did you convince him to free me?"

"That was my idea," Nell said. "We dined in the hall at the same time you did—after you'd met with Modred. To our eyes, Cedric didn't object to your company; although we didn't know how you'd met, it seemed fortuitous, given the discussion you and I had at Garth Celyn."

"So when the guards hauled you away," Ifan said, "and Cedric protested, albeit not loudly and not to Modred, we decided to take a chance on him."

"What did you do? Walk up to him and say, *Greetings. We're with Myrddin. Will you help us free him from the dungeon?*"

Ifan laughed from deep in his chest. "Yes. If I'm ever in a tight place, I'd prefer to have Nell with me. She was as bold as Queen Gwenhwyfar herself."

"He deliberated only briefly before he agreed to help you escape," Nell said. "We watched for Modred to come to you again, but he didn't. He went to his bed, and then we acted."

"Thank you for freeing me." Myrddin realized he hadn't yet said it. "It was quite a chance you took."

"I hope Cedric doesn't suffer for it," Nell said, "once Modred realizes you're gone."

The crisp air, along with their story, had perked Myrddin up considerably, even as his muscles stiffened from the cold. "He's Cedric ap Aelfric. He gave the guards wine and women, and if they remember what passed in the night, it will be a miracle. When Cedric tells Modred that he had nothing to do with my escape, if it even comes to that, it will be good enough for Modred."

"Cedric said he wouldn't leave Rhuddlan until the guards discovered your absence, after which he and his men would travel south to Brecon." Ifan paused, thinking. "I'm missing something, aren't I?"

"As in, the why of it? Why did he risk his own neck to free me?" The sight of Cedric in the doorway was fresh in Myrddin's mind and he felt a weight lifting from his shoulders. "He is willing to consider an alliance with King Arthur."

"He said that?" Nell said.

"He showed it," Myrddin said.

Chapter Six

15 November 537 AD

"CAN YOU HEAR ME, MYRDDIN?" Nell leaned over Myrddin's inert form.

Although Myrddin didn't reply, he did open his eyes to look into her face. The room was dark, except for a candle on the table at the foot of the pallet on which he lay. Nell smiled, even though it cost her. Myrddin didn't smile back, just stared, unseeing, and then let his eyes close. Nell stroked his cheek with one finger. And then she did smile, albeit mockingly, at what he'd think when he discovered that she'd shaved his mustache in order to tend to the gash above his lip.

It had been a long, grim ride from Rhuddlan Castle. Myrddin had been so much weaker than usual, and the last few miles had almost been his undoing. It had been all she could do to hold him on the horse. Modred's men had wounded him inside and out, though she wouldn't know how bad the damage was inside him until the rest of him began to heal.

"Would you like to hear a story?" she said.

Again, Myrddin didn't answer. He'd squeezed the hand she was holding earlier, but now his grip softened. She gazed down at his closed eyes, thinking of what story to tell, and whether it was time to tell him a true one. "Once upon a time, there was a little girl ...

SHE WAS JUST LIKE ANY other little girl—shocking red hair, green eyes, pointed chin—doted upon by her father, especially as he'd lost his wife at her birth.

One day, as she was wandering in the trees along the river near her home, looking for any winter herbs that had survived the snow, she heard voices—men's voices—very close. They shouted at one another. Hooves pounded on the soft earth, and then, not ten feet from her, a company of five men wearing King Arthur's crest rode out of the woods, swords and shields raised high. They splashed through the water and up the bank on the other side.

The girl was frightened. She ran the opposite way, but instead of running into her father's field as she expected, she found herself in a clearing, next to a church. All around her men called, and horses neighed. She ran for the entrance to the church, but, just as she reached it, the door opened. A man appeared, older than her father, his dark hair shot with grey. She'd never seen him before, but somehow she knew he was their king. He pulled his sword from his sheath, shouted at the men behind him, and retreated back inside.

Oddly, the man didn't see her. A moment later, the men who'd ridden through the water returned, racing their horses towards a line of Saxon soldiers that had burst from the woods on the other side of the clearing. All around her men fought and died.

Then, one man in particular caught her attention. He'd lost his helmet, and his black hair had come loose from its tie. His shield was gone too, and, between forcing his sword through a Saxon's belly and turning to race for the front of the church, he thrust his hair out of his face with his free hand.

In that space of time, she caught his eye. They stared at each other. They couldn't have been more different: Nell—a small, scrawny child, not yet blooming into womanhood; and Myrddin—a tall, dark-haired soldier, older, with lines around his eyes.

Then he broke away, racing to defend his king. She watched him barrel into a Saxon soldier; she watched him fall. She watched the Saxon soldiers celebrate their victory. And it was she who pulled the man to the side, off of the body of his king whose head the Saxons soldiers had taken while they left the rest of him to rot. And it was she who wept over his grave ...

"SO NOW YOU'VE SAVED *me*," Myrddin said. From the way the light reflected from the hallway through the open door, it was late afternoon. He'd slept a long time.

"Does that make us even?" Nell said.

"Do you want it to?"

She smiled and didn't answer, looking down at her hands. She'd tucked her hair into her cloak, but the end of her thick braid peeked out from underneath the hood. Then she looked up. "It hurts me to see you this way."

"It hurts me too," he said, trying to make light of it.

"I wish we could have reached you sooner."

"I'll heal," he said.

"Hidden away in my convent, I forgot the horror one man could do to another. I've been reminded almost daily since then."

"Believe me, Modred is capable of much worse."

Nell nodded. "I stitched the back of your head while you were asleep. I kept waiting for you to wake in the middle of it and argue with me about the proper method." She smiled. "I would have had Ifan cosh you on the head to put you back to sleep."

Myrddin laughed and then tried to suppress it, moving his hand to his chest. "Don't!" He swallowed the mirth and the pain the laughter had caused. "Where's Ifan now?"

"He stayed up with you most of the night," she said. "Did you know *he's* in pain nearly all the time?"

"It's his back," Myrddin said. "He injured it ten years ago—doing less than nothing, mind you—and it's never been the same since. But a soldier who can't ride and fight isn't a soldier anymore."

"I told him I'd make a rubbing salve for him when we returned to Garth Celyn." She turned her head to look through the doorway. The scent of greenery and outside air wafted through it, indicating that the temperature had risen. "It's peaceful here, isn't it? I didn't notice the first time we came through."

"We're at Caerhun?" Myrddin said.

Nell nodded. "That was the longest twenty miles I've ever ridden."

Footsteps sounded along the corridor. "You're awake." Rhodri poked his head through the doorway.

"In a manner of speaking," Myrddin said. "Thank you for your hospitality, as before."

"I thought you'd like to know that the Saxons patrol the eastern bank of the river. Three separate companies have ridden to the ford, to turn around at the water's edge. I would not have said you were that valuable." A grin split Rhodri's face.

"Nor I," Myrddin said.

Rhodri shrugged. "Let me know if you need anything, miss," he said to Nell.

"Thank you."

Rhodri left.

Myrddin gazed up at the ceiling, thinking about the past and the future and all that lay between them. He didn't fear death. He hadn't for many years, not with living it every night in his dreams. But despair was as close a companion for him over the years as for Nell, and it had overwhelmed him after Modred had left the dungeon. To have come so close to making a difference in whether Arthur lived or died, only to die at Modred's hand, had left him bereft. Now that they'd fled the castle and were safe in Arthur's lands again, the emotions he'd been holding in check came flooding back.

"I should have guessed that you were up to something," Myrddin said. "When I turned to look back at the castle and saw you and Ifan on the battlements, I should have been suspicious. Had you already decided what you were going to do?"

"I'd already decided to come after you, but Ifan wouldn't let me come alone."

"I should hope not," Myrddin said. "Were you afraid?"

"Not during the journey; not even when we reached the crossroads at St. Asaph. Ifan is a strong swordsman, or you wouldn't trust him. I was afraid for you and afraid that Modred would have already murdered you before we could reach Rhuddlan."

"I was afraid of that too," Myrddin said.

"The only comfort," Nell said, "was the assumption that you knew what you were doing."

Myrddin started to laugh and then swallowed it, trying not to move. "I'm not so sure you should have relied on that notion."

Nell smiled. "Once Cedric said he'd assist us, however, things moved quickly, and I hardly had time to think. He had it all in hand."

"Thank you," Myrddin said. "I don't know that Cedric would have freed me unless you encouraged him."

"I'm not so sure. It would depend on how much he thought he could gain from sticking his neck out."

"He stuck it pretty far," Myrddin said.

"He did," Nell said. "What did you say to him to make the two of you so friendly?"

"I told him that Arthur wanted to negotiate—to talk to him—even to work out an alliance."

Myrddin had closed his eyes again, as keeping them open was just too much work, but at Nell's silence, turned his head to look at her. A range of emotions crossed her face: shock, disbelief, puzzlement, and then understanding.

"Given that the king has never said any such thing, you took a risk," she said. "Suppose King Arthur doesn't want to talk to him?"

"Why wouldn't he? The king is willing to talk to Edgar, and he's far less likely a turncoat than Cedric. Cedric, at least, has a history of rebellion. Edgar is the son of the only Saxon lord with interests in Wales never to waver in Modred's cause, for all Modred has angered him now."

"What are you going to tell King Arthur?"

"The truth. Even your part of it—provided you do not object?" He studied her face. She had a smudge on her nose and a second along one cheek.

Nell lifted her hands and dropped them in an expression of resignation and helplessness. "Ifan and I made our choice. I don't regret it. Given that we rescued you, I'd hope King Arthur wouldn't either."

Myrddin nodded. "I'm glad you've told me everything now. I'm glad you know that you can trust me."

Nell sat silent for a long count of ten. "You weren't asleep."

"No."

Nell stayed frozen, her legs in front of her and her back against the wall.

"You have visions," Myrddin said, not as a question. "You've had them of me."

Nell swallowed hard. "Since I was a girl."

"Back at Garth Celyn, you cried my name in the night. You've done so often in the nights that followed."

"You've haunted me all my life," she said. "The story I told you was a waking dream—my first and only. It's why I've always known that you were real, even when all I had were dreams."

Myrddin nodded.

"You're not upset by this." Nell canted her head to one side, looking at him curiously. "Why aren't you afraid of me? Or at the very least, suspicious?"

"On December 11th, a month from now, if we do not stop it, King Arthur will die at the hands of a Saxon soldier, near a church by the Cam River," Myrddin said.

"That's what I see in my dreams," Nell said. "I just told you that story last night. That's what I dream nearly every night now. It's changed a bit in the last few days. But—"

Myrddin interrupted. "That's *my* dream, ever since I was twelve years old."

The relief he felt in admitting it to Nell—and that she would understand everything he felt—filled him. His was a true seeing, and they'd been given this vision for a reason. It appeared to be *their* job—his and Nell's—by what means he didn't know and couldn't imagine from where he lay—to ensure that his king did not meet Edgar by the Cam. He met Nell's eyes as understanding entered them: *their* vision; *their* task; *their* destiny.

Nell stared at him. "It isn't just me, then!"

Myrddin shook his head. "It isn't just you."

Chapter Seven

16 November 537 AD

MYRDDIN SLEPT AGAIN, woke in the early evening, and then slept in fits and starts throughout a second night at Caerhun. Every time he tried to roll over, he awoke in pain, but either Ifan or Nell was there to ease him into a more comfortable position. Ifan had a soldier's ability to watch or sleep in whatever situation he found himself, but the times Nell sat beside him, she talked. Some of what she said Myrddin remembered, but mostly he let the sound of her voice wash over him as she related a story from her girlhood, or another from the tales of the *Dôn*. She didn't speak of the dreams again, but then, Myrddin knew that story too well himself.

At dawn, Myrddin came to himself enough to realize that he couldn't delay any longer, and neither Nell nor Ifan protested that they should stay. They knew as well as he that King Arthur awaited word of Myrddin's journey. Soon, the king would begin to fear that Myrddin would never return. Most importantly, Myrddin had information for him and Myrddin didn't want him doing anything rash because of lack of knowledge.

In the pouring rain, which was a match to the companions' low mood, they made their slow way out of Caerhun. By late afternoon, they had reached the last stretch, descending down the road from the standing stones to Garth Celyn. The men-at-arms on the battlements saw them coming and opened the gates, welcoming them home.

In the muddy bailey, Nell slid off the horse. Myrddin climbed down with Ifan's help, his body stiff and a hand at his ribs. Even though they'd walked the horses the whole way, Myrddin could barely move from the effort the journey had cost him. Most of the day was gone, as slowly as they'd taken it.

"Your face looks much worse." It came out as a matter-of-fact comment as Nell steered him towards the hall. "I have something inside to help with the bruising."

"It's my ribs that ache the most," Myrddin said. "I'm glad Modred's lackeys didn't puncture a lung."

"From my examination, all your bones are whole," she said. "Not to diminish the pain, but I felt you all over when you were unconscious and you're only bruised."

"*Only*," Myrddin said.

Nell tsked through her teeth. "Infant."

They'd taken one step up the stairs to the double doors that guarded the hall when one of the doors opened to reveal King Arthur. Nell and Myrddin froze, their heads tipped up, looking into his face. He pursed his lips and then took two steps down to where they stood. Without saying anything, either admonishment or praise, he placed Myrddin's arm over his shoulder. Taking most of the weight off Nell, he hobbled with Myrddin into the hall, across it, and down the corridor.

"I need to rest." Myrddin's breath came in gasps.

"In here." Arthur maneuvered him through the door to his receiving room and onto his own padded chair. He motioned to Nell to shut the door behind them. "Better to talk in private."

The room contained two more men: Bedwyr, as always, since he never left King Arthur's side while he was at Garth Celyn except to sleep, and a much younger man standing with him, a youth, no more than sixteen or seventeen, albeit full grown—tall and well built—with shoulders used to wearing armor. Arthur straightened as Myrddin collapsed into the chair, and Nell put a hand to his upper arm to keep him from falling out of it.

Not giving Myrddin a chance to catch his breath, King Arthur held out a hand to the boy, who took a step closer. "Myrddin."

Myrddin looked up. Arthur's tone had been abrupt, but now an uncharacteristic smile—one Myrddin might even call gleeful—covered his face.

"Meet Huw ap Myrddin. Your son."

The boy looked straight at Myrddin, staring with an unrelieved intensity, and gave Myrddin a slight and very stiff bow. "Father."

"Wha—" Myrddin gaped at the boy, his head empty of any thought with which to work. "Who?"

"Huw ap Myrddin." The boy's spine matched his words, taut, like a bow string set to loose its arrow.

Myrddin's eyes ranged from the top of the boy's head to his boots, stunned speechless.

"My mother was Tegwan. From Brecon," Huw said, still quivering.

Tegwan. Dear God. He stared at the boy, this unexpected gift, and managed a nod. He remembered her—if the vague image of shape and form could be called a memory. Then Myrddin caught Huw's choice of words. "Was? She *was* called Tegwan?"

"My mother died two months ago," Huw said. "I've been looking for you ever since."

"I do remember her," Myrddin said, not exactly lying.

Huw released a long breath, and his shoulders sagged.

It was as if Myrddin had passed a test he hadn't known he was taking. If he'd had the strength to pace, he would have, but as it was, Myrddin shifted in his chair, hot and uncomfortable. "She never told me about you. I would have acknowledged you as my son had I known you existed. Surely Tegwan knew that?"

"My mother married someone else." Huw paused, swallowed hard, and continued, "A Saxon. He knew I wasn't his son because she was already pregnant by the time they married, but he preferred to say I was his. I grew up thinking that he was my natural father.

They had no other children, and when my father died two years ago, my mother told me the truth."

Myrddin waited for more. He could hardly accuse Huw of neglecting to search for him sooner, given that Huw knew nothing of Myrddin or where he was. And he'd been raised half-Saxon. That wasn't easily put aside.

"My mother was ill herself by then, a wasting disease, and I couldn't leave her beyond my regular duties to my lord," Huw said. "I came north to Gwynedd as soon as he gave me leave to find you."

"And who is your lord?" Myrddin said.

Huw bit his lip and glanced at Arthur, who nodded. Huw hemmed and hawed for a few more moments, and then blurted it out. "Lord Cedric of Brecon."

"Ho!" Nell said from beside Myrddin. "Well, that's a tangle, isn't it?"

"Did you tell him my name?" Myrddin said. "And that I served King Arthur?"

"Of course," Huw said. "For what it was worth, as you go only by your first name. My lord Cedric had less need of me during these few weeks of the Archbishop's truce. He didn't want me to come with him to Anglesey so he gave me permission to search for you."

And to act as his spy in the Welsh camp? The thought rose unbidden, but once admitted, couldn't be ignored. Myrddin looked at the king. "It was Cedric, with Nell and Ifan's assistance, who freed me from Rhuddlan's dungeon."

"Did he now?" Arthur scanned Myrddin's wounded body. It was impossible to hide the damage to his face or the awkward and uncomfortable way in which he was sitting. Every square inch of him, hurt, except perhaps his eyebrow, as Nell had noted.

Huw, too, perked up at the mention of his patron's name. "My lord freed you? But who did this?" Uncertainty entered his eyes for the first time. "Surely not Modred!"

"Surely it was Modred," Myrddin said. "Or rather, Modred's guards on his behalf."

"Tell me that Lord Cedric wasn't present at the time!"

"He was not," Myrddin said. "I spoke with him at length earlier in the evening. We were dining together when the guards took me away."

"I have always found Lord Cedric to be fair and honorable," Huw said.

"We know." Myrddin flapped a hand in his direction and managed not to laugh at him openly. "Stand down."

Arthur turned to Nell. "Perhaps you could find our young man some food and drink."

"Yes, my lord." Nell released Myrddin's hand, which she'd been holding tightly. Myrddin nodded at Huw and hoped that Nell understood that it was not she who was being dismissed, but Huw.

The boy made to leave too, but Myrddin held out a hand to stop him. "Wait." With one hand on the table in front of him for support, he got to his feet so he could stand face to face with his son. They possessed similar coloring and were of a height, although Huw was perhaps a half inch taller. The boy had Myrddin's straight nose but his mother's blue eyes, where Myrddin's were hazel. Myrddin settled a hand on each of Huw's shoulders and gripped them. "I'm glad you came to find me. Any man would be proud to claim you as his son."

Huw held Myrddin's arms, his fingers tight around his biceps. "Thank you, sir." He still carried himself with a tenseness that kept his shoulders back and his jaw firm, but some of the anxiety seemed to have left him.

"Nell is a good friend," Myrddin said. "She'll take care of you."

"Yes, Father." With a last, direct look, Huw left the room with Nell.

Myrddin sank back into his seat, his head in his hands. King Arthur, having lost his usual chair to Myrddin, perched on the edge of the desk. Bedwyr found a seat on the bench under the window.

"I'd be delighted to know what's going on," King Arthur said.

Myrddin looked up. "Damned if I know, my lord. Huw—" Myrddin made a helpless gesture towards the door. "I didn't know."

Bedwyr spoke from his corner. "Didn't your mother neglect to divulge the identity of *your* father before she died?"

"Yes," Myrddin said. "At least Tegwan gave the boy my name and encouraged him to find me, once her husband was dead."

"What was your mother's name again?" Bedwyr said.

Myrddin glanced at him, not sure why he wanted to know. "I don't know that I've ever told you. Her name was Seren ferch Gruffydd."

"An unusual name, Seren," Bedwyr said.

"Did you know her?" Myrddin checked Bedwyr's face again, but Bedwyr kept it blank. Lord Cedric could take lessons from him.

"I never met her," Bedwyr said.

Myrddin nodded and clutched at his hair. Arthur had risen from the table while Bedwyr and Myrddin talked, and now he moved to stand at the window, looking out at the flickering lights of the torches in the bailey, his hands clasped behind his back. "I did."

Myrddin's jaw dropped.

"Her father was an ally of mine until he defected to King Icel of Mercia the year before my uncle died. His action left his daughter alone, here at Garth Celyn, as one of my Aunt Juliana's ladies."

Towards the end of the 490's, King Icel of Mercia had appeared unstoppable. He'd wooed many a Welsh lord away from Ambrosius with promises of land and power, were he to conquer Wales once and for all. Instead, King Ambrosius and Arthur had defeated the allied Saxon forces in the summer of 500 AD at Mt. Badon. Unfortunately, Ambrosius had died in February of 501, followed six months later by Arthur's father, Uther. This left a gap in authority, filled instantly—if inadequately—by Arthur himself, then aged twenty-one.

Myrddin had been born into Madoc's household in September of 501—into a year of upheaval and strife. Each of the remaining Welsh lords, along with all of the Saxon barons, saw themselves as possible heirs to Ambrosius' throne. They'd fought among themselves for control of Wales. Though it was Arthur, of course, who triumphed. It was to avoid that horror again that many Welsh lords supported Modred now, preferring an orderly transition to possible war.

"I didn't know that," Myrddin said. "I thought my mother had grown up in Madoc's charge."

"No."

"But—"

"Speak to me of Cedric," King Arthur said.

Myrddin blinked, not wanting to leave the subject of his mother, but unable to disobey. "I don't know if you're going to like what I have to say, my lord. I took some liberties—"

"And paid for them, by the looks." Bedwyr's lips curved into a smile.

Myrddin coughed and laughed at the same time. "You could say that. Although as I told you before, these wounds were courtesy of Modred." Myrddin took a breath, his abdomen aching at the effort. "After I gave Modred your letter, he directed me to bring Lord Cedric of Brecon to him. Thus, Cedric and I had a few moments of privacy in his room. I took the opportunity to suggest that you, my lord, would be open to a discussion of the disposition of various lands in Wales if Cedric reconsidered his allegiance."

King Arthur swung around to stare at Myrddin.

"I apologize, my lord," Myrddin said. "It seemed like a good idea at the time, and the odds of him agreeing, or of anything coming of it at all, seemed worth the slight risk to my neck."

"It was obviously worth far more than that to Cedric," Bedwyr said. "And the fact that he had already heard your name from Huw sheds new light on the entire matter."

"It does," Myrddin said, although he was having a hard time figuring out what exactly it told him. He was feeling more and more wobbly and desperately wanted a drink, a bed, and Nell's gentle hand on his forehead, not necessarily in that order. "One more thing. Modred knows that you've sent Lord Gawain to Powys to marshal men against the Saxon lords there. Worse, Cedric told him of Edgar of Wigmore's letter to you. I don't know how he knew of it, except if Edgar himself told him."

The two men observed Myrddin, unspeaking, too well-practiced at absorbing bad news to show it openly, but clearly nonplussed. Bedwyr put down his cup of wine and leaned forward. "Go on."

"They are convinced, both of them, that Edgar is not sincere in his desire to ally with you and intends to lure you into an ambush, my lord king," Myrddin said, and then ventured to assert his own opinion. "I would think that likely."

"Thank you, Myrddin," Bedwyr said, implying he wasn't at all thankful for his advice, and then continued, half under his breath to the king—"The uncertainty in the air reminds me of the days after your uncle and father died, before you fully grasped the reins of Wales, my lord."

"Go to your son." King Arthur's expression softened at Myrddin's evident distress. He canted his head towards the door. "I don't want to see you in the hall tomorrow."

"And watch Huw closely," Bedwyr said.

Myrddin looked up, dismayed at the warning in Bedwyr's tone—and yet understanding it, for he'd had the same uncomfortable thought.

"He is Cedric's man," Bedwyr said. "He's already seen too much. I would be wary of allowing him to return to Brecon."

"Yes, sir." Myrddin didn't like Bedwyr's observation but knew he was right. He also didn't want the presence of his son to jeopardize Arthur's new found trust in Myrddin himself.

Still, Myrddin didn't move. His head felt like it weighed fifty pounds. Before he knew it, Arthur and Bedwyr were on either side of him. They pulled him up, just as the guards had done in the hall at Rhuddlan, but more gently, and half-dragged, half-carried him down the hall, out the door and across the courtyard to the sleeping quarters in the guest house. The small closet space in which Nell and Myrddin had slept before was vacant. The pallets lay on the floor, beckoning Myrddin with their softness and warmth. He reached an arm towards one. Bedwyr and Arthur laid him down.

"I'll find Nell," Bedwyr said.

It seemed Myrddin nodded agreement, but he couldn't be sure because an instant later, he was asleep.

Chapter Eight

17 November 537 AD

"MYRDDIN, DAMN IT, GET over here!"

"Coming, sir!" I hurried towards Gawain, my boots slipping in the snow, and we met in the center of the clearing by the church. In the growing darkness, the temperature had dropped, and snowflakes had begun to drift down from the sky, filling in our footprints. I would have been happier to have had four more eyes in order to see in all directions. The Saxons were coming. I sure as hell wanted to be ready when they did.

"The king is inside, waiting, but I'm impatient with Edgar. I expected him here by now," Gawain said. "I think we need to leave this place."

"Yes, sir," I said. "I'll tell King Arthur."

I strode towards the door to the church, glad that Gawain had decided to follow his instincts. I reached the bottom step and was just beginning to mount the stairs when the world blew apart. An arrow whipped by my left ear. I ducked and spun around, my sword in my hand.

"The king! The king!"

THE FIRST TIME MYRDDIN woke, Huw sat beside his pallet. A low candle guttered in a dish on the floor, the light flickering and reflecting off the walls of the room. Someone—Nell, perhaps—had removed his boots and covered him with a wool blanket or three. Myrddin was warm enough, even if his nose was cold since the room was one of the few in the manor house without a fireplace.

He rolled onto his back, noting that someone had also taken his cloak. He spared a thought for his armor, left behind at Rhuddlan, and reconciled himself to the knowledge that it was gone forever. He trusted that Arthur would see him properly protected when it came to it again.

Pushing aside the changing dream and what it meant, Myrddin turned his head to study his son. Huw sat upright against the wall, his eyes closed. At Myrddin's movement, Huw opened them.

"Hello, Father." He didn't appear to mind saying it. Myrddin certainly wouldn't ever grow tired of hearing it. He still couldn't believe that Huw could be his.

"What is the hour?" Myrddin said.

"The chapel rang Matins not long ago," Huw said. "Your friend, Nell, said she'd relieve me at Lauds."

"You don't have to stay."

Huw shrugged. "After the events of the day, I doubt I could sleep anyway." He smiled. "It's an honor to watch over you."

His obvious admiration—a sharp contrast to his earlier near-hostility—confused Myrddin, until he considered a possible source. "Someone's been talking."

"You have many friends," Huw said. "Ifan, certainly, but Lord Geraint joined us for the evening meal. They spoke of you at length."

"Do *not* believe everything they say."

Huw laughed. "Ifan said you'd say that."

"He was there when your mother and I met. Did he speak of it?" Myrddin said.

"Only that you were a squire in King Arthur's company. You came to Brecon in the fall of 520," Huw said. "But I knew that already from my mother."

"I was nineteen. Older than you, but in no way ready to be a father." Myrddin looked at Huw. "Your mother must have known it."

"I believe she did, else, why keep you a secret? It isn't as if you ever came looking for her again."

Christ. What do I say to that? "I did love her. I was careless with my heart and hers."

"And that's your excuse?" Huw's voice rose, and the admiration of a moment ago was forgotten in favor of long-suppressed resentment.

"Is that why you came to find me?" Myrddin said. "To accuse me of abandoning your mother? Of abandoning you?"

Huw looked down at his hands, clenched in his lap so tightly his knuckles whitened. Then he relaxed them, smoothing the palms on the fabric of his breeches.

"Yes. My anger just now caught me unawares, but I've felt it ever since my mother told me the truth."

"I served my king," Myrddin said. "I was with your mother in the fall and winter but even with the upheaval in Brecon the following year, King Arthur never called me south of Buellt again. It's my fault that I never asked leave to go." He paused, hesitating. The real truth shamed him; yet, at this late date, it was a truth from which he should not hide and which his son deserved. "And I did not ask to go because I was afraid to see your mother—I was afraid that she would ask for a commitment from me which I felt unable to give."

"Did you ever think of her?" Huw's voice didn't reveal anger now so much as pain.

"I was a coward, Huw," Myrddin said. "The longer I waited to see her, the worse the guilt. And after a year or two, I told myself that your mother would have forgotten me; that it was better for both of us if I didn't return." Huw didn't answer straight away and

158

so Myrddin added, his voice as gentle as he could make it, "For all that our acquaintance was short, your mother and I enjoyed each other's company."

"My mother said as much to me."

"But she still never wanted you to know about me."

Huw shifted, discomfited. Myrddin sensed he'd only added to his son's questions. "My father's family has served Lord Cedric for many years. My—" he licked his lips, "—father was a knight to Cedric's grandfather." He paused and glanced at Myrddin, a rueful smile on his face.

"Go on," Myrddin said. "I know the history."

"After Badon, Lord Cedric's family lost Brecon to King Arthur, but not their interest in it. My stepfather was often in the area," Huw said. "He'd had his eye on my mother for some time. She was with you, and then she was with him. She wouldn't tell me more than that."

Myrddin sighed, not even remembering the nineteen-year-old he'd been. It was so long ago, he had to wade through misty memory to catch a glimpse of those long ago battles. All Myrddin truly remembered of Tegwan was the hint of a laugh when he touched her, and his own eagerness.

"I was a fool to let her go." Myrddin noted the sturdy lankiness of his son and knowing how different all their lives would have been if he'd had as much courage in his personal life as on the battlefield.

"I loved my father—my mother's husband, but I've always been half-Welsh." Huw turned his head to look at Myrddin, his face intent. "I have resented you, it's true, but it is my hope that I will no longer have to be torn in two."

Myrddin had been a father to Huw for half a day and already the boy needed counseling. Myrddin didn't know that he was the right one to give it, but as he was the only one available, he had no choice. "Help me to sit up."

Huw grasped Myrddin's hand and hauled him to a sitting position. Myrddin swung his legs over the edge of the pallet so he could rest next to Huw, their backs to the wall. Myrddin reached for the water cup and took a long drink.

"The world is not divided as simply as the lines between countries make us think." Myrddin set down the cup. "You are full Welsh, by blood, but you were raised by a Saxon."

"Yes," Huw said.

"A man who loved you."

"Yes." Huw paused and Myrddin let him say what he was feeling, not at all offended. "And I loved him."

"I'm glad," Myrddin said. "If I wasn't a father to you all these years, I would much rather you had a different father, than none at all."

"Was that how it was for you? You have no paternal name. You are just Myrddin."

"My mother took the name of my father to her grave," Myrddin said. "Apparently, she never told him either—or he was dead too, before my birth."

"That must have been hard."

Myrddin was a bit surprised that Huw would speak to him of it. "It certainly made it difficult to dress me down as my betters would have liked." Myrddin smiled. "Nobody could say, *Myrddin ap Geraint ap Bedwyr, get over here!*" As Myrddin hoped, Huw smiled too. "I was not unique, certainly. Many of my companions growing up had lost their fathers early in life."

"But they knew who they were," Huw said.

"Yes," Myrddin said, "but as I had no choice, I didn't dwell on it." Myrddin paused. "Although, admittedly, I learned to fight almost before I could walk."

160

"And nobody seems to have any difficulty remembering who you are," Huw said.

Now Myrddin laughed. "Apparently not."

"When I began my search, I still called myself Huw ap Tomos, after my ... father," Huw said. "But as I approached Gwynedd, I met more people who knew you, or had heard of you. They mentioned one battle in particular, many years ago in the south, along the border with Mercia. You saved King Arthur's life that day."

Myrddin nodded at his son. "The king knighted me after that. It's his way to choose one man after each battle upon whom to confer the honor, and that day it was mine."

"I would like that for myself," Huw said. "Or, at least, I always saw myself serving in my lord's retinue. But now, I don't know what I'm meant to do; whom I'm meant to be or which lord I should serve."

"If you live honorably within yourself, it doesn't matter so much whom you serve," Myrddin said. This was Huw's real concern, and what had hovered over their conversation from the first.

Huw turned his head to look at Myrddin. "You believe that?"

Myrddin's eyes crinkled at the corners, and his mouth twitched with sudden laughter, because Huw had caught him out. "Except in this case. If King Arthur loses this war, our country will fall to the Saxons. Modred cares only for himself and his own power—despite the fact that he himself is half-Welsh. He desires to completely subjugate my people—your people too—and all evidence suggests that he will settle for nothing less. Your lord, Cedric, knows this."

"Which is why he might be willing to ally himself with King Arthur," Huw said.

"Possibly," Myrddin said. "Cedric fears that were Arthur to die, or lose this war, it will embolden Modred. Cedric himself does not possess such a high standing with Modred that he might not lose everything too."

"Even though he and Modred are cousins through their fathers."

"Yes."

"So you're saying that it matters this time," Huw said. "You're saying that it has reached a point where I have to decide the greater loyalty."

"Yes, if Cedric sticks with Modred. You can't both be Welsh and serve him. When Cedric himself freed me from Modred's grasp, however, he took a step towards shifting allegiance. It is also possible that Modred wanted me free, but wanted me freed covertly."

"Lord Cedric ap Aelfric has always dealt forthrightly with his men," Huw said, back to being a staunch supporter. "He is a good leader."

"I'll grant you that, but I must warn you, my son, that not everyone in this castle trusts your motives." Myrddin had deliberated with himself as to whether he should mention it, but the time seemed right.

"They fear I would betray King Arthur?" Huw said, eyes wide, a typical youth who still saw everything in black and white instead of realizing the world was mottled shades of grey.

"Think, Huw," Myrddin said. "This shouldn't surprise you. King Arthur has been betrayed by family, friends, and hidden foes more times than he can count. Is it any wonder some of his counselors would look askance at my newly claimed son who so conveniently rides to me from Brecon?"

"I see your point." Huw nodded, although Myrddin wasn't sure if he quite did.

"Just watch yourself," Myrddin said. "Better to keep silent and your eyes open."

"Yes, sir."

They were quiet a moment, and then Huw spoke again. "It was only chance, you know, that had me risk crossing the Conwy River and entering Eryri."

"Chance?" Myrddin said.

"In a tavern in Ruthin, I came upon a man who claimed to know you—or at least know the man whom the king knighted back in 525—but he told me you were dead. My heart fell. It seemed it was time to turn aside and return to Brecon."

"But you didn't," Myrddin said.

Huw shook his head. "Later in the evening, an argument developed between the man to whom I'd spoken and another. That man accused the first of being a liar and a traitor. The latter owed fealty to Arthur while the first had supported his brother, Cai, throughout his years of treachery." Huw glanced at Myrddin, his eyes thoughtful. "That was the tipping point. With my Lord Cedric on Anglesey, I was still free to search. I decided I wouldn't take the word of one man who did not hold with your allegiance."

"Praise God for that," Myrddin said.

"So what happens now?" Huw said.

"Cedric asked me to come to him at Brecon for the return of my horse. He isn't ready to turn wholly away from Modred or turn to King Arthur. He intends, I think, to continue our discussion."

"Lord Cedric and his father once fought with Arthur." Huw tipped his chin upwards and stared at the rafters.

"They did," Myrddin said. "God willing, Cedric will again. I hope that once I've healed, you and I can journey together to convince him to honor that history."

MYRDDIN THOUGHT A SINGLE night at Garth Celyn should have been enough to heal him. Nell, on the other hand,

163

was quite happy to have him more contained than usual. Bruised ribs could take weeks to mend. If they were right about what was coming for Wales and the king, Myrddin wasn't going to have the luxury of that much time. At least he was mobile, even if he looked and felt terrible.

The second evening back from Rhuddlan, Nell helped Myrddin hobble into the hall to share a meal with Ifan and Huw. The joy of Huw's very existence filled Myrddin's heart each time he said *my son*, as if no man before him had ever had one. She could see it. It brought her nearly to tears every time—for Myrddin's sake and because her own heart lifted at the thought of one of her long-dead sons walking through the door. Huw was only two years older than her Llelo would have been.

They were halfway through the meal when instead of a beloved son, Deiniol pushed open the great doors and walked into the hall, an enormous grin on his face. Immediately behind him were Lord Gruffydd and his son, Owain. Cai, who'd been sitting at his place at the high table on Arthur's right, rose to his feet. "By God, I prayed you'd come!"

He headed around the table and, in several long strides, he and Owain met in the center of the hall, careless of who watched or what they thought of this development. As Owain and Gruffydd had been co-conspirators with Cai eight years before when they'd plotted to assassinate Arthur, it was understandable that some of Arthur's men might give them a rather less-than-effusive greeting.

Arthur, a smile on his lips that didn't reach his eyes, canted his head in greeting to Gruffydd, who strolled down the aisle between the tables until he reached the point opposite Arthur's seat.

"My king." Gruffydd bowed his head, although not perhaps as far as he could have.

"Gruffydd." Arthur gave his guest a similar, slight nod. The king gestured with his hand to the space beside him on his left, which Geraint had hastily vacated two heartbeats before. Normally, Bedwyr, Arthur's closest confident, sat next to him on the other side, but he hadn't appeared for the meal. Could be, he didn't want to sit next to Cai, who'd taken his customary chair.

Then, inexplicably, Deiniol detached himself from Cai's side and headed directly towards the four of them.

"What's he doing?" Myrddin said.

Nell put a hand on his arm, just in case he acted first and thought later. She didn't want Deiniol to insult her again, but she also didn't want Myrddin to cause a scene either. In his weakened condition, Myrddin was more vulnerable than she. Deiniol, for his part, remained polite. He stopped two feet from their table, put his heels together, and bowed to Nell.

"Madam," he said.

"Deiniol," she replied, aiming for graciousness, although she couldn't stop the twitch of a smile that lurked in the corner of her mouth at having to be polite to him. Perhaps humor might conquer Myrddin's loathing.

"So you didn't have a death wish after all," Myrddin said.

Nell elbowed him under the table, hitting a painful spot that left him gasping, and then she smiled at Deiniol. "It was a great thing you did, bringing Gruffydd and Owain here. It must have been a dangerous journey."

Deiniol smiled, his eyes scanning Myrddin's bruised face. "It looks as if you've had it rougher than I."

"It's been an eventful week in your absence," Myrddin said.

"Was the road difficult?" Nell said, still speaking as sweetly as she could.

"It was no trouble to serve my lord and bring new allies into his circle," Deiniol said.

Nell wasn't so sure about that.

"Does Modred know that Gruffydd's here?" Myrddin asked Deiniol.

He shrugged. "I doubt it. Gruffydd has always followed his own road." He lifted his chin, pointing at Huw. "Who's this?"

"My son," Myrddin said.

"Sir." Huw held a cup in his hand and motioned to Deiniol with it, the same bemused expression she'd seen on his face at times when he talked to Myrddin, as if he couldn't quite believe he was actually in Garth Celyn, sitting beside his father.

Deiniol gave a laughing cough, saluted Myrddin with a slight motion of his hand, and moved on towards Cai, leaving the four companions staring after him.

Myrddin's lips twitched. Nell was glad to see his anger easing.

Wearing a half smile, he sat back in his chair. "Three days ago, who would you have said were the three weakest links in Modred's control of Wales and the borderlands?"

"The lords Cedric, Edgar, and Gruffydd," Nell said.

"And now all three have come to call," Ifan said.

"Can he have all three, do you think?" Nell said. "Will they work with each other as well as with us?"

Myrddin made a 'maybe' movement with his head. "They've each fought Arthur in the past, but they've also fought each other. It's Modred's response when he finds out that should give Gruffydd pause."

"If it's so dangerous, why is Gruffydd here?" Nell said.

"Because he's worried that Arthur will win," Ifan said. "He's afraid that if he waits too long to change sides, Arthur will no longer need him and, when he wins, give his land to someone more deserving and loyal."

"Are we that close to victory?" Nell said.

"Gruffydd appears to think so," Myrddin said. "Perhaps the pressure from the Saxon barons Modred is trying to unite is greater than we thought."

Chapter Nine

19 November 537 AD

"EXCUSE ME—UH—FATHER—WHAT are you doing?"

"I'm up," Myrddin said. "I am alive. I refuse to lie in that bed one hour longer."

"Are you really planning to ride today?"

Myrddin had entered the stables, thinking to get out of the hall and put aside his endless dreaming. It seemed that every time he closed his eyes, some new manifestation of his dream of Arthur's death swam before his eyes, each one different from the last.

"No." Snow had begun to fall, and at his son's words, Myrddin swung around to look behind him at the flakes floating in gentle wisps from the white sky. It had the look of continuing all day. "Up until right now, I'd forgotten Cadfarch wasn't here. I was going to brush him."

"I'm sorry," Huw said. "My lord will take good care of him."

"No doubt." Straw crunching underneath his feet, Myrddin walked to where Huw was brushing his own horse and picked up a brush to work alongside his son.

"I'm surprised Nell let you get up."

"She's seeing to a birth," Myrddin said. "She doesn't know."

"Is she your woman, like everyone says?" Huw carefully combed his horse's mane rather than looking at Myrddin.

"I don't know that she'd characterize herself that way," Myrddin said. "To her mind, she's nobody's woman but her own. At the same time, between you and me—and the rest of the garrison—no man should think otherwise."

Huw nodded. "I've spoken to Ifan of your injuries. When you said that they were at Modred's behest, I hadn't realized that he was actually *present* when his guards administered them."

"Yes." Myrddin ran his hand down the horse's legs, feeling his sturdy hocks for damage. "Modred does as he pleases."

"My lord!"

The call shattered the peace, and in four strides Myrddin and Huw arrived at the entrance to the stables to look out on a small company of men just coming through the gate. Gareth led them, the white plume on his helmet fading into the snowy landscape. The man beside him wore the garments of a member of the clergy, although he'd drawn up his hood to protect himself from the weather so Myrddin couldn't see his face. *Surely that's not one of Gareth's cousins?*

But then the priest turned to hand his horse's reins to Adda and Myrddin saw the face beneath the covering hood. The man was Anian, the Bishop of St. Asaph, who'd been party to the excommunication of King Arthur at Rhuddlan Castle.

"What's he doing here?" Huw said.

"Joining the fold, it seems," Myrddin said.

Huw turned back to his horse. As he did so, he asked casually—although the question was anything but casual. "You distrust him?"

"I trust very few men."

"Not Deiniol, certainly. Nell told me of your quarrels."

"It's more than a quarrel," Myrddin said, "for all that we've spoken no more than three sentences to each other in twenty years."

"And Cai? You loath him."

"That goes without saying," Myrddin said. "These men are known traitors to King Arthur. It's the ones who hide behind their loyalty while pocketing coins from Modred that concern me. Of them, there may be none or many, even here."

Huw picked up the brush for currying his horse and plucked at the hairs in it.

169

Myrddin watched him, waiting for the question he knew was coming.

"And me? Do you trust me?"

If Myrddin could have told Huw without humiliating him that he was transparent, he would have. As it was, he clapped his son on the shoulder. "I trust you. When I told you earlier that some here didn't, I did not mean me."

"What if my lord really did send me to find you in order to act as his spy among your people?" Huw said.

"Did he?"

"No," Huw said, indignant, despite the fact that he'd been the first to pose the question.

"Lord Cedric undoubtedly hoped that you would serve him in that capacity anyway." Myrddin said, and at Huw's stuttered protest held up a hand to stop him speaking. "Imagine you are a lord of Mercia and one of your men, one of the younger squires, tells you that his real father is someone other than the staunch companion of your youth. He's a Welshman you've never met. The boy asks to seek this new father out. You know that the boy's mother is Welsh. You understand how his two allegiances could pull him apart, regardless of how noble you believe him to be."

"So you send him north." Huw nodded. "And hope that he finds his father and that through that relationship, whether or not the boy wishes it, you discover something you didn't know about King Arthur's plans."

"It is a sensible approach," Myrddin said. "Logical too. It isn't even deceitful."

"If the boy comes home empty-handed, he has information about the disposition of Arthur's men and the interior of Wales you hadn't known before." Huw paused. "I would have been eager to tell Lord Cedric all I'd learned."

"It is the perfect plan," Myrddin said. "Cedric risks only you, who have requested this mission. At best, he gains knowledge; at worst, he loses a good squire."

"At worst." Huw studied his boots.

"When I met Cedric," Myrddin moved closer to Huw and took the brush so Huw would look at him, "he was surprised at first. But he recognized my name, and because of that, he freed me from Modred's clutches."

"So I would find you. So I would spy for him."

Myrddin shook his head. "Cedric's position in Wales is unstable. You cannot blame him for using whatever weapons come to hand, especially if he can wield them at so little cost to himself."

This was too much for Huw. The knowledge that he'd been used by his lord stuck in his throat, and he couldn't swallow it. He turned to Myrddin and stepped close, his face right in his father's. He wasn't angry as much as fierce. "Would you ever do that to me?"

"I would tell you," Myrddin said, "and make you a willing party to my plans. I promise you that."

Huw shot Myrddin an unreadable look from those pale eyes, nodded, and stepped away, back to his horse. Myrddin didn't know if Huw was truly reassured or if he no longer knew what to believe.

"But I am your father," Myrddin added. "In his present, precarious state, Cedric doesn't have time for niceties. Don't be too hard on him."

Huw didn't answer. Instead, he pawed through the saddle bags that rested on a hook in his horse's stall. He took out a wad of cloth that looked like nothing more than a bandage yet to be used on an injured man. He unfolded it and held his hand out to Myrddin. A heavy gold cross on a thick chain lay in Huw's palm. At the sight of it, Myrddin stepped closer, his breath catching in his throat.

"Christ's bones, Huw, I've not seen that cross ..." Myrddin's voice died as he realized where he'd last seen it.

"Since you gave it to my mother," Huw said. "I know."

Myrddin reached out a finger and touched it, feeling the smooth metal and remembering when he'd given it to her. The cross had weighed on his neck, dangling between them as Myrddin had made love to her. He'd placed it around her neck instead. In his mind's eye, he saw it settle between her breasts and warm there.

He'd spent the night in her bed, and then left in the early hours of the morning at the command of his king. At the time, he'd meant for Tegwan to keep it. Myrddin had been nineteen years old, in love and a romantic. It seemed appropriate to give her the one thing of value that he possessed, barring his sword.

"It was my mother's. I've always assumed that her father gave it to her, although it has crossed my mind that she could have gotten it from mine." He looked into Huw's face. "It's yours, now."

"No." Huw shook his head. "You're still young enough to marry. Although my mother cherished it, I have many things from her, including sixteen years of memories. If you want to give it away again, give it to Nell." He pushed his hand towards Myrddin, and Myrddin didn't resist him. He lifted the cross from Huw's palm by its chain, caressing the smooth links.

"Thank you." Myrddin forced the words past the thickening in his throat. "My nurse gave this to me when I was twelve, believing that I should have something of my mother. She had kept it hidden all those years, knowing that if Madoc found it, he could claim it for himself as payment for giving me house room until I became a man."

Myrddin slipped the chain over his head and tucked the cross under his shirt. It was an unfamiliar weight against his breastbone, but a comforting one.

"May it protect you wherever you go," Huw said, "as it has me."

"I DREAMED LAST NIGHT." Nell stood in the doorway of their room, gazing down on Myrddin who lay spread-eagled on his pallet. Huw remained in the hall where he would spend the night amongst the other squires and men-at-arms who were arriving in increasing numbers with their lords, in preparation for the meeting of the Welsh High Council.

Nell had asked Huw if he would prefer to share their room even though Myrddin no longer needed watching over. The appalled look on his face had prompted laughter from Nell. Myrddin and Nell had become more than friends, but what exactly they were to each other, Nell wasn't quite sure. The rest of the castle assumed they knew, however, and if that meant she could continue to stay with him, then that was fine by her. Like the breeches she'd worn to Rhuddlan, the idea was freeing.

"I dream every night," he said.

"Will you tell me about them?" Nell would have asked him about his dreams days ago, but he'd been ill, and she almost hadn't wanted him to share them with her because once he did, they'd both be laid bare. While they'd admitted the truth to each other, what that truth entailed, and what they were going to do about it, wasn't at all clear.

"Do I have a choice?" Myrddin said, and then he smiled, taking the sting out of his words. He gestured to Nell with one hand.

She closed the door behind her, and then walked to the pallet on which Myrddin lay and knelt on the end of it.

Myrddin pushed himself upright and braced his back against the wall. "All right." He scrubbed at his face with both hands. "Talk to me."

"My dreams have changed."

"Have they?" he said. "How?"

"Except for that first instance, I've always fought as you when I dream. But since before you went to Rhuddlan, it's been different.

Sometimes you're not even there. Last night, more men filled the clearing than before, and there were no archers. In fact—" she paused, trying to think how to say this, "—although you were there, you didn't die."

"Really." Myrddin dropped his hands to his lap. "And that's different?"

"Yes, of course."

"Certainly, I have no interest in dying just yet." They sat silent for a moment, before Myrddin said, "I don't just want to save King Arthur because I want to save Wales—I have this odd idea that if I save him, I save myself."

"There's nothing wrong with not wanting to die by a Saxon's sword," Nell said.

"In my dream last night, I didn't have Cadfarch," Myrddin said. "That might be the first time. And since just before I met you, I haven't worn a mustache."

Nell's eyes widened. "And that's my fault! But I didn't know!"

"No," Myrddin said. "Only because I didn't tell you, and yet ..."

"Does that mean that the actions we take in the real world change our dreams, which in turn indicates a new course in the future?" Nell said. "Does it mean we're making progress?"

"What is progress?" Myrddin said. "We have no idea if everything we're doing right now is exactly what we need to do to ensure that King Arthur dies on December 11th. There's no reason to think otherwise."

"Except that if King Arthur's death is inevitable, why dream?"

Myrddin snorted under his breath. "You're assuming these dreams don't come from the devil."

"Oh, yes," Nell said. "I thought it at first, of course. I told my father of the vision the first time I had it. I ran home, screaming of the battle I'd witnessed and the dead men. Once past the clearing, the world reverted to what it had been. But when my father searched, he found nothing by the river. He was afraid for me, then."

"Did you ever tell a priest?"

"Did you?"

Myrddin gave a sharp laugh. "No."

"So what *did* you do?" Nell said. "Up until now, I mean."

"I came to serve the king as soon as I was able," Myrddin said. "But otherwise, I ignored the dreams. I drank."

"You drank." Nell strove to keep her voice even. "And what good was that supposed to do?"

"Goddamn it, I don't know!" Myrddin said. "Who am I to change the world? Who am I to have these visions?"

Nell bit her lip as she looked at him, realizing she'd pressed too hard. "You're Myrddin. Why not you?"

"What about you, then?" Myrddin said, still angry. "You were doing no more than I. Less, in fact. You were leaving Wales."

Nell looked down at her hands folded in her lap and then back up at Myrddin. "No, I wasn't."

"That's what you told me."

"I lied." Nell forced herself not to look away from Myrddin's face.

"You lied." He mimicked the flatness in her tone.

Nell nodded. "I was going to Rhuddlan, as I said, but my intent was to enter the castle."

"For what purpose?" Myrddin said. "As a spy?"

Nell shrugged. "Not exactly." She glanced away, unable to maintain eye contact. Now that it came to it, perhaps he'd find the truth far worse than his basest suspicions. She felt his gaze on her, and still she wouldn't look at him. "I wasn't a nun anymore, you know."

"Christ!" Myrddin leaned forward to grab her chin. "You weren't going there as a spy! You were going as—as a—as a whore!"

There it was, the truth at last. Nell pulled away, pummeled by Myrddin's horrified stare. She shrugged again. "It was an idea."

"My God! What were you thinking?"

"I'll tell you what I was thinking!" Nell said, her anger flaring. "The solution to our problems certainly wasn't to drink myself into a stupor every night. I was going to get close to Modred! And kill him if I could! It might even have been easy—just a knife in the back after I refilled his goblet. I might not even have had to sell myself to do it."

Myrddin's mouth was open as he stared her.

Nell gritted her teeth, determined to tell him everything. "My sisters had already suffered worse at the hands of Wulfere's soldiers. It was the least I could do! And it was the only thing I could think of that *I* could do to change the future."

Myrddin leaned forward and gripped her arms. "You must have realized that Modred's men would have killed you immediately afterwards."

"Of course."

"*Christ!*" Myrddin blasphemed again. "That was the stupidest idea I've ever heard!" He shook her. Once. While she glared at him, trying to hang on to her anger even though tears pricked at her eyes. She opened her mouth to speak but then he put one finger to her lips to stop her, his voice softening. "And the bravest."

With that, she couldn't hold back the tears. They spilled out the corners of her eyes and down her cheeks. Myrddin made a 'tsk' noise from between his teeth and pulled her to him. Nell wrapped her arms around his waist and sobbed into his chest.

"Sweet Mary, mother of God, that you would think that was your only choice," Myrddin said. "You would have died."

"That was, in part, the point," Nell said. "By then I would have done anything. Anything to stop the dreams. Anything to stop King Arthur from meeting Edgar by the Cam River."

"Thank God I found you. I wish I'd done so long ago."

"You didn't know of me," she said. "Better that I'd tried to find you. Silly of me not to think of it. I don't know why I didn't."

"I'll be damned if I'll ever bow to a Saxon lord again!"

The fierce tones of Lord Gruffydd carried loudly through the wall. Nell froze in Myrddin's arms. As Gruffydd's words sank in, they eased back from each other. Nell wished she could see right through the wall to the other side.

"We've had little choice—" another voice said.

"He's talking to Cai," Nell said.

"You have had a choice!" Gruffydd hammered at him. "You would rather see Wales fall under the Saxon boot than lose an acre of what you possess? Even if Modred wins this war, you have no guarantee he will confirm you as Lord of Gwynedd. Look what has happened to Edgar of Wigmore!" Gruffydd sounded so much like Arthur, it was as if he'd become a different person.

"That's just one instance—"

Gruffydd cut off Cai again. "One instance that we are to take as an example for all of us! If he can do this to his loyal cousin, the man who stood by him through every war this century, he can do it to any of us."

"You've stood at Modred's side many times," Cai said, still defiant and forceful. "Why not now? Why not this time?"

"Because he betrayed me with my wife!"

The silence in both rooms was deafening. Gruffydd had married a much younger woman after the death of Owain's mother. His confession had Nell holding her breath, one hand clenching and unclenching around Myrddin's arm. Surely they must realize that the walls had ears?

Finally, Cai spoke again. "How do you know?"

"She told me that he'd asked for her. When I confronted him, he laughed. He admitted he'd taken her." Now, Gruffydd lowered

177

his voice, forcing Nell to lean in to hear the conversation better. She pressed her ear to the wall that separated the two rooms. "He thinks he controls me."

"Admittedly, Modred consorts with many women," Cai said. "It is well known."

"But never *my* woman," Gruffydd said.

"I can see that you are confirmed in your opinion." Cai returned to his normal speaking voice. "I will not try to change it."

"And you?" Gruffydd said. "You stand beside your brother for all to see, yet you mean to tell me that you spy for Modred?"

"I do not spy." There was a distinct *clunk* against the wall. Nell imagined Cai had pressed Gruffydd to it, and she shrank back, as if Cai might be able to sense her through the wall. Ten heartbeats passed and then feet retreated across the floor. A door to the hall slammed.

"I see," Gruffydd said, presumably to himself.

"I don't see. Are we to understand that Cai's faithfulness is a front? A sham to gain power and land?" Nell turned to Myrddin, whose jaw was set in a more grim line than she'd ever seen it.

"Yes. That is precisely what we must understand. It is as it has always been. I just don't know what to do about it."

"You could tell King Arthur."

"Just like I can tell him about our dreams? He would not believe me, *could* not believe me without proof."

"Then Bedwyr or Geraint," she said.

Myrddin shook his head. "Not yet. We still have time."

"We hope we still have time," she said.

Book Three: Of Men and Dragons

Of Men and Dragons

THOUGH OVERJOYED TO have been joined by a son he never knew he had, Myrddin struggles to come to terms with his dreams and faces treachery on every side in his quest to save King Arthur from the fate that awaits him. Nell, in turn, must choose between the life she left behind and the life before her, even if neither can last for even one more day.

Of Men and Dragons is the riveting third act of *The Lion of Wales* series.

Chapter One

"HAS IT OCCURRED TO you that any one of these men could be your father?"

Myrddin turned his gaze on his son, amused to find the boy's eyes alight with mischief. "No," but then he amended, "not for many years."

"Since my step-father's death, I wondered about you often," Huw said. "My mother told me that you served in Arthur's forces when she knew you, but that wasn't to say you still did. Or were even alive. I'm sure there are many Myrddins throughout Wales who wondered at the boy who questioned them about their activities when they were younger."

"I wish I'd been there, son." Myrddin rested a hand on his son's shoulder. "I can't say it often enough."

"You're here now," Huw said.

"So who looks most like Myrddin, Huw?" Nell sidled to Huw and looked with him. "Huddled in the corner are those cousins named Rhys and there's three Gruffydd's over by the high table."

The other great men of Wales had come far for the meeting. Many had vacillated between Arthur and Modred over the years, depending upon who had the upper hand. Could it be that position now belonged to King Arthur?

"Stop it, Nell," Myrddin said. "My mother dabbled with a pig farmer. If he were noble, she would have named him."

Nell laughed, ignoring his protest. "I hate to say it, but I think you resemble Modred a bit." At Myrddin's glare, Nell laughed again. "I doubt, however, that he's your father, as he was just four years old when you were born and even for him, that would have been mighty precocious."

"Thank heaven for small mercies," Myrddin said. "How would I ever live that down?"

They surveyed the company a while longer, and then Bedwyr and Geraint appeared. It was almost time to start the meeting. Men began filling the seats around the tables in expectation of King Arthur's arrival.

"Modred would murder half the people in this room, given the chance," Nell said.

"And how many of them will turn to him anyway, seeing an opportunity, whether tomorrow, next week, or—" Myrddin glanced at Huw, who had moved a few feet away in response to another man's query, "—if Arthur falls?"

Nell met his eyes, showing sympathy for what could be, squeezed his hand, and headed for the rear of the hall and her herb hut. She'd made noises about dressing in her male garb so she would be allowed to stay in the room, perhaps to serve as a page, but Myrddin had dissuaded her of it. Whether she remembered it or not, these men knew her as a former nun, and all hell would break loose if someone exposed her as a woman when she was thus disguised.

The commotion subsided. King Arthur had ordered the tables arranged in a large square, and a sense of equivalence, if not equality, permeated the room. The king took his seat with Geraint and Bedwyr on either side of him as was his custom. Cai sat opposite Arthur, some twenty feet away, more in the position of a rival than a brother.

As a mere knight, Myrddin was lucky to be in the hall at all. With Huw, who was doing his best to make himself as unremarkable as possible, Myrddin found a place against the wall where they could see the faces of both brothers. Unfortunately, their spot turned out to be two spaces down from Deiniol. It was too late to move, so Myrddin stayed where he was and resolved to focus on the proceedings.

King Arthur had designated Anian, the Bishop of St. Asaph, as convener of the Assembly. Anian had spent as many years opposed to Arthur's rule as for it, but when he'd greeted the king upon his arrival at Garth Celyn, he'd said that he'd come to his own conclusions about who should rule in Wales and that the excommunication to which he'd been a party was not the Will of God. In matters of faith, he would follow his conscience as he always had.

Anian began with an opening prayer, calling the assembly to silence. At its completion, he made a show of unrolling the letter to the Council that King Arthur had received back from Modred on November 8th and read it aloud. The letter was short and said, in a nutshell, that Modred wouldn't discuss what had happened on Anglesey or the status of the four cantrefs of Wales, nor would he offer the council any promises in exchange for peace other than that he would deal with them mercifully as befitted an overlord. Anian then read the secret terms Modred had conveyed to Arthur and Cai, to which they had already responded.

By the time Anian's voice fell silent, the room was in an uproar. Many of the lords had heard rumors of what the letters contained. Cai had made no secret of his (false) new-found hatred of Modred, but Arthur hadn't shared the exact wording with any of his barons since that first day, wanting them all to hear it at the same time. Now, King Arthur himself had to rise to his feet to silence them.

"I've already responded to Modred's letter, as has my brother." Arthur nodded his head to Cai, who raised a hand, in acknowledgement of his action. "As the bishop has just explained, Modred demanded that we, in exchange for peace, give up all claim to our lands in Wales and our patrimony, and to leave our subjects in the hands of the Saxons. We have, of course, refused."

Again the uproar and King Arthur raised his hand to settle the room. Every man perched on the edge of his seat, even those who'd never wanted to listen to the king before.

"As a council, we must respond to Modred's letter with one voice," Arthur said, "but before we do, it is important that each man be allowed to air his opinions, grievances, and suggestions freely, in the company of his peers. From this hour, we all rise, or we all fall, together."

That calmed the assemblage somewhat. The Welsh were a more egalitarian people (at least among the elite) than many peoples, and everyone was used to this method of resolving problems. Thus, each of the lords stood in turn to state what he had won or lost in the war with Modred since the council had last met, and what he thought of Modred's letters. Nobody was happy; the list of grievances against the Saxons grew longer with every man who spoke. Once these preliminaries were over, Anian stood again.

"King Arthur has asked me to open discussion regarding the future of Wales," he said. "If she is to have a future, now is the time to speak of it."

Utter silence fell. Then, to no one's surprise, it was Cai who rose to his feet. "I have something to say."

"By all means." King Arthur gestured that he had the floor.

"What I want to know," Cai said, his voice level and conversational, "is why the Council has not disowned Modred long since?" He lifted his hand to show the scroll of paper he'd received from Modred. "Is this any kind of letter to send to a member of his own family?"

"No!"

Myrddin craned his head to see who'd spoken, whether a supporter of Cai, or just one of the many men who knew injustice when he saw it. A number of men shook their fists, presumably at Modred.

Huw leaned in to whisper. "That was Owain ap Gruffydd."

Myrddin glanced at Huw. "You don't like him."

"I don't like traitors, even when they're on my side."

Myrddin smiled, hearing the echo of Cedric in Huw's voice.

"I say we throw off that yoke, once and for all," Cai said. "It is well and good that we defeated the Saxons at the Strait, but Modred doesn't yet believe himself defeated. He thinks us beholden to him, a people in rebellion. He is already measuring his head for the crown. He has called my brother a usurper, when it is he who seeks to take the crown from us!"

"Excommunicate, by God!" That was Gareth, whom Myrddin had never pegged as one for spontaneous outbursts.

Cai nodded. "What gives Modred the right to stand between us and our God?"

"No right!"

Far more heads nodded and there were more clenched fists than before. Even Huw was moved, his hands gripping his knees and his back stiff as he hung on every one of Cai's words.

"I say *no*! I say we should be free of the constraints that Modred imposes upon us. No half-Saxon lord has a right to our throne!" Cai gestured to his brother. "King Arthur has no heir of his body, but that is not to say that he doesn't have an heir of his heart!"

At those final words, the men around Myrddin swallowed hard, Cai paused, and Arthur gripped his goblet so tightly his knuckles whitened. Cai leaned heavily on the table, supporting his weight on both hands, and Arthur stood. When he spoke, his voice was gentle.

"What would you have us do, brother, that we have not already done? Did I not write to Modred that we spoke with one voice? Did not you? Did I not say that even were I willing to acknowledge

Modred as my heir, the people of Wales would be unwilling to do homage to one such as he who has no respect for their laws and customs?"

A murmur of approval swept through the hall.

"I say we do not write it," Cai said. "I say we shout it! From the highest peak of Yr Wyddfa, we must cry aloud as one people and keep crying it until Modred heeds our words. I say we take what is ours for Wales and only for Wales! I say we tell Modred what we think of his rights and his armies! I say we are a free and independent people and I, for one, am tired of living at Modred's sufferance!"

Cai's eyes were alive with triumph. He seemed to tower over the company with his power and eloquence.

Arthur, however, remained unmoved.

"To deny his claim to the throne will only spur Modred to greater heights of aggravation," he said. "He will take it as we mean it—as an open declaration that our people will never abide a half-Saxon overlord, even if he is also half-Welsh and my nephew. It treads hard on his divine right to rule."

Cai shot back. "We are already at odds with him. We thwart him and his church at every step. What more can he do to us that he has not already done? If you fear to place yourself at the head of such an endeavor, I do not!"

His shout rang throughout the hall. Then, silence settled, and it was as if everyone was holding his breath—Myrddin and Huw among them—waiting for Arthur's answer.

"You are not afraid to renew the fight, brother?" Arthur said.

"I am not afraid, brother," Cai said. "For the good of her people, I would stand tall and never again bend to a Saxon lord or allow Modred to set his boot on the back our necks."

Another pause. The energy hummed among the men, just below the surface, threatening to come out.

Arthur released it.

"Then, so would I. I will take that chance." For the first time, Arthur's voice boomed out to every corner of the room. "Who will stand with me against Modred and his Saxon toadies, now and forever? Who would see the Kingdom of Wales renewed?"

Bedwyr shot his fist into the air. "Aye!"

A half second behind him came Cai, and almost in the same instant, Myrddin was one of dozens of others who matched him. Even Deiniol, who must have been taken up in the excitement and Myrddin feared would find himself with second thoughts by the time the doors to the hall opened, thrust his fist into the air.

Everyone shouted together. "Aye! God is with us!"

Arthur focused on his brother, who met his eyes. Cai's glowed with exhilaration and something else that Myrddin read as deceit. Then Arthur nodded, straightened, and turned from the table. Leaving Bedwyr to sort out the other lords, he strode from the hall.

"I HEAR THAT THE BARONS have promised Arthur more money and men," Nell said, when Myrddin found her in her herb hut, boiling a concoction on the brazier. "Is it true? I didn't dare believe it until I heard it from you."

"That is what they've pledged. That's what King Arthur has sworn. He promised to push Modred out of Powys by Christmas." He paused as their eyes met. "If we live that long."

"What does Huw think?" Nell said.

"He has discovered what it means to be Welsh," Myrddin said.

"We all feel it." Nell forcefully set down the jar she held, and it almost tipped over. She righted it and then put it on the shelf above her head. "If the lords of Wales would stop fighting among themselves and unite, as they did at Mt. Badon, we would have the peace we need—not the peace that Modred wants."

"Modred has more men at his disposal than we do," Myrddin said. "This won't be easy."

"He is a vicious man, Myrddin. You do understand that if you ever cross paths with him again, you're dead." She held his eyes, like she once might have focused on one of the novice nuns, unsure if he was really listening. Myrddin went his own way, with a strong sense of *rightness* that Nell trusted, but that she feared might cost him his life.

"I know it," Myrddin said.

"You say that so casually," she said, "but I don't want you to die."

Myrddin's mouth twisted. "Nor do I." He glanced away.

Nell studied his profile and then turned away herself. Her back to him, she rummaged among her vials in the cupboard behind her. After the deaths of all her family, she'd carefully buried that part of her heart that cared too much—loved too much. But despite her best efforts to suppress it, she'd started caring for this man from the moment he'd stormed into the clearing to rescue her at St. Asaph, even before she knew him as the Myrddin from her dreams. That she'd loved that man since she was eight years old didn't help.

"Are you well?" Myrddin said.

Nell found herself smiling, her back still to him, studying the label of each of her jars in turn. "I am well, Myrddin. Thank you for asking."

Chapter Two

24 November 537 AD

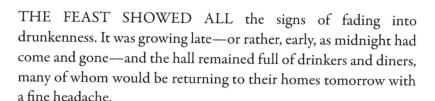

THE FEAST SHOWED ALL the signs of fading into drunkenness. It was growing late—or rather, early, as midnight had come and gone—and the hall remained full of drinkers and diners, many of whom would be returning to their homes tomorrow with a fine headache.

The lords of Wales had met one more time that afternoon, to give final approval for the wording of the letter to Modred. If the Welsh were anything, they were lawyers and the national pastime was suing each other over the smallest issue. A man moved a boundary stone, his opponent moved a fence, and they went to court to dispute their differences. They would settle them and then repeat the process the following year—sometimes over the same stones and fences. It was a wonder it had taken only three days with clerks and vellum to agree on the wording of the letter to Modred. There were years when it would have been too thorny an issue and tabled.

Bishop Anian had read the letter aloud to the general approval of the hall:

THE PEOPLE OF WALES, for their part, state that even if their king desired to give his nephew rule of them, they themselves would not do homage to any Saxon, of whose language, customs and laws they are utterly ignorant. For by doing so, they would be brought into perpetual captivity and barbarously treated ...

KING ARTHUR HAD RETIRED from the hall long since; Cai had been absent since before the last course. His behavior at the Council, once again, had been patriotically Welsh. How could Myrddin accuse him of betrayal when all eyes saw differently?

"I need you to help me with something." Nell plopped herself between Myrddin and Huw.

"Help you with what?" Myrddin said.

"I've felt something. Again."

"Felt, or *seen*?" Myrddin said.

"Not *seen*." Nell turned her body to shield them both from Huw's eyes, put her hand on Myrddin's, and gently squeezed. "I can't explain it. It's like when you went to Rhuddlan. Ever since we overheard Cai speaking to Gruffydd, I've been afraid. I can't articulate it, but something bad is going to happen tonight."

"All right," Myrddin said, intrigued.

"Tunnels lie underneath Garth Celyn. Will you poke around them with me? I thought you'd be angry if I followed one of the passages and didn't tell you, especially after what happened at Llanfaes."

"I surely would." Myrddin was glad that at long last she was paying attention to what was good for her without him having to tell her.

Huw, whose mental image of himself definitely included tunnel exploring, perked up too. Huw and Myrddin followed Nell out of the great hall, past Arthur's receiving room, to one of the towers that buttressed the administrative building. This particular tower was the most northwestern; the garrison used it to watch the sea for enemy ships and to store equipment, beyond what was regularly kept in the barracks across the courtyard by the gatehouse.

When they entered, two men sprawled in chairs on either side of a table set against the far wall. They'd been drinking, but were sober enough to think of duty as Myrddin entered.

"Sir," said the first, a man named Tristan.

"We thought we'd see to the security of the sea tunnel," Myrddin said, working hard to keep a straight face.

"It's dusty down there." Tristan walked to the trap door, set in the exact middle of the floor, knelt, and stuck his fingers through the recessed iron ring. He yanked on it. As the trap door came up, Myrddin grasped the edge to help him lift it. Below, a stairway led downwards.

Myrddin met Nell's eyes and she mouthed, *thank you.*

"It's been a long time since I trod these steps," Myrddin said.

"There's another tunnel that leads into the mountains behind us," Tristan said. "It empties into a meadow below Aber Falls."

"We'll have to try that next," Nell said.

Myrddin swallowed a sarcastic reply about unbecoming behavior in an ex-nun, not wanting to squash her enthusiasm and because her concern was forcing him to reassess how seriously to take this.

Tristan handed Myrddin a lantern, and in a file they walked down the surprisingly broad treads. Huw and Myrddin had to duck their heads so as to not hit the floorboards above them as they descended. Fifteen steps down, they arrived in a small room, much like the foyer in front of the cells at Rhuddlan, except there were no cells with prisoners, just a closed door.

Myrddin didn't recall a door there at all from his forays with Ifan or other boys as a youth but, admittedly, it was a long time ago. He raised the lantern high to inspect the stones around the door and the dust at its base.

"Look, Father." Huw pointed to fresh footprints in front of the door. Myrddin crouched to inspect them with him.

"Someone got here ahead of us," Nell said.

Huw lowered his voice. "Do you think something's really wrong? The hinges on the trap door were oiled, and the stairs were swept clean. Everybody knows about the tunnels."

"I realize that," Myrddin said. "But whoever swept the stairs, pushed the dust right onto the floor here. Everything would have been cleaned in preparation for the Council meeting, up to and including the stairs. That means that these footprints are very recent."

Nell, her arms folded across her chest, stared down at the footprints. Myrddin glanced at her and then beyond her, up the stairs to Tristan who still stood at the top.

"What is it?" Tristan said.

Myrddin straightened. "Did someone come through here tonight before us?"

"Not on my watch," he said.

"Keep your eyes open." Myrddin lifted the latch on the door and a gust of air wafted through it. "And you might tell Lord Geraint where we've gone."

"Yes, sir," Tristan said.

"I can smell the sea," Nell said.

Huw loosened his sword in its sheath. Myrddin took Nell's hand and led the way into the tunnel. It was five feet wide. Every six feet along it, a stone archway supported the wooden roof, which itself was at least six and a half feet high. Both Huw and Myrddin could walk comfortably along it. Water seeped through cracks in the walls; eventually the wood in the roof would rot, given the wet climate, but it was still solidly holding up the tons of earth that pressed down from above.

Huw stared around them. "Who built this, Father?"

"I believe the Romans started it."

"You can see the footprints again." Nell pointed at the ground.

Huw had his sword in his hand now. "Do we go on?" He stepped past Myrddin and Nell and along the corridor.

"Yes." Myrddin's eyes strained to see beyond the rim of the circle of light thrown out by the lantern.

Huw gestured at the floor with the tip of his sword. "There are two sets of footprints. One man walked behind the other, and over there where the tunnel widens, the footprints go side by side."

He paced ahead of them, his left hand on the wall. Myrddin gripped Nell's hand more tightly and put his head close to hers. "How did you know, Nell?"

"I didn't." Nell shook her head. "It's like when you left for Rhuddlan. I can't believe—" She broke off.

"Well, *feeling* or not, you may have saved all of us."

The smell of the sea grew stronger. The tunnel curved to the left in front of them and, as they came around the corner, a light flickered, reflecting off the moisture on the stone pillars. They retreated back around the curve and Huw doused the lantern. It wasn't entirely dark, as the light in front of them continued to flare.

Myrddin peered around the corner, making sure he stayed low to the ground in case someone looked their way. The light came from a source a short distance outside the entrance to the tunnel. The sound of the sea was louder now, but with it, when he stayed still, voices echoed.

Myrddin listened, trying to understand what they were saying. Then Nell moaned. "Oh, no."

"What?" Huw and Myrddin spoke together.

"Listen," she said. "Those are Saxon voices."

Myrddin didn't need to hear them himself to believe her. He pushed her towards Huw. "Relight the lantern and run as fast as you can to Geraint. Tell him there are Saxons outside the sea tunnel, who are being aided by two men from Garth Celyn."

Huw hesitated, but Nell understood immediately.

193

"It's better if just one of us stays, Huw. Myrddin speaks Saxon just as well as we do, and better Latin, if it comes to it. Someone needs to warn the king so he can plan our defenses. They must think to sneak into the castle with us unaware. Come!"

That Huw understood. With a quick strike of flint, he relit the lantern and then took Nell's hand to run back the way they'd come, Nell holding her heavy skirts off the ground with one hand. Myrddin spared them a last glance before swinging back to face the sea. He swallowed hard. He had no doubt that whoever these Saxons were, they would kill him if they caught him. Nevertheless, he hugged the wall and crept around the corner.

As Myrddin moved closer to the exit, the individual voices became clearer. Ten paces from the opening to the tunnel, he crouched low and listened. Several different conversations were going on at the same time, but the one occurring closest to the doorway was in Saxon.

"I will return to the castle overland to ensure that no alarm is raised and that the men I left guarding the exit remain true." The voice belonged to Owain, who'd evidently decided to continue his stand with Modred. Myrddin shook his head, choking down bile at this betrayal and fearing for the safety of Nell and Huw—and everyone in the castle.

A second man spoke, his voice ringing clearly down the passage even through what had to be clenched teeth. "No! That is not part of the agreement!"

"You dare threaten me?" Owain said. Feet scuffled and Myrddin imagined them facing off against each other, swords drawn. "Modred will hear of this!"

"He certainly shall," said the second man, "especially when I tell him that our Welsh traitor lost his nerve at the last moment!"

A third man spoke, this time in Welsh. "Be reasonable, Owain. They are looking out for their own interests, just as you are. I, for one, will be glad when this night is over, but we said we would lead them into Garth Celyn, and that we must do."

The second voice spoke again, still in Saxon. "Enough! I will leave five men with the boats. The rest of the company must march now if we are to have the cover of darkness for our work. Let's see this tunnel of yours, and then I alone will judge if you are true to your word."

Myrddin backed away from the entrance. A second later, he was around the corner and running, as fast and as urgently as he'd ever run before. He worried briefly about the echo of his pounding feet, but hoped he would be far enough away when the Saxons entered the tunnel such that the sounds of their movements would mask his own.

Myrddin ran the first quarter mile flat out, brushing his fingers along the right hand wall to guide his steps in the dark. He settled into a slower jog for the second half of the journey, which brought him into Garth Celyn with breath still in him. Huw had left the door to the tunnel cracked open.

Myrddin hit it with his shoulder and nearly impaled himself on a half-dozen swords, their owners ready for a fight. He skidded to a halt and blinked—and the men-at-arms gave way.

"Pardon, my lord," Tristan called to Myrddin's back as he ran past him to take the stairs up three at a time.

Huw waited for Myrddin at the top. "Lord Geraint was still awake. He sent me to Gareth, who is rousting the men in the hall and barracks. He sent Nell to wake the king."

They crossed the courtyard between the administrative building and the sleeping quarters. Once inside, they jogged up a stairway and turned down the hallway to King Arthur's room. Nell had just knocked.

Arthur's deep voice boomed through the oak. "Enter!"

Nell pushed the door open and hovered on the threshold with Myrddin just behind her. The fire burned hot in the room, and a wave of warmth met them. Arthur had been lying on top of his bedcovers, fully clothed. When he saw them, he sat up and swung his legs over the side of the bed. It seemed likely he hadn't slept at all.

"My lord." Myrddin bowed.

Arthur made an impatient gesture, as if to say, 'you woke me, now tell me what the trouble is'.

"A Saxon company is coming through the sea tunnel as we speak, led by Owain ap Gruffydd," Myrddin said.

Arthur had surged to his feet before Myrddin finished his sentence. A second later, Geraint brushed passed Myrddin, already booted, cloaked, and in full armor. Arthur's valet, an old fellow named Daffi, followed immediately behind. He hurried into the room, fixing the ties on his jacket. Geraint flung open the chest in which Arthur kept his armor.

"Keep talking," Arthur said, with a nod to Myrddin.

"The traitors spoke of allies in Garth Celyn who guarded the trap door entrance." Myrddin turned to Nell with a questioning look.

She shook her head, denying any knowledge of it. "When we returned to the stairs, Lord Geraint stood in the tower room, talking to Tristan with four other men."

"Tristan had come to find me," Geraint said, "but I needed more information before I raised an alarm."

While they spoke, Daffi helped the king with his armor and boots and then Geraint tightened the sword belt around Arthur's waist.

Arthur nodded, ready to ride. "I'll see you in the courtyard when you've armed yourself. We must ride to the beach if we're going to catch them, once they discover we've barred the way into Garth Celyn."

The Saxons could be back at their boats in half an hour. The king's company needed to intercept them before they could put to sea.

The king left the room.

Although Huw and Myrddin wore boots, cloaks, and the swords they always carried, neither were dressed in mail armor, which they'd need to fight the Saxons. "Help us arm, Nell?" Myrddin said, as they hustled after the king and Geraint.

"Of course," she said.

Together, they burst through the front door, ran down the stairs, and crossed the courtyard of the castle, heading for the barracks. Myrddin's new armor lay in a chest in the armory, alongside the equipment belonging to the rest of the men in the garrison. Once in the armory, Myrddin had to brush past Ifan to reach it.

"A wild night, eh?" Ifan shrugged into his surcoat which he'd pulled over his mail tunic. He stretched his arms to the sides, loosening his muscles. "It feels good!" He shot a smile at Nell, who patted his shoulder as she passed him.

Huw stripped to the waist, and Myrddin tossed him his thin shirt, padding, and mail vest. All of them were rushing. In her haste, Nell fumbled with the fastenings to Myrddin's bracers.

"Damn you, Myrddin," Nell said as she finally managed to buckle them. "Another battle. More dead men. Haven't you done enough?"

"I love you too, Nell," Myrddin said.

She stopped, frozen, her hands at his belt and her head bent forward.

When she didn't give him the reply he expected and wanted, he gripped her arms. "I feel what I feel. I can live with it if you don't feel the same." He pulled her close, wrapping his arms around her. "This fight is not an end in itself. It will be a small battle with a hundred men, perhaps fewer." He looked over at Huw. "Stay close to me when it comes to it. Get the horses and meet me in the courtyard."

"Yes, sir." Huw's eyes were bright.

"Quickly now!" Myrddin said to his retreating back, and then added under his breath, "There's nothing more exciting than a chance to get oneself killed."

Nell had her forehead in Myrddin's chest and was clenching and unclenching her fists around the edges of his cloak. She choked on sob that she turned into a laugh and lifted her head to look into his face. "I don't want you go."

"I'll be back."

She nodded and at last wrapped her arms around him for a hug, which he returned, thankful to have reached her at least that far. "Go with God, Myrddin."

Myrddin pushed past the few men still in the armory and out into the courtyard which seethed with men and horses. As he forced his way through the crowd to where Huw stood with Myrddin's new horse, christened Gwynfor because of her size and color, he searched for King Arthur. He eventually found him near the gatehouse, Cai already mounted beside him.

Myrddin gritted his teeth at the sight of him, not wanting Cai within a sword's length of Arthur.

Owain's father, Gruffydd, had stopped Arthur as he was mounting his horse, and his bellow carried over the uproar. "What is it you claim? You accuse my son of treason?"

"Where is your son?" Arthur said. "He would have us murdered in our beds and the castle fired. Produce him, and we'll see if he has betrayed us. You have spent your life in service to

Modred and his Saxons. Is it any wonder that I suspect treachery from your house?"

"Where is the proof?" Gruffydd said.

His challenge hung in the air. Then other men shouted. A few spilled from the tower in which the trap door was located.

A man called. "They've reached the door!"

"We need more men!"

Arthur hissed. "There's your proof." He threw a leg over his horse's back. "Now is the time to make clear where your loyalties lie. I tell you there's no room in my country for the Saxons or their Welsh spies who betray us." Arthur gathered the reins and stood in the stirrups. He called to the men around him. "We ride to the sea! Let all who will, follow me! We will show no mercy for those who would have none for us!"

Men cheered, as men do when they are fired up, and two guards pulled open the gate. Ifan joined Huw and Myrddin and they followed Arthur and Cai through the gate and down the old Roman road, three abreast, moving faster than was reasonable in the dark, but trusting to their horses' sight. They followed that road for a short way before turning onto a smaller track that took them the last quarter mile to the sea.

At that point, the three companions trotted their horses along the side of the column until they reached Gareth, who nodded at Myrddin as he approached, having been expecting him. They'd worked well together when they'd fought at the Strait. Huw and Ifan fell in behind.

"We'll keep the men out of sight until the Saxons issue from the tunnel's exit," Gareth said. "Then we will fall upon them."

"That sounds nice and simple," Myrddin said, "provided they aren't expecting exactly that."

"Even if they are, they won't be able to do anything about it," Gareth said. "Bedwyr sent men ahead of us the instant Huw sounded the alarm. We'll know soon where we stand."

Myrddin glanced back at Huw, who gave him a sickly smile, just visible in the half-light of the waning moon.

Gareth noted Myrddin's attention and smirked. "This is a battle we can't lose. We have over a hundred men on horseback—far more than Garth Celyn's normal garrison. The Saxons intended a lightening raid, not a siege. As we saw at the Strait, when the enemy is on foot, a cavalry charge across open terrain is impossible to turn aside or survive."

"I don't understand why the Saxons are taking this risk." It was the first time Huw had referred to their enemy as *the Saxons*, as if he was no longer one of them. He didn't seem to notice what he'd said, and continued, "Even with a hundred men, they couldn't have hoped for more than a momentary surprise."

"Where's the risk?" Gareth said. "At worst they'll lose a company of men. At the Strait the commitment was much greater, and thus the loss. Any lives lost here are a small price indeed, compared with the opportunity to kill three dozen Welsh noblemen—and King Arthur. Their captain had no reason to think Owain couldn't have brought them successfully into the castle. It's only because of you that we hold a position of strength now."

Gareth paused, with a glance at Huw, and then turned to Myrddin. "Do not think the king is unaware of your role in this. You will be well rewarded."

Myrddin tipped his head in acknowledgement.

Ifan spoke for the first time. "Myrddin didn't do it for a reward." Myrddin turned to glower at him and Ifan shrugged. "It's the truth."

"All the more reason to acknowledge your loyalty." Then Gareth caught his breath at a shout from the head of the line.

Arthur had raised his sword above his head. With Cai beside him, he charged forward.

The Saxons had abandoned their attempt to enter the castle through the trap door, admitted their defeat, and turned back the way they'd come. As Gareth had supposed, the cavalry caught them on the beach, just short of the water.

Huw and Myrddin raced towards the ranks of Saxons with a dozen of their companions, spread out across the length of the Saxon line. His eyes wide and his face pale, Huw killed his first man with a slash across the neck, blood soaking him and his sword. Myrddin moved with him, his arm rising and falling with a deadly monotony, while Myrddin tried at the same time to keep his eyes on Arthur, who fought just ahead of him.

But Arthur and Cai were working together, fighting side by side, first one slicing through an opponent and then the other. All the while, Cai buttressed his brother with his own horse, body, and shield.

With Ifan emitting a steady stream of curses beside him, Myrddin, for his part, killed four Saxons in succession. When he had no more opponents, he turned to come at them again. But there was no need—so many men had already fallen.

Huw and Myrddin came to themselves simultaneously and sighted three Saxons heading up the beach, looking for safety in the woods that lined its edge. Myrddin spurred Gwynfor after them with Huw, who'd reacted a heartbeat sooner, just in front of him. Huw had his sword raised high, ready to thrust it into the neck of the first man he came upon. When he reached him, however, he hesitated—only for a heartbeat, but it was enough.

The man sensed Huw's approach and didn't waste his opportunity. As Huw aimed a blow at his head, the man stopped abruptly, spun on a heel, and swung his sword two-handed. He would have sliced right through Huw's arm if Myrddin hadn't reached him in time to grasp the man's wrist with his left hand, preventing him from completing the downward stroke. While Myrddin had arrested the man's movement, his own overbalanced him and he went down, falling off Gwynfor and pulling the man with him.

The Saxon fell at an awkward angle and Myrddin heard—and felt—an ominous crack when he landed on top of him. Unfortunately, Myrddin's momentum also brought him in contact with the Saxon's sword and it sliced through Myrddin's leather armor into his thigh above the knee. As Myrddin rolled off the dying Saxon, Ifan arrived, his eyes wide and staring at the blood soaking Myrddin's leg.

"It hurts," Myrddin said. "*Christ.*"

"You might as well call on Him," Ifan said. "He'll be more forgiving than Nell. She's going to be very put out that you've given yourself another injury."

The sight of the wound brought spots to Myrddin's eyes. The fire that had rushed through him—through all of the warriors—died and he breathed heavily, curling inward on the pain. At the sight of Myrddin down, a Welsh man-at-arms ran over with a lighted torch.

Huw threw himself from his horse to crouch beside his father. In the flickering light, Huw's face showed more white than its usual Celtic pale.

Myrddin caught his eyes. "Is that what is taught among the Saxons?"

Huw bit his lip, unable to avert his eyes from Myrddin's wound. "No, sir."

Ifan unbuckled Myrddin's armor to get at the wound and pulled the torn fabric of his pants aside. Gritting his teeth, Myrddin straightened his back. With Huw supporting his shoulders, they both looked at the damage. Ifan's hands shook as he tended the wound. Myrddin's eyes blackened but Huw's grip kept him conscious as he fought the buzzing in his head. Fortunately, the cut was not deep, just bloody.

"That man was as much our enemy as any other, Huw," Myrddin said, after all three had regained some measure of control. "Why did you hesitate?"

"I meant to kill him."

Ifan ripped a strip from a scrap of cloth he kept in his scrip and began to bind the wound so Myrddin could no longer see it. That was all to the good. Myrddin had doctored many wounded men in his time, but he'd never been quite as sanguine about his own injuries.

Myrddin took a deep breath, still staring down at his leg. "I know you did, son. You fought well, up until the end."

"I'd already killed three men," Huw said. "As I chased this last one down, he was one too many. I didn't want to kill him, not from behind. If he'd been facing me, I wouldn't have cared, but from the back—"

"It isn't wrong to regret the loss of a life or to show mercy, but this war we're fighting ..." His voice trailed off too as Ifan wound the last cloth around his leg and pulled it tight. Myrddin felt like puking.

Ifan finished for him. "This war isn't about honor or justice or mercy. Only winning matters, by whatever means necessary. Neither side is going to have any honor left by the end of it."

"The one with honor is going to be the one that's lost?" Huw said. "That's what you mean?"

"We didn't make the rules," Myrddin said.

"You don't mean what you're saying." Huw gripped Myrddin's hand. "Not you."

"He doesn't." King Arthur had dismounted ten paces behind Huw, who now jerked around to face him.

Myrddin reached a hand out to Ifan. "Help me up."

"Father!" Huw turned back to Myrddin. "You can't! You're wounded!"

"I've had worst cuts than this," Myrddin said. It was no less than the truth. Besides, he wasn't going to get back to Nell any quicker by lying in the sand. Ifan grasped Myrddin's forearm and, with the help of his sword, Myrddin levered himself to his feet. He was shivering badly now, most likely from shock as well as the cold November air. He grasped Ifan's shoulder with his left hand to stay upright.

Arthur studied Myrddin as he wove in front of him on his one good foot, nodded, and then gestured with his sword to Huw. "Kneel before me."

Huw hesitated, blinking, and then walked stiff-legged to within five feet of the king.

"Give me your sword." Arthur pointed the tip of his own sword at Huw.

Eyes wide, Huw turned his sword, bloody as it was, and presented it hilt out to the king. King Arthur, in turn, gave it to Cai, who grinned as he cleaned the blade with quick, efficient movements. He handed it back to his brother, who gestured to Myrddin. Finding that his pain had faded, and by using Ifan as a crutch, Myrddin took short hobbling steps to stand beside Arthur. Myrddin grasped the sword and drove it tip down into the sand in front of the kneeling Huw.

"I would have your oath," Arthur said. "Are you man enough to give it?"

Huw stared up at King Arthur and Myrddin, standing side by side before him. "Yes, my lord."

"Do you swear to fear God, to obey His laws, to serve your lord, to protect the weak, and to be honorable, chivalrous, generous, and truthful in all things?" Arthur said.

"I swear." Huw's voice cracked as it probably hadn't for months.

Myrddin tried to take a step towards Huw, but before he'd moved his foot three inches, his leg buckled underneath him. Ifan grabbed Myrddin's arm to keep him from falling, and it was Arthur who stepped forward and backhanded Huw across the face.

Huw rocked from the blow, and then straightened, letting no emotion show on his face, knowing that was expected of him as a man. Arthur pulled Huw's sword from the sand and held it out to him. Huw took the hilt, astonishment clear on his face.

"Stand as a knight, Sir Huw ap Myrddin," King Arthur said.

Huw popped to his feet as only a youth could, his initial nervousness transformed from disbelief, to astonishment, to joy. He crossed the sand to Myrddin in two strides, a smile a mile wide on his face. Myrddin put a hand to the side of Huw's head and pulled him closer. He grinned, no longer feeling the pain in his leg. Suddenly, they found themselves in the center of a ring of men, cheering and pummeling them, jubilant in their victory.

Ifan wrapped his arm around Huw's shoulders. "You're a good man."

Huw laughed, and everyone laughed with him.

Into the midst of the joviality, rode Gruffydd. "Where is my son? I don't see him among the dead."

Cai and Arthur had stepped out of the ring of men, once it became raucous, and now it was Cai who strode forward to stand at Gruffydd's stirrup. The rest sobered, recalling the seriousness of the morning's events.

"He is not among the Saxons," Cai said. "My brother sent men through the tunnel, as well as overland to Garth Celyn, to inform those who guard the trap door that it should be safe to open. We should have news soon of those who never left the tunnel."

Gruffydd didn't look satisfied, but it took only a short wait to prove Cai's words true. One of Arthur's personal guards jogged from the entrance. "If it pleases you, my lords, Lord Bedwyr asks that you return to the castle. Owain ap Gruffydd lies at the foot of the stairs."

Myrddin stared up at Gwynfor's back, sure he was never going to be able to mount her. Still, between Huw and Ifan, they got him astride and heading home. They entered Garth Celyn through the main gate, and Myrddin dismounted awkwardly. Along with many other men, he limped to the top of the stairs that led to the tunnel.

King Arthur was just ahead. "This way, sire," Bedwyr said, his expression grave.

He and Arthur walked down the stairs and through the door at the bottom. Nobody stopped Myrddin from following, although the bandage around his thigh received more than one look. The activity had him bleeding through the cloths. Nell was *not* going to be happy.

Owain lay just inside the doorway to the tunnel, propped against the wall and alive—barely. A body sprawled on the other side of him, a knife thrust through his midsection.

Myrddin didn't recognize him, but Cai did. He stood at the man's feet with his hands on his hips, staring down at the body, his eyes narrowed in recognition and disgust.

Owain was speaking to Nell as Myrddin arrived. "Don't try to save me. If I survive until dawn, I'm for the gallows."

Nell had been pressing hard on his wound to stop the flow of blood, but now he pushed at her hands, and she removed them. Owain rested one hand on the spot just above his left hip. The blood began to flow freely through the cloth.

Choking on a sob, Nell got to her feet.

Just as she moved away, Gruffydd rumbled up and fell to his knees in the place Nell had vacated. He took Owain's hand. "What is this, my son?" His voice was gruff. "What are you doing here?"

Owain's face twisted into a grimace, and his voice, when he spoke, came harshly. "I followed your example, Father. All my life we've fought against Arthur. You meant me to believe you sided with him this time? I'm afraid that I could not."

Gruffydd bowed his head, and his shoulders sagged.

Owain's next words were for Cai. "I understand you've been looking for this man." He tipped his head towards the fallen traitor.

Geraint spoke softly in Myrddin's ear. "He belongs to Cai's own guard, from the former garrison at Denbigh. Do not forget that we cannot trust this man."

As if I could.

Cai said nothing, merely toed the dead man's heel and shot a glance at Arthur, who didn't notice it, as he still watched Owain.

"What do you want from me?" Owain had his eyes on the king.

"From you, nothing," Arthur said. "For Wales, peace. That is all I have ever wanted for her. We'll leave you to say goodbye to your father."

As Arthur moved towards the door, Myrddin reached for Nell's hand and led her away, his vision etched with a picture of Gruffydd, his head in his hands, kneeling beside the failing body of his son.

Chapter Three
27 November 537 AD

"YOU'RE THE LAST PERSON I'd have expected to see here, Myrddin," Gareth said. "When was the last time you darkened the door of a church?"

Myrddin half-turned to look at Gareth, who continued smirking. Myrddin opted not to mention to Gareth that he set foot in a church every night in his dreams, on the way to dying.

They were standing at the rear of the packed Church of St. Deiniol to honor the date of the church's dedication. They might be in the middle of a war and all of Wales might be under interdict, but Arthur ap Uther lived a pious life. It was a holy day, and all of Garth Celyn had turned out to celebrate it.

It had been an amusing scene, in fact, when the king had arrived at the church. Neither Brother Rhys, who ran the church, nor Brother Llywelyn, who led the adjacent monastery, had been prepared for the crowd that had ridden the three miles from Garth Celyn and descended on Bangor on a Friday afternoon in order to celebrate the service before sunset.

"What is this? What is this?" Rhys had run around the sanctuary in a panic, unable to waylay either the king or Anian, who'd accompanied him. Because Rhys then refused to hold the service, Anian himself had ordered the candles on the altar lit.

Now, they were two hours into the service and Myrddin was tired of standing. But as was increasingly the case, he wasn't going anywhere without Nell. He lifted his chin, indicating to Gareth where she stood with bowed head, Huw beside her. A few feet beyond stood Cai. He'd found religion, apparently, and no longer left King Arthur's side. If that wasn't irritating enough, Arthur had reminded the company a dozen times these last three days how brilliantly Cai had fought. To Myrddin's mind, it was as if he was spitting into the wind, daring the fates to disagree with him.

"I see," Gareth said. "Do you trust your son to see her safely back to Garth Celyn?"

"Of course." Myrddin looked at Gareth more closely. "Why?"

"All may not be as it seems."

Myrddin snorted under his breath. He could only agree with that assessment. He despised standing in the same room with so many traitors. While Rhys had disappeared, refusing to countenance the use of the church under these circumstances, Brother Llywelyn had stayed, hovering on the margins of the crowd as if to prevent someone from stealing the candlesticks. It was insulting.

"Tell your son you'll be staying behind," Gareth said.

Myrddin nodded. "Yes, my lord."

Eventually, the service ended, at which point Myrddin caught Huw's eye as he approached with Nell on his arm. "I have a task to do. I'll see you back at the castle."

"That will be fine," Nell said. "One of the villagers from Bangor tells me her niece is laboring with some difficulty. Huw can see me there and then home when it's over."

Huw nodded, obliging as always, although his eyes on his father were intent. Myrddin clapped him on the shoulder to indicate all was well and watched them leave, heading towards the horses with the rest of the crowd, the bulk of which was easily visible from the dozen torches that lit up the clearing in front of the church steps.

King Arthur was among them, bareheaded, half a head taller than most of the men. He mounted his horse and rode away, flanked on one side by Gruffydd and on the other by Bedwyr.

By Bedwyr?

"You note it too?" Gareth looked past Myrddin to the king's entourage. "His mistake was to be *too* attentive. The king may think nothing of his absence—in truth may even be relieved to ride without him—but it's glaring to me who has tailed our traitorous prince these last three days."

"What is it you suspect?" Myrddin said.

"Cai wanted to be here alone—he said as much to King Arthur when he broached the subject of the holy day. Cai discouraged King Arthur from coming—but Arthur refused to take the hint."

"So all of Garth Celyn came. No wonder Rhys and Llywelyn were taken aback," Myrddin said. "Does King Arthur know you're spying on his brother?"

Gareth snorted a laugh. "No. He would not countenance it. But I do what is best for Wales. Come."

They re-entered the church, slipping back into the nave to wait for the last of the parishioners to leave. Anian hadn't extinguished the candles he'd lit and they flickered on the altar, moments from going out. Eventually, all was dark and quiet.

"There's no one here," Myrddin said.

"Isn't there?" Gareth said. "Cai hasn't left the church."

"Could he have used a different exit?"

"There's only the one," Gareth said. "I suspect he's in the belfry, if only because I saw Llywelyn's skirts disappearing up the stairs earlier."

With a tip of his head, Gareth indicated a curtain on the northern wall. Myrddin realized he'd never looked behind it, never thought to. Together with Gareth, he poked his head past it, observed the shadowed stairs, and hastily retreated at the sound of voices above them.

"Hide," Gareth said.

Myrddin slipped behind one of the limestone statues that lined the walls of the nave, an older one, but with a large base. Gareth spun on his heel, and at first Myrddin thought he was looking for a similar spot for himself. But he wasn't. Instead he waited, planted in the center of the floor with his hands on his hips.

Three men came through the curtain, Llywelyn in the lead. He lit the way with a lantern, which threw shadows on the wall that separated the nave from the foyer. Because they spoke among themselves, distracted by their own issues, the three men were almost upon Gareth before Llywelyn halted abruptly.

"You!"

"Cousin. I thought I'd find you here among your betters." Gareth nodded his head at Cai, who stepped out from behind Llywelyn.

"What do you want?" Llywelyn said.

"I knew you had to be up to something," Gareth said. "And now I know what it is."

"Just kill him," the third man said. Myrddin didn't recognize either his voice or his shape. Nor did he dare stir from behind his statue to get a better look.

"Ahh," Gareth said. "My dear Agravaine." And Myrddin understood that Gareth said the man's name for his benefit. "*You're* the secret they've been keeping. King Arthur might rationalize a meeting with my slippery cousin, but you—you he wouldn't forgive."

"Which is why we need to kill him," Agravaine said.

Gareth spread his arms wide. "Go ahead. I suspect the consequences might be greater than you know." Myrddin's hand went to his sword, his stomach churning and his head spinning with shock. If he'd expected anything, it wasn't this.

Agravaine made to step forward, but Cai put out an arm to stop him. "He's Modred's. You can't touch him."

"You tell me false!" Agravaine's tone dripped with disdain and outrage. "He can't be."

"He was spying for Modred as early as 532," Cai said. "I know because I was at Modred's court then."

"Why didn't I know of this?"

"Perhaps because you don't know everything! Be quiet and let me think." A pause, and then Cai spoke again, directing his words at Gareth, who was the only man he appeared to view as more-or-less an equal. "What do you want?"

"Assurances," Gareth said.

"Don't listen to h—" Llywelyn said.

Cai cut him off. "Shut up, monk." And then to Gareth. "You have them. What is your concern? That Modred won't like what we do?"

"More that you'll muck it up, just like the attack on Garth Celyn," Gareth said.

"That was Owain's plan," Cai said. "He's always been long on ideas and short on follow through."

Llywelyn sneered. "It would have worked but for this Myrddin. I told you we should've removed him sooner."

"He'll be taken care of before too long," Cai said. "Agravaine has it in hand."

"Good to know as Myrddin's a nosy bastard," Gareth said.

"Are we done here? I have a boat to catch." Dismissing his fellows with a wave, Agravaine strode towards the exit and flung open the door. The cold night air blew over Myrddin, and he heard the staccato of rain on the slate roof of the church.

Llywelyn and Cai followed, though Cai paused on the doorstep in order to direct a few last words to Gareth. "We'll speak later."

"Yes, my lord."

The door swung home, leaving the foyer completely silent but for the drip of water from the roof. Myrddin was loath to rise from his hiding place lest they return—and even more reluctant to face Gareth.

"You heard some things I would have preferred you hadn't," Gareth said, into the quiet.

"Does King Arthur know your role in this?" Myrddin finally stood and stepped from behind the statue.

"He knows Modred thinks I spy for him," Gareth said. "He doesn't know that I once truly did."

"Am I to believe you remain loyal to King Arthur now? After what I heard?"

"It's the truth."

Myrddin contemplated Gareth's face. He seemed sincere, but Myrddin felt manipulated. "Admittedly, you could have come alone and confronted them without me. It would have been safer for you."

"But not safer for the king," Gareth said. "Knowing that Cai and Agravaine are allies, I cannot now believe that he should go south. They may well be using Edgar for their own ends. You should know, in addition, that Modred confirmed Edgar in his inheritance a few days ago."

"*Cnych*!" Myrddin said.

"I share your sentiments," Gareth said. "I brought you as witness because I found what I was looking for, but I am not in a position to speak to the king of the dangers that face him in the coming weeks."

Myrddin stared at him. "What? Why ever not?"

"I play a dangerous game, Myrddin," he said. "Modred trusts me; Cai trusts me. So does my king. Few could have played this role so well for so long. But if I speak to King Arthur of Cai's betrayal, I throw all to the fates."

"You're afraid," Myrddin said.

"Cautious," Gareth said. "What if Cai discovers I've deceived him? I will have lost all ability to serve Arthur effectively."

"So you leave it to me?"

Gareth waved a hand dismissively. "You're one of his household knights. Your loyalty is without question. He will listen to you."

"I pray you're right."

Chapter Four

28 November 537 AD

"HE THREW ME OUT OF his office, Nell." Myrddin paced around the work table in the center of her herb hut. He and Gareth had ridden home, and Myrddin had gone straight to Arthur, leaving Gareth drinking in the hall as if nothing untoward had happened.

Myrddin's subsequent conversation with King Arthur had been short, lasting only as long as it took for Myrddin to explain what he'd seen. Arthur had shouted Myrddin down before the words were half out of his mouth. Even Geraint, who was witness, was taken aback by Arthur's rare display of temper.

"Sit, Myrddin," Nell said, "before you upset all my tinctures and salves. Besides, it's very late. You'd do better to sleep than think."

Myrddin sat but was on his feet again an instant later, too restless to stay still. "He and I have always maintained a good relationship, and now he thinks I'm a traitor."

"Tell me what happened again."

"I told him that Cai, Llywelyn, and Agravaine had met in the belfry at Bangor. I told him that I believed the letter from Edgar a trap and asked if I could go in his stead or, as an alternative, travel south to Brecon as Lord Cedric suggested. Arthur ignored my request, instead asking if I knew what the meeting had been about. I told him I didn't know. He asked if I'd actually seen Agravaine's face. I hadn't, and since I couldn't reveal Gareth's role in all this, the king instantly disbelieved my whole story. He didn't want to believe it.

"And then Cai came into the office, that incessant sneer on his face, before he wiped it clean and denied everything."

Nell moved to stand beside him, her hand on his shoulder. "The king loves his brother, all reason aside. And without Gareth, you have no proof. This isn't your fault."

Myrddin grunted his disagreement and disgust, moving towards the brazier to raise the fire. When he'd left the hut earlier, he'd banked the coals so they'd continue to burn low, but he'd been gone so long they were almost out. Soon, Myrddin had the coals glowing again. The hut was small enough that the heat from it would make some headway against the cold.

The activity calmed him, and he found his shoulders sagging with his acceptance of his failure. "I must return to the hall and speak to Geraint. I cannot leave it there."

Now it was Nell's turn to pace, and she circled her table. The light glinted off the blonde highlights in the wisps of hair that escaped her coif. Myrddin had never noticed them before; he knew he'd never seen anyone as beautiful as she. He'd lost track of his sensible decision to keep her at arm's length. It sucked the air from his lungs to realize how much she still kept inside her own head. He could only hope that she, too, loved despite herself.

At last she stopped in front of him. "Tell Geraint everything."

He studied her face. "Everything?"

"Yes," she said. "I'll come with you if you think it will help."

"Not yet. Let me try again alone first." He moved away, ready to leave and glad to have the decision made. But Nell caught his arm before he'd gone two steps.

"What you did was very brave."

"It had to be done." He turned back to her. "Time is too short to waste." He started to pull away but she didn't let him go, tugging him closer and forcing him to focus on her again.

"You be careful," she said. "I told you the only way to prevent myself from weeping was to laugh, but I can't face the coming weeks with laughter."

He looked down at her, seeing the concern in her eyes. "I lived thirty-six years with nobody to worry about me. I can take care of myself."

"I know." She stepped closer, placing her hands flat against his chest. "And is that what you want?"

Myrddin didn't look away. His hands found her waist and rested there, one on each hip. He looked into her eyes. "I've never had a choice before." He leaned forward and kissed Nell's forehead, his lips lingering in her hair.

"I shouldn't have let you go into battle without an answer," she said.

Their faces were inches apart, hers upturned looking into his. Time and silence stretched out as Myrddin stared down at her. Then without a conscious decision on his part, he brought his lips down on hers. She wrapped her arms around his neck, and he pulled her tight against him.

"God, Nell." He forced himself to take a breath. "I don't want to lose you."

"You won't," she said. "No matter what happens, you won't."

His arms encircled her. He didn't want to let her go, but knew he had to. He groaned, his forehead to hers, and his desire for her a deep ache within him. "I must see Geraint." He eased away.

"I know that too." She allowed him to lift her hands from his chest. He squeezed them once, and then left the hut, heading down the garden walkway to the kitchen, his mind full of Nell.

Halfway there, Geraint stepped out of the darkness. "What is it that you cannot leave?"

Myrddin pulled up short.

"The king leaves for Powys in three days. I must know what it is you aren't telling me." Geraint's tone was forceful, but not menacing. Urgent, rather.

"Over here." Myrddin glanced around to make sure that nobody had followed him and that Nell had shut the door to the herb hut. It wasn't so much that he didn't want her to overhear their conversation, but rather he didn't want her to suffer for his failings if this went as awry as the conversation in Arthur's office.

"Speak," Geraint said, once they'd retreated to the far corner of the kitchen garden where the side of the keep met the garden wall.

"If you're worried that Modred turned me to his side in his dungeon at Rhuddlan," Myrddin said, "that is not the case."

"I have no such concern," Geraint said. "If you'd been bought, there'd be signs."

The compulsion to tell the truth had Myrddin pressing his lips together to keep the words back. And then, for better or worse, he gave up the fight. "I fear for the king's life because I already know the future. I know what will happen by the Cam River if he goes to meet Edgar of Wigmore."

Geraint stared at him. "What in Christ's holy name is that supposed to mean?"

"I've seen it," Myrddin said. "I've seen him fall, stood over his body to protect him, and fallen myself. I've seen all Wales weep."

In the darkness, Myrddin couldn't read Geraint's expression, but he stood so still that if not for the light coming through the open kitchen door he would have been indistinguishable from the wall at his back. The scar that slashed across his forehead stood out white against his darker skin.

"No." Geraint shook his head. "You can't know what you're saying."

Myrddin stepped away, rethinking his approach. "Come, my lord. A cup of wine wouldn't go amiss."

Geraint hesitated, and then nodded. They returned to the hall, Geraint walking several paces behind Myrddin. By the time Geraint lowered himself onto a bench near the fire, a cup and carafe in front of him and Myrddin settled across the table, his intensity had lessened. He took a swig and wiped his mouth with the back of his hand.

"Let's try this again." A twinkle appeared in Geraint's eye that told Myrddin he didn't believe a word he'd said, and for that, Myrddin was almost grateful. Geraint might treat him like a lunatic from now on, but not so much that he'd hang him as a traitor. "I'd like to hear the rest."

Geraint's expression was such as a man might wear when he was settling in to hear a bard's tale of how Gwydion, son of Dôn, brought pigs to Math ap Mathonwy when he ruled Gwynedd as its king, or how Gwydion and Math conspired to make a wife for Gwydion's nephew out of flowers. They were stories that he didn't believe but, at the same time, thought might provide good entertainment for an evening.

Myrddin folded his hands around his cup, took a sip, and set it on the table in front of him. "On the 11th of December, King Arthur will go to St. Cannen's church at the request of Edgar. It is a trap, as I told you before, and he and the eighteen men of his personal guard will die. The Saxons will remove King Arthur's head and send it to Modred."

"And you know this how?"

"Since I was a boy, I've dreamt it. I have fought and died for our king more times than I can count—always at the church by the Cam River; always straddling the fallen body of the king. Lately, I've had the visions even while awake."

"So you're what? A saint? A seer? A wizard?" Geraint's amusement of before was gone.

Myrddin leaned forward across the table, determined to defuse Geraint's skepticism before it turned to anger if he could. "This is me, Geraint. Myrddin. I've ridden with the king for twenty years, and I tell you I've *seen* it. I've lived it. This is what is coming, and it has haunted me my whole life!"

"And you've kept these visions hidden all this time?" Geraint said, mocking. "I'm the first to know?"

"If this is your response, is it any wonder I've told no one?" Myrddin said. "Look what happened when I tried to tell the king about something I saw with my own eyes! I only tell you now because we are so close to the end."

Geraint rubbed his chin with one hand. "All right. Say I believe you. What do you propose?"

"It's as if I've had a path laid before my feet—like footsteps in the snow—that I've followed time and again to my death. I refuse to follow that path any longer. We must forge a new one."

Geraint leaned back in his chair, ran his fingers through his hair, and then scrubbed his face with both hands. "Christ, Myrddin." He dropped his hands to rest them helplessly in his lap. "I don't want to know this. I don't want to hear this."

"I know," Myrddin said. "As long as you protect the king, I don't care if you believe me, but you mustn't stop me from doing whatever I can to help him and Wales."

"I will protect the king," Geraint said, "but perhaps it would be best if you do as you suggested and ride south to Brecon and Buellt."

"So I don't embarrass you with my delusions?" Myrddin said.

Geraint looked straight at Myrddin, meeting his eyes, his jaw set. "No. That's not it at all. You must ride south so that what you describe never comes to pass."

"I NEED YOU TO GET UP, Huw," Nell said.

Huw rolled over, and his eyes met hers. Instantly, he was awake and attentive. "What's wrong? Father—"

"Myrddin's fine. He's getting the horses. I'll tell you on the way."

"Where are we going?"

"Brecon. And Buellt after that if we have time."

Nell was already moving away. Huw, fortunately, had slept close to the door and had been easy to find. The other men were used to Nell by now and nobody else, even if awake, had stirred to stop her.

Huw caught up with her by the time she reached the door, shrugging into his coat and cloak. "I'll need my armor." He slept with his sword, as befitting a newly dubbed knight.

"Your father has it," she said. They left the barracks and trotted across the courtyard towards the stables.

"And you're coming with us?" Huw said.

Nell glanced up at Huw. "Yes. Don't you dare take Myrddin's side in this!"

"He's trying to stop you," Huw said, not as a question.

"Of course he is, but he's wrong to. I can help. I've cobbled together a nun's habit. If I wear it as we travel, it will provide an adequate ruse for our journey."

Huw pursed his lips in thought. "That's a good idea, actually." They turned into the stables and came to a halt in front of the horses. Myrddin was adjusting the stirrups on the last.

"No it isn't." Myrddin straightened and glowered in Nell's direction.

Nell whirled on him, finger pointing. "You don't get to decide this! I already cleared it with Geraint."

They glared at each other for a count of five, and then Myrddin gave way. "I don't like it."

"I know you don't," Nell said. "But you won't regret it."

Regardless of his doubts, Myrddin had saddled three horses, not two, one for each of them. As she grabbed the bridle of her horse and prepared to mount, Nell smiled inwardly, not so much at his capitulation or that she'd *won*, but because he respected her enough to bring her even when every fiber in him protested.

"*Jesus Christ*!"

Nell had half-pulled herself into the saddle when the curse came from behind her. She swung around to see Myrddin, his hands up and helpless, with Deiniol behind him pressing a knife to Myrddin's throat.

"Well, well. You're leaving Garth Celyn in the wee hours, *mochyn*? Have I caught myself a traitor?"

"You would know far more about that than we would!" Nell took a step towards the pair but arrested her movement as Deiniol tightened his grip on Myrddin's hair. The knife pressed far enough into Myrddin's skin to draw blood.

"Stay back, love." Myrddin had placed his hand on the hilt of his sword, but could do nothing more than that. Huw had moved beside her but was helpless as she, staring at Deiniol and Myrddin.

"What do you want?" Nell said.

Deiniol gazed at her through narrowed eyes and then spit out the truth—maybe for the first time ever. "I've caught him now. He can't get away with his treachery this time. He's always had it easy—the one touched by God, the one everyone always trusted and believed, and for whom everything came easy. He's a nobody! He took from me what was mine!"

That was such a different perspective from the one that Myrddin had expressed, Nell couldn't reconcile the two. She met Myrddin's eyes, trying to speak without speaking and discover a way out of this predicament in which Myrddin's throat didn't end up cut.

"Let him go, Deiniol," Huw said.

Huw was drawing his sword, despite the danger to Myrddin when, a finger to his lips, Gareth appeared out of the darkness of the stalls. He approached silently from behind Deiniol, his sword out, and he pressed the tip into Deiniol's back. "That's enough."

Deiniol started.

"Your grievances have no place here," Gareth said. "Let Myrddin go."

Deiniol clenched and unclenched his hand in Myrddin's hair, and then eased up on the knife. He straightened and slipped it into the sheath at his waist. "My lord." He bowed stiffly in Gareth's direction.

Myrddin swung around to face him. "The next time you touch me, I will run you through, even if it would anger my lord and yours!"

"Why are you here, Deiniol?" Gareth placed a hand on Myrddin's chest and stepped between the two men.

"Lord Cai believes we have a traitor among us. He charged me with discovering his identity." Deiniol gestured towards Myrddin. "Who but a traitor would leave Garth Celyn in the middle of the night?"

"You know what Modred did to me," Myrddin said, "and what it took for me to escape."

Deiniol smirked. "I admit, to suffer those wounds simply to put on a show would imply an unprecedented devotion to duty, even for you, Myrddin."

"There are men among the king's company who are more deserving of your knife than I. Including your own lord."

Gareth shot Myrddin a quelling look. "How long have you been following Myrddin?"

"Long enough," Deiniol said.

"Be off." Gareth threw out a hand and stepped back. "Your duties lie elsewhere."

Deiniol gave Myrddin an evil look but turned away, disappearing through the far doorway of the stables.

Gareth turned back to Myrddin. "I heard what happened with King Arthur. I'm sorry."

"You set me up," Myrddin said.

"Myrddin—" Nell took his arm. She'd never seen him this angry. Gareth's appearance, instead of easing his temper, appeared to have increased it. He was vibrating with the effort it took to contain it.

"I did not foresee this outcome," Gareth said. "But I do not believe all is lost. Cedric could be a valuable ally. Even Edgar might turn out to be sincere—I find it more likely now than before I knew of the alliance between Cai and Agravaine, since Edgar despises them both. I take comfort in the fact that you, of all people, are going south to determine the truth."

Myrddin's jaw remained set. "I, at least, will do my duty. We will see you along the Cam at the king's camp—or I will see you in hell." With that, he threw himself onto his horse and urged her out of the stables.

Gareth moved to help Nell mount, and she opted not to shake him off. Still, she couldn't quite be civil. "I don't trust you. You are far too concerned about your own neck."

"And your man is too noble for his own good." Gareth paused. "I'm glad of it."

Nell looked at him for another heartbeat, and then pulled at the reins, turning her horse's head to follow Huw and Myrddin. Geraint waited for them by the wicket gate, having apparently missed the exchange in the stables entirely. It was by his power that they were leaving, and he'd sworn to assuage Arthur's anger when the king discovered their absence.

"May God go with you," Geraint said, as they passed through.

Chapter Five
6 December 537 AD

"YOU WERE RIGHT NOT to leave her behind." Huw leaned across the space between him and Myrddin to murmur the words. "It's always better to do as Nell suggests."

"I heard that." Nell gave Huw her sweetest smile. "But you are correct."

The three of them were jogging along well down the old Roman road to Brecon. The weather had eased, turning warmer and bringing overcast skies and threatening rain instead of the snow of the past days. Huw and Myrddin flanked Nell, as her escort and protectors. Even masterless men would find the prospect of attacking two armed men and a nun daunting.

The eastern slopes of the Cambrian Mountains were as rugged and barren as their northern counterparts, but as they followed the road eastward, towards the farmlands along the Welsh border, the air warmed further. The snow was reduced to pockets, mostly tucked into the northern slopes of the hills.

Nell was looking forward to reaching Brecon not long after nightfall, which always came too early this time of year. They'd slept safe but not overly warm in a series of castles and hunting lodges that linked Eryri with Powys and whose castellans were loyal to Arthur. She was cold, tired, and smelled of horse—and they hadn't even arrived at the hard part yet.

They'd skirted the hill of Yr Allt to the north of the Usk river valley and were continuing east, expecting nothing untoward, when up ahead a horse whinnied, the desperate pitch carrying through the still air. The sounds of men shouting and swords clashing followed.

Huw slowed to listen. "That can't be good."

"Definitely not," Myrddin said.

The two men shared a glance and then spurred their horses forward. Nell hung back, knowing that she would only hinder the men in a fight. Twenty yards ahead, Huw outpaced Myrddin, his sword held high. In that formation, they rode around a corner, heading towards the ford of the fast-running Cilieni River, swollen from the autumn rains. Another eighty yards farther on a dozen men battled—or what remained of them. One group had caught another in an ambush at the ford.

Dead men and horses lay in the water. A cry rose in Nell's throat at the sight of a lone man in Cedric's colors standing astride another, who sprawled on the ground, unmoving. The knight held off four others in red and white surcoats from a good position, even if a desperate one. In order to reach him, his enemy had to climb the bank leading up from the river.

In the excitement of the fight, only one of the men noted them coming and half-turned in his seat. He had a single heartbeat to register Huw's approach, without even time to raise his shield to defend himself, before the boy swung his sword in a mighty sweep of his arm and severed the man's head from his body.

"Huw!" Nell found her voice, afraid Huw would barrel right into the other men and fall under their combined assault. The taste of fear was sour in her mouth.

But Huw was a good soldier and, while his horse carried him another few steps down the bank, he was able to recover. Before he went into the water, Myrddin caught up with him. In parallel formation, the two men charged towards the three remaining soldiers, two of whom were struggling to turn their horses in the river. The third was still intent on running the lone defender through.

One of the attackers danced around Myrddin. Their swords connected. To Nell's eyes, it was the same as she imagined any other fight: hack, slash, twist, each trying to gain advantage over the other. Then Myrddin's horse found a hole, and her leg twisted. Going down, Myrddin threw himself from her back, barreling into the man he was fighting to bring him off his horse and into the water.

They landed with a terrifying clunk, instantly soaked, their boots filling with water and their soaked clothing adding to the weight of their mail. The man's head hit the stones under the water, and he lay stunned, with the wind knocked out of him. Myrddin pushed up on one knee and, having lost his sword and shield in the fall, drove his fist into the man's jaw.

At first the man's head fell back into the water, but then he coughed and sputtered and tried to rise. Myrddin held his head under the water for a count of ten to subdue him, and then he grasped his arm and began to haul him to the far bank of the river.

Huw, meanwhile, had dispatched his opponent. Bleeding from a mortal wound, the man lay on the southern end of the ford, before floating off of it, heading downstream. Turning away, Huw urged his horse out of the water and up the bank towards the final enemy soldier.

That man noted Huw's approach. Rather than continue to fight a battle he might not win, and having dispatched Cedric's last knight, he spurred his horse eastward, down the road that led to Brecon. Huw visibly warred with himself as to whether or not he should follow, and then he didn't. Instead, he dismounted and fell to his knees beside the body of the man who'd had such a staunch defender.

"It's Lord Cedric himself!" Huw looked back at Nell, still on the other side of the river.

Myrddin dragged his combatant up the slope and dumped him half-in and half-out of the water. Forcing herself to push aside the violence she'd just witnessed, even if the memory of it would haunt her forever, Nell trotted her horse into the river and across the ford. Once up the other side, she dismounted and crouched opposite Huw.

"Let me." She felt for a pulse, which was hard to discern as her own heart still beat in her ears, her outward calm a false front for the choking horror inside her. "He's alive. His heart is strong."

Soaked, Myrddin limped up the bank. After a brief inspection, he rolled the body of Cedric's defender off his shins where he'd fallen. "The wound is here." Myrddin gestured to a slash across his right thigh, not dissimilar to Myrddin's own healing injury. The stroke had slid in just under his mail armor, cutting the thick muscle but not the bone or tendon.

Long ago, Nell's husband had explained to her why so many soldiers were wounded in the same way when fighting well-armored opponents. A man must direct his attack toward legs or faces, or deliver crushing blows, because it was nearly impossible to pierce an opponent's mail in hand-to-hand fighting.

In this case, Cedric's opponent would have driven his weapon underneath Cedric's shield while Cedric was astride his horse. The man then hoped to deliver the killing blow once he'd put Cedric on the ground, but Cedric's man-at-arms had protected him from that.

"He's out of his senses. Perhaps he hit his head." With gentle hands, she removed his helmet, set it to one side, and then felt at the back of Cedric's head. She glanced at Myrddin who'd slumped beside her on the ground and looked a bit green around the edges too. "Give me a moment to get my supplies."

Myrddin sat with his legs splayed in front of him, spent. His horse had righted herself on the far bank and now stood, one leg lifted, on a grassy verge. If her injury was a sprain, they might be able to save her. Otherwise, it would be more humane to slit her throat right now.

"I'll see to her." Huw met Nell's eyes, acknowledging their joint concern for Myrddin's well-being.

"Thank you." Nell removed her healer's pouch and flask from her saddlebags and returned to Cedric.

Myrddin, meanwhile, was regaining control of himself. While she crouched again beside the wounded lord, Myrddin grabbed one of the linen scraps from her bundle and ripped a strip off of it with his teeth. Nell held the flask of alcohol above the wound, hesitating, knowing that if Cedric was at all conscious when she poured it on him, he would leap from the ground, shrieking in pain. As it was, when she tipped the liquid over the wound, Cedric's body stiffened, his back arching. And then he bucked.

"Help me hold him!" Nell said.

Myrddin dropped the bandages on top of her leather pouch and pressed down on Cedric's shoulders while Nell mopped up the remaining liquid and smeared calendula salve along the length of the wound.

"You sew him up," Myrddin said. "You've the finer hand."

She nodded, while adding, "Riverside medicine. Not my favorite." With a hand that didn't tremble, she threaded her needle.

Myrddin leaned in to hold together the edges of Cedric's skin above his right knee while she sewed. Then he lashed the bandages around Cedric's thigh and, with his stronger hands, tied them. About the time Myrddin finished, Cedric opened his eyes.

"I know you." Cedric looked into Nell's face. "Am I in heaven?"

"I'm a nun, not an angel—although I'm not even that anymore." With a swipe of her hand she removed her headdress. Her thick braid swung loose, the end tied with a leather thong.

Cedric turned his head as he sensed Myrddin on the other side of him. "It's you." He blinked.

"Myrddin, again, my lord. I've come with Huw, my son."

"Ah," Cedric said. "He found you, then."

229

"He did."

"Help me up."

Nell opened her mouth to protest and then closed it. *Riverside medicine* was not subject to the conventional rules of healing. The man needed to stay prone, but the sun had set and the light was fading. None of them wanted to be caught out at the windy ford once it grew dark, fair game for marauders, both animal and human.

With Nell's help, Myrddin levered him to his feet. Upright, Cedric surveyed his dead companions. "Did any of my men survive?"

"None that I know," Myrddin said. "One of the enemy fled, and we chose to care for you rather than follow him."

"Under the circumstances, I can hardly protest," Cedric said.

Nell was glad to see that his dry humor was still in evidence, despite his pain. "Are we going to talk about whose men they were?" She studied the man Myrddin had felled, still lying by the river. He'd begun to moan, and he put a hand to the back of his head.

"Their colors tell me they belong to Arthur," Cedric said, matter-of-factly, "but your presence here makes me question it."

"Thank you for that." Myrddin walked down the bank, his boots sliding in the mud, to the injured man-at-arms. At his approach, the man opened his eyes.

"Just because a man wears certain colors, doesn't mean they belong to him," Nell said. "Remember Modred at Shrewsbury." At the battle where Cedric's father died, Modred had deceived him by raising a friendly standard. He'd allowed Modred's men to get too close and ultimately trap his entire army.

"Such was my thought." Myrddin's tone was as flat as Cedric's had been. He squatted beside the injured man and spoke in Welsh. "What's your name?"

The man didn't answer, and his eyes remained unfocused. Myrddin repeated the question in Saxon.

"Carl." The man's face had been flushed when Myrddin first crouched beside him, but now it paled, and he twisted towards his left side, his pain evident.

"Was it truly your mission to kill Cedric ap Aelfric?"

The man didn't answer. All of a sudden, he just ceased to be.

Myrddin checked his pulse. "He's dead. I didn't think I'd done enough damage to kill him."

Nell refused to chastise herself for the fact that she didn't seem to care that another man had died and turned to Cedric, all business. "You shouldn't be able to stand, but given that you're doing it anyway, can you ride?"

"Of course," he said, and then amended, "with help."

Just then, Huw returned, leading a single horse: his own. His face said, *I'm sorry.*

Myrddin sighed and stood.

Cedric's own horse had strayed along the river bank, cropping the short grass along its fringe. Huw and Myrddin retrieved it, along with another, whose owner no longer needed it, for Myrddin. Between the three of them, they managed to get Cedric astride with Nell behind him, to hold him should he weaken.

"You all right?" Myrddin asked her, once she was seated.

She gazed down at him, warring between disbelief and humor. "I held you like this. I've been around you long enough to get used to wounded men."

Myrddin grinned back at her, and then he mounted the extra horse himself.

Despite their efforts, it was immediately clear that Cedric couldn't ride one mile, much less the eight that would bring them to his castle at Brecon. His head lolled back onto Nell's shoulder.

"Is there anywhere else we can go?" Nell said.

231

Myrddin had brought his horse closer so he could brace Cedric with his right hand.

"There's a small manor house not far ahead, perhaps a quarter of a mile," Huw said. "I've ridden by it a time or two."

"Its owner was one of my men," Cedric said, his voice a rasp. *Was*, meaning *dead*.

They plodded forward, Nell clutching Cedric around the waist, Myrddin with one hand out, holding Cedric's shoulder, and Huw leading the way. The horses picked their way along the road and then, within a dozen yards, they reached a trail and turned onto it, following it north. A half-mile on, they found the house of which Huw and Cedric had spoken, squatting in a clearing amidst the trees.

It wasn't quite what Nell expected for a manor house, although it was a cut above the huts that dotted the countryside, in which lived families like the ones who'd worked her father's land. Still in good condition, despite being abandoned, the house was roughly built, one story and a half high, with a wooden door and one shuttered window. Beside it sat an empty paddock, fenced with wooden poles, and a barn. The house might even have a wooden floor instead of dirt.

Anxious to get Cedric to safety, they approached the house, ghostly in the moonlight that filtered through the shrouding trees. They arrived at the deserted front door, and Myrddin dismounted to allow Cedric to slide off the horse into his arms.

Despite the possible indignity of it, Myrddin bent forward and threw Cedric over his shoulder. Huw lashed the reins of their horses to the stockade fence to prevent them from escaping, while Nell reached around Myrddin and lifted the latch to allow them to enter the house.

Nell and Myrddin pushed at the door simultaneously, with Myrddin nudging the bottom of the door with the toe of his boot.

When it didn't immediately give way, he shoved it hard. It opened halfway but then stuck on something behind it.

They froze on the doorstep. "*Mary, Mother of God*," Nell said.

The smell of blood and death, oppressive in such a small and enclosed space, wafted over them. Huw, who'd had a hand on Cedric's back to keep him in place—and perhaps because he didn't quite believe he was still alive—stepped to the corner of the house and retched. Myrddin backed away from the door, swallowing hard.

"Let's get him into the barn," Nell said. "We can deal with this later."

She led the way across the paddock and through the barn door, which was open. The barn was bare in a way the house was not. Hay had drifted across the floor to pile near a broken shovel a past resident had left on the floor near the door. Myrddin followed Nell and, after a bit, Huw came as well, holding his belly, but recovering. Once inside the barn, Huw kicked at a bed of straw to make sure it wasn't moldy, and Myrddin laid Cedric on it. Nell knelt beside him to check his leg wound and feel again at his head.

"He's not fevered," she said.

"Maybe he'll get lucky," Myrddin said.

She shot him a look, a cross between hopeful and skeptical, and then turned back to her patient. "He needs warmth, or he'll go into shock."

"If we could get into the house, we could make a fire," Myrddin said.

Nell and Huw looked at him in disbelief.

Myrddin held out his hands. "All I'm saying is that it would be preferable."

"But not possible," Nell said. "Even if we moved the bodies, we couldn't stay in there with the stink. We need to build a fire here."

"I'll get the flint and start it," Huw said. "If I build it at the entrance, we won't choke on the smoke."

Nell nodded, glad that Huw was capable. Then Myrddin put a hand on Nell's shoulder. "Can you manage if I find us firewood?"

"I'm as fine as I can be." She grasped his hand, squeezed once, and let go.

As Myrddin turned away, Cedric opened his eyes. "Thank you. You could have let me die."

"No." Nell leaned in to better assess his wounded leg. "We couldn't."

WITH A LAST CHECK OF Nell's face, and Cedric's pale one beyond her, Myrddin stepped out of the barn and set off towards the house. Huw was already gathering handfuls of straw. Myrddin worried that the light might alert an enemy to their presence—whether Saxon or Welsh, the choices were near limitless—but a night out here without a fire might well mean Cedric's death.

Holding his nose and without entering the house, Myrddin latched the door to the manor, not wanting to draw wild animals to the smell of blood. Shutters blocked the window in the lower level, meaning that an animal couldn't have strayed inside and died. The remains were human.

Myrddin was tempted to return with a torch and discover who was dead, but the pressing needs of the moment had him skirting the corner of the house and heading for the woods beyond it.

Once among the trees, Myrddin slowed, allowing the darkness to envelope him. The luminescence of the snow in the mountains had given way to dark earth and fallen leaves of the more balmy lowlands. Still, the moon was playing cat and mouse with the clouds, which were not as thick as before, so Myrddin wasn't blind.

As he moved from tree to tree, picking up every likely piece of wood—wet or dry—he listened hard to the forest. Once he'd circled around to the far corner of the barn, he stilled and let his senses expand. The smell of smoke from Huw's fire filtered towards him, mixing with the scent of pine, but otherwise he was alone in the world.

It had been a long time since he'd stood this way. He could be anywhere in Wales, at any time in his life. He felt as young as the twelve-year-old who'd had that first vision, and as old as the man in his dreams, whose only thought was the cold certainty of death as the Saxons closed in around him.

He'd always thought it strange that his *seeing* showed him the end of his life but never what it might take to avert it. He'd never *seen* this location before and had no prior knowledge of rescuing Cedric. Myrddin didn't know what was going to happen tomorrow. He tipped his head back to look up at the familiar stars and breathed in the cool, moist air.

Amidst his fear for King Arthur's life, there was an excitement, and a joy, in that fact.

Chapter Six

7 December 537 AD

THROUGHOUT THE NIGHT, Myrddin, Huw, and Nell took turns with Cedric, staying near him and checking his breathing and pulse every hour to make sure his concussion wouldn't settle him into too deep a sleep.

As dawn approached, while Myrddin was sitting by him and Huw and Nell were sleeping, Cedric woke fully for the first time. Myrddin had just tended to the fire, so it burned hot and gave off enough light to see the outline of the ceiling of the barn, the rusting farming implements and equipment that hung on the walls or were stacked along them, and the shapes of his companions.

"It's been a long time since I've slept in a barn." Cedric's voice was strong enough for Myrddin to note the amusement in it. "I must have been no older than nine."

"How do you feel, my lord?" Myrddin rested the back of his hand on Cedric's forehead, trying to sense whether he had developed a fever. He was cool enough.

"You've fought for Arthur your whole life." Cedric shifted and then winced as pain shot through his leg. "I'm sure you know how I feel."

"True," Myrddin said. "In fact, I have a new scar on my leg that mirrors the one you will have on yours. I received it a few weeks ago when a Saxon company tried to take Garth Celyn."

At that, Cedric, who'd been gazing up at the ceiling, turned his head to look at Myrddin. "You say, 'tried'. I'd heard your enemies burned the castle to the ground."

Myrddin stared at him. "Why would you say that?"

Cedric pursed his lips. "Because that's what the messenger told me."

Myrddin had a sudden fear that the Saxons had attacked Garth Celyn since they'd left—that the first attempt had been a ruse to make them think they were secure.

Warily, Myrddin said, "On the 24th of November, a fortnight ago, Owain ap Gruffydd and a company of Saxon soldiers attempted to enter Garth Celyn through a tunnel that runs from the beach, north of the castle, into Garth Celyn. We stopped them."

Cedric pushed up on his elbows, trying to straighten enough to sit up. Myrddin grasped him under his arm to help him.

"You tell me truly?" Cedric said. "The date is correct, but the outcome is not what I was told."

"Did the rider say who'd been killed?"

"He said that Arthur's daughter was captured and taken to Mercia, and a host of the king's personal guard killed, although King Arthur himself escaped." Cedric paused. "I can see from your face that this is not true."

"None of it," Myrddin said. "Not even a morsel. Whom did the messenger serve?"

Cedric pressed into his forehead with two fingers, his eyes closed. "Agravaine."

"I don't understand it," Myrddin said. "Why lie?"

"To counter your victory at the Strait, of course," Cedric said. "To convince all of us who've wavered at times to stay true to Modred."

"But eventually you'd find out ..." Myrddin's voice trailed off at the subversive logic. With helpless understanding, he nodded. "By then, Agravaine assumed he'd have killed King Arthur or severely weakened his cause. Agravaine isn't worried about you learning of his deception next year or even next week. He wants you steadfast now."

"News of a Welsh defeat could stiffen the spines of the lords in Modred's cause long enough for Agravaine to achieve his aims." Cedric settled back into the straw, a look of satisfaction on his face at learning the truth. Then he changed the subject. "So Huw's been blooded?"

"He has," Myrddin said. "More than once. He's had some adventures since you sent him to me."

"He and I must have a long speech together."

When Myrddin didn't answer him, just allowed his eyes to meet Cedric's, Cedric nodded. "Ah. His allegiance isn't what it was."

"He was the first to wade into the fight at the ford," Myrddin said. "It was four against one and yet he didn't hesitate. He thinks of you as a father."

"But you are his true father and have claimed him." Cedric nodded again. "It was a risk I thought worth taking."

"You saved my life at Rhuddlan," Myrddin said. "I owe you that."

"Then we are now even." Cedric gestured to indicate his wounded leg.

Perhaps we are, at that. "Do you remember the events of the day before we arrived? Why were you at the ford?"

"Simple scouting mission," Cedric said. "I try to ride with my men when I can. I'm not an old man just yet—younger than you I warrant—and we were about to cross the river when men I thought were Arthur's set upon us. I admit to entertaining dark thoughts about your lord. And yet, you came in on my side."

"They couldn't have been King Arthur's men," Myrddin said. "But whose they were—Cai's? Agravaine's?—I couldn't tell you. This move makes even less sense to my mind."

"Does it?" Cedric said. "You know as well as I that we border lords wage war against each other when we aren't allied with one another to fight the Welsh or perhaps our own Saxon allies."

"But why would anyone want to kill you?" Myrddin said, and then added with a smile, "beyond the obvious that is."

"Who knows of your journey? Could someone want to prevent you and me from speaking?"

That got Myrddin thinking grim thoughts. "Definitely. But it's more than that. Many would gain by your death. Your son is only six. You would die without a strong heir."

"My God, man," Cedric said as Myrddin's assessment sunk in. "I'm of the royal house of Mercia! This is unconscionable!" In his agitation, he struggled to return to a sitting position, even to go so far as to bend his good knee to get to his feet. His voice woke Huw, who hurried to his side.

"My lord," he said. "You'll start the leg bleeding again."

"I can't sit here," Cedric said. "I have to return to my castle!"

Myrddin put out a hand to stop him from rising. "We have a slight problem to deal with first."

Cedric spied an overturned wooden bucket and snapped his fingers at Huw to get it for him. Huw brought it, and Cedric lifted himself onto it, his wounded leg outstretched. "I'm not going to like this either, am I?"

By now, Nell had also risen and come to sit on the overturned water trough to re-braid her hair. "Not much, my lord."

A hint of a smile flickered at the corner of Cedric's mouth as he took in her clothing, still the nun's habit, and loose hair. Then he turned back to Myrddin. "What is it?"

"Something lies dead in the manor house, just there." Myrddin pointed at the house with his chin. "The stench is oppressive."

Cedric sighed. "You say 'something'. You don't know who or what?"

"We've not yet found out," Huw said. "Whoever it is wasn't going anywhere, and we couldn't sleep in the house even if we knew. Better to wait until the sun rose."

Myrddin checked the sky. It was still dim in the barn, but the sun shot rays that glittered on the puddles in the paddock. The temperature had dropped over the last hours and their breath hung in the air in front of them.

"None of my men came through here in the night?" Cedric said.

"No," Myrddin said.

"I pray Brecon isn't under siege," Cedric said.

"Surely not," Huw said.

"I wouldn't have thought the ford would prove dangerous either." Cedric turned back to Myrddin. "Let's see this, then."

With Huw on one side and Myrddin on the other, Cedric hobbled across the snowy paddock to the front door. Myrddin lifted the latch and pushed the door open. The smell was the same. Cedric pulled a handkerchief from his scrip and put it to his nose. In a row, they stepped into the main room, angling so they'd all fit through the door, and surveyed the chaos inside.

Two men lay on the lower floor, the first behind the door. It was his body that had kept it from opening all the way. Black boots, smaller than the ones Myrddin himself wore, stuck out, but the rest of the man remained hidden by the door. The second dead man lay in plain sight, leaning against the wall underneath the loft, his legs sprawled in front of him. Someone had skewered him through the gut.

"Check the loft," Myrddin said to Huw, who obeyed, heading towards a ladder on the right side of the room.

Nell remained in the doorway, hovering on the threshold without entering. "They're all dead?"

Myrddin turned to her. "Yes. There's nothing you can do."

She nodded and stepped outside again, moving out of sight and smell of the dead men in the house.

Huw called down to them. "There's another one up here."

"What are the man's colors?" Cedric said.

"Gold lions on blue," Huw said. "Same as the others."

"Christ's bones," Cedric blasphemed. "Mine."

"But who killed them, and why?" Myrddin said.

He left Cedric propped against the door frame and went down on one knee near the dead man behind the door to roll him onto his back. He too wore Cedric's crest. In his left hand, however, he grasped a piece of torn cloth. Myrddin pulled it from his grip and held up the prize. The emblem on the cloth was the same as that worn by the men at the ford: a crimson dragon on white.

"Gwynedd's colors again," Myrddin said.

"Enemies are friends, and friends are enemies," Cedric said.

Huw now came down the ladder. "This becomes more and more strange."

"And less and less to my liking." Cedric's face was very pale, although Myrddin thought that was less a result of the dead men than from the effort of staying upright. "We must return to Brecon Castle immediately."

Nodding his agreement, Myrddin threw Cedric's arm over his shoulder as before and hobbled with him towards the barn and the horses.

With Cedric boosted onto his horse and Nell behind him once again, they left the manor, riding south along the trail to the main road, and then east as they'd intended the day before. Cedric didn't speak until they were within sight of his castle. Myrddin had left him to himself, not wanting to disrupt his focus on staying upright.

But Cedric had been considering his situation. "When I invited you to retrieve your horse, I could not have predicted the events of yesterday."

"No, my lord," Myrddin said.

"I am reconsidering your king's proposal," Cedric said.

"He will be pleased to hear it," Myrddin said.

Cedric shot Myrddin a quick glance. "I cannot meet with him myself at this time, but perhaps a small gesture on my part wouldn't go amiss."

"A gesture that doesn't commit you fully, but indicates to the king your goodwill?" Nell said.

The smile flashed again. "Exactly, my dear."

"Give a company of your men leave to ride north with us when we depart from Brecon," Myrddin said. "As you told Modred last month, Edgar of Wigmore—and Agravaine with him—intend to lure King Arthur into a trap near the Cam River. I fear the king will meet them with too few men."

"That I can do," Cedric said, satisfaction in his voice.

Myrddin congratulated himself on latching upon the perfect solution. It was a way for Cedric to show support, without showing too much. At worst, if Agravaine accused him of switching sides, Cedric could claim his men had been in the wrong place at the right time and waded in on Arthur's behalf. Cedric was justified in not wanting to see Arthur, a noble kinsman, struck down, even if he was ostensibly an enemy.

Agravaine might not believe Cedric. Nor might Modred. But they could prove nothing. If Arthur did die in four days, God forbid, Myrddin wouldn't have Cedric lose everything just because he'd had honor enough to listen to him.

Chapter Seven

8 December 537 AD

SNOW SPIT ARRHYTHMICALLY against the pane. Nell gazed through the chapel's unusually large glass window at the accumulation—more than enough for this early in December. It sifted and swirled in the bailey of Brecon Castle. The small chapel was decorated with intricate carvings, stained glass windows with Cedric's crest, and family tapestries on the walls. All trace of King Arthur, who'd held it for decades, had been erased, not just here but everywhere.

Myrddin walked to stand behind her. He hesitated—she could sense his tentativeness—and then placed a hand on each of her shoulders. She trembled beneath them. "What are we doing here, Myrddin?"

"We've come a long way from St. Asaph haven't we?" His hands rubbed gently on her arms to warm her.

"Do we trust him?"

"Can we trust anyone at this point?" Myrddin said. "But yes, I do. I have no reason not to, and we're so close to the end now that the price of failure is no worse than that which already faces us."

"Your dreams consumed the whole of last night," Nell said.

Myrddin shrugged. "And yours didn't?"

She canted her head in acknowledgement of his point, though in truth she'd hardly slept. "And what do you see? Is it still the same dream?"

"It's odd. You've told me I'm no longer present in yours, which is something in which I find great comfort, but I'm watching from above in my own dreams now too. It's disconcerting, frankly, and I find myself trying to force the dream into the long-remembered patterns."

"But it won't go," Nell said.

"No," Myrddin admitted.

"Shouldn't that mean we're doing something right?" Nell said.

"The king still dies, Nell," Myrddin said. "I can no longer see his face, but the Gwynedd crest is bloody on the ground every time, just like at the ford."

Nell turned to him, wrapped her arms around his waist, and put her face into his chest. "We're doing everything we can. If King Arthur goes to meet Edgar, it's out of our hands."

"We are *so* close—not only to saving the king but to *winning* this war," Myrddin said. "I refuse to back down now."

Nell breathed deeply and squeezed Myrddin once more. "It's time we started for Buellt. How soon can we leave?"

"I would have liked to have left this morning," Myrddin said. "The last thing I want is to be late to the castle or the church."

"I share your concern, but you can't ride today," Cedric said from behind them.

Myrddin swung around, pulling Nell with him. Cedric stood framed in the doorway to the chapel.

"You shouldn't be up—" Nell cut herself off. Telling Cedric he shouldn't be up and around two days after a sword sliced through his leg was just as effective as saying it to Myrddin.

"And why is that?" Myrddin said.

"Because it would do you no good to arrive at Buellt Castle when Edgar is not there. You don't want to spend two days waiting for him under the eyes of Agravaine."

"How do you know this?" Myrddin said.

"Edgar has just sent me word that he intends to leave Wigmore tomorrow, at the head of a host of men, break his journey at Buellt, where he will see to the status of the garrison and confer with Agravaine, and then journey on to Brecon after hearing mass on Sunday."

"And his men?" Nell said. "What of them?" The combined forces of Agravaine and Edgar would be considerable, more than enough to counter the men that King Arthur might be able to collect once he reached Powys.

"Likely, he will leave the majority of them with Agravaine, to bolster his numbers and prevent King Arthur from besieging Buellt Castle," Cedric said. "Both sides are wary of each other now. They see the end game and are maneuvering their forces to strike at the most opportune time."

"As are you," Nell said.

Cedric canted his head at her, an amused glint in his eye, but he didn't answer. Instead he turned to Myrddin. "I trust your horse is undamaged from his stint in my stables?"

"Yes, my lord," Myrddin said. Nell had been there when he'd located Cadfarch, and Myrddin had been very pleased. "He's an old friend."

"Always the best kind to have at your back," Cedric said.

Nell didn't know how to interpret that, since even if Cedric was their friend (not yet determined), he certainly wasn't an 'old' one. Meanwhile, Cedric turned on his heel and departed.

As he disappeared down the corridor, heading for the stairs, Nell shook her head. "I can't read him."

"Neither can I," Myrddin said. "I wouldn't want to cross him."

"Do we know what we're doing?"

"No," he said. "We don't."

MYRDDIN FOUND HUW IN an open space between the stables and the smithy. The wall and buildings sheltered it from the worst of the wind, and the ground, although frozen, was clear of snow. Huw had grown to manhood in this castle after King Arthur's defeats earlier in the decade. In the last day, he'd fallen into old patterns, willing to take up where he'd left off to the point of holding a dull sword to face down a boy of similar age to him.

Unlike Huw, the boy was not yet a knight. By the look in his eye and the determined set of his jaw, he was ready to put Huw back into the place he thought Huw belonged.

But Huw, for all that he was young, had earned his title and was equally determined to show it. As they fought, Myrddin recalled another castle and a different fight, this one overseen by the captain of Arthur's guard, a man long dead but much revered. Those first months Myrddin had lived among Arthur's court, the captain had taken Myrddin under his wing. Even now, he could hear the man's words:

'A man is divided into four quarters,' he'd said, gesturing to Myrddin with the point of his sword. 'Every attack you make should draw your opponent's defenses to a new quarter, degrading his ability to counter you. At the same time, your opponent will be trying to attack you in the same way, and you must parry his blows. Remember that, and that we slash, not thrust, unless it is for the final blow when you force the point of your sword through a man's mail.'

It had been a lesson Myrddin had heeded. Despite Huw's hesitation at the battle at Garth Celyn, it was one he'd learned well too.

"I will miss the boy." As was his custom, Cedric had silently come up behind Myrddin in a manner Myrddin found disconcerting. Then again, it seemed to be his way and an extension of his desire to hide what he was thinking and feeling at all times. As a Saxon lord, this ability had undoubtedly stood him in good stead.

"Thank you for giving him leave to find me," Myrddin said. "It isn't every lord who would have done so."

"It was either that or find him gone one day, the imperative of his birth overcoming his allegiance to me," Cedric said. "It would have cost him more than needful to have refused him."

Huw parried another blow. Then, in a quick movement, he upended his opponent to pin him to the ground. Watching with Myrddin, Cedric gave a snort of satisfaction. "As I said, I will miss him."

"I will do my best to ensure that you never find yourselves on opposite sides of a fight," Myrddin said. "If I can protect him from that, I will."

"When I was sixteen, I saw my father cut down in front of me. There will be worse things for him in this life than having to fight in a battle not of his choosing."

Huw left the ring of boys and men, stripping off his tunic as he walked away. Steam rose from his torso. Even in the cold and snow, his young blood ran hot from the fight.

Cedric glanced at him once more and then turned to Myrddin. "Come. I have something to show you."

Myrddin followed Cedric into the great hall, both walking with identical stiff right legs, though Myrddin told himself his was the more limber, and then up the stairs to Cedric's office. Like the chapel, it had one window with glass in it, which in this case looked northwest. Snow had built up along the window ledge and ice coated the inside edges of the glass. Black clouds lay ominously low on the horizon, threatening more snow. Cedric's steward sat at a desk near the fire. Upon Cedric's entrance, he stood, bowed to Cedric, and left.

Myrddin faced Cedric across his desk, expectant but not expecting anything. Cedric reached up to a shelf above his head and brought down a box. Setting it on his desk, he opened it. Several cloth bundles nestled inside. Cedric chose one and unwrapped it, revealing a gold cross. Myrddin stared at it, speechless, for it was a match to the one he wore.

Wordlessly, Myrddin lifted his own cross over his head and laid it on the table beside the box.

"Your cross fell on your chest during the fight beside the river, and I noted it," Cedric said. "Where did you get it?"

"From my mother," Myrddin said. "She died at my birth, under the protection of one Madoc, a household knight of Lord Cai, King Arthur's half-brother."

"But Madoc was not your father."

"No." Myrddin's stomach lurched at the thought. "At least, he never claimed me, for all that he allowed me house room until I became a man." Myrddin paused. "And yours?" He almost didn't want to know.

"My mother died when I was two. She left this cross for me, her eldest son," Cedric said.

Myrddin absorbed his news, wondering and uncertain. There was no doubt the crosses were brothers, made by the same goldsmith and likely purchased together.

"There's more you should know." Cedric watched Myrddin carefully as he spoke, while Myrddin endeavored to copy him—to give nothing away of what he was thinking. "This cross was a gift to my mother from her sister, Juliana, when Juliana was near death."

"Juliana had it made?" Myrddin kept his eyes fixed on the matching crosses, recalling what King Arthur had said: that Myrddin's mother had been a lady-in-waiting to Juliana for a time before Myrddin's birth.

Cedric shook his head. "Juliana's husband had it made for her. He gave it to her the Christmas before he died."

Myrddin's head came up at that. Together, yet unspeaking, he and Cedric contemplated the import of his words. Juliana's husband had been Ambrosius, uncle to King Arthur and ruler of Wales after the death of Vortigern.

Myrddin ran his finger along the intricate carvings on the cross. Celtic in appearance, the crosspieces flared at the tips. "How is it that you came to me?"

The cross lay on the table, not answering. Shaking his head at all he didn't know, about his father and everything else, Myrddin picked it up and hung it around his neck, tucking it under his shirt as usual.

Cedric studied Myrddin's face and then scanned his clothes, his worn scabbard with its fine sword, and tattered cloak. "Who was your father, Myrddin?"

Myrddin shook his head.

"You really don't know?" Cedric said.

"No," Myrddin said. "Once I was grown, it no longer seemed to matter."

"Has your king ever seen that cross?" Cedric said.

"No," Myrddin said again. "Not that I'm aware."

Cedric picked up his own cross. "You might show it to him. Sooner, rather than later."

Chapter Eight
10 December 537 AD

MYRDDIN HAD NELL TUCKED against him under their blanket—fully clothed—with Huw sleeping not far away. They'd found shelter halfway to Buellt at a small castle whose owner swore allegiance to Cedric.

The place was primitive in the extreme, but it was warmer than outside. The threatened snow had turned into a whiteout in the higher elevations that rose between Brecon and Buellt. It was the difference of a few hundred feet, but it was enough to turn a snowstorm into a blizzard. Thus, they'd come all of five miles from Brecon in an entire day. They had only eight more miles to go, but it could have been eighty for all the difference it would have made. Nothing could have been more pathetic—or impossible.

Nell had lain quiet against Myrddin a long while, neither of them sleeping, just absorbing each other's company and their growing closeness. She knew now that if nothing else in the entire world made sense, she was sure of him. She was no longer nervous or afraid that she was risking her heart. Better to risk it than not live the life she'd been given, even if it lasted only one more day.

"We're going to have to ride on in the morning, no matter what," she said. "Even if we lash ourselves together with rope."

"I know," Myrddin said. "And we'll be losing Cedric's men at Penrhiw."

"I suppose, at the very least, they're loud and good at plowing snow." Nell laughed. But then she sobered and turned in Myrddin's arms so she could see his expression. The small amount of light given off by the candle they'd not yet blown out made his face just visible. "If something goes awry in Buellt, you save yourself."

Myrddin took her face in his hands and studied it. "Meaning what?"

"There's so much here we don't know or understand," she said. "I'm afraid of what may happen. If you need to flee, you do it, even if it means leaving me behind."

Myrddin shook his head. "I will not desert you. I'm no longer the unthinking warrior I once was." Then his voice gentled, and he rested his forehead against hers. "I'm not afraid of dying, Nell. I've died in my dreams more times than I can count."

"And I've died with you. As you. I don't want to live in a world without you in it." She reached up and stroked a stray hair off Myrddin's forehead. "We need a place to meet if the worst happens, and we get separated. I need to know where I can find you."

"Some place safe," Myrddin said. "Some place that one of us can stay until the other one gets there."

"A tavern?"

"In what village?" he said. "If this goes bad, the Saxons will control the coasts, the border, and be pushing inward."

"Then an Abbey," she said. "Cwmhir, where Arthur himself might be sleeping tonight."

Myrddin nodded. "That's a wise choice. The monks are loyal to Arthur and always will be. Wait there, no matter how long it takes for me to arrive."

"And if you don't find me?" A tear leaked from the corner of her eye. Myrddin wiped it away with his thumb.

"I will find you." Myrddin brushed his lips across hers.

Unable to resist, she tightened her arms around his neck. "I want to see this through with you. I love you."

"You do?" Myrddin pulled back.

She smiled through her tears. "For a man as old as the hills, you certainly are thick."

251

Myrddin stroked a second, stray tear from her cheek. "It's going to be all right. When next we see the king, all will be forgiven. He'll give me land on which I can settle with my new wife, and I can retire from fighting forever."

"Wife, is it?" she said. "A second ago you didn't know how I felt about you!"

"Ah, Nell," Myrddin said. "You are my world. Marry me. Say you will."

"We may have no future—"

"All the more reason. Say you love me," he said. "I need to hear it again."

Nell buried her face in Myrddin's shirt, her hands entwined in the cloth. "I love you, Myrddin."

"Marry me." Myrddin threw off the blanket and got to his feet. He kicked at Huw who grunted and rolled over. "Right now."

"Now?" she said. "How are we going to do that?"

"There's a castle chaplain. We'll wake him up."

"I'm supposed to be a nun!"

Myrddin flapped a hand at her. "It's a disguise. Everyone here knows that."

She stared at him, her mouth agape, and then she laughed. "You're crazed."

"The king could die tomorrow; I could die tomorrow." Myrddin reached down and shook Huw.

Huw opened one eye. "Wha—?"

"Get up," Myrddin said. "Nell and I want to get married and we need you as a witness."

Huw was instantly alert. "Excellent." He popped up from his pallet and onto his feet, pulling on his boots a second later. "But wait." He paused. "As King Arthur's men, we are under interdict. The priest can't bless you."

"The chaplain's is sympathetic," Nell said. "If we ask him, he'll do it anyway."

"I know we've no contract—" Myrddin swung around to look at Nell, the first sign of hesitation in his eyes.

Nell laughed. "We've no money, Myrddin. No possessions other than what we stand up in. No family other than Huw. The priest will make it right."

After rousing one of Huw's squire-friends as witness, they filed into the chapel on the top floor of the keep.

"What's this about a wedding?" The priest came into the room, buckling the belt to cinch his tunic at the waist and shrugging into his cloak of office.

"Nell and I would like you to bless our marriage," Myrddin said.

The priest took in Nell's loose hair and green dress which she'd worn under her habit. "Have you asked her father?"

Momentarily at a loss for words, Nell looked at Myrddin and then back to the priest. "My father is dead. No one is alive to gainsay us."

The priest's face turned very serious. "Do you have the king's permission, my lord Myrddin?"

"King Arthur told me to find myself a wife, and he would give me land to support her in the new year," Myrddin said, praying it was still true.

The priest nodded. "That's very good. I will bless you, even if some will say that I can't see to my parishioners in this fashion."

"Those men are not Welsh," Myrddin said. "Even the Bishop of St. Asaph refused to put out his candles. If it matters to you, we can ask again for a blessing when the interdict is lifted."

"If the interdict is lifted." The priest grumbled under his breath and then said something about, "Upstart half-Saxon telling me how to do my job."

Nell and Myrddin exchanged a look, and both smiled. The priest placed a cross about his neck, turned back to them, and lifted his hands to the heavens to begin his prayer. Myrddin moved his hands to Nell's waist to pull her closer, bending to touch his forehead to hers.

After the priest finished speaking, Myrddin lifted the chain that held his mother's cross and settled it around Nell's neck. Surprised, she looked down at it, and then up into his eyes. "Myrddin—"

"Sshh." He put a finger to her lips and then recited, "*For as long as there's wind in the mountains; for as long as there's salt in the sea; for as long as rain falls on these green hills; I will stand with thee.*" It was the native ritual with which they'd both grown up. "Nell ferch Morgan, I claim thee as my wife."

Nell brought her hands up, one in each of his, and Myrddin clasped them to his chest. They stood close, breathing each other in, as the priest called down the blessing they wanted but didn't need.

Chapter Nine
11 December 537 AD

THE STORM HADN'T LESSENED by dawn. Myrddin lay on his back, listening to the wind howling around the castle, not wanting to face the morning. The king couldn't see the chasm opening at his feet, but Myrddin had already fallen into it and, with only ten hours between now and the rendezvous, there was no way he and Nell were going to get everything done that needed doing.

"It's time," Nell said from the doorway to their room. As they'd agreed, she wore her habit. That was going to be a surprise to the priest if he saw her before they left. "Huw's got the horses ready."

"I'm coming." Now that Myrddin was awake, he noted the stamping of the two dozen horses in the castle bailey, just on the other side of the wall. "How did you sleep?"

"Did I sleep?" She smiled. "When this is over, they'll be plenty of time for sleeping."

Myrddin got himself upright, kissed Nell on his way out the door, and walked with her into the bailey. He had some hope that the snow wouldn't be falling quite as hard as yesterday, but once they left the shelter of the castle walls and were again on the road to Buellt, the wind picked up. It shrieked down the canyon through which the road ran and into their faces.

They bent forward into the storm, cloaks clutched and shoulders hunched. Myrddin pulled his cap more securely over his ears and his scarf tighter around his neck. He'd tied his helmet to his saddlebags. He would put it on only in great need, since metal and cold were synonymous in a snowstorm.

As Cedric and Myrddin had agreed, they said goodbye to Cedric's men at a crossroads. The company turned northwest to St. Cannen's church where they would wait for Arthur—or for

Myrddin once he'd finished his business with Edgar. Nell, Huw, and Myrddin carried on the last miles alone.

Myrddin had hoped to have easily reached this point the day before. He'd wanted plenty of time to determine the lay of the land, even if it meant sleeping in a ditch or an abandoned barn last night. But they'd run out of time for maneuvering. The eight miles to Buellt took them long hours of hard slogging, pushing on past the point they wanted to stop and refusing to give up. Thus, noon had come and gone by the time they reached the castle.

"We have to find a way to talk to Edgar," Nell said as they approached the gates, which rose up black before them. Agravaine had a small army outside the walls, but the encampment showed no signs of imminent movement, which was a great relief.

"We're walking in like blind men," Myrddin said. "I don't like it."

"Aww. This is what makes it fun," Huw said, parodying Ifan and trying to cheer up his dour elders.

"No question of that, son," Myrddin said. "Go on, then. Your face and Cedric's colors can get us inside."

Myrddin hoped the garrison and its leaders were so busy with the threat of Arthur's approaching army that they'd not question Myrddin's presence. In contrast to Huw, he wore a deep green surcoat that claimed allegiance to no lord. Nell said his tunic brought out the green in his hazel eyes. It occurred to Myrddin that, if it pleased her so much, he would wear only this color from now on, even if it clashed with Arthur's crimson and white—and if he still had leave to wear those colors.

As they hoped, at such a busy hour of the day and with all the coming and going through the gatehouse, few marked their presence, and those who did were appropriately dismissive. The man-at-arms who allowed them through the gate looked them over and then waved a hand to let them pass.

Given that the snow still fell unrelentingly, a man would have had to be pretty hardened to turn away a nun and her escorts—one of whom wore Cedric's crest—under those conditions. They found housing for their horses in the sprawling stable complex and then made their way to the great hall.

"This needs to be quick if we are to reach the church in time," Myrddin said. "We are already too late to warn the king before he reaches it."

"That's what Cedric's men are for," Nell said.

"I spoke with a stable boy," Huw said. "He told me that no one has seen Edgar since he arrived. Could he have returned to Wigmore Castle or left already for Brecon?"

"No. If he'd gone to Brecon, we would have passed him on the road. Edgar is here." Nell tipped her head to indicate a man-at-arms walking from the barracks to the stables. "Those are his colors."

"I would have to agree," Myrddin said. "Modred finally approved Edgar's inheritance. He'll want to be in the thick of things to emphasize that Modred chose right in restoring his lands to him."

"Which is why we don't think Edgar ever intended to betray Modred in the first place," Nell said. "Or if he did for a fleeting moment, he certainly doesn't now. There's too much at stake for him to risk Modred's disapproval."

"But then why isn't he in evidence?" Huw said. "We have to find him—for Lord Cedric's sake, if not for King Arthur's."

The rescue of Cedric had done nothing to dampen Huw's admiration of his former lord, and Myrddin couldn't blame him. What most concerned Cedric was his own power, but you had to admire the man for making it this far, given what had happened to his father at Modred's hands.

Like the bailey, the great hall was full of soldiers. Huw led the way to a spot on the end of one table. But before they could sit, a jovial shout split the air.

"Huw!" A young man rose from his position on the other side of the hall and walked towards them.

Huw smiled, somewhat sickly Myrddin thought, and held out his hand. The two grasped forearms, and then Huw introduced him. "Father, this is Peter, one of my companions growing up. Lord Cedric sent him to Agravaine as a squire several years ago." Huw turned to Peter. "I'm glad to see you are well. You've found a place here."

"That I have." Peter slapped Huw on the back. "Come. Eat!" Then, Nell's habit registered, and he turned fully to her, his face flushed with embarrassment at his lapse. "Madam." He gave a slight bow. "Might I be of some service to you?"

Nell stuck her nose in the air and sniffed. "I wish to speak with Edgar of Wigmore. On a private matter."

At the mention of Edgar's name, Peter reacted swiftly, moving closer and waving his hand at her in a shushing movement. "You cannot see him! Don't say his name."

Huw studied his friend. "Why? What's happened?"

"Lord Agravaine believes him a traitor to Lord Modred!" Peter said, relishing his role in imparting the news. "Supposedly, Edgar is unwell and confined to his bed at the top of the keep, but in truth, my lord leaves men to guard his door."

Nell opened her mouth to speak but Myrddin put a hand on her shoulder to stop her. "Thank you, Peter. We appreciate the news."

Myrddin caught Huw's eye, and he tipped his head at his son. Catching on, Huw said, "I'm starving. I'll sit with you, and we can catch up."

"For a short while only. I'll be riding out soon." Peter winked. "We have a mission."

Huw shot Myrddin a look of pure dismay, and Myrddin caught his arm before Peter could lead him away. "Watch your back, son."

"I can do this, Father," he said. "Trust me."

Myrddin nodded, reluctance sickening his gut, but he let him go. As soon as Peter and Huw had turned away, Myrddin steered Nell towards the back of the hall, to the stairwell that led down to the kitchen or up to the apartments above.

"That boy is one of the men Agravaine is sending to the church," she said.

"I know," Myrddin said. "We can't stop them now. Given that we've made it here at this hour, Cedric's men should have reached the clearing too. The king will have allies, and it won't be the uneven fight for which Agravaine is hoping."

"But what are we going to do?"

"We're going to speak to Edgar," Myrddin said. "Agravaine distrusts him and that's good for King Arthur. Then we're going to get out of here as quickly as possible. If Modred's dungeon was bad, the one here would be catastrophic."

Nobody stopped them from climbing the stairs to the rooms above, although when they reached the landing on the second floor, intending to continue to the third, a guard confronted them. He dropped a pike to block the way, looking apologetic once he took in Nell's apparel.

Myrddin had to give Nell credit. Bringing her along on this journey dressed as a nun had been one of her better ideas.

"I have orders to let nobody pass."

Nell opted for her cloak of meekness, rather than authority; all Myrddin could do was admire it. "Please, sir. I had word that Edgar requested someone with whom to pray. Since it is uncomfortable for me in the hall, the priest sent me here. My former husband served the old lord before both of their deaths. I believe Lord Edgar would want to see me."

The man gaped at her. "I've had no orders—" He stumbled over the words.

Myrddin looked at him with his best *how foolish do you want to be?* stare.

"Yes, Madam." The guard recovered enough to shrug his shoulders. "Tell the two men on the door that Walter sent you."

"Thank you," Nell said, befuddling him further with an uncharacteristic giggle, and moved past the guard, Myrddin hard on her heels.

"You simpered at him," Myrddin said as they circled the stairs to the uppermost rooms.

"It worked, didn't it?"

Myrddin couldn't argue with her, although surely it was unbecoming conduct in a nun, not to mention his wife. He shook his head and remembered Ifan's laughter. *Myrddin with a wife.* He prayed they'd have more than just this one day together.

In short order, they arrived at the landing of the third floor. Two guards occupied the space. A ladder to the battlements rose from the middle of the floor. A locked door, barred from the outside, lay behind it.

"She's here to speak with Lord Edgar," Myrddin said. "I was to tell you that Walter sent us."

One of the men sneered, but he didn't argue. He peered through the narrow window in the locked door. "Got a nun to see you." Myrddin couldn't hear the reply, but the man nodded. "Go on in."

Nell smiled and tipped her head. "Thank you."

The guard unbarred the door, and she slipped past him. Myrddin made to follow, but the guard stopped him with a hand to his chest before he could pass through the doorway.

"You stay here." He closed the door.

Myrddin had expected as much. He stepped to the side and leaned against the wall, ready for when Nell and Edgar came through the door—if that was indeed what was going to happen. He would find out soon enough. He'd caught a glimpse of Edgar before the guard had blocked the way. He'd been facing away from them, staring out the lone window, which was located high up in the northwestern wall.

Although it couldn't have been far into the afternoon, the sky was dark, less because the sun was setting than because of the storm clouds that had been their constant companion for the last four days. Blessedly, the rate of falling snow had lessened over the last hour since they'd arrived.

The moments stretched out in silence. The guards returned to their table and their dicing, and Myrddin waited. He couldn't make out the conversation beyond the door, just low murmurs between Nell and Edgar. Then the voices stopped, booted feet paced the floor, and a strong hand banged on the door.

"We're done here," Edgar said.

Earlier, Myrddin and Nell had agreed that if Edgar said those words, then she believed he was on King Arthur's side, and Myrddin was to do what he could to facilitate his release.

The guards looked up, surprised they were needed again so quickly. One stood and came to the door. The other turned to Myrddin. "Our lord is cleansed of sin, is he?"

"It seems so." Myrddin returned his smirk.

Myrddin stayed where he was beside the door frame, seemingly unconcerned but inwardly bracing himself for action. The guard unbarred the door and pulled on it. As it began to open, Myrddin moved. Shoving his left shoulder into the gap between the door and the frame, he put the full force of his weight behind it to slam the top edge of the door into the guard's forehead.

The man stumbled backwards. Before he could recover, Myrddin came around the door, hit him with the heel of his right hand and, with a swipe of his right foot, had the guard's legs out from under him. The man fell hard on his back and cracked his head on the wooden floor.

Meanwhile, Edgar had bounded out of the room. The second guard had tried to pull out his sword but was still fumbling with it when Edgar drove Nell's knife into his chest to the hilt. With two downed men between them, Edgar and Myrddin faced each other. Myrddin gave the former prisoner a long look, taking in his short-cropped dark hair, narrow face and black eyes, which, like Cedric's, gave nothing away.

Edgar raised his eyebrows. "I think we're done here."

Walter called to them from the stairs below. "Is everything all right up there?"

"Prisoner's giving us a bit of trouble," Myrddin said, in as gruff a voice as he could manage and speaking in Saxon, the language of the guards.

"I'll come up." Walter's feet sounded on the steps. They had ten seconds to prepare.

Without Myrddin having to say anything, Edgar leapt to a position on one side of the archway that led to the stairs while Myrddin occupied the other. Nell stood some ten feet away in the middle of the room, just in front of the ladder that led upwards. For a count of three, she waited, her hands twisting in her skirt. Walter spied her with five steps to go to the top and then bounded up the rest.

"Madam!"

That was all he managed to say before Myrddin wrapped his arm around Walter's neck. Edgar pressed the knife to his breastbone. In the end, however, he didn't have to use it. Walter lost consciousness and slumped against Myrddin, who lowered him to the ground.

Then he turned to Edgar. "You sent a letter to Arthur ap Uther."

"I did." Edgar had started to ease away from Nell and Myrddin, as if unsure of his safety, but now he arrested his movement.

"Was it sincere?"

Edgar coughed and laughed at the same time. "Was it? Do I even know? It doesn't matter now. Agravaine sends men to intercept the king. He's emptying the castle of his knights and men-at-arms in pursuit of this endeavor."

"It isn't too late to warn him," Myrddin said to Nell. "If we leave now, I can ride hard to the church."

"It is too late," Edgar said. "Agravaine has been communicating with King Arthur in my name for three days. The meeting will occur in less than an hour's time. He told me of it last night. As Nell entered my room, I saw that Agravaine's second-in-command had gathered his men in the bailey of the castle. They left in the time we were occupied in talking."

Myrddin spun on his heel and strode through the open doorway to Edgar's cell and then to the window. "The devil take him. We *are* too late." He swung around to Edgar. "Has Agravaine gone too? Does he lead them?"

"Does the man fight himself? Ever?" Edgar gave a laugh that came out an ironic snort. "Of course not. He's too important to tarnish his sword with Welsh blood."

Myrddin had heard enough. "Do you want to get out of here?"

"And damn the consequences?" Edgar said. "Yes. I never intended, as Agravaine does, to murder my uncle. I do not want his death on my conscience."

"Then let's go." Myrddin covered the distance to the stairwell in a few steps, glad he didn't have to kill the Saxon lord.

They hurried down the stairs to the second floor, and then to the first. Before they continued to the kitchen, Myrddin held out a hand to stop his companions. Huw had been dining in the great hall but, if Peter had left with the rest of the garrison, there was no telling where Huw'd got to.

Myrddin peered around the doorway that led to the hall, looking for his son. The tables were deserted as Edgar had warned they would be. Only two men remained: Huw—his back to the fire—and another man. The man's voice had risen, berating Huw while Huw shifted from one foot to another, pained and uncomfortable. Myrddin recognized the tone. *Damn it! Agravaine.*

Huw didn't acknowledge Myrddin other than with a flicked finger, held down low at his side. Understanding, Myrddin waved him off and retreated around the corner, furious at the cock-up this mission had become, and running through potential ways to rescue his son. "Huw needs help."

"Let me see." Nell peered around the corner before he could stop her. Almost immediately, she popped her head back, her face drained of all color.

"What is it?" Edgar said.

"That man." Her breath choked her.

"You recognize him?" Myrddin said. "Have you *seen* him?"

"No." Nell switched to Welsh. "I didn't have to. But I know him. He's one of the men at St. Asaph. He was one of the knights who escaped."

Christ.

Meanwhile Edgar, not understanding their words, even if their tension was evident, had taken a quick glance through the doorway. "It's Agravaine. It would be better if he didn't see me."

They needed to get out right now. "Go through the kitchen," Myrddin said. "Bring the horses into the bailey. I'll send Huw to join you, and then I'll meet you as soon as I can."

Nell grabbed his arm. "No, Myrddin! We can't leave you here!"

"I'll be fine." Myrddin spoke in Welsh as she had, for her ears, not Edgar's. "I don't wish to die. I have a life with you to look forward to. I'll meet you. I promise."

Nell clasped his hand tightly. "I'm not ready for this. We've had so little time!"

"What are you going to do?" Edgar said.

"Rescue Huw." Myrddin looked at Edgar over Nell's shoulder. "And maybe kill Agravaine."

Edgar appeared amused at that, but not Nell, who'd regained control of herself again. "Don't be an idiot. King Arthur is more important now."

She was right, of course. Myrddin pulled her to him in a brief hug and then let her go. Edgar grasped her arm. "I'll take care of her."

They turned from Myrddin, hurrying down the stairs to the kitchen. Once they moved, Myrddin strode from the stairwell. Agravaine was focused on Huw but Myrddin hadn't walked five paces before he drew Agravaine's attention.

For his part, Agravaine paled at the sight of Myrddin and stopped speaking in mid-sentence. He stood with his mouth open, staring. "You!"

Myrddin checked his stride. Agravaine stepped backwards towards the fireplace, distancing himself from both Huw and Myrddin. He yanked his sword from its sheath and held it out, keeping them both at bay. Meanwhile, Huw sidled sideways towards Myrddin.

"What are you doing here?" Agravaine said. "You shouldn't be here!"

"Have we met?" Myrddin came to a halt ten paces from Agravaine.

"You should be at the church!" Agravaine said. "I've *seen* you there!"

Agravaine's words hung in the air, the echo of them twisting between them—and, in a single heartbeat, upended Myrddin's world. He'd thought himself unique all these years until he found Nell. And yet, even with their union, it had never occurred to either of them that they were not alone in their *seeing*. That there could be others like them. The implications were staggering.

"Get the horses, Huw. Get out of here." Myrddin drew his sword to match Agravaine and pointed it at him.

"But—"

"Now!" Myrddin said. "Nell will explain."

"Yes, sir," he said, and Myrddin was grateful that he didn't say 'father' and reveal to Agravaine their connection.

Huw walked quickly towards the stairs and disappeared down them.

"You've *seen* me there?" Myrddin said to Agravaine, once they were alone.

Agravaine brought up his chin, his eyes blazing. "You've died every night in my dreams since I was a boy." And then amended, "until recently."

Dear God, to borrow Nell's favorite phrase. Myrddin's stomach curdled with a strange sort of sympathy for Agravaine, which he immediately gagged down.

Agravaine didn't share it. "You're nothing but a trouble-maker. I should have known as my dreams became more confused these last weeks, and then ceased to come at all, that something was wrong."

"If you knew what was to come, why harm the woman at St. Asaph?" Myrddin said. "What did that gain you?"

"Why not take her? I knew the future."

Myrddin took a step back, involuntarily distancing himself from Agravaine's amorality. Agravaine had been haunted all his life, just as Myrddin and Nell had been. But in Agravaine's case, the result had been a life without consequences.

"You're a child." Agravaine's sneer was affixed permanently to his lips. "There is so much you don't know."

At that, Myrddin refocused on Agravaine's words and stepped towards him again. "If that's true, then we can help each other. We can pool our knowle—"

Agravaine cut Myrddin off, shouting his disbelief. "I need nothing from you!" He brandished his sword at Myrddin, ready to fight even if Myrddin wasn't.

Realizing that Agravaine was in earnest, and that he couldn't consider him an ally of any kind, Myrddin met Agravaine's blade with his own. The swords rang out as they clashed, and then the men backed off from one another.

"So how did you discover who I was?" Myrddin said. "Did Cai tell you?"

Agravaine's eyes glinted with amusement now instead of anger. "I have always known your name and your allegiance, of course. I *just* missed you at Rhuddlan. I shouldn't have talked Cai out of running you through at the first opportunity."

Myrddin had heard enough. The dreams might have overtaken Agravaine's reason, but he was still powerful. He still stood between Myrddin and the exit. "The king isn't going to that church alone, you know." Myrddin advanced on Agravaine.

Agravaine laughed. "You think you can prevent his death?" His query echoed off the walls of the empty hall. "You can't. I imagine he's dead already!"

At these final words, he attacked, driving at Myrddin with all his strength. Myrddin fell back, stepping away from him and allowing him to expend his energy unnecessarily. Every defense a swordsman made should have an attack associated with it, and as Myrddin parried his blow, he positioned himself more strongly.

Then, when Myrddin caught Agravaine's cross guard with the tip of his own weapon, the movement pulled the sword down and away from Myrddin, and he took the opportunity to close the distance between them. He wanted Agravaine on the ground and his sword in his throat.

But Agravaine was too quick and spun away. The two men clashed swords again—four, five, six times—and with every movement, Myrddin allowed Agravaine to push him closer to the door of the hall. This couldn't go on much longer before a member of the garrison—one of the few left in the castle—would hear, and then Myrddin would be outnumbered. Anxious to put an end to it, desiring Agravaine's death, but not willing to die himself to achieve it, Myrddin contemplated making a run for it.

At that moment, one of Agravaine's boots slid on a piece of abandoned food that a diner had dropped on the floor. The rush mats provided a poor footing, almost as bad as muddy grass. It was ignoble of Myrddin, and he knew it, but as Agravaine went down on one knee, Myrddin moved in, batted Agravaine's sword to one side with his gauntleted left hand, and drove his own sword through the man's midsection.

Agravaine fell backwards, his breath guttering as he lost air. Myrddin ripped his sword from Agravaine's body and then kicked Agravaine's fallen sword away. It went skidding underneath a nearby table. Without a second look, Myrddin turned to the door, wiping his sword on the edge of his cloak as he did so, and then sheathed it on the run. He didn't want to reveal to all who might see him that he was fleeing from the aftermath of a fight, and that a Saxon lord lay dying in the muck of the hall.

When Myrddin burst through the great doors and into the bailey, Edgar, Huw, and Nell were passing between the main gates out of the castle. Each sat astride their own horse, while Huw led Cadfarch.

Myrddin called in Saxon, on the off-chance that avoiding Welsh might give him a few more seconds before the guards caught on that he was an enemy. "Wait!"

Myrddin raced down the steps towards the gatehouse and across the courtyard. Nell had turned her head at Myrddin's call but the others didn't notice him until he threw himself onto Cadfarch's back, delighted to have had such a close shave and survived again—and also knowing that the delight was a mirage, a false emotion that would fade as soon as the fire inside left him.

As he'd hoped, the guards had seen him coming but hadn't known if they should block his path. Usually their charge was to prevent people from entering the castle, not leaving it. Besides, no hue and cry rose from the hall, and Lord Edgar, whom the guards would expect to be able to come and go as he pleased, rode at Myrddin's side.

At a steady canter, they left the castle, moving into a gallop once they came down from the gatehouse. They traveled the mile between the gatehouse and the bridge across the Irfon River in short order. It was distressingly dark by the time they crossed it, at which point Edgar pulled up.

"I cannot ride farther with you," he said. "Tell King Arthur, if he lives, that I would talk with him, but not here. Not now. I must first speak to Lord Modred."

"What was that?" Myrddin's heart was still beating hard since he hadn't recovered fully from the fight or his flight from it. He forced himself to take a deep breath and encompass what Edgar was saying. "Do you think Modred doesn't know of the letter you sent? I assure you he does! Agravaine suspected you of treason. You cannot doubt that Modred does too!"

"Modred confirmed me in my lordship," Edgar said. "He deserves to hear my concerns from me. He needs to know that Agravaine seeks only his own power."

"Not anymore," Myrddin said. "To bring the news of Agravaine's death will not make you welcome in Modred's court."

"And yet I must go," Edgar said, "and accept the consequences of doing what is right. I am my father's son."

The man was too noble for his own good. Turning from Edgar, Myrddin and Nell faced off in the growing darkness. "What would you have me do?" Myrddin said.

She shook her head, looking from him to Edgar and back again without an answer.

Edgar stepped in. "I have a manor house not five miles from here. I will shelter Nell and Huw there until such a time as it is safe to send them to you."

Nell put out a hand to Myrddin. "We'll be fine on the road—especially given my habit—while you, a Welsh knight, will not. Find King Arthur. He is alive. I know it. And then we'll find you. Huw and I will come to the Abbey, as we agreed."

"I can't leave you," Myrddin said. "Agravaine's men—"

"Were met by ours, Myrddin," she said, and then switched to Welsh. "The king is alive. Even if he went to the church, even if Agravaine has tricked him into going, Cedric's men would have arrived in time to save him."

"All right." Myrddin nodded, wanting her to be right, wanting to believe that the future they'd envisioned together would really come to pass.

"Did you say Cedric?" Edgar said, catching the reference. "What has he to do with this?"

"We're not yet sure." Myrddin turned back to Nell. "Don't do anything stupid."

"I wouldn't," she said.

He reached for her, pulling Cadfarch close to her horse so he could kiss her.

Edgar muttered under his breath. "Some nun."

"They're married," Huw said.

"Of course they are," Edgar said, deadpan.

Myrddin released Nell who shot Edgar an amused look. Then Myrddin held out a hand to Huw, who grasped his forearm as one knight to another. "Take care of each other." Myrddin wasn't used to caring so much about the immediate prospects of survival for people other than Arthur, but fear for Huw and Nell roiled his gut.

"I will, Father," Huw said.

Edgar threw up his hands in mock exasperation.

"I love you, Myrddin," Nell said.

Myrddin nodded, unable to speak through the knot in his throat. All three turned away. Myrddin watched them until they disappeared around a bend in the road. The ache in his chest flamed higher until it burned him. And then it went out as cold certainty set in. Nell might hold hope in her heart still, but with her absence, Myrddin couldn't share it.

Turning Cadfarch's head, he acknowledged that it was better that Huw and Nell were out of it. To the east was Mercia and, for all intents and purposes, peace. The danger was to the west. Alone, he could make better time and approach the church more circumspectly. If Agravaine's men had attacked King Arthur's, there was nothing Myrddin, as one man, could do to help them. At this point, he'd just be happy to find the king had stayed in bed, even if all his other plans had come to nothing.

Then Myrddin cursed himself for the questions he had forgotten to ask Agravaine, not that he would have answered: first and foremost, how many of the dangers that faced the king were his doing? The attack on Garth Celyn? On Cedric? *Ah well. Too late now. The man is dead.*

It was less than two miles from the Irfon Bridge to St. Cannen's Church. The road kept close to the Cam River and Myrddin followed it. The river rushed by, not quite in flood, and the wind howled in the trees, blowing the snow directly into Myrddin's face. The weather raged around him, but as he approached the churchyard, the strife of men drowned out all else. Up ahead, shouts came in Saxon and Welsh. As Myrddin got closer, a great column of smoke rose into the air. It flew above his head, a dark smudge blowing east. The smell of death and mortified flesh enveloped him.

Retreating to the safety of the trees that lined the river, Myrddin bowed his head and closed his eyes, a sickening horror in his stomach. Sure enough, after a short wait, a troop of men—thirty at least—marched around the corner, coming from the church. They bore torches that lit up the night as their light was reflected off the snow on the ground and in the air and the white clouds above their heads.

The trees and the darkness beyond the torchlight hid Myrddin. Even without the protective trees, the troop made so much noise they wouldn't have noticed Myrddin if he'd shouted. Several of the men in the lead whooped and called their triumph.

One call rose above every other, this one in Saxon: "He is dead at last!"

Not all the men were so exuberant. Towards the tail end of the company, five or six men rode straight and solemn. Every so often, one of them glanced upwards and Myrddin gagged at what rose above their heads: A severed head bobbed on a pike, blood matting the dark hair, a grisly testament to their accomplished task.

They passed Myrddin without a glance. He stayed in the trees, doing nothing, too late to save his king. When they'd gone, vanishing into the whirling snow, Myrddin directed Cadfarch towards the ruin of all his hopes. Men and horses had packed the snow in the clearing in front of the church so the blood stains showed clearly where they'd pooled on the icy ground. Here and there, grass poked through the snow where a heel had dug into the earth, evidence that men had dragged other men across it.

It was the first time he'd ever seen the place while he was awake. Myrddin noted the differences and similarities to his dream—and knew they mattered not at all. He followed the signs to a spot to the northwest of the church. The Saxons had built a bonfire, their only tinder the bodies of the men they'd killed.

Upwards of two dozen men burned in the pyre, most marred beyond recognition. The fire hadn't yet consumed their gear but the torn clothes and disarrayed armor told Myrddin all he needed to know about how they died. His friends lay as they'd been thrown, haphazard and in every direction. Each man wore the dragon crest on his surcoat.

Myrddin walked around the pile in a daze, the smoke stinging his eyes, although he would have been blind from tears regardless. At the far end, he spied the headless and mutilated body of his king, fallen off the edge of the pile and stripped of its fine armor. Choking on the horror of it, he dragged the remains to one side, unable to look more closely at the other bodies for fear he'd find the faces of his friends staring up at him, lifeless and empty.

A lament rose unbidden in his ears. Its relentless rhythm drove Myrddin's movements as he labored to put out the fire, to throw dirt on bodies, and to provide some semblance of a decent burial for his king, although all that was decent had disappeared from the earth:

Can you not sense the turmoil amongst the oaks?
Do you not see the path of wind and rain?
And that the world is ending?

Cold my heart in a fearful breast
For the lion of Wales, that oaken door
our warlord, our dragon-king
Our Arthur ... is dead.

EXHAUSTED AND SPENT, knowing he'd done his best, and it hadn't been enough, Myrddin wept over the fallen body of Arthur ap Uther, his lord, and the last hope of his people.

Chapter Ten

12 December 537 AD

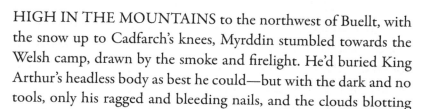

HIGH IN THE MOUNTAINS to the northwest of Buellt, with the snow up to Cadfarch's knees, Myrddin stumbled towards the Welsh camp, drawn by the smoke and firelight. He'd buried King Arthur's headless body as best he could—but with the dark and no tools, only his ragged and bleeding nails, and the clouds blotting out the stars and moon, the body was more under rock and brush than earth.

It had taken far longer than Myrddin had wanted. Once he'd finished, he'd given Cadfarch his head, merely directing him west towards what he hoped were the remains of Arthur's camp. Arthur's men might face a battle tomorrow that they could easily lose, now that they had no king to lead them.

And after that, if Myrddin survived the battle, he had to find Nell and Huw. They needed to decide what they were going to do next: if they were going to stay in Wales and live as best they could, or walk away. Or maybe die where they lay. The part of him that refused to surrender, that held onto hope amidst the desolation, died a little inside with every step that led him farther away from them. With so many dead, his family was the only thing that mattered anymore.

Myrddin had just reached the first of the outer sentries, posted some two hundred yards from the camp, when a voice from behind hailed him. "My lord!"

Wearily, Myrddin swung around, every muscle protesting even that slight movement. Cedric's men, torches lighting up the forest, rode towards him. In response, the sentry beside Myrddin raised his pike. It was a brave stance, though what he thought two men could do against a company of soldiers Myrddin couldn't guess.

Myrddin raised a hand to Godric, the young captain, while reassuring the sentry. "They are friends."

Godric began speaking before he'd come to a halt. "We've just come from the church. I'm sorry. We were too late. We were lost for hours and ended up miles out of our way. The snow—" he broke off at Myrddin's look, knowing as Myrddin did that excuses were merely that, when the price of failure was the loss of a king and a country. If the blizzard had not delayed them, these twenty men could have been enough to change the course of history.

"Come," Myrddin said. "I was too late as well."

Myrddin turned from Godric, gave the sentry a nod, and led the company the short distance through the woods to the camp. If he'd had the energy to think on it, the scene when they reached it was far calmer than he would have expected: men walked around the fires; they ate and drank, but their movements held no urgency. If anything, the emotion Myrddin felt from them was positive—even cheerful—without the expected drunken despair.

And then it hit him. *Could they not know?*

If it was possible for him to feel more despairing, the emotion would have overtaken him then. He faced the truth: the Saxons had killed everyone else who could have reported back, and it was he who would bring the news. Only he had survived and that by chance.

Myrddin dismounted in front of the pickets. "My lord Myrddin," the guard protecting the entrance said, "we've missed you."

It took a moment for Myrddin to recognize the man as one of Cai's—and then his already cold heart collapsed in on itself. *Of course.* Cai had come. It would be just like him. Perhaps it was he who'd convinced Arthur to meet Edgar, setting up his brother to die as he'd plotted with Agravaine back in the belfry at Bangor, and now he would get to act the grieving brother and take up the mantle of Wales in his stead.

Myrddin's stomach churned in a foul pit, and he felt like puking. Instead, he looked for Deiniol among the men at the fire pits for he was sure to be here too, but he didn't see him.

Myrddin and Cedric's soldiers left their horses with the boys whose job it was to tend them and trudged through the camp to what had been Arthur's tent. When they reached it, voices inside rose and fell. Myrddin hesitated at the entrance, gripping the hilt of his sword. He speculated if it would be better to run the traitor through now, or see Nell and Huw safe first and then return to finish him. While he was deliberating, a man spoke from behind him:

"You're late, but I forgive you since you've brought so many friends."

Myrddin spun around at the familiar voice. Gawain smiled his greeting, leaving Myrddin unable to speak. *He should be dead! Why isn't he dead like in my dreams?* Oblivious to Myrddin's shock, Gawain leaned across Myrddin and held out a hand to Godric, who took it. He remained mute, but Myrddin managed to stutter, "You—but I saw—how can you—the king —?"

"What's wrong with you?" Gawain said. "You look as if you've seen a ghost."

"The church—"

"The king didn't go to the church." Gawain looked from Myrddin to Godric whose mouth was opening and closing like a landed fish.

"Didn't go?" Myrddin was unable to think coherently. "Then who—?"

Gawain shook his head at Myrddin's evident stupidity and gave up on him. He gestured towards the entrance to the tent. "Go on. The king is waiting."

"He's dead!"

The shout came from the entrance to the camp, and Myrddin turned to see Deiniol riding towards them, threading his horse between fire pits. He was bent over his horse's neck, haggard of face and worn to exhaustion. He pulled up and dismounted.

Once on the ground, he staggered towards Myrddin, wrapped his arms around his neck, and to Myrddin's combined horror and astonishment, wept into his cloak.

"Who's dead, Deiniol?" Myrddin grasped him by the arms and pushed him away so he could see his face. "Who's dead?"

"Lord Cai," Deiniol said. "At the church by the Cam River."

"Cai is dead?" Gawain's voice held disbelief.

Deiniol nodded. "When Lord Cai learned that his brother had passed up the chance to ally himself with his nephew, Edgar, he went in his stead. It was his right."

Gawain stared at Deiniol. *"Sweet Mary, mother of Christ!"*

Deiniol continued, caught in his own misery yet still defending his lost lord. "Lord Cai had arranged to meet with Edgar in the nave of St. Cannen's church, or so we thought. But shortly after we arrived, Saxon soldiers set upon us. Everyone is dead! Everyone but me."

Myrddin gazed into Deiniol's smoke-blackened face. Ordinarily he would have found some illicit pleasure, even triumph, at seeing Deiniol so unmanned by grief. Now, Myrddin stopped to take in a breath and refocus on the part of Deiniol's story that mattered most to him. "Then King Arthur—"

"What's this I hear about my brother?" The door to the tent swept open, and a dark head ducked through the doorway.

The sight of his king walking toward him, with Gareth and Geraint behind him, had Myrddin weaving on his feet, his hollowed limbs barely holding him upright. "I thought you'd gone to the church."

"Of course I didn't go," Arthur said.

"Of course—" Lost, Myrddin swallowed the rest of his sentence.

Arthur shook his head at him. "How could I go to that meeting when you made it so clear I shouldn't? You who have served me unswervingly for twenty years. You who had the courage to speak the truth."

"But you didn't listen to me. I failed."

Geraint, coming to stand beside the king, smirked. "Only if failure means saving King Arthur's life—and Wales."

"What do you mean?" Myrddin said. "What has any of this to do with me?"

"My dear boy," Arthur said. "It has everything to do with you. Cai's increasingly desperate attempts to unseat me resulted from *your* continual interference in his plans. Who escaped from Rhuddlan to warn me that Edgar's letter might not be what it seemed? Who thwarted the attack on Garth Celyn? Who told me of Cai's treachery when no one else dared speak of it? Who related to Geraint your fears of my death? Who is possessed of the *sight*?"

This struck Myrddin speechless, but Geraint nodded. Arthur glanced from one to the other before continuing. "Yes. You have a friend in Geraint. If more of my men had your courage, Modred would not have been able to constrain us as he has." Now his eyes narrowed. "I have underestimated—and you have downplayed—your abilities until now. We will not allow that error to continue another day."

"I thought you didn't believe me!" Myrddin recalled his desperation and the hours he and Nell had agonized over their choices, or lack thereof. "I feared for twenty years that I couldn't avert your death. Until just now, I believed I *had* failed."

"And that is my fault," Arthur said. "That is my lapse for not seeing that one of my staunchest defenders and counselors had gone unacknowledged all these years."

"What changed your mind?" Myrddin said.

"The evening after you left for Brecon, I dined with my brother. It was as if I saw him for the first time. Noting my attention, he turned to me with a smile that never reached his eyes. I recalled your parting words when you spoke to me of his treachery."

"Thou practice deceit through confidence; Alas! my brother, must that be?" Myrddin said. "From a poem by St. Llywelyn."

"I'd refused to listen to you. But you were right. Cai opposed me at every turn, even as he professed his support. My brother was the same man he'd always been, just as you were the same as you'd always been. In that moment I knew it, knew that I should be listening to you and not to my brother."

Arthur sighed. "I informed Cai that I would not be going to meet Edgar—though not why."

Gareth moved into the circle of men. "Cai was angry but he acquiesced, lest he reveal his duplicity. With that, I came forward to confess my part in all this—that I also knew of Cai's treachery—that he had been working with the Saxons, specifically with Agravaine, for many months."

"But how did Cai end up at the church when he *knew* it was a trap?" Myrddin said.

"It is as I told you," Deiniol said in a loud voice, speaking for the first time since Arthur had appeared. "He sought Edgar's support for our cause."

"More like he thought to concoct a new plan to overthrow King Arthur," Geraint said, "and wanted Agravaine's help with it."

"You have the truth of it," Gawain said, with a half-laugh.

Myrddin was filled with a sudden compassion for the wayward lord. "Except that neither Edgar nor Agravaine went to the church

280

to meet Cai, and instead Agravaine sent men to kill him. Cai went to the church thinking he was among friends, only to find he'd outlived his usefulness. It was an opportunity to get rid of a rival, and Agravaine took it."

Myrddin had dreamt his own death at that church, lived again and again the moment when he realized he was going to die. Cai must have known that feeling, there at the end. Myrddin hoped that as he died, he'd repented, and that he'd understood he couldn't trust these Saxons and should have remained loyal to his brother.

"Edgar betrayed him," Geraint said.

"Mmmm," Myrddin said. "Not Edgar, in truth."

"What did you say?" Arthur peered into Myrddin's face.

"Edgar's initial letter to you *was* genuine, my lord," Myrddin said. "Agravaine imprisoned him in Buellt Castle because of it. We released him. Nell and Huw are accompanying him north even now. Agravaine, however, is dead."

Myrddin's companions openly gaped at him at that.

Myrddin shrugged. "It needed doing."

Arthur met the gazes of each of the men in his circle in turn: Geraint, Gawain, Gareth, and Myrddin, Godric, with his men crowded up close to hear the conversation better, and Deiniol, who stood a little behind Myrddin, listening but not one of them. "In one day, Modred has lost four allies: Cai, Cedric, Agravaine, and Edgar. In the morning, we will seal his loss by taking Buellt Castle from him too." He stepped back and gestured towards his tent, indicating that the men should enter. "We have much to do before dawn."

Myrddin, for his part, hung back to the last, coming to a halt in front of King Arthur after everyone else had entered the tent. The two men studied each other for a long moment, and then Arthur stuck out his hand to Myrddin. For the first time in his life, Myrddin clasped forearms with his king, one man to another, before they turned together into the tent.

For once, despair was in abeyance. A potent mix of joy, awe, and relief flooded Myrddin. Arthur ap Uther ... lived.

Historical Background

Historians are not in agreement as to whether or not the 'real' Arthur—the living, breathing, fighting human being—ever existed. The original sources for the legend of King Arthur come from a few Welsh texts. These are:

1) *Y Goddodin*—a Welsh poem by the 7th century poet, Aneirin, with its passing mention of Arthur. The author refers to the battle of Catraeth, fought around AD 600 and describes a warrior who "fed black ravens on the ramparts of a fortress, though he was no Arthur". http://www.missgien.net/celtic/gododdin/poem.html

2) Gildas, a 6th century British cleric who wrote *De Excidio et Conquestu Britanniae* (*On the Ruin and Conquest of Britain*). He never mentions Arthur, although he states that his own birth was in the year of the siege of Mount Badon. The fact that he does not mention Arthur, and yet is our only historian of the 6th century, is an example of why many historians suspect that King Arthur never existed. http://www.fordham.edu/halsall/source/gildas.html

3) Taliesin, a 6th century poet, who wrote several poems about Arthur. Including the lines: "...before the door of the gate of hell the lamp was burning. And when we went with Arthur, a splendid labour, Except seven, none returned from Caer Vedwyd." http://www.maryjones.us/ctexts/t30.html

4) Nennius – "History of the Britons" (Historia Brittonum, c. 829-30)

"Then it was, that the magnanimous Arthur, with all the kings and military force of Britain, fought against the Saxons. And though there were many more noble than himself, yet he was

twelve times chosen their commander, and was as often conqueror."
http://www.fordham.edu/halsall/basis/nennius-full.html

5) *Native Welsh Tales*: These connected works of Welsh mythology were named *the Mabinogion* in the 19th century by their first translator, Lady Charlotte Guest. These include the story of *Culhwch and Olwen*, in which Arthur and his men track down the thirteen treasures of Britain, and *The Dream of Rhonabwy*, a tale of Arthur that takes place after the Battle of Camlann (thus indicating that he survived it) and includes directions to 'Mount Badon' or Caer Faddon, as the Welsh call it. These stories are found in the *Red Book of Hergest* and/or the *White Book of Rhydderch,* both copied in the mid-14th century. http://www.maryjones.us/ctexts/index_welsh.html

6) *The Annales Cambriae*. This book is a Welsh chronicle compiled no later than the 10th century AD. It consists of a series of dates, two of which mention Arthur: "Year 72, The Battle of Badon, in which Arthur carried the cross of our Lord Jesus Christ on his shoulders for three days and three nights and the Britons were victors. Year 93, The Strife of Camlann in which Arthur and Medraut fell." The early dates of the above works indicate little or no relation to the later English/French embellishments of Arthur, which Geoffrey of Monmouth popularized. http://www.fordham.edu/halsall/source/annalescambriae.html

LATER TEXTS THAT ARE built on the above works, in chronological order, are:

1) William, Chaplain to Bishop Eudo of Leon – "Legend of St. Goeznovius, preface" (c. 1019)

2) *William of Malmesbury* - "The Deeds of the Kings of England (De Gestis Regum Anglorum)" (c. 1125)

3) *Henry of Huntingdon* – "History of the English" (Historia Anglorum, c. 1130)

4) *The History of the Kings of Britain*, by Geoffrey of Monmouth, dating to the middle 12th century. This is the beginning of the King Arthur legend as we know it. Geoffrey was born in Wales, but worked for his patron, Robert of Gloucester, who was particularly interested in legitimizing the claim of his sister (Matilda) to the English crown. Thus, the confusion of landmarks which moved Arthur from Wales to England proper, and the romanticizing of the tale, including the notion that Britain was originally conquered by Brutus, the son of the Trojan hero Aeneas, and thus Britain was 'classical' in origin.

5) *Roman y Brut (The Romance of Brutus)* is the translation of Geoffrey's work into Anglo-Norman verse. It takes much of Geoffrey's story and adds the round table, courtly love, and chivalry, thus transforming Arthur from a Welsh warrior to a medieval, Anglo-French knight. From this point, the Welsh Arthur is all but lost, and the Anglo/Norman/French 'King Arthur' is paramount.

BY 1191, THE MONKS of Glastonbury were claiming knowledge of his grave, and soon after, the link between Arthur and the Holy Grail, which Joseph of Arimathea supposedly brought there. By 1225, monks in France had written The Vulgate Cycle, telling of the Holy Grail from the death of Jesus Christ to the death of Arthur, and included the romance of Lancelot and Guinevere. This story became the standard version used throughout Europe.

Whether or not King Arthur was a real person is an either/or query. He either was or he wasn't. Many scholars, researchers, and Arthurophile's have strong opinions on this topic, both for and against. Because of the paucity of written records (most notably, Gildas fails to mention him), much of the academic work has come down on the side of 'wasn't'—or at least if Arthur was a real person, his name was not 'Arthur' and possibly he wasn't even a king.

As a side note, the Welsh sources, particularly *The Dream of Rhonabwy*, make Modred Arthur's nephew and foster-son, not his illegitimate son as many readers might know him. This version of events is carried through to Geoffrey of Monmouth's version of the Arthurian story. Arthur's illicit/incestuous relationship with his sister, Morgause or Morgan, is a later (French) addition.

For the purposes of my book *The Lion of Wales* series, I choose to believe that Arthur was real, that he was backed into a corner by his duplicitous nephew, Modred, and—as in the *Dream of Rhonabwy*—he did not die at Camlann as the Norman/French/Anglo version says, but lived to see his country securely in the hands of a worthy heir. At the same time, the world of *The Lion of Wales* series rests in the balance between the historical Wales of 537 AD, and the quasi-medieval Arthurian world that readers have grown to love throughout the ages.

SOME POINTS IN PARTICULAR where *The Lion of Wales* series is less than historically accurate:

1. The Christian Church was not as full blown and organized as portrayed in *The Lion of Wales* series. Although St. Dafydd was appointed Archbishop around this time, he did not have ecclesiastical control over Christianity throughout Wales and organized Christianity tended to center on small groups of monks/nuns or hermitages. Many people remained pagan.

2. Saxons had only just begun to fight on horseback. They rode horses, of course, but cavalry weren't necessarily part of their repertoire. Nor the use of bows.

3. A 'knight' is a much later medieval notion, but it is impossible to portray Geraint, Bedwyr, Gareth, and Gawain without using the word. Forgive me.

Book Four: A Long Cloud

A Long Cloud

KING ARTHUR LIVES, but the war isn't over, and distinguishing between friends and foes has never been more difficult. *A Long Cloud* takes Myrddin and Nell into England. And it is there, in the heart of Modred's domain, that the truth about Myrddin's parentage is finally revealed.

A Long Cloud is the fourth book in the *Lion of Wales* series.

Cast of Characters

<u>The Welsh</u>
King Arthur ap Uther (born 480 AD)
Ambrosius—King of Wales (deceased 501 AD), uncle to Arthur
Uther—Arthur's father (deceased 501 AD), brother to Ambrosius
Myrddin—Knight (born 501 AD)
Nell—Myrddin's wife (born 507 AD)
Ifan—Myrddin's friend

Geraint—Knight
Gawain—Knight, Gareth's brother
Gareth—Knight, Gawain's brother
Bedwyr—Knight, Arthur's seneschal
Cai—Arthur's half-brother (deceased)
Dafydd—Archbishop of Wales

<u>The Saxons</u>
Modred—Arthur's nephew (born 497 AD)
Cedric—Lord of Brecon
Edgar—Arthur's nephew, Lord of Wigmore
Agravaine—Lord of Oswestry (deceased)
Godric – Cedric's captain

Arthur ap Uther's Family Tree

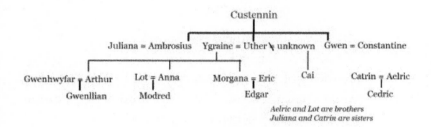

Custennin

Juliana = Ambrosius   Ygraine = Uther \ unknown   Gwen = Constantine

Gwenhwyfar ⊤ Arthur   Lot ⊤ Anna   Morgana ⊤ Eric   Cai   Catrin ⊤ Aelric

Gwenllian   Modred   Edgar   Cedric

Aelric and Lot are brothers
Juliana and Catrin are sisters

Chapter One

—◈—

There drew he forth the brand [Caledfwlch],
And o'er him, drawing it, the winter moon,
Brightening the skirts of a long cloud, ran forth
And sparkled keen with frost against the hilt ...
—Alfred, Lord Tennyson

—◈—

12 December 537
Myrddin

—◈—

KING ARTHUR'S HANDS *were tied in front of him, and his face*
was bloody and bruised. As he knelt in the snow, the king lifted his
head to speak to someone behind Myrddin. Myrddin wanted to turn
and look, but the dream wouldn't let him, and then his attention was
drawn to the woman crouched at the king's feet. She turned slightly
and raised her arm to protect her head, as if warding off a blow—and
Myrddin saw that it was Nell.

—◈—

"NO!" LOST IN THE VISION, his whole focus on protecting
Nell from the man who was attacking her, Myrddin pulled his
sword from its sheath and swung around, slicing the weapon
through the air.

"Myrddin! What are you doing?"

Myrddin gasped, blinked, and his eyes cleared. King Arthur's
foremost captain, Geraint, had fallen backwards in the snow in

his haste to escape Myrddin's unexpected action, which could have severed Geraint's arm at the elbow.

"I'm sorry!" Horrified at what he'd almost done, Myrddin dropped his sword and, in mimicry of King Arthur, fell to his knees.

Geraint was still staring at him, his face completely white. "You *saw* something, didn't you? A vision. What did you *see?*" Recovering more quickly than Myrddin, he scrambled to his feet and crouched beside Myrddin, every line of his body intent on Myrddin's response. Even at noon, it was cold enough that his breath fogged in front of him.

Myrddin passed a trembling hand over his eyes. The remnants of his vision remained, like a thin veil that hadn't yet been pulled aside, and his soul was exposed. He could still see the pain and despair evident in Nell's face as she begged him to save her.

With Geraint so close, Myrddin couldn't lie. He had no intention of ever lying about his visions again. "I saw King Arthur bound and on his knees before an unknown captor. And Nell with him!"

To Myrddin's surprise, Geraint let out a breath that was almost a laugh, and his intensity diminished. "Myrddin, the king is well. I spoke with him less than an hour ago—and your Nell is safe with Huw a few miles from here. Look there." Geraint tipped his head to indicate a position on the other side of the Wye River, in the opposite direction from Buellt Castle, which lay behind them. "After we battered down the gate, I convinced King Arthur that Gawain and I had the siege well in hand, and we couldn't afford to lose him to a stray arrow or a lucky blow. He's in the command tent with Gareth, planning the next course of action. He asked that I send you to him when I found you. I believe that after you speak to the king of our victory, he will give you leave to go to Nell."

Although the tent itself was pitched on a low hill, and thus screened from view by the trees growing along the river bank, the red dragon was just visible on its long pole above them. From now on, Myrddin would never be able to look upon Arthur's banner with anything but utter joy. To see it flying, to know that his king lived for one more day, made the previous twenty years of dreaming worth every moment of lost sleep.

"Did he say what he wanted me for?" Myrddin said, trying to speak normally, even though he was finding the contrast between his vision and reality as impossible to reconcile as it always had been.

"Undoubtedly to bestow some new honor upon you." Geraint smirked. Before the battle, he'd cropped his brown hair short to keep it out of his eyes, and the white slash of the old scar across his forehead stood out against his browner skin. He was taller and thinner than Myrddin. And, for all that they'd won the battle, Geraint looked older today than yesterday—and certainly older than his thirty-five years.

By contrast, until Myrddin had the vision, the knowledge that Nell waited for him—that he had a life to live when this was over—had him feeling younger than he'd felt in years.

Myrddin shook his head. "I didn't do nearly enough, and what I did do was almost too late."

"The king doesn't see it that way."

Myrddin curled his hands into fists, clenching them until the knuckles turned white. He didn't know what was happening to him, but the power of his vision had been straight out of the ancient tales of Wales, which told of seers and saints who advised and admonished kings with their foretelling of the future. "I *saw* him, Geraint."

It was one thing to have dreamt of King Arthur's death for twenty years. At least it was the same dream every time. And because it had turned out to be a true *seeing*—and one that had brought him and Nell together—Myrddin had been grateful for it in the end.

It was quite another thing, however, to find himself overcome with a different vision entirely—and terrifying to think that more visions were in store for him. He knew the fate of those cursed with the *sight*. Eventually they lost the ability to distinguish between the dream world and the real one and retreated to a cave on Mt. Snowdon, to eke out the rest of their existence apart from the lives of men. He did not want that for himself.

"You're tired." Geraint picked up Myrddin's discarded sword and handed it to him, hilt first. "When was the last time you slept?"

"Long enough ago that the castle Nell and I stayed at after leaving Brecon is a faint memory," Myrddin admitted. "I *am* tired, but Geraint, this was a vision, just like before. You don't have to believe me, but it was as real to me as you are right now."

At Geraint's pitying look, Myrddin turned his head away, and his eyes fell instead on the body of a fallen compatriot. He leaned over to pick up the tail of the dead man's cloak and used it to clean the snow from his sword.

Then Myrddin gestured towards the castle. "Where are we with the defenders? Last I heard, a dozen Saxons had barricaded themselves in the guardroom."

"The debate is whether to leave them to starve or to fire the door and haul them out. Gawain is waiting to hear of my conference with the king before deciding," Geraint said.

"Let them rot," Myrddin said. "They can't get out, and why ruin a good door?"

"That's what King Arthur said." Geraint held out a hand to Myrddin, who'd remained kneeling in the snow to mask the weakness in his legs. "Your brother, Deiniol, is with him, by the way. He survived the battle too."

Instead of correcting Geraint—Deiniol was Myrddin's foster brother, not his blood brother—Myrddin took Geraint's hand, grunting as he rose to his feet. He supposed he no longer wished death on Deiniol. He didn't care enough about him for that. Last night he'd even pitied him a little.

Once on his feet, Myrddin gave Geraint a nod and set off towards Cadfarch, who was picketed by the ford that would take him across the Wye River. Geraint might pity him even more for his haste, but Myrddin had dallied in the snow long enough. He needed to see the king for himself, and he had come too far to be put off with easy assurances, even if they came from King Arthur's right hand man.

"Myrddin—" This time when Geraint said Myrddin's name there was exasperation in his voice, but then Geraint's feet thudded in the packed snow behind Myrddin, and he fell into step beside him. "Before I speak to Gawain, I will come with you to see King Arthur."

"I thought he was well-guarded, so I had nothing to worry about?" Myrddin picked up his pace.

"You just had a vision of the king's capture. Obviously my instinct is to dismiss what you saw as the imaginations of an exhausted warrior. But given what happened yesterday and that you have the *sight*, I have thought better of it. Who am I to ignore the word of Myrddin?"

By contrast, now that he was moving, Myrddin was feeling steadier, and the vision was fading. If he hadn't just related what he'd seen to Geraint, he might have been able to dismiss it outright as Geraint initially had. Still, Myrddin carried his sword bare in his hand, just in case.

They mounted their horses, trotted towards the small company of soldiers guarding the ford across the Wye, and passed through them with hardly more than another lifted hand from

Geraint—though as Cadfarch entered the water, one of the men gave Myrddin a real bow and said, "My lord."

Myrddin shivered. He could almost accommodate being a seer more easily than being a lord. He'd never been lord to anyone and hardly deserved the title now. He was a landless knight from an unknown house, risen to the station he now possessed by the strength of his arm and the grace of King Arthur. Another shiver went through him—this time from the cold. He was wet to his knees from kneeling in the melting snow, and from his sweaty undertunic, which had cooled around his torso under his armor, leaving him clammy.

"Is Lord Cedric's young captain, Godfrid, about?" Myrddin said as Cadfarch picked his way across the rocks. The ford was a good one, but it was two hundred feet wide, and one misstep could break a horse's fetlock.

Geraint guffawed. "He and his company took out an entire troop of Agravaine's men all by themselves."

"I thought I saw them over to the right," Myrddin said. "I'm delighted Godric decided to join us, but I'm also glad he had sense enough not to fly Cedric's banner."

"Though he hated not flying the swans, he understood the step he was taking," Geraint said. "Once he fought beside us under Cedric's colors, there would be no going back for his lord, and that wasn't his decision to make. I told him that if Lord Cedric was truly loyal to Arthur now, fighting under the king's banner should be honor enough for him, as it is for all of us."

Myrddin managed a mocking laugh. "I don't see how Cedric could ever have fought for Modred. He may be more pragmatic than I'd like, but he has honor—enough to have won the loyalty of men like Godric."

"And Huw," Geraint said.

Myrddin's eyes brightened at the mention of his son, though he was glad that neither Huw nor Nell had witnessed the battle and more glad than he could say that they hadn't been here to participate in the grisly task he'd set himself before the vision—and Geraint—had overtaken him. He'd been looking for survivors among his own men and among the Saxons too. It was heart-breaking work, monotonous in its desperation as he looked into familiar face after familiar face that would never smile again. Had Nell been here, she would have insisted on searching with him. She was a more knowledgeable healer than he, and while he could have used her, she was well out of the fighting, safe at Edgar's manor to the north of Buellt.

If King Arthur really gave him leave, Myrddin would set out to find them before dark, and when he did find them, all would be right with the world again. He just had to survive the next few hours first. It was the memory of Nell's parting touch and the knowledge that he would be able to hold her again that was giving him the strength to carry on despite his fear for the wellbeing of everyone he loved.

And for all that the field behind him was full of dead men, the Welsh had suffered far fewer losses than the Saxons.

Myrddin had initially been concerned that Agravaine's death would have excited the Saxons to greater heights of self-sacrifice, but it turned out that Myrddin had done the Saxons a favor. Although Cedric had insisted that Agravaine was unpopular, Myrddin hadn't counted on how thoroughly Agravaine had been hated by those he led. For some, to lose Agravaine, even if he was Modred's foremost commander, while at the same time murdering King Arthur (as they believed they had done), had piled good news on good news.

King Arthur's scouts had reported that the subsequent celebrations had gone on well into the night. Buellt Castle was too small to hold the majority of Agravaine's army, so many had camped between the castle and the river. Most had been asleep when the Welsh forces had attacked at first light, bypassing the castle in the first forays in favor of engaging the men outside who defended it.

Agravaine's second-in-command led them, but with Agravaine himself dead, his men lacked the force of his will to keep them together. Because the Saxons truly believed they'd murdered King Arthur the night before, the dawn attack surprised them completely, and they struggled to raise an adequate defense. Myrddin had been in the forefront of the resurgent Welsh army and had been among the first to fall upon Agravaine's men as they slept off their drunken revelry of the night before. It had felt almost dishonorable to kill them in cold blood.

Almost.

And then, in the heat of the fighting, King Arthur threw off his helmet and pointed his sword at the sky, calling his men to him. In that moment, the clouds parted, and a ray of sunlight shone down upon the king's gray head, glinting off his mail and enveloping him and his sword in a halo of light. The heavens themselves were signaling their approval of his right to rule.

Welsh and Saxon had been stunned into momentary inaction. Then the sign from God spurred the Welsh to greater heights of bravery, and many (though not all) of the Saxons turned tail and ran. That single ray had been a precursor of what was to come. By noon, the clouds had cleared and the sun was bathing the Welsh victors in gossamer light, which followed Myrddin and Geraint now across the ford.

Geraint shrugged. "Cedric served Modred because he told himself it was foolish to win the battle only to lose the war. He's been playing a long game, and I don't pretend to understand his ultimate goal."

"Cedric wants the power to care for his lands and people. I can respect him for that, even if I wish he'd been less accommodating of Modred up until now."

Then they were up the opposite bank and heading towards King Arthur's tent, located downstream and still screened from the ford by trees. Before they were halfway there, however, Myrddin frowned, and he urged Cadfarch faster, passing Geraint, who was only a heartbeat slower to realize that something had gone wrong.

When they entered the clearing at the bottom of the low hill where King Arthur's men had pitched his tent, dead and wounded men greeted them, nearly a dozen, most struck with arrows. Whoever had shot them had planned the assault well, taking out the king's men from a distance before moving in on the king himself.

Heedless of the possible threat to himself, fearful that the danger had passed, which would mean that they'd come too late, Myrddin urged Cadfarch up the hill. At the top, he threw himself from the horse without even reining in. Sword still in hand, he burst through the entrance to the tent.

One man with a gash on the side of his head lay face down in the wreckage of a table. It looked as if he'd been thrown on top of it.

Myrddin went to him and turned him so that he could see his face—and if he was alive. "Gareth!"

Gareth moaned and tried to sit up. "He's gone. He's gone." The young lord was too handsome for his own good, which the new scars he would have on his right temple and on his chin would do nothing to diminish.

"How long ago?"

"I don't know."

Myrddin looked over at Geraint, who stood in the entrance to the tent, his face drawn and white. "Several remain alive outside, but only one can walk—he was just stunned like Gareth. I sent him for help tending to the wounded, though with the caution not to raise a general alarm until we know what we're dealing with."

"Good," Myrddin said. "When exactly did you leave the king's presence?"

"As I said earlier, it must have been nearly an hour ago," Geraint said. "All was well then. I swear it!"

That Geraint would feel he had to justify his behavior to Myrddin revealed the true extent of his guilt at what had been done and left undone. For his part, Myrddin chastised himself for kneeling in the snow on the battlefield as long as he had, lamenting the delay it caused, and he told himself that the next time he had a vision, he wouldn't question it nor allow anyone else to do so either.

He turned back to Gareth. "Who was it?"

"Modred's lackey, Beorhtsige." Gareth was crawling on his knees now and conscious enough not only to be articulate, but mocking as well. "There were more than a dozen of them and, once the arrows stopped flying, only a few of us remained to defend the king. I tried, but even I can't fight off that many men at once."

Not long ago, Myrddin might have questioned Gareth's loyalty, but in recent weeks he'd proved himself a true son of Eryri—enough so that Myrddin merely held out a hand as Geraint had done to him earlier and helped Gareth to his feet.

He swayed at first, but then he steadied himself. "I'm not badly injured. I fear for the king, however, who could even now be dead."

"No," Myrddin said. "I *saw* him alive. That was what brought us here in haste."

Gareth put a hand to his head. "It doesn't make sense that they'd keep him alive. Only last night they had orders to kill him."

Geraint let out burst of air. "I am as much at a loss in this as you."

Myrddin stood looking between the two of them. "I can't say what was in the minds of these Saxons, and I won't pretend that the king's abduction isn't a disaster, but take comfort in my vision, for it seems it was a true *seeing*. King Arthur is a captive, not a casualty, and if he isn't with Nell, he soon will be."

Myrddin felt a surge of anger at the thought that the Saxons might hurt his wife, but her presence in the vision meant she was alive too.

All was not yet lost.

Chapter Two
12 December 537
Nell

NELL AND HUW FACED off in the darkness of the stable. Where they were standing and what they were talking about reminded Nell of another scene, but one which contained Myrddin instead of his son. Unfortunately, Huw was taking the same position that Myrddin had taken at that time, to his detriment and hers.

"You're a nun, Mother." Huw's blond hair stuck up on end where he'd run his hand through it in frustration and in a manner that reminded her very much of his father. But even the reference to her new relationship to Huw wasn't going to make her give way. Huw knew everything now about Nell's and Myrddin's long quest to save King Arthur. She'd even told him about her intention, before she'd been rescued by Myrddin, to enter Rhuddlan Castle and kill Modred. Unfortunately, knowing the truth about his parents had only made him more protective of her, not less.

"One—" Nell gestured to the plain gown she wore rather than the habit she'd traveled to the manor house in, "—I'm married to your father, so I'm clearly not a nun. And two, going our separate ways is not the answer. I know you want to discover if your father survived the battle at the church. I do too, but you can't leave me here."

"Edgar will protect—"

"Edgar is a Saxon lord who doesn't yet know his loyalties and seems determined to give Modred his head on a platter!"

"That's where you're wrong, Nell. I have no wish to die." Edgar's dry tone came out of the darkness, and Nell swung around to look in the direction of his voice.

Nell glared at him. "That may be, but you're doing an excellent job of behaving as if you do. If you go to Modred, if you tell him that you have lost faith in his leadership, he is going to skewer you on a long poker, and you know it."

Edgar licked his lips, which were chapped, a reminder of his days spent in captivity. He'd cleaned himself up otherwise, and once again wore the fine tunic and cloak of the nobleman he was. Even his black leather boots were newly polished. "As I told your husband, I have an obligation to my line."

"Your obligation to your line is to father a son to carry on after you," Nell said tartly and completely without embarrassment in mentioning the delicate topic, "and not to die before you have that opportunity."

Edgar pressed his lips together. "Modred will not murder me."

Nell tsked under her breath at Edgar's innocence. "You can't assume that."

"He won't murder me, because I am not going to tell him that I've changed my allegiance. Agravaine suspected me of treachery, but all Modred knows is that I wrote that letter to Arthur in order to lure him into a trap. Nothing more."

Nell studied him assessingly, comparing these words with those he'd spoken before on the road from Buellt. "You would spy for Arthur?"

"You're thinking that after all my talk of honor, I've just thrown it away."

"No! By the saints, no! It is exactly what you should do, but I would never have dared suggest it because I didn't think you'd do it."

Edgar cleared his throat. "Things have changed. I have just received word from Buellt that the trap laid by Agravaine was successful only in that it lured Prince Cai, not King Arthur, into it. At Agravaine's orders, Cai was killed and his head removed from his body. What's more, the Welsh forces attacked Buellt with the dawn and have taken the castle."

Huw punched the air and shouted inarticulately, but the news had Nell wavering on her feet. "Are you sure—"

She had assured Myrddin that he had nothing to fear, that King Arthur hadn't gone to the meeting at the church. She'd held that belief tightly to her heart, even as she'd had to ride away from him, and then through the long hours as they waited for word of what had befallen the king. She hadn't dared ask Edgar sooner if he'd heard anything, in part because she hadn't wanted to know. She hadn't wanted her golden dream shattered. And now—she couldn't take in the news that she and Myrddin had *won*.

Unaware of Nell's trembling, Huw scooped her up in a hug and danced around the stable with her. "You did it, Mother! You did it!" Nell managed a laugh and allowed him to turn her in a pirouette before coming back to face Edgar.

He'd waited patiently through their celebration, a small smile on his lips. "The news comes from one of my own scouts. He reports that few Saxons were able to get away. Agravaine's army—what's left of it—is vanquished. The scout feared for his own safety, afraid that he would be mistaken for one of the combatants, so he didn't stay to learn more."

Huw still had an arm around Nell's waist, and now she found that she needed him to hold her up. He put his lips to her ear. "Father survived too. You know he did."

Nell put a hand to her chest and took in a breath. She nodded at Huw, emotion overwhelming her, and her joy turning to relief as tears streamed down her cheeks. She reached for one of the low stools upon which the stable boys rested between tasks and sat for a moment with her head in her hands.

But then she looked up, wiping at her cheeks with the back of her hands. "So what is it about Cai's death and the loss of Buellt that made you change your mind? Yesterday, you were riding to Modred to tell him to his face that you were changing your allegiance."

"I want to know that too." Huw's brow furrowed. "If King Arthur had died last night, you never would have had to say anything at all to Modred about your allegiance. With Agravaine dead as well, you're the last man standing."

Edgar barked a laugh. "What changed? That King Arthur lives is what changed. That Agravaine failed means the war will continue. Last night, I didn't believe King Arthur would be saved, so I said what I said to make sure that you and Huw survived the onslaught that I was sure was coming from Agravaine's army. If King Arthur had died, Modred would have mercilessly hunted down and executed every one of his captains, Myrddin among them. Modred could not have allowed even a single one to live, for fear that he would rally the people to him and renew the fight."

Nell stared at the Saxon lord and shook her head in disbelief. "You lied."

A corner of Edgar's mouth twitched. "I did have a manor five miles to the north of Buellt, and by bringing you here, I kept my promise to your husband, which I believed to be the greater good. It seemed to me that you and Huw would be safe here as long as you needed shelter." Edgar took in a breath. "But that was last night. You are no longer safe here, not if I am to return to Modred's side and spy for Arthur."

Nell bit her lip, thinking back through all the interactions she'd ever had with Edgar. Now that she thought about it, riding to tell Modred to his face that he was betraying him was not in keeping with Edgar's character. Like Cedric, and all the Saxon lords who served Modred, he'd had to be pragmatic all his life. No man who ruled lands on the border between England and Wales and was caught between two powerful overlords could afford to put an ideal above the practical matter of caring for his people. In fact, now that she thought about it, lying to save her and Huw was *exactly* like Edgar.

Huw nodded. "We should go. I might not agree with your methods, but I can honor your choice." He looked at Nell. "My mother and I have no possessions other than what is in our saddle bags, so there is no barrier to leaving immediately.

"I believe to do so would be wise," Edgar said.

"If anyone questions where we've gone or asks why we rode here with you, you can say that we were innocents who you took from Buellt," Nell said. "Which, in a way, we were."

"My men already believe that, and if anyone wonders where you've gone, they'll soon be too busy for you to be more than a passing thought."

"If the news from Buellt is accurate, we should have no trouble finding our lines." Huw put out a hand to Nell to help her to her feet.

"You should know, also," Edgar said, "that whatever Agravaine's men did to Cai, it was on Agravaine's orders. Modred never wanted King Arthur dead."

"How can you say that?" Nell said. "Killing King Arthur at the church was always the plan."

Edgar's eyes narrowed, perhaps at Nell's use of the word *always*, and she hastily backtracked so that she wouldn't have to tell him about her and Myrddin's visions. "I mean, they wouldn't have killed Cai in Arthur's stead if they hadn't been ordered to."

"Yes—but those orders came from Agravaine, and my refusal to be a party to Arthur's death was part of the reason he imprisoned me at Buellt. Modred wanted—and still wants—the king captured and in his hands. He still intends to convince Arthur to name him as his heir."

Huw frowned and took a step toward the Saxon lord. "King Arthur said he wouldn't."

"Modred believes, not perhaps without justification, that a few days in captivity might change his mind," Edgar said.

Huw scoffed. "King Arthur wouldn't bend to torture."

"You misunderstand. Modred has no intention of harming the king physically. But tell me this: if Modred told Arthur that he would lay waste to one Welsh village for every day that Arthur refused to name Modred as his heir, what would the king do? If Modred threatened to kill in cold blood twenty of Arthur's citizens for every hour the king delayed would not the king bow eventually to Modred's demands?"

Huw gaped at Edgar. "He wouldn't—"

Nell put a hand to her mouth. Unlike Huw, who couldn't imagine such evil, Nell had already seen what Modred—and his men—could do. They'd raped and murdered all the women in her convent. What was another village compared to that?

"Edgar is right, Huw." Nell put a hand on her new son's arm. "And Modred is right. King Arthur could withstand his own pain and death, but he would rather take his own life than allow Modred to murder innocents—perhaps hundreds of innocents—if he knew that by giving way he could stop it.

"At one time, King Arthur would have believed—and been right to believe—that the greater good was served by holding fast, no matter how many Modred murdered. I don't think he believes that anymore—not because he has grown weak, but because he has lived every day of his life at war, and he no longer believes that his throne is worth more than the life of even one child, who might die to keep him on it. By threatening King Arthur thus, and following through with his threats, as Modred always does, Modred would force King Arthur's hand."

"But think of all who will lose their lives if King Arthur names Modred as his heir!" Huw said. "Knowledge of that future is what has kept you fighting all this time. Men died today to take Buellt from Modred out of the knowledge that they would rather die than surrender their country to him."

"I don't deny what you're saying," Nell said. "But for children to die now to avoid future deaths that might not come to pass is a bargain King Arthur might not be willing to make—especially because he has no heir, and he can't live more than another few years, whether or not he defeats Modred. He's old now, Huw. And nobody can predict the future."

Huw put his face right in Nell's. "You can! Father can!"

"Can you really?" Edgar had been listening to her exchange with Huw with evident interest. "See the future, I mean."

Not in this," Nell said shortly, ignoring Edgar's incredulous look. "When we reach our lines, I will tell the king what you said and what you have offered. I will impress upon him the importance of staying out of Modred's hands above all else."

Nodding, Edgar reached for the bridle of Nell's horse and began to lead it towards the entrance to the stable. "Up until now, King Arthur has led his army himself because he knows that his men need to see his strength, but it makes him vulnerable. For some time, the capture of King Arthur has been Modred's single-minded goal. That was why he looked upon my letter to Arthur with favor. I was to lure him into a trap to capture, not kill."

A cheer went up from the men in the courtyard beyond the doorway, and a look of concern crossed Edgar's face. He made a clicking sound to get Nell's horse moving out of the stable, and Nell and Huw followed, with Huw leading his own horse.

Though it was early afternoon, because it was winter and each day gave them only eight hours of daylight, the sun had never risen to a point directly above them and was well down in the sky now.

When Nell entered the courtyard, however, the space was lit up like a summer's day by the arrival of a host of men holding torches, each one with a smile a mile wide on his face.

Their leader, dressed in mail and sporting Modred's colors, dismounted. Edgar, tossing the leading reins of Nell's horse to Huw, strode towards the Saxon newcomer. "Beorhtsige. I'm glad to see you alive."

Most Welshmen complained that Saxon names were incomprehensible, but Nell and Huw had lived among the Saxons for many years, and the harsh tones of the names didn't bother them.

"No thanks to you," Beorhtsige said.

Huw leaned in to whisper in Nell's ear. "That's one of Modred's captains. I didn't see him last night at Buellt."

Nell nodded, though her eyes didn't leave the scene before her. Beorhtsige was taller than Edgar, with broad shoulders and a thick neck, as befitted a warrior. Edgar's problem had always been that he was slightly built and had been destined for scholarship—before his elder brother had died and left him heir to their father's lands.

Edgar was dressed like the nobleman he was, however, and he emanated a quiet strength. He'd certainly had no trouble dispatching the guard in the tower at Buellt. That same confidence had him straightening his shoulders and lying through his teeth to Beorhtsige. "Lord Modred shall hear of your impertinence, Beorhtsige! He gave me a mission that he did not share with Agravaine, and he would have punished Agravaine for thwarting me. I had no choice but to escape if I was to serve our master."

Beorhtsige gave a stutter that might have been the beginnings of an apology. In a few heartbeats, Edgar had reduced Beorhtsige to a supplicant.

"Fortunately for Agravaine, he was spared that fate, since he is dead," Edgar concluded.

Beorhtsige stared at Edgar. "What? Agravaine is dead?"

Edgar's brow furrowed. "Last night King Arthur sent a spy into Buellt who killed Agravaine in the hall. You didn't know?"

"No! How could I? Modred sent me—"

Edgar overrode him. "And then, while Agravaine was dying an ignominious death, your men murdered King Arthur's brother, Cai, who was a spy for him in Arthur's court. Modred will be none too pleased about that!"

A flash of annoyance crossed Beorhtsige's face. "I don't know what you're talking about."

Edgar laughed mockingly. "And if the man at the church had, in fact, been King Arthur, your men would have murdered him too, and then where would we all be? Modred wanted the king captured, not dead! I look forward to being present when you tell our lord what you've done."

Beorhtsige made a dismissive motion with his head, as if shaking off Edgar's accusations. "That wasn't me or these men. We weren't even at Buellt last night. I too had my own mission for Modred, and *we* have done well." Beorhtsige's confidence reasserted itself.

"Have you? How?"

"From your misplaced ire, I see you were aware that we were sent to track King Arthur, but our task was not to meet him at the church. Modred never believed he would go and, as always, our lord was right. King Arthur didn't." Beorhtsige drew Edgar's attention to his men, most of whom had remained mounted and still wore wide smiles, despite their leader's dressing down by Edgar. Several shifted aside to reveal, in the center of the company, a man with a cloth bag over his head and his hands tied at the wrists. "Show him."

One of Beorhtsige's men ripped the bag from the man's head, revealing him to be King Arthur himself.

Nell couldn't suppress the reflexive gasp, and her gesture drew the king's attention. To her astonishment, as he caught her eye, he winked.

Bloody and beaten he might be, but even in captivity, the Lion of Wales remained unbowed.

Chapter Three
12 December 537
Myrddin

LEAVING GERAINT TO make sure Gareth wasn't bleeding from any place he didn't know about, Myrddin went to the back of the tent. The intruders had slashed through the cloth, and three more of King Arthur's guard lay on the ground outside, all dead, all with arrows sticking out of their chests. The king had been well guarded, but his men had been surprised in a way they should not have been.

He came back inside the tent, feeling sick inside rather than vindicated that his vision had been proven true. "Is anyone missing among the fallen that you can see?"

"What do you mean *missing*?" Geraint said. "We've lost a dozen men!"

"Yes, I know, but that wasn't what I was asking." Myrddin tried to speak with patience since it seemed Geraint's mind wasn't working as quickly as it usually did. "Whose body should be here but isn't? Who was here when you left and no longer is? Who is the traitor?"

"I-I don't know." Geraint went to the entrance to the tent and looked out. "Caradoc, maybe. He isn't among those who lie here."

"Nor among those at the back," Myrddin said.

A voice hailed them from beyond what Myrddin could see from inside the tent, and Geraint responded, striding through the opening. Myrddin followed after him. Three men had come up the hill at a run, two newcomers and the wounded soldier, a man named Rhys, who had blood seeping from a wound just above the temple. He indicated the two men he'd brought. "I found them some yards from the ford and hoped they'd do. You told me not to raise a general alarm—"

Geraint cut him off with a slashing gesture and pointed to two wounded men, who lay in the snow halfway down the hill. "You did as you were bid. See to the others—and yourself!"

"Yes, my lord," Rhys said.

Gareth had also followed Geraint from the tent and spoke as if their conversation of earlier hadn't been interrupted by the newcomers. "Caradoc has served the king for many years. Longer than I have."

Myrddin held his tongue rather than express the derision that statement deserved. According to his own testimony, Gareth hadn't stood with the king very long himself since for months he'd been secretly spying for Modred—a falseness Modred still believed. Myrddin frowned. "Why didn't Beorhtsige's men know you, Gareth?"

"I have never been introduced to Beorhtsige. He might know my name, but he doesn't know my face."

"So Cai wasn't present the day you defended me to King Arthur?"

"No. My confession was for the king's ears alone. And even if Cai did hear of it later, with both him and Agravaine dead, I don't see how word of my loyalty to Arthur could have reached Modred."

"Your life may one day depend on you being correct in this," Myrddin said.

Gareth waved his hand, dismissing Myrddin's concerns, and turned to Geraint. "We have no time to lose as we're an hour behind already. Myrddin and I can ride after the king. With just the two of us, we can move faster and without drawing suspicion, especially since we both speak Saxon well. Myrddin can ride as my man-at-arms, and if we leave now, we could catch them before nightfall—perhaps even before they leave Wales."

"Modred isn't going to be fooled like he was last time when you escaped Rhuddlan, Myrddin," Geraint said. "You can't use Nell's plan a second time because the king will be guarded by far more men than you were."

"We will think of something else," Gareth said.

Geraint shook his head. "Someone else should go. Even I would be better, since Modred knows Myrddin's face."

"If we do as I suggest, Myrddin won't go anywhere near the king—only ensure that I do," Gareth said. "He'll be missed here far less than you, Geraint."

Geraint's expression showed skepticism. "Surely you don't mean for me to hide from our men that King Arthur has been taken?"

"Surely I do," Gareth said.

"What am I to do with the dead men?" Geraint was aghast. "Shall I bury them in secret and say that King Arthur rode north with this company to rally the people to him after his great victory here?"

"That's a really good idea," Gareth said. "I wish I'd thought of it."

Geraint was shaking his head vehemently before Gareth had finished speaking. "No, Gareth. You have spent too long amongst the Saxons if you think King Arthur would approve of such a plan."

"We have to keep King Arthur's abduction a secret if the alternative is telling the truth," Gareth said. "Or, if you feel that you can't bury these men in secret, leave them among the others who are dead on the battlefield, so that their families can grieve them properly. Nobody is going to question their deaths or wonder who among the king's guard remains alive."

Myrddin didn't want to lose any more time arguing. Standing between them, he put a hand on each man's shoulder. "Give us four days, Geraint. If we haven't located the king by then, it won't matter what we tell the men, because King Arthur will probably be dead and Modred will be our king despite the victory here."

Geraint chewed on his lower lip, his head turned towards Rhys, who was crouched over one of the fallen men and was closing his eyes with a gentle touch. "I will do as you ask if only because I don't have a better plan, but I wish you weren't going alone. If you find the king, how are you to send word to me that you've found him? And how are you going to free him with only the two of you? You need a company of soldiers."

Gareth tsked through his teeth. "I don't see the benefit of being seen coming a mile away, Geraint, but you're right about the messenger."

Myrddin rubbed his chin. "It may be that being seen doesn't matter, Gareth. We know where Beorhtsige is taking the king: he's riding to Modred, who's at Wroxeter, sixty miles from here."

Gareth gave a mocking laugh. "We can't attack Wroxeter with twenty men."

"We can't attack Wroxeter at all," Myrddin said. "It's the most defensible fort in England, and it's twenty miles from the border. It's impossible with the army we have, even with weeks or months of preparation."

"King Arthur doesn't have weeks or months, which means I am right, and we are better off going alone. We will rescue the king, or we will die trying." Gareth's whole focus was on the mission now. Geraint might as well not have been there. "You get the horses, Myrddin. I will gather provisions from King Arthur's stores. He won't be needing them now."

"You still don't understand." Myrddin caught Gareth's arm before he could return to the tent. "I'm not suggesting that we take a company of Welshmen. We need Saxons, a company of which we just happen to have to hand!" He pointed down the slope to one of Godric's men, who had waded into the river some distance from the ford, which was off to the west, in order to wash the blood from his hands.

"I should have thought of that." Gareth gave a disgusted snort before returning to the tent to gather supplies as he'd suggested.

Geraint put a hand on Myrddin's shoulder and shook him. "Go."

Myrddin went, loping down the hill towards the Saxon rider, ultimately scrambling down the bank in order to draw the Saxon's attention.

The man recognized Myrddin at once. "My lord?" he called across the water.

"I need Godric and all your men. Now."

"Yes, my lord!" the man said, as if the prospect of some new adventure couldn't have been more welcome, despite being awake all night and having fought a battle at dawn. He hastened away, back up the southern bank towards where Godric's men had gathered fifty yards from the river.

Within a quarter of an hour, Myrddin had collected the horses; Gareth had come down the hill with a bag full of provisions; and Geraint, Rhys, and the two guards had started the gruesome work of dragging dead men to lie in rows by the river bank. Getting the bodies across it to lie alongside their fellows wasn't a task that Myrddin envied, but if anyone could accomplish it with a minimum of fuss, it was Geraint.

Gareth waved Myrddin to him. "Your plan was better than mine or Geraint's. I apologize for doubting you."

"Your plan would have worked too." Myrddin held out his forearm to Gareth for him to grip, as he might do to a friend, though a month ago the idea that the two of them could be friends would have been laughable. Gareth grasped Myrddin's forearm, both men heedless of their blood-stained hands.

Then the blond Saxon captain arrived from the direction of the ford, flanked by his dozen men, and he dismounted in front of Myrddin. "What do you require of me?"

In a few succinct sentences, Myrddin told him, and then added at the end, "If we're planning to go into England, which it seems can't be avoided if we are to save the king, I need a disguise. Modred would recognize me on sight."

"Between all of my men, we should have something that should fit you," Godric said.

Myrddin looked up the hill towards the tent and the pole where the Red Dragon of Wales still flew. "We'll get him back, my lords."

"Go now," Geraint said. "I will see to this."

"We're already gone," Gareth said.

Chapter Four
12 December 537
Nell

"GET ON YOUR KNEES, Welsh swine!" Beorhtsige was in his element, and proving—if anyone had ever doubted—that the day the Saxons conquered Wales would be the end of the world as the Welsh knew it.

Two of his men wrestled Arthur off his horse and pushed him down into the snow. His hands were tied in front of him, so he fell awkwardly on them for a moment before he managed to straighten up. Nell's heart hurt at the sight of him kneeling before Beorhtsige and looking up at him like a supplicant.

Beorhtsige shot a smirk in the king's direction, and then he turned back to Edgar. "We have a quarter of an hour to stock food and water, and then we'll be off again. Because of the snow, our trail is clearly visible. The Welsh were foolish to have left their king so ill-protected, but they will notice eventually that we've stolen him away. We need to get as far away into England as we can under the cover of darkness."

"You can take what you need," Edgar said. "What's more, I and my men will accompany you to Wroxeter."

Beorhtsige's expression turned fierce. "King Arthur is *my* prize!"

"Heaven forbid that I deprive you of the honor of presenting him to Modred." Edgar's voice showed mild amusement. "But I have news for our lord too, and if you and your men really weren't at Buellt last night and witness to Cai's death, then you can't be the ones to explain how it came about—not to mention, someone has to tell Modred that he lost Agravaine at nearly the same hour."

"You'll take that burden on yourself, will you? Why?"

Edgar chortled. "Because I have with me the wife and son of the man who killed him—his name is Myrddin."

Nell and Huw each took one step back but then found themselves corralled on all sides by Edgar's men, who had gathered to listen to their lord's exchange with Beorhtsige and stayed to do his bidding. Nell stared at Edgar, horrified at the betrayal and hardly able to believe he could be so two-faced. In a single hour, he'd gone from a man who felt the need to speak to Modred in person about his allegiance, to being their captor.

Beorhtsige's eyes widened, though he had enough control to mask his surprise otherwise. "The man who escaped from Rhuddlan?"

"The very one," Edgar said.

One of Beorhtsige's men dismounted and approached, "May I speak, my lord?"

Beorhtsige canted his head in a gesture of permission. "You may, Caradoc."

The young man lifted his chin to point to Nell and Huw. "I've seen them at Garth Celyn, Arthur's seat. The woman is indeed Myrddin's and the boy is his son, Huw, just as Lord Edgar says."

"And you would deliver them to Modred? You are a cold man, Lord Edgar." Beorhtsige shook his head, but his tone was admiring.

"The longer we delay here, the more likely that Modred will hear this news from someone else. Personally, if I am to speak to him of the disaster that Buellt has become, I'd rather be riding into Wroxeter with King Arthur and these two prisoners to soften the blow."

King Arthur spoke for the first time. "And the Saxon called *me* swine. I was right not to meet you at that church." He spat in the snow. "My brother is dead because of you."

Edgar took a step forward and backhanded the king across the face.

"No!" Nell ran forward and fell on her knees in front of the king, who'd rocked backwards at first but now steadied and put his bound hands to his lip. When next he spat, the spittle was bloody in the snow.

"Mother!" Huw struggled against his guards. For a moment, he gave as good as he got, his hands curled into fists, punching at his captors in his desperation to get free. But then one of them moved in under his guard and slugged him twice in the belly. He bent over, gasping for breath. Other guards hauled his arms behind his back, forcing him upright, and the same guard punched him in the face. Huw collapsed in the arms of the guards behind him, and when they hauled him to his feet, he had a nasty cut on his left cheek, and his eyes glowed with anger and pain.

Nell shook her head at him, one quick jerk, and he yielded, though perhaps that was simply because he didn't have the breath to fight anymore. Tears streaming down her cheeks at how wrong this had gone so quickly, she pulled a cloth from her waist and dabbed at the bloody gash at the corner of the king's mouth. "I'm so sorry." Her voice broke.

King Arthur looked into her eyes. "It is nothing, my dear. Just one more atrocity in a lifetime of war. Tell Huw not to fight them. He should save his strength for when it is truly needed."

Nell swallowed down her tears around the giant lump in her throat and turned to look up accusingly at Edgar. "You—"

"I do what I must." Edgar's tone was steady, and he didn't look away.

She couldn't read him. She didn't know how her world had turned so completely upside down. The victory at Buellt meant nothing with the king in chains.

Meanwhile, Beorhtsige made a sound of disgust and turned away to see to the disposition of his men, leaving several to guard the king, but otherwise paying him no more attention.

Both she and the king were soaked to the knees now, but she stayed where she was—still unbound herself, but unable to leave him.

"It's all right, Nell." King Arthur's hands were tied at the wrists, but they were in front of his body, and he touched her chin with one finger, asking her to turn back to him. "All will be well." His words were patently untrue, and he said them only to make her feel better.

Then a curious look came into the king's eyes as they strayed downwards to the cross around her neck, which her sudden forward movement had revealed. Usually she kept the cross tucked underneath her bodice. He used the same finger to touch it. The movement was almost intimate and very out of place in this gathering of hateful Saxons. And yet, it was as if he and she were alone on an island, speaking Welsh amidst a sea of English. "Where did you get that cross?"

"From Myrddin at-at our wedding two days ago." Nell stuttered, suddenly terrified to be telling the king that Myrddin had married without his overt consent, though, of course, King Arthur had himself suggested the possibility to Myrddin in the days leading up to the fight at the Strait. "It came to him from his mother—" but that was all the explanation Nell managed before two of Edgar's men hauled her away from the king. She ended up beside Huw, whose arms had now been tied at the wrists like King Arthur's. He was breathing somewhat shallowly and holding himself stiffly.

King Arthur had been lifted bodily to his feet as well. He kept his eyes on Nell, however—on the cross, it seemed—until he was forced with a cuff at his head by one of Beorhtsige's men to turn towards his horse. That little display of brutality, following hard on the heels of Beorhtsige's and Edgar's actions, was designed to show him how little power he had here.

It had shown her too, and she told Huw (in Welsh) what the king had said to tell him. "Do as they say, son."

"But—"

Nell turned her head away from the king and looked into Huw's face, meaning for him to read authority there. Huw stopped speaking and gave her a jerky nod, subsiding entirely. "Yes, Mother. We, and he, must stay strong in order to live to fight another day."

"With King Arthur prisoner, I can think of no better place for us to be than by his side," Nell said.

Huw looked past her to where the king now sat on his horse. "I have learned so much these last weeks. Father isn't here, so I must do what he would do."

Nell nodded. "For better or for worse, Myrddin would do everything in his power, up to and including sacrificing all honor, to aid the king."

It took so little time for Edgar to gather his men that Nell wondered if he'd been prepared for something like this to happen. Or perhaps it was just that, ruling border lands as he did, his men were always ready to leave at a moment's notice. Either way, within the quarter of an hour Beorhtsige promised, they were ready to go.

They formed up outside the gate of Edgar's manor, and Nell and Huw, now mounted on their own horses, were crowded off to one side of the path—though they were still buttressed by Edgar's soldiers so they couldn't escape. They'd been positioned many paces behind King Arthur, who was secured amongst Beorhtsige's men.

Edgar, however, was to ride at the head of the company beside the Saxon captain. Huw kept a fixed glare on him, and finally he leaned in to her and spoke in Welsh. "How could everything he spoke of back in the stable have been a lie? How could any man lose himself to such an extent that he becomes so capable of so profound a deception?"

Nell raised one shoulder and let it drop. "I read truth in his eyes from the moment I entered his prison back at Buellt. I still see it, but now I don't know what truth he is conveying. He said he would spy for Arthur in Modred's camp. What better way to ingratiate himself with Modred—and to convince Beorhtsige of his allegiance—than to bring us with him? What better way to ensure Arthur's survival than to ride to Wroxeter at Beorhtsige's side?"

"Or," Huw said, "he truly intends to give us to Modred and never had any intention of serving King Arthur."

Nell's hands still weren't tied, and she made a helpless gesture with one of them. "And yet I still say, how convincing is his disguise if we, his allies, can't even tell his true intentions?"

"You may no longer be a nun, Mother, but you still want to see the best in people." Huw paused and shook his head. "We have to find a way to let Father know where we've gone."

"I've already thought of something, though it isn't much, and he would have to come here to find it." Nell motioned with her head that Huw should look at the ground. Beneath Nell, a single red drop had fallen onto the snow.

Huw was horrified. "You're bleeding!"

"No." Nell leaned in close to whisper to him. "The man who helped me mount my horse allowed me to remove the wineskin from my saddlebag so that I might drink from it as I wished." Nell put her hand briefly on the wineskin, which was slung around her waist by its strap. As the horse shifted, another drop fell to the snow. "I pricked it with the pin from my sewing kit."

Huw laughed under his breath. "I should have thought of that."

Nell smiled, and she was amazed that even under these conditions, she could feel a little warmth of humor. "You don't have a sewing kit."

As the miles rolled away beneath them, the wineskin slowly emptied, and the night passed. Nell's anticipation of rescue drained away too, leaving her in a haze of exhaustion and despair. Beorhtsige allowed them short rests every two hours, for a quarter of an hour only, but even that wasn't enough, and once on the ground, Nell could barely put one foot in front of the other.

At their third stop, somewhere in the vicinity of midnight, Nell could tell they'd reached England because the terrain was flatter. The Welsh mountains and valleys had given way to the rolling hills, fields, and fences of Powys and the March that bore little resemblance to her homeland. She threw herself down on the ground and pillowed her head in her elbow, desperate to be horizontal and to close her eyes for at least a few moments.

"Mother." Huw knelt beside her to place a blanket over her.

She stirred. "If you don't sleep, you'll be no good to me or the king."

"Do I hear Father in your voice?" Huw actually managed a laugh.

"You should."

"I slept in the saddle," Huw said. "I'll keep watch until Beorhtsige orders us to ride on again."

Nell closed her eyes—and instantly she was swept into a dream.

Bong. Bong. Bong. A church bell tolled long and low. Instinctively Nell looked up and saw the tower looming above her head. She was standing on the steps of a stone church, which had been built of great marble blocks the likes of which she'd rarely seen, and then only in the ruins of the long-abandoned Roman forts that were strewn across

the landscape in Wales. Caerhun was full of similar abandoned blocks that were so big it made more sense to leave them as they lay and build in wood than use them for anything more than the base of a wall.

Slowly and without urgency, her surroundings beyond the church came into focus. She turned her head and was surprised and happy to see Myrddin, his breath freezing in the cold air before him, standing beside her. Except he held a sword bare in his hand, and blood dripped from the tip. She tried to talk to him, but as in every dream before this one, he was completely unaware of her presence.

And then another bell sounded, this one in a tone that was higher and more urgent. Nell knew without Myrddin's shout that the sound was a warning call and might as well have been accompanied by cries of Awake! Awake! To arms! To Arms!

The moon came out from behind a cloud, illuminating the area around the church and revealing the faceless forms of a dozen Saxon soldiers. With another shout, Myrddin threw himself into their midst—not to fight them, but in order to take his place among them. They were his companions.

She wanted to fight beside Myrddin too, though she had no weapon, and as she pressed forward as Myrddin had done, her vision expanded to include Myrddin's opponents, who were also Saxon, one of whom was aiming a blow at Myrddin's head ...

—⟨∽⟩—

"MYRDDIN!" NELL WOKE with a gasp.

Huw stood a few paces away, keeping watch as he promised, but at her cry he hastened towards her and crouched at her side. "What is it, Mother? You said you were going to try to sleep."

"I did—I did sleep, didn't I?"

"For ten heartbeats, maybe," Huw said.

Nell bent her head with a sigh. She could never tell while she was in a dream how long it lasted. Some took up the whole of the night, and in others, a lifetime could pass in the dream in the time it took for the man who guarded them to pace to the nearest tree and back. That seemed to be the case tonight. But even with hardly closing her eyes, Nell wasn't tired anymore. She wrapped the blanket around herself and stood.

"I just *saw* Myrddin, Huw. I was with him as he was fighting with Saxons against Saxons."

"Does that mean he's tracking us?"

"It means he's alive, which is all I can hope for just now." Nell took in a breath and let it out. "I am afraid both that Myrddin will come for us and that he won't. We are his weakness, you know. All these years, he never allowed himself to grow close to anyone because he feared he would fail in his mission if he did. With us in his life, he succeeded in saving Arthur only to find that he's more vulnerable than ever."

"Love is not a weakness, Mother. Father worked so hard to save King Arthur because he loved him. Without that love, he would never have despaired at his failure. He would never have rescued you."

Nell put her face into her hands, struggling for composure. "You're not wrong, but I fear that Edgar has latched upon the one thing that will prevent Myrddin from saving the king, and that's his need to save us."

"Your visions don't always come true, Mother," Huw said. "We know that now. They show one possible future, and they show you that future so you can prevent it. Don't lose hope."

She clenched her hands into fists, struggling to find the strength to keep believing. She was losing hope, and it was wrong of her to do so after they'd come so far. "I can only pray that you're right."

Chapter Five
12 December 537
Myrddin

AS GARETH HAD FORMULATED his initial plan, all he'd been thinking about was secrecy and speed. Now, however, they rode in a company of fifteen, thirteen of them Saxons, which gave them the ability not only to take the high road, but to ride openly along it.

As Myrddin had suspected, the Saxons who'd taken King Arthur were easy to track, because of the snow and the fact that they were riding hard so as to enter England before they were caught. The only drawback now was that the sun was going down, and if King Arthur's captors turned off the trail or found shelter for the night somewhere along the way it would be easy to miss them in the dark.

Myrddin's vision had shown him King Arthur with his hands bound, but it hadn't given him any guidance as to where he and Nell had come into contact. Best case, it was at Edgar's manor, because Beorhtsige had sought shelter there—the worst, it was in Wroxeter, in which case Myrddin would have words with Edgar when next he saw him, because that would mean that Edgar had betrayed them.

And yet, the knowledge that Nell was with the king was comforting. It was just too bad (and annoying) that his *sight* was so unreliable that it hadn't told him about the danger to King Arthur *before* it happened.

Myrddin didn't know this part of Wales well, so he was forced to rely on the others for guidance. He'd spent his life doing exactly that but, somehow, without him realizing it was happening, since the fight at the Strait he'd grown used to making important decisions for himself and the men he led. But even if he had to rely on others here, he could still track, and he held up his hand to stop the company.

"The tracks go both west, and on," he said to Gareth and Godric. "Do either of you know where the western path leads?"

"To a manor owned by Lord Edgar of Wigmore," Godric said, as if Myrddin should have known that already—and perhaps he should. "It's about a quarter mile in."

Myrddin heart skipped a beat, and he had to refrain from raising his hands to the heavens in thanks. "Edgar was supposed to ride there with Nell and Huw last night. Perhaps they are still there. Perhaps we are not too late!" Myrddin jerked his head at Gareth. "Stay with the men. Godric and I will have a look."

"I should go," Gareth said.

"No," Myrddin said, trying to keep the impatience out of his voice and undoubtedly failing, "you are memorable and that's the last thing we want right now. If Nell and Huw are there—and by some miracle the king too—we can take a quick look around without drawing undue attention to ourselves and then return here to formulate a plan for rescuing them."

Mollified, Gareth gave way. Myrddin's intent hadn't been to butter him up. Gareth *was* memorable, and the last thing they wanted, if King Arthur was being held prisoner at Edgar's manor, was to worry the defenders of the fort with the appearance of a Welsh nobleman whom the Saxons might not quite trust—no matter whose side he claimed to be on.

Godric waved a hand to his men to indicate they should stay with Gareth, and then he and Myrddin rode on ahead, cantering the promised quarter of a mile in hardly any time at all, even if Myrddin's heart was in his throat the whole time. Edgar's manor house was protected by a ten-foot-high palisade. The wide gate was currently closed, and the snow in front of it had been trampled, indicating that a large company had passed through it since the snow had stopped falling.

With calm assurance, Godric tipped up his chin to call to the sentry on duty. "I wish to speak to Lord Edgar of Wigmore. I am sent from Lord Cedric of Brecon."

A man leaned down. The descending darkness was hiding all of his features but his chin and half his face, which were visible in the torchlight that shone from the guard tower. "He is not here."

Godric looked appropriately puzzled. "Where has he gone?"

"To Wroxeter."

"To Lord Modred?" Godric said. "Why?"

The man shouted laughter. "Because in the aftermath of the battle at Buellt, King Arthur was captured by Beorhtsige and his men. They came here looking for provisions, and my lord aided them."

Myrddin cleared his throat and tried for a Saxon accent in mimicry of Godric. "Do you have there with you a woman and a young man, who rode in with Lord Edgar last night?"

The guard made a motion with his head that came off as to mean both yes and no. "They were here but they left with Edgar. Something about presenting them as a prize to Modred. I didn't understand why Modred would care."

Myrddin's face darkened with a sudden boiling anger that threatened to burst out of him, and it was just as well that it was too dark for the guard to see him properly. Godric put out a steadying hand to Myrddin, while at the same time calling up to the guard, "We'll be on our way to Wroxeter then. Did they take the high road?"

"Straight and fast. With King Arthur among them, Beorhtsige had no intention of stopping for more than a few moments' rest until he reached Modred's palace."

"Thank you." Godric turned his horse.

The guard disappeared from above the palisade before Myrddin could trust himself to formulate a reply. As he made to follow Godric, however, out of the corner of his eye he saw a crimson splotch on the ground, somewhat off to one side of the main path. Even in the near darkness, the color stood out like a beacon on the patch of white snow. Afraid even more now than before, Myrddin dismounted to crouch low to the ground.

"What is it?" Though Godric had set off from the gate, he returned when he realized Myrddin hadn't followed him.

Myrddin touched the drop with a finger and brought it to his tongue. "Wine." He heaved a sigh of relief.

The darkness was growing, but the torches on the wall walk still threw out enough light for him to see another twenty feet in front of him. "There's another." He pointed to a spot ten feet away.

"And another," Godric said, having walked his horse further along the path. "Someone has a leaky wineskin." He looked back at Myrddin. "Could the leak be intentional?"

"Intentional or not, someone has left us a path to follow." Myrddin remounted his horse, and the two men cantered back to where Gareth waited with the rest of Godric's company, who must have heard them coming because they were already mounted by the time Myrddin and Godric appeared along the path.

Myrddin slowed to a stop and snapped his fingers for a torch held by one of Godric's men. He wanted to find the next drop of wine to make sure they were truly going in the right direction.

Meanwhile, Gareth urged his horse forward and spoke to Godric. "What did you find?"

Godric made a growling sound under his breath. "We were right that King Arthur was captured by a company of Saxons. They came here, to Edgar of Wigmore's fort. Edgar, Nell, and Huw are riding to Wroxeter with him—Nell and Huw as captives too. According to the guard, they are riding openly and with little rest—and someone has very kindly left us a path." He pointed to the droplet of wine beside which Myrddin had crouched.

Gareth was appalled. "I thought you said Edgar had shifted his allegiance to King Arthur?"

Myrddin turned to look up at him. "I did, because that's what he said. I see now that he would have used any excuse to effect his escape from Buellt." The anger rose in him again, but he swallowed it down. He had to maintain a cool head if he was going to have any chance to save not only the king but his wife and son too. "I fear for whoever is responsible for the leaky wineskin. If he's caught—"

Gareth shook his head. "The Saxon band has to know we are following—and also that we are well behind them. I'm far more concerned about them luring us into an ambush."

"Since we know where they're going," Godric said, "we should take a different road."

"What other road is there?" Myrddin said.

"All roads lead to Wroxeter, Myrddin," Godric said. "The Romans built theirs, yes, but my people have lived in this land for a hundred years, and we have our own pathways."

Gareth's jaw was set. "My people lived here for a thousand years before any of you came, and we had ours too." He looked at Myrddin. "I assure you that from here, the high road is not the only road."

"As I said." Godric glared at Gareth.

The two men were no more than a year apart in age, and their training was of a kind, but one had been raised a Welsh lord and the other a Saxon knight. Their minds had been forged in worlds apart—except in this case, they were in complete agreement, even if they couldn't see it themselves.

Myrddin made a chopping motion to stop their fruitless argument. "We will do as you both suggest. I don't know this region of Wales, so I need the two of you to work together to find us the best path, whether Welsh or Saxon I do not care—and nor should either of you."

Gareth and Godric glared at each other for another two heartbeats, and then, as if each had taken the measure of the other and found him not as wanting as initially supposed, they subsided.

"Fine," Gareth said, "I would say that the best path runs to Castell Collen, where we can strike out due east for Leintwardine."

"I agree." Godric's eyes narrowed as if he couldn't believe he'd just said that. "The Roman road goes north from there, and then turns east again to Wroxeter."

"So we go east from there and then north to come at Wroxeter directly from the south," Gareth said. "If Godric is willing, we should send three or four men to follow Edgar's company—and the drops of wine—in case he diverges from this road. At least that way, if Beorhtsige lied about where he was headed, we won't lose them completely."

Myrddin nodded, satisfied that the pair had become companions in this. He found himself amused as well, which was an odd emotion to be feeling under these circumstances. "I will follow your lead."

Chapter Six
13 December 537
Nell

THEY'D RIDDEN FOR NEARLY sixteen hours through night and day to reach Wroxeter. Nell would have lauded it as a triumph of horsemanship if she hadn't been falling off her horse herself in exhaustion. Every muscle in her body ached—and she hadn't even had to ride the whole way with her hands tied as had King Arthur and Huw.

At various times during the long ride, Huw had wanted to attempt to free the king, but Nell had watched his guards closely, and at no time throughout the whole of the journey had they left him guarded by fewer than three men. As Beorhtsige had insisted, King Arthur was his prize, and he was taking no chances that the opportunity to stand victorious before Modred was going to be taken from him.

At one point, Nell had contrived to collapse on the ground on the other side of a tree from where they'd thrown down the king, and she'd managed a few words with him, but he had ordered her not to risk herself or Huw for him. After that, they'd had no choice but to obey.

For now.

She had no intention of doing nothing for King Arthur. While it might turn out to be a far more difficult task to free the king from within the walls of Wroxeter than it had been to free Myrddin from Rhuddlan, Nell thought she had the measure of her enemy now. She recognized Beorhtsige as a typical second-in-command: gruff, very good at following orders and relaying them, but not nearly as good at coming up with plans himself. The brutal exterior masked an insecurity about who he was and his place in the world that

Edgar, for all that he'd been ridiculed throughout his life for his size and inclinations, didn't exhibit.

"What's going to happen to us, Mother?" That Huw would ask such a question revealed how worried he was. He wasn't bothering to hide his fear behind a brave show.

"So much depends upon Modred, Huw. I honestly don't think he will kill us. He knows, as does Edgar, that Myrddin will move heaven and earth to rescue us." Even if Nell hadn't guessed it already, the conversations around her during the night had made it clear that if there was anyone Modred hated more than King Arthur, it was Myrddin, odd as that seemed.

Her new husband had said more than once that he was the least of the knights in the king's company. Except ... Even Myrddin himself didn't believe that anymore—and Modred's hatred of him proved that Myrddin's most pernicious enemies didn't either. Modred would keep her and Huw alive if there was the slightest chance that their captivity meant Myrddin might fall into his clutches again.

By the time they reached the river crossing that would take them into Wroxeter, the sun had risen well into the sky and shone starkly down on the old Roman city, once known as Viriconium. The stronghold acted now as a symbol of the power that Modred held in Mercia, and which he hoped soon to hold in Wales. Once upon a time, the city had encompassed an unimaginable number of people, but under Saxon rule it had been reduced to a tiny fraction of its former size. Modred's hall squatted in the middle of the city and even though, in another setting, the Saxon fortifications would have appeared formidable in size, they took up less than a tenth of what had once existed here.

The bards sang of the Romans—how they'd conquered Britain in bloody battle after bloody battle. They killed the druids and cut down the sacred groves on Anglesey and brought Christianity to the island. But Rome had fallen to barbarians; the soldiers who'd kept the peace for four hundred years had been called home; and Britain had been left wide open to the Saxon hordes, who'd attacked in wave after wave almost from the moment the last Roman soldier had set sail.

The first invaders had ravaged Kent and the whole eastern shore of Britain, raiding and pillaging wherever they went. The most successful of these made themselves overlords of the Britons and married local women, as the Romans had done in their time, binding their lines to native families, but never becoming British. Then the Saxons had discovered the rich farmlands of southern England. The next waves of invaders, once they'd pillaged the countryside and murdered those who fought back, sent for their families.

Mile by mile, Britain had been taken over by Saxons, such that few even remembered that the whole of the Island had once been British, and that the British had been pushed west and then farther west into the mountains of Wales and had become Welsh.

The Welsh had fought back, but it was King Arthur's belief that four hundred years of peace under the Romans had left them soft. It was only after many generations of loss that they'd learned to fight again. King Arthur himself—though he hadn't been king then—had turned the Saxon tide at the battle of Mt. Badon, after which he'd held off the Saxons for nearly forty years.

But Modred presented an unanticipated threat. He was Arthur's nephew, his sister's child, half-Saxon/half-Welsh, and to many the perfect man to bring peace to Britain. He straddled the line between two peoples, and if he'd been anyone else but Modred, the Welsh might have welcomed him with open arms as their king.

But he *was* Modred—cruel, remorseless, and more power hungry than all of his Saxon forbears combined. With his rule, many Welsh feared that their country would be overrun entirely and that they would lose their language, their laws, and their very right to exist.

Here at Wroxeter, Modred had showed himself to be more Saxon than the Saxons themselves, building himself a Saxon fort that rivaled any of those which the kings of old had built before him. And, unlike those great kings, his fort was protected by the Roman stone walls and gate. Looking up at them, Nell understood that by claiming Wroxeter as his seat, Modred was declaring himself the heir to the Romans as well as Arthur, as if somehow his line was the legitimate heir to what they'd once created.

But as they passed through the gate, with much jubilation on the part of the Saxons who admitted them, Nell was struck by the extent to which the apparent mightiness of the fortress was a façade—a false-front for crumbling walls surrounding a space far too large for Modred's army to protect. Behind the gate lay a cobbled road, which led to Modred's seat. Again, like the walls, it was larger than any she'd seen before, consisting of an enormous stone hall with mighty doors, each at least eight-feet high. But it sat in the center of a traditional Saxon wooden palisade, which was the only real fortification at Wroxeter.

Nell had never seen any structure as large as Modred's stone hall. Even Rhuddlan Castle could fit inside it. And yet, proving again how vain Modred's imaginings truly were, the open gates of the palisade also revealed dozens of wattle and daub Saxon huts and craft halls that had been built up against the sides of the stonework and around the inside of the wooden palisade. The magnificence of Modred's seat was dwarfed by what had once been, and the farther they progressed inside the ruined city, the more the truth of Modred was revealed: he was a stunted offshoot of a once-noble house, now brought low by ambition and avarice.

They passed within the palisade and received the same jubilant and jeering reception as at the front gate, and then the whole lot of them crossed the courtyard and were admitted into the hall, which could have held a thousand people. Modred sat on a throne at the far end and waved a hand, commanding that they should come forward. Archbishop Dafydd had a seat in front of the step leading up to Modred's chair, and the hall was lined with other Saxon noblemen, all come to Wroxeter to pay their respects to Modred and take part in what they believed to be the coming conquest of Wales.

Beorhtsige himself held King Arthur, his arms still tied at the wrists, and marched him towards Modred's seat. Edgar caught Nell's elbow and urged her forward too. "Come on."

"Traitor," Huw muttered in Welsh under his breath.

"Oh ye of little faith," Edgar said in Latin, a language which Huw didn't understand. Nell didn't know if Edgar realized that she did, or if he was speaking only to himself.

For her part, Edgar's words had Nell trembling with sudden hope, even if in his ignorance Huw remained unforgiving. Whether intentionally or not, Edgar had just told her that his course had not changed: he had brought them to Modred to give himself instant credibility in Modred's eyes. Edgar was playing a long game, and while he'd said that he was loyal to Arthur and he promised Myrddin that he would see to her and Huw's safety, it wasn't clear if the show he was putting on for Modred would extend as far as forfeiting Nell's and Huw's lives entirely. If he still adhered to the sense of honor Nell detected in his eyes, he would view both prior promises as binding.

Leaving Nell and Huw under guard twenty paces from Modred's chair, Edgar walked the last few feet to stand at Beorhtsige's side. Beorhtsige might demand the reward for capturing Arthur, which Nell couldn't disagree that he deserved, but Edgar wasn't going to give him any more accolades than that.

"We can't trust Edgar, if that's what you're hoping," Huw said in Nell's other ear.

"We can't trust anyone," she said in reply.

"What of your vision of Father?" he said.

Nell shook her head, her eyes on the men in front of them. "He is coming, but we have to assume that you and I are King Arthur's only hope."

Beorhtsige was assuming there was no hope, and he was triumphant in his victory. "I bring you King Arthur, my lord!"

Modred sat with a finger to his lips, not quite smiling. "Well done, Beorhtsige. I gather you have Lord Edgar to thank for this achievement?"

"Er—"

Nell had never seen Modred before, never heard him speak, but according to Myrddin, the question was typical for him. She didn't think Modred could yet know what had happened, but somehow he'd cut through what should have been Beorhtsige's great moment and deflected his glory to someone else.

Edgar cleared his throat. "If my lord recalls, I sent a letter to Arthur suggesting my willingness to change my allegiance to him and asking him to meet me at the church by the Cam River."

"That is the meeting to which I was referring." Modred's tone was dry, and Nell had the impression that he thought Edgar was wasting his time by reiterating an obvious point.

Edgar continued calmly as if Modred hadn't chastised him. "I was not able to follow through with that meeting because Agravaine took it upon himself to imprison me in my own tower. He suspected me of betraying you. I did not, in fact, betray you, while it seems Agravaine did, to his detriment."

"How?" The word came out as an order rather than a question.

"King Arthur disbelieved in my sincerity, so he sent his brother, Cai, to the church in his stead, where he was subsequently killed on Agravaine's orders."

Even Modred couldn't hide his surprise at this. "Agravaine ordered Cai killed?"

"Agravaine did not go to the church, and thus did not know that Cai had been sent in Arthur's place. Regardless, he'd ordered his captain to kill the Welsh soldiers who did go, and his orders were carried out."

The only part of Modred's body that moved was his eyes, which went first to Arthur, whose head was thrown back in defiance, and then to Beorhtsige.

"He speaks the truth, my lord," Beorhtsige said.

"Where is this captain now?" Modred said.

"Dead," Edgar said before Beorhtsige could answer, "killed this morning in the battle of Buellt which followed."

Nell didn't know how Edgar knew this. Perhaps his spy had reported it, but he hadn't seen fit to mention it during their conversation in the stable.

"Why isn't Agravaine here to explain these matters to me?"

Edgar cleared his throat. "He is also dead, killed in the hall at Buellt by one of Arthur's men, one Myrddin, whom I believe you've met."

Modred's eyes unexpectedly lit. "Myrddin killed Agravaine?" He barked a laugh. "The pure cheek of that man. If even one of my men had his loyalty and intelligence—"

Every man in the hall flinched at this backhanded compliment to Myrddin and insult to them. Edgar, however, remained unmoved. "What's more, it was Myrddin who released me from the tower, under the impression, of which I did not dissuade him, that I was willing to swear allegiance to Arthur. He believed in my loyalty to such an extent that he entrusted his wife and son to my care." Edgar stepped to one side and pointed to Nell and Huw.

Modred was openly laughing now. "And you brought them here to me." He shook his head. "Oh, Edgar. Had I known of your ability to prevaricate, I would have confirmed you in your lands long ago."

Edgar bowed. "All I asked for was a chance to prove myself."

"Which you have done."

From beside Edgar, Beorhtsige shifted, seemingly dissatisfied with the conversation. He hadn't even been thanked for bringing King Arthur to Wroxeter.

Modred noticed the movement too. "Something wrong, Beorhtsige?"

"No, my lord."

Modred tipped his chin to Arthur. "Why are his hands tied? Release him immediately."

"But, my lord—

In an instant, Modred's mood transformed from amused to raging. "He is my uncle and the King of Wales!" His voice thundered throughout the hall. "What kind of heir to the throne would I be if I treated my predecessor with less than the utmost respect and cordiality?"

Beorhtsige took two steps back in the face of the onslaught. "M-m-my lord, I d-d-didn't realize—"

"Obviously." Modred's voice held nothing but disdain, which was hardly fair. Beorhtsige had done his duty—beyond his duty—and instead of being honored for it, he was being chastised in front of the entire court. It was no wonder he was befuddled by what he'd done wrong. Nobody else in the room understood either.

Because the room had been frozen into silence by Modred's tantrum, the half-Saxon pretender to the throne came down from his chair and untied Arthur's hands himself. "I apologize, uncle, for any mistreatment you may have received at the hands of my men."

"It is to the wives and children of my men, who lost their lives today, and to my brother, that you should be apologizing, not to me," Arthur said.

"I have been misunderstood, by you, of all people, the most," Modred said. "I ask only that you give me the opportunity to make amends."

"You cannot bring back the dead."

Modred dismissed that concern with a gesture. "Sit with me tonight at table; let me show you how I manage my kingdom. Tomorrow, I open my affairs to your inspection. At the end of the day, if you can look me in the eyes and tell me that I have mismanaged my rule and that I am not worthy to be your heir, I will send you on your way. You can renew this war, if that's what you really want."

"I didn't start this war, Modred."

"But you can finish it. We can finish it together."

Nell wanted to grab the king's shoulder and pull him away from Modred. This was a trick. Modred wouldn't release him in a dozen lifetimes, but King Arthur gazed at his nephew for a count of five and then said, "I have a condition."

"Name it."

Arthur motioned with his chin towards Nell and Huw. "The woman and boy stay with me."

Modred didn't like that. He wavered for a few heartbeats, but then his jaw firmed. "Of course, uncle. They are of no importance."

Of all the things he could have said, nothing else would have been a bigger lie. But Modred gave a clap and spun on his heel, to then wave at one of his men, who was dressed in the gown of a steward and who'd been standing to one side of the hall. "See to my uncle's comfort."

As they were herded out of the hall with King Arthur, Nell grasped Huw's hand. She understood Saxon—she might even be considered fluent—but that didn't mean she understood what had just happened in there. There was one thing she did know, however. While King Arthur was no longer bound, the danger facing them had in no way lessened.

Chapter Seven

13 December 537

Myrddin

THEY'D FALLEN FAR BEHIND, but not for lack of effort. They'd started out from Buellt at least an hour after King Arthur's abductors, and while they'd worked hard to catch up, the going had been rough. The Saxons and Welsh might have worn roads through the landscape over time, but the Romans had built theirs with rock and sand and, quite frankly, there was a reason they'd done that. Those roads were better.

"What can you see?" Myrddin said to Gareth, who was known for his perfect vision, which Myrddin no longer could pretend to possess.

"Wroxeter," Gareth said.

Myrddin made a guttural sound in his throat. He'd known that, of course, and Gareth was being deliberately obnoxious. "I mean, what can you see on the walls?"

Myrddin had worried for the whole journey about the risk they'd taken in following a circular route instead of tracking King Arthur directly. But Gareth had been right that an ambush was well within the realm of possibility, and the consensus when Godric had questioned those in nearby farms and villages was that Modred was indeed at Wroxeter.

"Nothing that's going to make rescuing the king with the few men we have any easier," Gareth said. "We have to go in there. You know we do."

Myrddin did know it, but the knowledge didn't make him any happier. "What about waiting until nightfall and sneaking into the city over the eastern wall. That end of the city is far less well guarded."

"You are thinking like a Welshman instead of the Saxon you're pretending to be," Gareth said. "Modred has spies in the lands around Wroxeter. Even now we are being watched. If we don't ride straight to the gate, the guards will know something is amiss."

"They could even fear that we have come for King Arthur and tighten their watch on him." Godric said, having ridden up beside Gareth. The two men hadn't become friends on the road from Buellt, but they'd learned to respect each other. "It would make it many times harder to free him."

Even though riding as a Saxon had been Myrddin's idea in the first place and he would have much preferred to stay in the shadows, he gave way. With the exception of Gareth, who retained his Welsh garb, though he'd removed the surcoat that proclaimed him to be one of Arthur's men, they looked like a company of Saxons. Thus, a quarter of an hour later, as the sun was setting behind them, the company turned onto the high road and made directly for the bridge across the Severn River. The bridge would take them to the main gate at Wroxeter, located on the north side of the town. As they did so, to Myrddin's huge relief, the four men of Godric's company who had been sent to follow the wine drops trotted out of the trees to the north of the road and joined them.

"They're there all right," one of them said without preamble. "They took many short rests, and we took fewer, so we caught them ten miles before Wroxeter. We didn't approach for fear of spooking them."

"You have done well," Godric said.

Myrddin clenched his hands around the reins. He imagined himself driving a fist into Modred's nose, a pleasure he would surely never have. He ached to have Nell's arms wrapped around his waist, where they belonged, and he was glad he hadn't had the opportunity to sleep for fear of seeing her battered face looking up at him again.

Of course, the vision of King Arthur had been a waking dream, and part of him prayed he'd have another sooner rather than later because he needed to know where Modred was keeping his wife and son. Myrddin knew that he should be thinking first and foremost about the king's welfare, but even King Arthur might accept that he couldn't.

The company cantered across the bridge that spanned the Severn River. Myrddin's Saxon helmet, with its long nose guard, almost completely blocked his face, and while his sword remained belted at his waist and he wore his own mail shirt, he carried a round Saxon shield and bore a spear. His tunic also proclaimed him as one of Cedric's men. All in all, he looked utterly unremarkable, but he kept his gaze averted from the guard, who stopped them at the gate and listened intently to the credentials of both Gareth and Godric. He glanced at the men accompanying them too, but after a cursory assessment said, "Quite a day we're having."

"How is that?" Gareth said.

"King Arthur is within, captured by Lord Edgar of Wigmore."

"Is that so?" Gareth said. "The king might be glad of my news, as well."

"Which is what?"

Gareth laughed. "What kind of servant would I be if I told you first?"

The guard laughed too. "You may be Welsh, but you understand our lord well."

"Modred is half-Welsh too," Gareth said.

And with that—perhaps unwise—rejoinder, they walked their horses along the cobbled road towards the entrance to the palisade. Here in the late afternoon, that gate had been left open. Given the comings and goings of Modred's forces, it might only be during an attack by an enemy force that the guards would close it, for the palisade was a secondary defense, intended to provide protection if the gatehouse was breached.

The stable wasn't located inside the palisade, and it was full anyway, with all the stalls set aside for the use of Modred's horses and those of a few of his highest ranking captains. Other horses were picketed all around the southern side of the fort, and thus everyone dismounted in front of the gate.

Myrddin had never been here before, so he couldn't tell if the number of men gathering around them was usual, or if they were on particular alert because Modred was preparing for King Arthur's army to come thundering towards them from the west. Regardless, Myrddin hadn't ever been in the company of quite as many men and horses as Modred had gathered to him.

"What news are you going to bring to Modred?" Myrddin said in an undertone to Gareth.

"I was planning on telling him that you're dead," Gareth said matter-of-factly. "I will say that you were killed at the end of the battle, after King Arthur left the field, which is why he hadn't yet heard of it."

Myrddin let out a surprised laugh. "That news will surely gain you admission."

Gareth wrinkled his nose for a moment. "Now, however, I'm having second thoughts. It is likely that Nell and Huw will be in the hall."

Myrddin's stomach clenched to think of how his death would affect them, but he answered the way he had to anyway, "You can't worry about them."

"If I am able, I will pull them aside and tell them the truth," Gareth said.

Myrddin shook his head. "It would be better if you allowed them to believe I'm dead, at least at first. Their acceptance of it will go a long way to reassuring Modred that you're speaking the truth."

"In which case, the sooner we get them out of here, the better," Gareth said.

Myrddin turned to the others and motioned that they should gather around him. "Godric and Gareth will enter the hall, which will leave the rest of us free to fraternize here. Nobody will suspect us of being anyone other than what we are unless we make a show of ourselves. Our mission is to find King Arthur. If he is still alive and in no immediate danger, we will confer as to a possible plan for getting him out tonight."

"In and out and gone by dawn," Godric said. "That is my preference."

Though Myrddin nodded at Gareth and Godric, and he'd approved of Gareth's plan—even encouraged him in it—he found his mouth going dry. While Gareth had sworn that he was loyal to Arthur, and Arthur had believed him, the ease with which Gareth moved among these Saxons had Myrddin reconsidering this entire plan.

What if Arthur's capture had been at Gareth's behest? What if he had been felled by a blow from Beorhtsige that was just hard enough to draw blood and look convincing, but not hard enough to do him real harm? During the ride, Gareth had shown virtually no ill-effects of his injuries.

Fortunately for Myrddin, at that moment Gareth turned away in response to a signal from one of the men on the palisade, who indicated that Modred had agreed to see him, and he didn't notice Myrddin's dismay. For his part, Myrddin kept his face averted, though his eyes searched the faces of the men who surrounded him, suddenly distrustful of them all. While they'd fought for Arthur at Buellt, and even Gareth hadn't revealed Myrddin's presence in Wroxeter to the guards, none here were truly Arthur's men. They were all Cedric's men. What Myrddin didn't know was how many of them might also be loyal to Modred and resent their lord's new found allegiance.

Anxious and exhausted, Myrddin walked Cadfarch to where the other men had gathered, off to one side of the palisade in the shelter of what might have once been a fine house but which no longer had a roof. He was a Welshman in a sea of Saxons, and the only people in the whole of the fort he knew absolutely he could trust were captive to Modred.

Chapter Eight

13 December 537

Nell

GARETH MARCHED DOWN the long corridor and came to a halt at Modred's seat. "Myrddin is dead."

An icy coldness began in Nell's belly and spread throughout her body. Huw put his arm around her shoulders and his face into her neck, his shoulders shaking, though he didn't make a sound.

At the initial sight of Gareth walking into the hall, Nell had been heartbroken at the thought that he'd been captured too. Then when she realized that he was accompanied by Godric, and that both men willingly made their obeisance to Modred, she'd been consumed with a rage that had her hand clenching Huw's arm so tightly she might have left a bruise. So much had gone wrong, at the very moment she had thought everything would be all right.

Nell kept her head up and her eyes fixed on Modred's seat, ignoring curious eyes turned towards her, not willing to share her grief with these people. King Arthur, who sat just to Modred's right, held himself very straight, as if he had an iron rod up his spine.

Nell felt for Myrddin's cross, which she'd worn constantly since her marriage, and clenched it in her fist, her whole body curving around it. The cross and Huw were all that she had left of him. She had lost everything when her sons had died. She had joined the convent because she'd never wanted to feel as sad again—and then Wulfere had come to her convent. She had intended to travel to Rhuddlan to kill Modred, giving her life in the process, because it had been all she had left to lose. Or so she had thought. She'd been wrong.

With the sorrow that her world had ended came a further realization that she and Myrddin had gotten it all wrong. They'd meddled with the future—and by doing so, they'd only made things worse.

Meanwhile, Modred sat with his elbows on the arms of his chair and his hands folded before his lips, studying Gareth. "You tell me truly?"

"Yes, my lord."

Modred dropped his hands and sent a sardonic glance in the direction of King Arthur, who was sitting to his right. "I am almost disappointed that he could have met such an unremarkable end." He tipped up his chin. "I gather Buellt is lost, however."

"Yes, my lord. Though—I understand that the Welsh victory was short-lived." Gareth nodded towards King Arthur.

"We are coming to an understanding," Modred said without looking at Arthur.

That wasn't true, in fact. Arthur had slept most of the day alongside Nell and Huw, and while the rooms were richly furnished, they were still a prison. It was tomorrow that Modred had promised the king free run of Wroxeter. They'd all wondered what might be happening tomorrow that wasn't happening today. King Arthur had muttered that Modred would be spending the day making sure that there would be nothing objectionable to find among his records. But without knowledge of what was beyond their prison walls, it was difficult to formulate any kind of plan.

The house in which they were being held captive had been restored to much of its former glory and, even in its reduced state, was possibly finer than any Welsh palace from which King Arthur had ever ruled. In all, Nell counted eight rooms, including servants' quarters, a tiled bathing room with a pool long since empty of water, and three sleeping rooms. Before the guard had closed the rear door, Nell had caught a glimpse of the property behind the house, which appeared to include a kitchen and pens for animals.

The interior of the house also included a courtyard open to the elements, which would have provided the owner a fine place to sit on warm summer evenings, even if they were few and far between in Britain as compared to the sunnier climates where the Romans had originated.

"I'm happy to hear that, my lord." Gareth bowed again. "It will be a great day when peace comes to Britain."

"It will," Modred said shortly, clearly impatient now with the audience and the platitudes.

Gareth and Godric, who hadn't said a word, bowed one more time and backed away until they were lost among the many men coming and going from the lower tables. Gareth was a Welsh lord, but fairly low down in the hierarchy of Modred's barons. Edgar, however, sat at the high table a few seats down from King Arthur, next to Archbishop Dafydd, who was the only one among Modred's nobles who looked stricken at the news of Myrddin's death. For all his faults, and though Nell thought he was mistaken in supporting Modred's bid for the Welsh throne, Dafydd was sincere in his hatred of war and the needless deaths that came with it.

At last, the attention of those in the hall was diverted to someone else and other problems, and Nell allowed herself to feel her grief. Tears rolled down her cheeks unashamedly, though she didn't sob. Once Huw had regained some measure of control, he spent the rest of the meal staring at his trencher.

Finally, she, Huw, and King Arthur were once again escorted from the hall to their prison. When they'd first arrived at the many-roomed, well-appointed house, her thoughts had focused on being rescued, because she still had hope that the king might have been followed from Buellt. Now, however, she swallowed down her grief and looked around her with a new eye. With every ally going over to Modred's side, they needed to find their own way out of Wroxeter, preferably before dawn when Modred would come for King Arthur.

As before, guards posted themselves at the front and back doors and patrolled the area around the house, at least ten by Nell's count, but none observed them from inside the house, for which Nell was truly grateful. With sleep elusive, the companions huddled together on a bench in what might have once been the reception room (given its size) to talk in private, far from whatever ears might be listening from the doors or windows.

King Arthur took Nell's hand. "My dear, I am so sorry."

Nell took in a trembling breath. "I loved him my whole life, even before I knew what real love was. I had a vision of him on the journey, standing side by side with Saxons fighting Saxons. I don't feel that he is dead, but Gareth would not be mistaken about something like that—not having come all this way to tell Modred of his death, knowing how important the news would be to him."

"We are surrounded by traitors," Huw said.

"Even had our Saxon friends remained loyal, they would not have been able to free us, not with us so well-guarded," King Arthur said.

"That just means we must rescue ourselves," Huw said.

"And then what?" King Arthur rose to his feet and walked to the entrance of the room in order to look towards the main door. "We have many hundreds of Saxons between this house and the Severn, and I cannot pass for one of them." He turned back to Nell and Huw. "You two, however, must try."

"We will not leave you," Nell said.

King Arthur made a shushing motion with his hand. "Modred wants me alive—for now, but with Myrddin dead, you are completely expendable."

"In which case, why are we here at all?" Nell said. "What use could we be to him?"

"It may be that he hopes to use you as leverage against me," King Arthur took a step towards them. "We cannot allow that."

Nell had stayed sitting on the bench, but now she stood and approached the king. "Modred can't possibly think you would value our lives over your throne."

"No, but he might murder you in front of me as an example of what he will do to many more of my people if I don't name him as my heir."

Nell shook her head to emphasize her denial. "You must never bow to Modred's demands, no matter what he does, no matter what he threatens."

King Arthur grasped both her hands. "I wish I could agree. Before today, I might have agreed. Unfortunately—and unbeknownst to Edgar and Beorhtsige—by bringing you two here, Edgar has delivered into Modred's hands the one person whose life I value more than my own."

Nell pulled her hands away, shocked. "Not me, surely."

"No, Nell, not you, as dear as you are to me." King Arthur lifted his chin to point to Huw. "Him."

In utter confusion, Nell turned to look at Huw. For his part, Huw stood with his hands loose at his sides, gaping at the king. "Me? Why me?"

King Arthur moved in a wide arc around the youth, studying him as he might a prized stallion. "My disgrace is in believing what I was told." He threw out a hand. "I wanted an heir of my own body. I didn't want to need Myrddin."

Nell's tongue stuck to the roof of her mouth. She had no idea what King Arthur was talking about or where he was going with this.

Huw asked the question she couldn't. "Why would you need Myrddin? He was born out of wedlock to the daughter of a minor lord and raised in the household of one of Cai's knights. His father was probably a pig keeper."

King Arthur barked a laugh. "Is that what Myrddin told you?" And then he went on without waiting for an answer. "Typical of the man."

"What is typical?" Nell said, finding her voice and not liking the king's mocking tone.

"It is typical of him that he never told you about the conversation he and I had just a month ago about his mother. Before she lived in Powys—before Myrddin's birth—Myrddin's mother was lady-in-waiting to my Aunt Juliana, King Ambrosius's wife."

"And why is that important?" Huw placed his hands on his hips, not liking the king's apparent disparagement of Myrddin any more than Nell.

"Her name was Seren," King Arthur continued as if he hadn't heard the question. "As she was lovely, she came to the attention of my uncle, though you must realize that I didn't know of his attentions at the time. I only learned of Seren's pregnancy after her death when my Aunt Juliana told me of it, on the way to assuring me that the child too had died and that I had no rival for the throne. I never thought to question what she told me, busy as I was with mourning my uncle and father, who also died in 501, and consolidating my own power.

"I can tell you that at the Christmas feast before his death, Ambrosius gave Juliana the queenly gift of a golden cross. He gave one also to me, his heir." King Arthur pulled a silver chain from beneath his shirt and held it up so Huw and Nell could see the cross that dangled from the end of it.

Her incipient anger forgotten, Nell found her hands trembling. She clasped them before her lips and looked at the king over the top of them, holding her breath and waiting for him to finish. If they had been speaking about a stranger, or hearing the tale from the lips of a bard, she could have guessed where the king's story was going but not when he was speaking of Myrddin, her husband.

King Arthur dropped the cross back inside his shirt and looked at Nell, whose own hand had strayed to the cross around her neck. "I did not know until yesterday that Ambrosius also had a third cross made, which he gave to Seren, his mistress, the mother of the longed-for son he would not live to see." The king took in a deep breath. "Myrddin's father was no pig keeper. He was Ambrosius, the king of Wales, and Myrddin is his natural son. As Myrddin's son, Huw has a greater claim to the throne of Wales than I."

Chapter Nine

13 December 537
Myrddin

MYRDDIN STOOD WITH his hands on his hips, staring with utter horror at Gareth, who was explaining how they would free King Arthur, Huw, and Nell from the clutches of the Saxons. Godric stood nearby, grinning, since it was one of his men who'd discovered the low tunnel and had brought to their attention the possibility of what Gareth now thought was the perfect plan.

"You want us to go in there?" Myrddin peered past Gareth to the opening behind him, which would require someone to travel a hundred yards underneath Modred's stronghold until he reached the house in which Modred was keeping Nell.

"I do." Gareth grinned. "I'm impressed at how easily you grasped the concept."

He was mocking Myrddin again, as was his habit. Myrddin had spent much of the evening doubting Gareth's allegiance, but after Gareth had returned with the news that Modred had believed without question the news that he was dead, Myrddin had to concede that he had no grounds for suspicion. Gareth had once served Modred, but it truly seemed now that he was staunchly on Arthur's side.

They were standing in an abandoned portion of the town, to the north of Modred's palisade and fifty yards from Wroxeter's exterior fortifications. Most of the wall here was ruinous, some portions as low as six-feet high, a fact which explained the need for the palisade that surrounded the main hall.

Myrddin had spent the early evening scouting out the area and felt he had a grasp of its dimensions. The houses were much smaller in this quarter, indicating that the poorer members of Roman society had once lived in this area of the city, and it was from here that waterworks that had fed the baths had been controlled and maintained. Although Myrddin would have chosen the task for himself, he'd allowed other men to keep an eye on the prison house for him, though their attention had needed to be sporadic so they wouldn't call attention to themselves. Godric had pulled them all back within the last half-hour in preparation for the rescue.

Myrddin stepped closer to the entrance, sniffing with distaste. A hundred and fifty years of neglect had left the tunnel, which had clearly once been an outtake for the sewer system, dripping in grime and smelling of mold. Myrddin sneezed violently three times.

Gareth put a hand on Myrddin's chest and pushed him away from the entrance. "What's wrong with you?"

"I don't know." Myrddin sneezed three more times, and his eyes streamed with tears. The first sneeze had caught him by surprise, but he'd managed to stifle the subsequent ones in the elbow of his coat. He didn't need Gareth's restraining hand on his chest to know not to approach the tunnel again, and he blew his nose into the dirt beside the road, trying to eject the vile smell of mold from his nostrils.

Gareth was disgusted by Myrddin's weakness. "I can tell you right now that the whole plan would end in an instant if we sent you in there."

Myrddin shook his head. "I can go if I have to, if it's the only way to rescue— " Another sneeze overtook him.

"As I said." Gareth gave a low laugh. "You would have been the perfect man to send too because you still need to remain hidden from Modred and his men. But as it is, it's impossible." He turned on his heel to survey the rest of the men, who'd gathered in a semi-circle around him. And then he sighed. "Maybe I should be the one to go, since my presence in the rescue party will be a way to prove to the king that I have not defected to Modred."

"No, my lord. We need you out and about, in case Modred demands your presence. I'll send two of my own men," Godric said. "They can reassure the king of your allegiance, and that in speaking of Myrddin's death, you were acting on Myrddin's own advice."

Though he'd been willing to go, Gareth looked so relieved it was almost comical.

"So what am I supposed to do?" Myrddin said.

"Keep watch?" Godric said.

Keeping watch went against Myrddin's nature, and he kicked at the cobbles beneath his feet in frustration. It wasn't as if Godric wasn't right, however. Myrddin never would have imagined that he could be undone by a few sneezes, but that certainly seemed to be the case. His eyes had failed him quite some time ago, and he'd learned to live with it. His friend Ifan's back was starting to go and was the main reason Myrddin hadn't considered bringing him on this journey, though he would never tell his friend that. It was disturbing to discover that Myrddin's breathing had failed him too—and like Gareth's relief, it would have been amusing if the situation hadn't been so serious and his family and King Arthur in such peril.

In short order, two men chosen by Godric for their smaller size disappeared down the tunnel with a torch to light their way and a spare in case the first one went out. According to Gareth, they would soon be crawling on all fours, a fact which made Myrddin somewhat less regretful that he wasn't among them. Godric sent an additional two men to wait in the tunnel, staged at intervals, so that the rescuers would have light and companionship to follow home. Then he went to see about the disposition of the rest of his men, who were spread out around the waterworks in an effort to keep watch and not be taken unawares in case a stray guard of Modred's wandered by.

"I can't believe a rescue of King Arthur, Nell, and Huw can really be accomplished this easily," Myrddin said to Gareth in an undertone.

"I wouldn't say this is easy. Have you had a vision that tells us otherwise?" Gareth said with apparent interest.

"No."

Gareth plucked at his lower lip. "It's *why* Modred is keeping King Arthur in a fine house that concerns me. Back at Buellt, Beorhtsige should have killed King Arthur so Modred could declare himself King of Wales immediately. Why didn't he?"

Myrddin kicked at some debris between two cobbles, thinking. "Maybe Archbishop Dafydd has something to do with it. He wouldn't countenance the murder of a sitting king in cold blood, even if he has become one of Modred's lackeys."

In fact, the more Myrddin thought about it, the more it seemed likely that Modred's conciliatory attitude, as had been the case a month ago before the Battle at the Strait, was a result of Dafydd's influence. The archbishop had excommunicated Arthur and Cai at Modred's behest and forbidden the holding of services and rites in Wales until Arthur surrendered to the Church's authority. The fact that Dafydd had taken that action did not mean, however, that he had given up all hope of reconciliation. Quite the opposite—he was still hoping to push King Arthur into giving way before Modred.

"Since it was you who escorted Lord Aelric across the Conwy River only last month and were present for the excommunication at Rhuddlan," Gareth said, "I suppose if any of us should know the archbishop's mind, it's you. Modred has always wanted to appear kingly and that has meant appeasing the archbishop—perhaps up to and including today."

Wishing now that he'd been given the opportunity to sleep because he actually *wanted* a vision to overtake him if it would help them rescue King Arthur, Myrddin left Gareth to his musing and went looking for Godric, who had paced down a narrow alley to the next street, which was closer to the center of the city. At the intersection, Godric had stopped, his hand on his sword hilt, as if in anticipation of drawing it. Myrddin came to stand beside him.

He didn't have to ask what had drawn Godric's attention: angry voices rose faintly from the central square of the town where the entrance to the palisade was located. Myrddin gave Godric a wary look. "We should find out what's happening."

"I will stay here to wait for my men to return," Godric said.

Myrddin loped back to Gareth, who'd remained at the entrance to the tunnel. As Myrddin clapped the Saxon helmet on his head again and pulled up the hood of his cloak to hide his features, he related to Gareth what he and Godric had heard.

Never one to need something explained to him twice, Gareth went with Myrddin through the maze of abandoned buildings between the tunnel and Modred's hall. From the position of the moon it had to be nearly midnight by now and, as dark shadows, they flitted from the corner of one building to another, avoiding main streets, until they reached a point where they were within hailing distance of the palisade gate.

A small circle of men had gathered around two soldiers who were arguing, each held back by two friends. The crowd watching grew larger with every moment that passed.

From what Myrddin could decipher from the shouted words, two factions within Modred's army were on the opposite sides of an argument, though for the life of him Myrddin couldn't figure out what they were arguing about. They were all well soaked in beer, however, so it could have been about anything. Then the two combatants simultaneously wrenched themselves away from the men trying to hold them and attacked each other, punching and grappling and trying to gain an advantage. The argument had progressed to a brawl.

"The time is now to free King Arthur from his prison," Gareth said, immediately seeing how they could turn the situation to their advantage.

But before he could set off in the direction of the house where the king was being kept, Myrddin grabbed his arm and said, "Look!"

Edgar of Wigmore edged himself out the back of the crowd and walked swiftly around the north side of the palisade, in the same direction they'd intended to go.

Myrddin had been trying not to think about Edgar's betrayal all day. He longed to find the Saxon lord alone in one of these deserted alleys. It would have been absurd of him to confront Edgar, however. A man didn't become a leader of men by following his heart as much as his head.

"What does he think he's doing?" Gareth said under his breath, and he started off after him, though at such a distance that Edgar wouldn't notice. "I spoke with Beorhtsige about the bruises on King Arthur's face, and he told me that Edgar himself gave them to the king."

Myrddin didn't answer because he couldn't speak since his hatred for Edgar was clogging his throat. He followed quickly after Gareth, again staying in the shadows and trying to both stay with Edgar and to keep out of his line of sight in case he looked around. Edgar followed the palisade, moving at a steady pace that didn't draw attention—neither too fast nor too slow—and headed, as Gareth and Myrddin had intended, for the house which served as Arthur's prison.

Gareth spoke from just ahead of Myrddin. "Am I crazed to think that it was he who started that fight?"

The front of the manor house was lit by torches shining from either side of the door. Two men guarded it, though they had the look of men who'd rather be elsewhere. They shifted and fidgeted, craning their necks to discover what was causing all the commotion a hundred yards to the west, and one took a dozen steps away from his post in the hopes that his new position would allow him to see the action better.

Edgar halted in front of the guard at the door, who managed to focus on him long enough to show his respect. "Good evening, my lord!"

Edgar inclined his head regally. "Good evening. I would speak briefly to the woman and boy, if I may."

The man's eyes flicked past Edgar to the fight, which had to be winding down by now, though from the continued shouting it wasn't. "We have been given orders to let nobody past us."

The moonlight and torchlight were bright enough that Myrddin could see the sneer that passed across Edgar's face, in an almost direct imitation of Modred, whose sneer was fixed permanently in place. But when Edgar spoke, his tone was reasonable. "I was the one who brought them to Wroxeter. Surely such a rule does not apply to me."

"The boy walks as if he's bruised all over," the guard said.

Myrddin frowned. He'd heard that Edgar had bruised the king face, but not that Huw was injured too.

"He is a prisoner," Edgar said, as if that was all the explanation required. And maybe it was. He cleared his throat. "Now see here—"

"Act like my servant, will you?" Gareth said in a whisper to Myrddin, and then he stepped out of the shadows and strode out of the darkness towards Edgar.

Myrddin followed, albeit a little stiffly, since he'd been told time and again to stay in the shadows, and he was uncomfortable with coming forward, especially with Edgar present. His helmet did cover much of his face, however, so Myrddin acted against instinct and brazened it out.

For his part, Gareth sauntered towards the front door. Earlier, many more guards had encircled the house, but Myrddin didn't see them now. Either they were in deep shadow, were no longer needed, or had abandoned their posts sooner than these guards. All soldiers drank, but beer appeared to be a more potent drink than mead, given that over-indulgence had diverted so many of Modred's men.

"Let him past, soldier," Gareth said in his accented English, though he still managed to infuse the words with a lazy drawl that marked him as a man of wealth and privilege.

The soldier saluted Gareth in a way he hadn't Edgar. "Yes, my lord."

Gareth lifted his chin to point towards the front of the palisade. "Why don't you two see what's happening at the gatehouse. My man will stand guard until you get back." He indicated Myrddin with a tip of his head.

"Yes, sir!" The first guard patted Myrddin's shoulder as he passed, muttering his thanks, and the two men disappeared around the palisade.

Gareth glared at Edgar. "What are you doing here?"

Edgar's teeth were clenched. "What are *you* doing here? I had this well in hand!"

Myrddin gave a low laugh, having finally realized that his suspicions about these Saxons, half-Saxons, and former traitors who surrounded him had been misplaced from beginning to end. "He's rescuing the king, just like you are. Now—can we get on with it?" He pushed through the door, ignoring the protests of both lords.

Nell must have overheard some of the activity, because she stood in the center of the floor, with Huw a half-step in front of her. At the sight of him, she put both hands to her mouth and then ran forward to throw her arms around Myrddin's neck.

"I'm all right, *cariad*." He reached out an arm and pulled Huw to him too.

Nell gave a choking sob. "Gareth said you were dead!"

Myrddin bent to rest his forehead against hers. "I'm so sorry about that, Nell, but we needed safe passage into Wroxeter, and we, unlike Edgar, didn't have you or King Arthur to barter with."

Edgar and Gareth had done a quick search of the house, and now Gareth returned to the foyer. "Where's the king?"

"He isn't here," Nell said. "Someone came for him a quarter of an hour ago."

"That explains why there are so few guards. Who was it, Nell?" Myrddin said.

Nell shook her head. "I don't know. It isn't as if the guards would tell me."

A tapping sound came from the recesses of the house, and Myrddin leapt towards the sound before he remembered the Saxons coming through the tunnel. He reached the bathroom in time to see the head of one of Godric's men poking through a three-foot door in one side of the pool, which maintenance workers had used back when the house had been lived in.

"That was ugly." The man swore under his breath in English. "What are you doing here, my lord? Don't tell me we did this for nothing!"

Myrddin reached down to grasp his hand while holding his breath at the same time at the smell emanating from the open hatch. "Sorry. Let's get you out of there."

Soon, both of Godric's soldiers were standing on the floor of the pool, breathing deeply. They were a matched set of curly blond hair and blue eyes, not unlike half the men in Modred's army, which had been helpful today since they were trying to blend in.

Nell went to the opening, sniffed once and frowned, and then looked back to Myrddin. "Do we need to leave the same way?"

"That was the original plan, before Edgar involved himself." Gareth laughed softly. "Madam, I apologize. I approved the idea."

"One of Godric's men discovered the tunnel, but you are noble, my lord, for taking responsibility," Myrddin said. "Is there a back way out of here?"

"That door has been sealed shut," Huw said. "We tried it, once we realized we were all but unguarded. I didn't think to leave by the bath."

To this point, Edgar had contributed nothing at all, but now he said, "Thus, my plan to bring them out the front is clearly the best one." He jerked his head towards the door. "We should go now while we still can."

Gareth indicated Godric's two soldiers. "Even better, we have guards to leave behind."

The first man, a fellow named Heard, said, "Karl is waiting for us in the tunnel. We should send him back to Godric so he knows we're coming."

While they waited for the Saxon to return, Myrddin edged open the front door and poked out his head. To his relief, the real guards hadn't returned, even though whatever fight Edgar had started seemed to be winding down. Myrddin felt like they'd been in the house for an hour, but as he thought back, he realized it had been less than a quarter of that time. He could still hear activity in the distance, but nobody was in their immediate vicinity.

Gareth said to Edgar, "This will be it. By entering here tonight, we have exposed ourselves as servants of Arthur."

"Is that what he is?" Nell gestured to Edgar.

It was only then that Myrddin realized that Nell had refused so far to look at the Saxon lord.

Myrddin motioned that Nell should come to him, and when she reached him, he put his arm around her waist. She was trembling.

Edgar bowed in their direction. "I did what I thought was necessary." When he didn't say more, Myrddin realized that was all the apology they were going to get.

"You could have left us behind and said nothing," Nell said. "We would have been safe enough."

"Is that what you wanted?" Edgar said. "I couldn't let Beorhtsige take King Arthur to Wroxeter without me. I assumed you felt the same, or I would have left you behind."

Nell gazed at him for a count of three, and she then took in a breath. "No, you're right. I was glad to go, and I even told Huw at the time that there was no better place for us to be than by the king's side."

Edgar nodded. "It's the fact that I hit King Arthur that angers you most."

"Yes," Nell said after another breath, "but you had to convince Beorhtsige. I understand that now."

Heard and Oswin came hustling back. "We're ready."

"Let's move." Myrddin pulled the door wide, but Edgar caught his arm before he could pass through it. "I will leave first. Nell and Huw should have their hands behind their backs as if they're tied, and you can hold their arms as if they're prisoners." He turned to Godric's men. "Get rid of your cloaks and tunics. That will help with the reek and make you less identifiable. You can stand guard after we're gone until the real guards get back. If we're lucky, they won't check the house, and they won't think twice about your presence, but simply be glad they didn't fail in their duty, once they remember it again."

Edgar was proving himself to be full of good ideas. Godric's men took their place, with strict instructions not to get involved in any conversation with Modred's men, and to meet back at the rendezvous point by the cistern entrance the moment they were free to do so.

Then, as they walked quickly away from the house, Edgar said, "We can't be concerned about our exposure. Finding King Arthur tonight is the important thing. Modred assures me that unless he is named heir at the evening meal tomorrow, King Arthur will not live to see the following sunrise."

Chapter Ten

14 December 537

Nell

UPON LEAVING THE HOUSE, in order to ensure they weren't being followed, they first lost themselves in the maze of houses in the abandoned quarters of Wroxeter before finally wending their way to the waterworks.

Nell was draggingly tired, and she kept her eyes on her feet, afraid that a loose cobble or fallen stone from one of the houses would trip her up. At one point, Myrddin caught her elbow to help her. She felt for his hand, and they walked the last hundred yards to the waterworks with clasped hands.

"When Gareth said you'd died, I thought I'd died too," she said in the lowest undertone she could manage that would still reach Myrddin's ears.

"Gareth told me what he was going to say, but I could think of no way to gain him admittance without that untruth."

"I forgive you," she said, "as long as you never do that to me again."

"To any of us," Huw said from Myrddin's other side.

As they came down the alley towards the entrance to the waterworks, clear relief crossed the young captain's face at the sight of Nell and Huw, though his brow furrowed at the appearance of Edgar beside Gareth.

"He's with us," Gareth said shortly.

"Where are Heard and Oswin?" Godric said. "My men came through the tunnel but their understanding of the situation was somewhat confused."

"Heard and Oswin are coming," Gareth said. "They were standing guard at the house until we got clear."

And even as Gareth spoke, the two soldiers came huffing up from the east, having apparently taken the same circuitous route their friends had. Oswin leaned over with his hands on his knees, breathing hard. "We weren't followed. I'm sure of it."

"No cry has been raised either," Heard said. "I told the two guards who came to relieve us that I'd checked the house and you two were asleep. We didn't stick around to make sure they took me at my word."

"Meanwhile," Edgar said, "King Arthur is missing, and we have to find him."

"The guard will change at dawn," Gareth said to Edgar, "and if the new men check on Huw and Nell, they'll discover they're gone too. By the time that happens, we need to be out of Wroxeter."

"Even then, we should be safe from Modred," Edgar said. "He drank more than usual and went to his bed with two doxies."

Godric frowned. "I'd heard he was usually more circumspect than that."

"Not on the day King Arthur is brought to his hall and he learns of Myrddin's death," Edgar said, implying that he had something to do with Modred's inebriation too.

"Those guards would know who ordered King Arthur removed from the house," Huw said.

"We can't go back there—any of us." Myrddin turned to Edgar and Gareth. "Who has the authority to alter Modred's commands other than Modred? Do we have another ally or an enemy?"

Edgar shrugged. "It must have been Modred, though I didn't hear him give the order, and I sat next to him all evening."

Nell took in a breath to brace herself for what she had to say next. She'd been dreading telling the others about her vision, afraid they wouldn't understand—and how could they? She didn't herself. "I may know."

All of the men swung around to look at her. "I thought you said the guards didn't tell you?" Gareth said.

"The guards who took the king away didn't say anything to me, but—" she hesitated just for a heartbeat and then allowed the words to rush out of her before she lost her nerve, "—I had a vision."

Myrddin put his hands on her shoulders. "When did this happen, and what did you *see*?"

Nell looked into Myrddin's face, though she couldn't make out much of his expression where they stood in the shadows, other than a certain brightness to his eyes and the flash of white teeth. "It was earlier, on the ride from Buellt. In the vision, I stood beside you, though you couldn't see me, and you fought against Saxons." She indicated the men behind Myrddin. "You fought *with* Saxons too."

"Where?" Myrddin's voice couldn't have been more urgent.

"We stood before a bell tower, which I remember tolling long and low."

"Could that mean King Arthur is being held in a tower?" Myrddin released Nell and turned back to the others. "The gatehouse tower at the palisade is *inside* the city walls. We'll never get to him there."

Nell drew his attention back to her with a hand to his arm. "I think it might have been a church—in my vision I thought it was a church—though built from huge Roman stones like these on the ground. I didn't connect my vision with the guards taking King Arthur away until now."

"Is there a church within the city?" Myrddin asked Edgar.

"Yes."

Nell gripped Myrddin's arm. "You-you didn't *see* anything like that?"

He shook his head.

Gareth cleared his throat. "It was Myrddin who *saw* you kneeling at King Arthur's side."

"That's what made Geraint and me check on the king's wellbeing after the battle," Myrddin said. "That's when we'd discovered he'd been taken. I've *seen* nothing since then."

"In my vision, we were horribly outnumbered," Nell said, deciding this wasn't something she would ever lie about again. "It was like the church by the Cam River all over again."

Myrddin made a guttural sound deep in his throat. "Has anyone seen Archbishop Dafydd lately?"

Gareth met Myrddin's eyes, and Nell saw something pass between them, a sign of recognition perhaps, as if they'd had a conversation about the archbishop earlier.

"He was at Modred's side in the hall earlier when I told Modred of your death," Gareth said.

"The archbishop appeared genuinely overjoyed to see King Arthur when we arrived this morning." Nell canted her head. "Who else among all of Modred's men would be obeyed as a matter of course? Who has the authority to move the king without Modred's knowledge or consent?"

"We can't know if he's in the church until we go," Gareth said. "We have no other leads, and I, for one, feel horribly exposed out here. We need to move now or not at all."

"Now," Myrddin said.

According to Edgar, the church lay a quarter of a mile to the southwest of the town center, very near the Severn River. The waterworks were located on the northeast corner of Wroxeter, as far from the church as it was possible to be and still be in the city. In order to reach the church, if they hoped to avoid crossing the main street that led from the city entrance to the palisade, they would have to skirt the whole of the city to the east.

The fight in front of the palisade had dispersed, and since it was well past midnight by now, they hoped they could travel without calling attention to themselves. They took it at the closest thing they could to a run, but they numbered more than a dozen, so they couldn't help but make noise. Here on the edges of the city, however, there were few guards. Before they were halfway there, Huw was clearly flagging.

"What's wrong, son?" Myrddin said.

Huw had a hand on his lower ribs. "It hurts to breathe."

"Several of Edgar's guards hit him hard. I think his ribs are bruised." Nell pressed her lips together, forcing herself not to complain again about Edgar's treatment of them.

But Edgar was loping along nearby—by accident or design she didn't know—and sensed her unspoken admonition anyway. "I haven't apologized, because I still believe I did the right thing, but I never intended for Huw to be hurt, and I am sorry."

"I'll heal," Huw said, with a glare at the Saxon lord. "I can still fight."

"We hope it doesn't come to that because you can't," Myrddin said shortly.

Once they were clear of the last guard station and had left the palisade far behind, they made directly for the church. Built of Roman stone, it was almost as large as Modred's hall and was surrounded by its own low wall. The winter moon had broken through the cloud cover again and shone thinly down. Four Saxons occupied the church yard, guarding the entrance, though without real attention being paid. Three men were gambling with dice. A fourth man snoozed on a bench with his legs stretched before him and his back braced against a gravestone. A fire blazed in a brazier at his feet, effectively ruining the night vision of the three men who were awake.

Myrddin spread his fingers wide, signaling that the men should spread out, circling around the church to come at the guards from the rear. As Godric passed Myrddin, he put a hand on his shoulder. "You stay with them. We'll handle this."

He was past them before Myrddin could protest, and so Myrddin, Nell, and Huw hunkered down together in the abandoned garden of a nearby building, a good hundred feet from the church.

Huw gazed up at the bell tower, which was all they could see from this angle. "I've never seen the like."

"The like doesn't exist in Wales," Myrddin said in an undertone. "It's a church fit for a king to worship in, which I'm sure is what Modred intends."

At Myrddin's words, Huw gave a gasp. "He doesn't know who he is, Mother."

Nell put a hand to her mouth. In all the excitement of their escape, she'd forgotten to tell Myrddin about his parentage.

Gareth scoffed as he moved to crouch next to Myrddin, looking with him through a crack in the wall that allowed them a narrow window on the churchyard. "Tell him quick, Nell."

"What are you talking about?" Myrddin said. "Tell me what?"

Gareth turned his head, looking appraisingly at the three of them, and then he gave a low laugh. "Myrddin, you are Ambrosius's son. Now ... can we get back to the task at hand?"

Chapter Eleven

14 December 537

Myrddin

"HOW DID YOU KNOW THAT when we only found out today?" Nell said to Gareth in a hoarse whisper.

Myrddin was barely listening, and could hardly credit what Nell and Gareth were talking about anyway. It was absurd to think he was Ambrosius's son. He glanced towards the churchyard in time to see Godric and six of his men rise out of the grass and fall upon the Saxon soldiers. Cursing under his breath, knowing he had taken far too passive a role in this adventure ever since he'd arrived at Wroxeter, he turned to the others, gesturing impatiently. "Enough. Tell me what is going on, in as few words as possible."

Gareth's expression turned smug. "After Ambrosius's death, Juliana discovered that Seren, your mother, who'd been her maid and Ambrosius's mistress, was with child. Juliana asked my mother to make arrangements for Seren to live with that Madog fellow in Powys. Neither Juliana nor my mother wanted to call the succession into question any more than it already was by introducing Ambrosius's bastard into the mix. Later, Juliana told my mother that you'd died at birth, along with your mother."

"She told King Arthur the same," Huw said.

"Why would she do that?" Nell said.

Gareth shrugged. "What wife wants to raise the bastard son of her husband? She probably figured you'd die before the age of five anyway. Many children do."

"And then Juliana died," Nell said, "and there was nobody to say different, especially if Madog didn't want to answer to anybody for Myrddin's care."

"How did you come to learn this?" Huw said to Gareth.

"My mother told me the story on her deathbed. She'd kept the secret, but it seemed a silly piece of information to take to her grave since the child had died." As Gareth spoke, he looked very pleased with himself.

"Then why tell it at all?" Nell said.

"I think a small part of my mother never believed Juliana had told her the whole truth. It was too easy an end, and since Arthur was still without an heir, she thought she should tell someone."

"And yet you failed ever to mention it," Nell said.

"I was ten years old!" Gareth said with some heat in his voice.

"Why didn't you tell the king?" Nell said.

"What was there to tell? Myrddin is ten years older than I and, until recently, we moved in different circles. I never questioned his origins, and it wasn't until a few weeks ago when I met Deiniol, Myrddin's foster brother, that it occurred to me that this unknown bastard of Ambrosius might be very much alive—and that he and Myrddin could be one and the same."

It was an incredible story, but he heard truth in Gareth's voice, and for all that the man could lie with the best of them, Gareth believed what he was saying.

"My father was a landless knight who'd died before I was born," Myrddin said. "Or a pig keeper. That's what Madog told me."

Gareth scoffed. "That's what he wanted you to believe. Maybe he believed it, though he wouldn't have wanted you on the throne of Wales any more than Juliana did, seeing how he was loyal to Cai, who, as long as Arthur remained childless, was as much Arthur's heir as Modred."

"Why didn't someone tell me?" The question sounded pitiful, even to Myrddin, but it rose out of him before he could stop it. "Why didn't my mother tell someone before she died?"

Gareth barked a laugh. "Telling anyone—Madog included—that you were Ambrosius's child would have marked you for death. At the very least everyone had much to gain by your ignorance, Myrddin. Until now, that is."

Nell's expression told him she understood the magnitude of the betrayal. "Until yesterday, King Arthur himself didn't know the truth."

"Of course he did," Gareth said. "He kept you close, didn't he? He knighted you, didn't he?"

Nell pulled her necklace from within her bodice. "He saw this cross for the first time at Edgar's manor. King Arthur wears an identical cross given to him by Ambrosius nine months before you were born."

Myrddin stared at it. "Cedric had the same cross, given to him by his mother, who got it from Juliana."

"As I said," Gareth said, "this has been a long time coming."

Laughter rose in Myrddin's chest, dispelling his earlier anguish. He knew exactly why Arthur hadn't told him—because he hadn't been worthy of the throne—and he still wasn't. "I can't be Ambrosius's son. I just can't."

"King Arthur says you are," Nell said gently, "and he ought to know."

Gareth made a chopping motion with his hand, in mimicry of Myrddin a moment before. "Myrddin, there's no point in denying this truth, so I say we don't. We have a job to do, and we should do it."

"That's the first thing you've said that makes sense," Myrddin said.

And then Gareth ruined it by giving him a deep bow. "My lord."

Thankfully, Myrddin was absolved from giving a response by a bird call that came from a spot nearer to the church. Godric signaled the all clear with a wave of his hand. The four Saxon soldiers were nowhere in sight.

"Stay here," Myrddin said to Nell, and then he put a hand on Huw's shoulder. "You too. Protect your mother."

Without waiting to see if he was obeyed, Myrddin sprinted for the church door, Gareth a pace behind. He didn't know where Edgar had gotten to, but revelation or no revelation, they did have a job that couldn't wait any longer. Myrddin was loath to draw any weapon in church, so he left his sword in its sheath, but he didn't dare enter unprotected. Once in the sheltering alcove by the door, Myrddin pulled out his belt knife.

After a glance at Gareth, who gave him a quick nod, Myrddin pushed at the door, which opened on silent hinges. A long nave lay before them, in the middle of which knelt the king. Archbishop Dafydd stood at the altar. Fifty candles flickered, lighting the space, though they almost went out because of the breeze wafting through the open door.

Myrddin walked towards the king, who didn't stir. "Sire?"

Dafydd left his post, moving around the king, to meet Myrddin and Gareth halfway. "Do not befoul this sanctuary with your weapons."

Gareth put away his knife. "We mean no harm. Our only concern is the king's safety."

Edgar's voice echoed from the doorway. "Your grace, Modred has betrayed your trust. If you do not release King Arthur into our custody, Modred will see him dead before the sun sets."

Archbishop Dafydd frowned. "Lord Modred swore to me—"

"He lied," Edgar said flatly, his boots thudding dully on the large flagstones that made up the nave. "If Arthur makes Modred his heir before his death, all to the good, but Modred will not allow the king ever to return to his people. I heard these words from the man's own lips."

"He wouldn't dare—" The archbishop was both affronted and disbelieving.

Nell and Huw hurtled through the doorway behind Edgar. "Men are coming. Modred's men. They must have discovered our absence from the house."

Arthur finally abandoned his prayers and rose to his feet. "I gave you my word that I would not escape, provided you saw to the safety of Huw and Nell. I will uphold that promise, even to my death, but you must also abide by yours." Standing in the center of the nave, even without his sword or armor, Arthur looked every inch a king.

"We have to move now, sire, promise or no promise," Myrddin said.

Such was Gareth's agitation that he strode forward and caught Dafydd's arm. "Why will you not see? You have before you Arthur, rightfully crowned King of Wales—and also Ambrosius's own son, who has been kept hidden for his own safety all this time. You would sacrifice them for your own pride—because you refuse to admit that you were wrong to support Modred? No king should be coerced into naming an heir. Kings rule by the Grace of God. Could the Welsh have survived this long without it? God does not support Modred."

The archbishop gaped at Gareth, not understanding—or maybe even not hearing—his meaning, and then he gasped as the sound of men shouting and the clashing of swords reached them through the open doorway. Godric's men were already engaged with Modred's.

Gareth still held the archbishop's arm in a tight grip. "Is there any way out of this church other than through the front door?"

"I-I—"

"Is there?"

More shouts and clashes came from the front of the church. Edgar drew his sword and ran forward to help Godric and his men, followed by Gareth, who, after a disgusted snort, gave up on the archbishop. Through all this, Dafydd hadn't moved, and therefore King Arthur hadn't either.

Myrddin faced the archbishop. "Please allow me at least to see to the welfare of my wife and son."

Archbishop Dafydd looked Myrddin up and down. "Are you truly Ambrosius's son?"

"Yes." King Arthur answered for him.

But Dafydd was still looking at Myrddin, who realized that he too had to answer. "It seems that I am. My mother was Seren, maidservant to Juliana and mistress to Ambrosius. I was conceived during the Christmas feast before Ambrosius died and born in September, seven months after his death. Seren died at my birth, and Queen Juliana told the few people who knew of me—King Arthur and Gareth's mother—that I'd died too. That is why my identity has remained hidden until now."

Myrddin paused. Listening to himself recite this story made his parentage suddenly far more real than it had been when Gareth had told him of it.

Dafydd looked Myrddin up and down, as if taking in his appearance and worth in one go, and finally nodded. "The church is built on top of the old public baths. The crypt connects with these and leads to a tunnel that empties into the Severn River."

Myrddin understood what the archbishop was talking about in a way he wouldn't have before tonight and went with Dafydd to the altar, hoping at the same time that these tunnels were better maintained than those on the other side of the city. With Huw's help, he pushed at one corner of the altar to reveal steps leading down. When the altar was in place, nobody could tell what lay beneath.

Nell squeezed Myrddin's hand once. "Defeat them quickly and join us." Then she hurried down the steps into the dark.

Arthur gazed down at where she and Huw had gone and then looked to Archbishop Dafydd. "You would have me follow?"

"I would, sire." The archbishop didn't even stumble over the honorific.

King Arthur turned to Myrddin. "I will guard your wife and son with my life."

The two men saluted each other, one cousin to another, and then the king disappeared down the stairs, leaving the archbishop at the top of the steps with Myrddin.

"Thank you." Myrddin didn't wait to see what the archbishop was going to do next. He ran for the door, reaching it in ten strides, and then he checked himself. A Saxon had broken through the defenders' line and launched himself up the steps towards the church door.

Godric's men were fighting in a half-circle in front of the church steps, so after thrusting his sword through the approaching Saxon's gut, Myrddin filled the space the man had come through. As he fought, the dream of King Arthur's death at the church by the Cam River rose before his eyes. This wasn't a waking vision, but merely a memory, and Myrddin prayed that he hadn't averted that future only to fall prey to an identical one two days later. That had been Nell's fear too.

The original company of attackers consisted of upwards of thirty men. Myrddin didn't know what had prompted them to come to the church. Perhaps they'd merely been on patrol or Modred's men had discovered that the Roman house was empty. A town-wide alarm had not yet been raised, however—and while Godric's men had been taken by surprise by the attack, they were a handpicked force and thus the better fighters.

The battle was brutal and yet, despite their greater numbers, within a quarter of an hour, most of the attackers had fallen. The remaining dozen or so retreated to regroup, and Myrddin took that moment to do the same. "Back! Into the church before the general alarm is raised!"

Myrddin wasn't taking charge because he was Ambrosius's son and heir to the throne of Wales—and his companions didn't obey with alacrity because of his new station either. They moved because they could see as well as he that if Modred's men returned in force, being outnumbered ten to one was not good odds.

They scrambled up the steps, closed the door, and the last man dropped the bar across it. The walls of the church were thick, but the windows were not, and through them Myrddin could hear—finally—the bonging of the warning bell at the top of the palisade tower. The alarm had been raised, and if they didn't get out of the church and across the Severn as quickly as possible, they were dead men.

Archbishop Dafydd had remained at the entrance to the crypt and, as Myrddin reached him, he handed Myrddin one of the flaming brands that had lit the nave. "I followed after them most of the way to the Severn to make sure they were safe. They should be waiting for you on the bank."

Myrddin allowed all his companions to file past him so he could bring up the rear. "Thank you again. I mistrusted your motives and judged you unfairly."

Showing a sense of humor for the first time, Archbishop Dafydd gave a low snort. "I excommunicated your king." Then he gave a slight jerk of his head. "I am sorry that Ambrosius did not live to acknowledge your birth. Illegitimate or not, any man would be proud to claim you as his son."

A man was deemed legitimate in Wales as long as his father acknowledged him, which Myrddin's had not and could not have done, since he'd been seven months dead by the time Myrddin was born. Still, Myrddin had royal blood, and with the succession hanging in the balance, it seemed that even Archbishop Dafydd was willing to overlook that failure.

"What will you tell Modred?" Myrddin said.

"The truth." The archbishop bowed slightly. "You, not Modred, are the rightful heir to the throne of Wales."

Myrddin gave a shake of his head, not understanding how Dafydd could have supported Modred all this time, but now that Myrddin had been named, he'd recanted. Myrddin didn't have time to argue, however, and he didn't think he'd waste his breath telling Dafydd that he should be fleeing with them. "What about his soldiers? They will batter down that door sooner rather than later."

"I will open it for them before that happens and berate them for disturbing the peace of my church," Dafydd said. "They will search the nave, but none of them would know about the crypt, and they will not learn of it from me. Most haven't darkened the door of any church, much less this one, in years."

Myrddin offered the archbishop his forearm, which Dafydd looked at for a moment before taking. Then he leaned forward and surprised Myrddin (and possibly himself) by embracing him. "God go with you."

"And with you," Myrddin said.

Once on the stairs, Myrddin assisted with the repositioning of the altar from below. It fell into place just in time too, as the first sounds of hammering on the door echoed through the stone church. As Myrddin loped along the low passage, he prayed that the archbishop could withstand the force of Modred's rage without breaking—and that the Saxon soldiers wouldn't expend their frustration on him rather than on the stones of the church. He estimated that they had a quarter of an hour—perhaps a half-hour at most—before it would occur to someone to send men outside of Wroxeter to look for them.

Fortunately for Myrddin, this tunnel was less like the maintenance tunnel he'd been unable to enter and more like the one under King Arthur's seat at Garth Celyn. Still, even taken at a run, the distance to the end seemed endless, but as a light appeared, Myrddin realized that he'd come hardly more than a hundred yards and had taken no more than a hundred breaths.

Gareth met him twenty feet inside the door. "Your wife is the most sensible woman I've ever met."

Myrddin allowed himself a momentary glow of pride before asking why Gareth would say such a thing.

"She sent Huw up the Severn looking for a boat, and he found one. They used it to cross safely to the far side, and then, once we appeared, Huw ferried Godric's men. You and I are the last."

Myrddin's boots slipped in the grass that lined the bank, and he caught the branch of an overhanging tree above his head. He would have swum the Severn if he had to, but he was very glad that he wasn't going to spend the rest of the night soaked from head to foot.

The boat was a typical Severn rowboat, flat-bottomed, eight feet by four. Myrddin accepted the hand of Heard, who was now manning the stern, and stepped over the side, wavering a little as the boat took his weight. He moved quickly to the front to allow Gareth room to climb aboard too.

"We could send the king, Nell, and Huw downstream in the boat while the rest of us cover the distance on foot," Myrddin said. "South seems to me the best way to go."

"We have very little time to decide, whatever we decide to do," Gareth said. "Modred's men will soon realize that we are not in the fort at all and will send out riders—whether or not he knows about the tunnel."

"And that's if Archbishop Dafydd can hold his tongue," Myrddin said.

The boat hit the bank, and Edgar reached down to grasp Myrddin's hand and haul him out of the boat. "I say we strike out west for my castle at Montgomery. It's twenty-five miles as the crow flies, and the closest stronghold."

"No," Gareth said immediately. "We should go south, even retrace our steps to Buellt where we left our men. Modred will expect us to go west." Still arguing, Gareth and Edgar came up the bank.

King Arthur stood with his hands on his hips, facing west, as if he could see any of the above-mentioned places from here if only he looked hard enough. He turned to Myrddin. "What say you?"

Gareth and Edgar immediately ceased speaking. A month ago, Myrddin would have stuttered out his reply, but Ambrosius's paternity aside, Myrddin wasn't the same man as he'd been then. "I say we make for Mt. Badon, if not Gaer Fawr a few miles further on, but even still not as far as Montgomery. The fort at Badon was destroyed and never rebuilt, but Gaer Fawr still stands and remains a formidable stronghold." He turned to look at the others, and he could tell that his idea was being met with interest by their thoughtful expressions.

King Arthur nodded and without looking at Gareth or Edgar, he instead settled a hand on Myrddin's shoulder. "I have been a foolish old man, but I have learned the error of my ways. No longer shall Wales be divided between king and heir. No longer shall we fear Modred's wrath." The king wore no sword himself, but he surprised Myrddin by pulling Myrddin's own from its sheath. "Kneel!"

Myrddin obeyed on instinct, as he'd obeyed every command Arthur had given him since he was sixteen years old. They didn't have time for this, but he didn't have the voice to say as much to the king. Edgar and Gareth, Huw and Nell, Godric and all of his men also sank to one knee and bowed their heads.

King Arthur settled the flat of the sword on Myrddin's right shoulder. "Ten years ago, it was my honor to knight you on the field of battle. Little did I know that I was knighting my own cousin." He drew in a breath. "Myrddin ap Ambrosius, I name you as my heir!" King Arthur's voice was exultant. "Rise, Myrddin, Prince of Wales."

"Long live Myrddin ap Ambrosius! Long live King Arthur!" The echoing chorus rose into the air, a triumphant call despite the danger and the dark.

"And now," King Arthur said, motioning with his hands that everyone should rise, "we run."

Book Five: Frost
Against the Hilt

Frost Against the Hilt

LOVE, MAGIC, FAITH. All roads lead to Camlann as Arthur gathers his men for a single battle—a final great contest against the full might of Modred and his Saxon army. Wales will win all or lose all in one last throw of the dice.

Frost Against the Hilt is the fifth and final installment in the *Lion of Wales* series.

Chapter One

---⚬---

---⚬---

NELL CROUCHED IN THE ditch, twenty feet from the nearest sentry posted on the outskirts of Modred's encampment, and trembled. Her own army lay a quarter-mile to the west behind the safety of Caer Fawr, the hillfort that had served her people for hundreds of years. For the last few days, Nell's dreams and thoughts, awake or asleep, had been full of nothing but Arthur's death by Modred's hand on the field of battle. A death that, if she did nothing, would come tomorrow.

Nell bent her head in the darkness and breathed deeply, focusing on the task before her. It was no coincidence that Modred had constructed his encampment over the top of Roman ruins, which centuries ago Caer Fawr had opposed. By choosing the ruins rather than the high ground, Modred was—as at Wroxeter—basing his right to rule in historic victories. He was telling the Welsh that his kingdom was the rightful heir of the Roman Empire, just as he was King Arthur's rightful heir, and for the Britons to defy him from Caer Fawr would be as ineffective now as it had been then.

Modred's men were in the process of throwing up a palisade that would protect their forces from a surprise attack from the Welsh, proving Modred had learned from the disaster of Buellt.

They'd cut down a great number of trees already, first to make room for the army of men at Modred's disposal and then to provide posts for the palisade. With each tree felled, the woods receded farther from the camp. If Nell had waited any longer to approach, she would have had hardly any trees to hide in.

The nearest sentry was well forward of the torches, almost to the tree line, which made sense because the fort was lit up like day. If he were closer, he'd have no night vision at all. As it was, he was squinting towards the forest, and the stiffness in his shoulders told Nell that he was afraid. The notion gave Nell courage, because she was afraid too.

Bracing herself for the endeavor, Nell rose out of the shadows, already having pulled off the headdress that marked her as a married woman. She sauntered onto the road that led to the main entrance to the fort and strolled past the guard, who merely eyed her for a moment before waving her through. He knew her kind—or so he thought. She'd been watching the fort for some hours now. The camp followers of Modred's great army nearly outnumbered the soldiers. It seemed as if the whole of Mercia had come to watch tomorrow's battle—not to participate in the way that the women of Wales, many of whom would fight beside their men tomorrow, would participate—but to gawk and cheer the final triumph of Modred's forces over Arthur's.

And a final triumph it would be. Even without her *sight*, she could have foretold that. Never mind that the lords of Wales had come at Arthur's call, the Welsh were outnumbered, as they always would be, by the great Saxon horde that filled the fields and valleys of what had once been British land—all the way to the English Channel. Their numbers were ten times greater than the population of native Britons; thus the army Modred could call upon was also ten times greater.

The moment Myrddin had told Nell that Modred's army had arrived, and in such numbers, Nell's decision had been made for her. The only way to win this war, the only way to ensure the survival of Wales and everyone Nell loved, was to do what she'd set out to do weeks ago. That day, she'd been waylaid by a stray party of marauding Saxon warriors, led by the now deceased Agravaine. Myrddin had rescued her from them and then been horrified when she'd finally told him her plan: she'd intended to infiltrate Modred's castle at Denbigh, disguised as a serving maid or a whore, and when the opportunity arose, put a knife into Modred's heart.

She hadn't killed Modred that night, thwarted as she'd been by Myrddin. At the time, she'd tried to shake him off, but he hadn't taken no for an answer, and she hadn't had the will to fight him. Since that day, she and Myrddin had done everything in their power to ensure Arthur's survival. They'd averted his death, which they'd dreamed of for two lifetimes. And still, King Arthur was back to exactly where he'd started: facing certain death on the battlefield. And this time it really would be at Modred's hands.

As if the loss of Arthur wasn't bad enough, it was what she knew would come afterwards that had made the decision to sacrifice herself an easy one. Although Myrddin would take Arthur's place, he would have no choice but to call a retreat. Secure in his victory, Modred would then pursue the Welsh army through Wales, scattering the other Welsh lords and sending their armies into disarray. Sadly, even once they eventually regrouped, the lords of Wales would descend into bickering, and Myrddin wouldn't be able to hold them together to face the Saxons when they came again. If Nell didn't act, not only would Wales be overrun before Easter, but Myrddin and Huw would fall in battle alongside their countrymen.

That Myrddin couldn't fill King Arthur's shoes wasn't a slight on Myrddin, but an indictment of the men Arthur ruled. Each one saw himself as having the potential to be high king and cared not how he achieved the throne. If nothing else, Nell understood two things. The first was that respect came with battle. Even if Arthur's immediate allies acknowledged Myrddin's worth, without Arthur's guiding hand, Myrddin would not be given the time to win the support of the rest of the barons.

The second thing was that her life was a small price to pay for peace. Arthur would live. Myrddin and Huw would live. Once she killed Modred, as she should have done weeks ago, the greatest threat to Wales' sovereignty for a generation would be eliminated.

More confident now, Nell passed the guards on either side of the not quite finished gate and entered the camp. Ahead, in the exact center, lay Modred's tent, and Nell decided not to put this off any longer. As unconcernedly and as casually as possible, she strolled over to the open-air kitchen. There was a slight chance that someone would recognize her, since it was only a few days ago that she'd been among them at Wroxeter, but Nell's attire and attitude were a far cry from what they had been there. She'd been a companion to King Arthur himself and the wife of Myrddin. Here, she was a serving wench at best, a whore at worst. Even if recognition of her face niggled at the back of someone's mind, it would be difficult to place her so far out of the context in which they'd last seen her.

"I have been sent to bring food to Lord Modred," she said in English to the cook. Nell had been raised in the borderlands between England and Wales, and her first husband had been Saxon, so she spoke the language fluently.

The head cook gave her the once-over and apparently didn't find her wanting; his accompanying grimace was not for her. "We're late with his meal, I know."

"Perhaps a carafe of wine will ease him until the meat is ready," she said.

The cook lifted his chin to point to where barrels of mead and beer waited to be tapped. "Over there. Tell Osric I sent you."

Nell went where she was bid. In short order, she held a carafe in one hand and a tray with three goblets in the other. Somehow, she was certain that Modred would not be sleeping alone tonight. With sure steps, she weaved in and out among the fires until she approached the two men who guarded Modred's pavilion. Twenty feet on a side, it was twice as big as those around it.

"I was sent to bring wine."

"He's been waiting." The man jerked his head to indicate that Nell should enter immediately.

Now was the tricky part. Modred had stared into her face not five days ago at Wroxeter. As with the guards and kitchen staff, she was counting on her loosened hair, coarse gown, and the low light inside the pavilion to confuse him. With breath held, she ducked through the doorway. As it turned out, Modred was alone, bent over a table on which a map had been laid. Nell's feet stuck to the bent grass that formed the floor of his quarters.

But Modred barely glanced at her. "Put it over there." He gestured with one hand to indicate a second table near his sleeping furs.

She moved to obey, but before she could set down the tray, she found herself caught around the middle, swung around such that the carafe and goblets went flying, and thrown to the ground. As she lay on her back on the bed, Modred leapt on top of her, his expression utterly gleeful.

"I never forget a face, my dear."

Even as Nell reached for the knife in her boot with which she'd intended to kill Modred, he pulled his own knife from the sheath at his waist and thrust it downwards towards her throat—

Chapter Two
14 December 537
Myrddin

MYRDDIN FELL TO HIS knees, gripping the post in front of him and hanging on for dear life. His breath came in choking gasps at the horror of what he'd just seen.

Huw's hand came down on his shoulder. "What is it, Father?"

Myrddin opened his eyes, gazing blindly around the barn in which they'd taken temporary shelter. His male companions gaped at him, but Nell knelt on the ground near one of the stalls, her arms wrapped around her belly and her face as pale as a new linen sheet.

"Did you *see*?" Nell and Myrddin said to each other at the same time.

He swallowed. "What did you see?" He realized in that instant that some of Godric's men were still coming through the open doorway to the barn. It had taken no more than the space between breaths to dream as he and Nell had.

The barn belonged to a minor Saxon lord, who had not yet ridden to Wroxeter at Modred's call. King Arthur had stood before the thane and demanded his horses. With only two warriors at his back—one his own daughter, who wore breeches like a man and carried a bow—against King Arthur's dozen, he'd had no choice but to give way. The thane had been angry at losing his horses but delighted at the gold he'd been given in return. "If Modred learns that I helped you—"

"We won't tell him, if that's what worries you," King Arthur had said in a rare moment of levity. "I suggest you run—as far and as fast as you can away from here. Come back in a few days."

The man had departed for a neighboring manor rather than help them further.

Nell put a trembling hand to her mouth. "I *saw* Modred's camp before Caer Fawr. And you?"

"The same." He staggered over to her and fell to his knees at her side. "You—you—I can't believe you would do such a thing."

She stared into his face, her eyes wide and unseeing, and then her eyes came back into focus, and she looked over his shoulder to where King Arthur stood. "Modred is gathering an army ten times larger than we have. We cannot overcome such a force, no matter how many men come to meet us at Caer Fawr."

"Then we don't go to Caer Fawr." Gareth's dark hair was plastered to his head from sweat and snow, which had started falling again in the last hour. "That seems obvious enough."

King Arthur put out a hand to stay the younger man. "Let her speak."

But Nell had transferred her gaze back to Myrddin. "What do we do?"

"What we always do: adapt. Gareth's suggestion is probably a good one, but I'd like to think we can do more than that." Myrddin pushed to his feet and looked at the men who surrounded him: Gareth and Edgar, two great lords in their own right, one Welsh, one Saxon; Godric, Lord Cedric's Saxon captain; Huw, Myrddin's son; and nine Saxon men-at-arms, who served under Godric, all that was left of the twenty men who'd left Buellt with him two days ago.

A lifetime ago.

"Gareth may be right that we would be wise to carefully consider the place where we make our stand, but our path is laid before our feet. The battle that is coming is a fact that we cannot change. It looms over me even after the dream has ended, and it is all I can see."

"It is all I see as well." Nell grasped Myrddin's hand for assistance in rising to her feet.

"One final stand?" King Arthur said.

Myrddin bowed his head to Arthur. "Yes. And whether it is in the field before Caer Fawr or on different ground, Modred not only will come, but *he is coming*."

"I still don't see why this battle is inevitable." Gareth stabbed a finger towards the door. "No Saxon lord seeks a fight in the middle of winter."

Edgar scoffed. "Did we not just suffer through a battle at Buellt? Did we not just leave Wroxeter under great duress and even now are fleeing the forces of Modred? He has hundreds of fighting men—thousands—all craving war. More importantly, they all need to be fed. I may not be able to see as Myrddin does, but he is right that Modred is coming and will bring everything and everyone he has to bear against us. The next time we face him, he will have all his might behind him. I suggest we be the ones to choose the ground."

Gareth was not to be persuaded. "I disagree. The Saxons have not forgotten Mt. Badon. Why do you think they have engaged us in skirmish after skirmish but Buellt was the closest they've come to committing to a definitive fight? They fear to lose again as they lost then."

"Other lords might fear to lose, Gareth," Nell said, "but Modred was a child when King Arthur fought that battle. He doesn't believe that fate will be his."

The heavy weight of the vision pressed on the space behind Myrddin's eyes. Gareth could think what he liked; it was Arthur whom Myrddin and Nell had to convince. He turned to the king. "You must face him, my lord. But unless we—" He broke off to stare at the loose hay scattered at his feet.

"Unless we what?" Arthur said.

Nell's eyes were bright as if she had a fever. "Unless we change the future in some way, do things differently from what Myrddin and I have seen, you will die in that engagement. We will all die."

"Thus, as I said, we don't meet him." Gareth grumbled under his breath and paced away to the door to look out at the snow, which was coming down harder than before—or seemed like it was, now that they were sheltered from the worst of it. "Maybe our more immediate concern should be who it is that chases us and how many come. Why have they not caught us? We're lucky to have come this far without being stopped. The dogs can't be far behind."

Nell stretched out a hand to Gareth as if to bring him back into the circle of counselors, though he was out of reach. "We will do what we must, Gareth, as we always have. There is no doubt that Modred has sent men after us—"

"—which means we must do what we can right now to prepare," Myrddin said, "and we don't have time for dithering."

"What do you suggest?" Gareth swung back around. "I say we send the king and you on your way immediately."

"That's exactly what we mustn't do. It's more important that we send you and Edgar west," Myrddin said. "You need to marshal your men, especially those that don't yet know their true allegiance."

Edgar blew out a breath. "You are referring to *my* men."

"Lord Cedric will come if you call, my lord." Godric spoke for the first time. Myrddin didn't know if he simply hadn't had anything to say, or if he had become lost in the rapid exchange of Welsh.

King Arthur nodded. "You are right that this is the time for choosing, and if ever I needed Cedric as an ally, it is now."

Gareth wasn't having any of that either. "We have sixteen riders and only three horses. What can we do with so few?"

"Six of you go now, riding double," Myrddin said. "As soon as each pair comes upon a settlement, get yourselves a second horse and then ride for Wales as if the hounds of Arawn were at your heels."

"Which they might well be." Arthur moved to Gareth, who still had not acquiesced. "What is it?"

"Gah! Don't you see?" He threw up his hands. It was rude and despairing at the same time, which revealed more about what he was feeling than anything else could have. "You three are Wales. Without you, we fall. And Modred won't forgive my betrayal a second time."

"All the more reason for you to ride as hard and as fast as you can for Wales to ensure that we don't fall," Myrddin said. "What would you have the king do—retreat to Anglesey? Hide in a cave in Snowdonia? Modred is marching on Wales. If we don't meet him, if we don't draw him to us for a great battle to decide all, he will ride through Wales like a hurricane, burning, raping, and pillaging until he finds each one of us defending our forts alone or until we finally come out to meet him. And by then the ground will be of his choosing, not ours."

Gareth stared at Myrddin. "That's what you saw?"

"Yes." Myrddin kept his gaze steady on Gareth's face. He didn't tell him that the fact of Modred's coming and the outcome of the battle had been ancillary to the dream—basic facts that he'd known in the moment he'd dreamt because Nell in the dream had known them. For now, Nell's death and the rest of what he'd seen would have to wait for a quieter moment with Nell, possibly Huw, and the king.

"That leaves ten of us remaining with more than fifteen miles to go to Caer Fawr," Huw said.

"Which is where you are *not* going, remember?" Gareth said.

"Wherever you go, you won't make it running." The thane's daughter stepped through the doorway, still dressed as she'd been in men's gear. Tall and slender and of an age with Huw, she'd braided her honey-colored hair in a long plait and wound it around her head to keep it out of the way of her bow and quiver. "You're going to have to stand and fight. They're coming."

Myrddin's head came up as he too heard the baying of Modred's hounds.

King Arthur went to the doorway and looked out. "They were so far behind, I hoped they hadn't been able to track us in the snow, but then, it wasn't as if our tracks weren't clear." He looked at the girl. "Why aren't you with your father?"

"He's not my father. My mother married him four years ago after the death of my true father. I'm Welsh and stand for you, my lord."

"You must go now!" Myrddin wasn't talking to the girl but to Edgar and Gareth. "Huw too."

"No." Huw shook his head vehemently. "I will not run away."

"Edgar and Gareth aren't running away," Myrddin said. "They're rousing the countryside."

"But if I went, I would be. You can't protect me, Father. Not from this."

Grief left over from the vision stabbed all the way through Myrddin. He wanted to force the issue, make Huw leave and take Nell with him. "If I send you riding to Wales with Edgar and Gareth, it could be a way to change the future just a little."

"I thought you said the future couldn't be changed—that the battle was coming no matter what?" Huw said.

Myrddin shook his head, finding it impossible to explain. The battle was inevitable. The events around it, however, were not, and he would not follow any path the dream had laid out for him. They needed to act otherwise, in as many ways as possible. But then again, maybe he was wrong. Maybe in that dreaming past, he'd sent Huw away, and Huw had still returned in time to fight and die at Myrddin's side.

Nell rubbed Myrddin's shoulder. "There are no good answers."

He nodded. Every way he looked showed him the same image of Nell in an unmarked grave, dead, as King Arthur would be dead, by Modred's hand.

"Nell and Huw are right, Myrddin. He has a right to make a stand as much as you and I do. We should prepare." King Arthur pointed to Edgar and Gareth. "And you should ride."

"Where will you go once you defeat these trackers?" Gareth said. "We can't bring men if we don't know where we're riding to!"

The girl, whose name Myrddin still didn't know, spoke again. "My uncle rules at Caer Caradoc, my lord. He has ever been a loyal ally, and his stronghold isn't far—fewer than ten miles from here."

Arthur swung around to look at her. "King Cador is your uncle? I did not know he still lived."

"Yes, my lord," the girl said. "He fought with you at Mt. Badon. He has held his lands for you for thirty years. He will stand with you again against Modred."

"He is a cousin on my mother's side, not that kinship is a reason to trust him, given my family." Arthur looked back to Edgar and Gareth. "You heard the girl. We will be at Caer Caradoc!"

The baying of the hounds had been growing closer by the heartbeat. Thus, Edgar, Gareth, and four of Godric's men—those who were lightest along with anyone who'd suffered wounds at Wroxeter and might not be fully capable in a fight—raced out the back of the barn in the opposite direction from which the hounds were coming. One of them would go to Cedric personally and tell him of King Arthur's need.

Meanwhile, Huw approached the girl. "You should leave this place. Find your father."

"I already told you that he is not my father."

"Why do you live with him if your uncle is such a great lord?" Huw said.

"After my mother died last year, Uncle Cador tried to arrange for me to live with him, but my stepfather thought to use me for an alliance with a neighboring thane. Either that or—" she indicated her quiver, "—as long as I was unmarried he didn't have to pay a man to hunt or to guard his home."

With a finger, Huw touched the fletching of one of the arrows in her quiver. "Have you ever killed a man before?"

For the first time, some of the girl's confidence wavered. "No. Have you?"

Huw's expression softened. "Yes."

King Arthur snapped his fingers at Huw. "Our need is pressing, and I will take all the help I can get. Girl, what is your name?"

"Anwen, my lord."

"I assume you are proficient with that weapon?"

"Yes, my lord."

"Are we going to kill the dogs?" That was Alan, one of the younger Saxons.

Myrddin rolled his eyes. "Of course we aren't going to kill the dogs—not unless we have to. The girl's bow is going to be used on men."

King Arthur turned to the others. "The dogs are easy. A few of us will lure them into the barn and shut the door behind them so they are trapped inside. The rest of us will take on the men who follow."

With an economy of motion afforded only to the young and agile, Huw swung up onto the rafter above his head and perched there. "Get me a rope. I will pull the doors closed behind the dogs while someone drops the bar on the outside. I'll leave by the hayloft door."

Nell shivered. "I'll bar the door behind the dogs. The rest of you go do whatever you have to do."

"I guess this is as good a way as any to get ourselves some horses." Myrddin grasped Nell by the waist and pulled her to him for a kiss. "We'll be fine."

"You'd better be."

Fortunately, the farmer's barn had no shortage of rope. Leaving Huw and Nell with their hasty preparations, Myrddin ran with the others out of the barn. He made sure to stay exactly in the tracks they'd made when they'd come in not even a half-hour ago. Dogs were smart, but they were single-minded creatures, and if one of Myrddin's companions veered away from the main track, one of the dogs might follow, and then they'd lose them all. Perhaps it would have been wiser to put the dogs on the trail of Gareth and Edgar since, on horseback, they could outpace dogs over time. But then the men who followed might catch up too. Better to end this here.

Once in the deeper woods through which the path ran, Godric caught hold of an overhanging branch and swung himself onto it, in much the same move that Huw had used in the barn. "Up!" He reached down and pulled the girl Anwen after him. "Climb higher and aim well."

"Yes, my lord." Anwen started through the branches as if climbing trees was something she did every day. Maybe it was. Maybe even this tree.

King Arthur stopped beneath Godric's branch and looked up at the grinning Saxon, who was looking down at him. "No."

Myrddin caught the king's elbow, pretty sure that he himself wasn't going to be as agile as Godric either. "I have another way."

Twenty yards on, a series of rocky outcroppings buttressed the path on one side. Myrddin and Arthur clambered onto them to crouch at the top so they could overlook the path. The snow continued to fall steadily, which was good. It would soon coat them completely, hiding their dark cloaks enough to allow them to blend in to some degree with the rocks around them.

"We forgot one thing," Myrddin said.

Godric groaned from his perch in the tree. "I know it."

"I'll do it." Alan, the youngest of Godric's men, swung down from his branch and dropped to the ground in the middle of the path. "I'm fastest."

"You'd better be," Godric said. "We can't afford to lose you, even if you are a worthless excuse for a soldier."

All of the Saxons chuckled at the obvious jest. Alan, as far as Myrddin could tell, had fought well at Wroxeter and, presumably, at Buellt too, since he'd lived. "Don't worry." Alan went up on his toes and down again, preparing himself. "As soon as I'm inside the barn, I'll swing up to the rafter like Huw did."

Arthur had been looking east towards the sound of baying hounds, coming closer and closer. They must have been at least a mile away when Anwen had brought the baying to their attention. The only reason Modred's hunters hadn't reached this spot already was because they'd started so much later than Myrddin and his companions. They were nearly ten miles from Wroxeter, and not even dogs could keep to a flat-out run for so many miles.

Myrddin braced himself on his rock. "Here they come!"

Alan didn't wait for the dogs to appear out of the snow but started running at top speed towards the barn. Myrddin was confident he would make it, but he was sorry that they'd be one short when they fell upon the men who came after. As much as he hadn't wanted to use her, they needed Anwen now.

"How many, do you think?" Arthur pulled a knife from the sheath at his waist. Modred had taken the king's weapons, including his fearsome sword, Caledfwlch, so Arthur had borrowed the knife from one of Godric's Saxons. Huw had also left Wroxeter without appropriate weaponry and had been forced to borrow. Fortunately, Saxons carried multiple knives as a matter of course.

Before Wroxeter, King Arthur might have said that his sword was more valuable than his life, but of course that hadn't proved to be the case. Hopefully, once Modred was defeated and Wroxeter fell into Welsh hands, Myrddin could get Caledfwlch back for him. In a moment they would have swords to spare, or they would have no need of swords ever again.

"It depends on how many men and dogs Modred sent and in how many directions," Myrddin said. "Presumably, this is not the only hunting party."

Arthur crouched lower on the rock. "I despise the need to presume anything. I didn't become High King of Wales on presumption."

Three long and rangy bloodhounds bounded into view, running flat out towards Alan, who had a hundred-foot head start. He was going to need it.

Once the dogs passed by, baying louder than ever, Myrddin and the others silently waited for the men who would follow, praying that there wouldn't be too many for seven men and a girl to handle.

King Arthur growled low. "You haven't seen this in any vision, have you?"

"No, my lord."

Arthur nodded, as if that was a piece of information he'd been missing. "I know that what you see appears sometimes like a path laid before your feet, and at other times like a stone wall in front of you. But you and I both know that you do not see all ends. Don't forget that our real task is to live the life we've been given, without regard to possible futures. We have only one future. That's all we've ever had."

Chapter Three

EVERY SOLDIER HUW HAD ever spoken to had told him that waiting was far worse than fighting. Once the battle began, there was no time for thinking, for fear, or for anything but immediate survival.

He had fought before, of course. He'd been knighted by King Arthur himself after they defeated a traitorous incursion into Aber. And he found that he had to agree with how hard it was to wait, especially today, since he was perched inside the barn and couldn't see anything that was happening outside. *Why oh why had he swung up onto this beam?* He could tell himself that it was because he was the youngest of the group, except perhaps for the girl, and that he'd felt at the time that his sacrifice would give them the best chance for success.

But the truth was that he'd been showing off for Anwen. This was her barn. She could have done this job instead of him, and then he could have been the one out there with his father. He cursed again at his stupidity and pride and swore that he wouldn't allow it to get the better of him again.

The baying of the hounds grew steadily louder until Huw felt like the barn was shaking with the noise. *He* was shaking with the noise, which was the entire intent of loosing them this way, he was sure. The hounds bayed to invoke fear in their prey. Intellectually, Huw knew this to be true, but every instinct told him to run screaming from them anyway.

He also knew that the hounds were the least of their problems. They would be dealt with, either by being locked in the barn or with a quick knife to the throat. It was the men who followed them that were the greater concern.

A shout came from the front of the barn. "Now, my lady!"

Huw recognized Alan's voice, and prayed that Nell had just leapt from the ladder on which she was perched at the back of the barn and was even now running around to the front to drop the bar across the doors, once Huw closed them. A heartbeat later, Alan burst through the door, the hounds hard on his heels. He reached for the same beam on which Huw was standing, even as one of the dogs leapt up and bit Alan's ankle, hanging on with a locked jaw.

Alan cursed. Though Huw wanted to help him, he had other business first, which was to yank on the ropes he held in each hand and the doors swung to. Once done, he didn't wait to hear if Nell had done her job and grasped Alan's arm to haul him upwards. The dog held on, and Huw lay on his belly on the beam in order to slash at the dog's muzzle with his knife. The dog yelped and let go of Alan's ankle, and Alan scrambled all the way up to lie on the beam like Huw, breathing hard and near to weeping.

"I thought I was a goner," he said.

"They're just dogs," Huw said. "They're only threatening if you don't have a blade and if you let them scare you."

Alan shivered. "Maybe to you."

Ignoring the barking dogs below him, Huw straightened. He was taller than the roof at this location allowed, so he had to hunch over to make his way along the rough beam towards the loft. "Come on. Let's get out of here. Can you move?" Alan's heel was bleeding profusely. Huw hoped the dog hadn't severed something important.

"Enough," Alan said.

In single file, they picked their way to the loft, which was half the size of the main floor below, climbed out the hayloft door, and took the ladder to the ground. Nell met them at the bottom, breathing hard herself. "It's done."

She'd left distinct footprints in the snow, coming around from the front of the barn, so he could have figured that out for himself. Instead of saying so, Huw hugged her.

The baying of the hounds resounded through the open hayloft door, but the dogs couldn't get out. Ignoring the sound as best they could, Nell took one side of Alan and Huw the other, and they helped him hobble to an overturned bucket near the well. Once they'd moved away from the barn, the noise of the dogs diminished slightly, muffled by the wood. Huw's heart began to settle into a more normal pattern.

"What happened to you?" Nell said as they sat Alan down. She picked up his foot and rested it on her knee. The snow was falling as hard as ever, but she ignored it. Blood dripped from the gash in Alan's heel. The dog had bitten all the way through his boot and ripped the leather away.

Alan grimaced as Nell gently worked the torn boot off his foot. "I wasn't quite quick enough, I guess."

With the boot on the ground, the puncture wounds from the dog's teeth were clearly evident in Alan's ankle. The gashes needed to be cleaned soon, or they would fester, and Alan could die.

"If you were afraid of dogs, why did you volunteer to lead them to the barn?" Huw said.

"I figured I was the best choice, since the dogs would smell my fear and come for me."

Huw gawked for a moment, and then he laughed in appreciation of Alan's bravery. "My father says real courage is doing what must be done despite your fear." He shook Alan's shoulder. "You are a brave man."

"Thank you, my lord."

Huw faltered at Alan's use of his title. He still hadn't quite gotten his head around the fact that his father was the heir to the throne of Wales, which meant that he was too. Inside, he was still just Huw.

Nell looked up from inspecting the damage to Alan's heel and gave Huw a rueful smile. Though she would never show it to anyone but him or Myrddin, he thought she might be feeling the same uncertainty. By marrying a knight, she'd become a lady, but that was still far and away different from being a queen.

Huw transferred his hand to Nell's shoulder and squeezed. "You two stay here. I'm off to help the others."

"Hey! Wait for me!" Alan struggled to rise, but Nell was still holding his foot, so he didn't get very far.

Huw couldn't wait, and since Nell didn't try to stop him, he set off at a run, avoiding the path and thinking it would be better not to come at the battle directly. He ran flat out for only fifty yards before the distinctive sound of clashing swords and cursing men came to him. Their location wasn't far from the barn.

Within heartbeats, the terrain turned from flat ground to rock and, before he could catch himself, he sprawled face down, tripped by a small tree growing out of the rock but hidden beneath the snow. Cursing, Huw pushed himself up, thankful for the gloves that protected his hands but wincing at the pain in his right knee and at his ripped pant leg.

The fighting continued ahead of him, and the longer it lasted, the more likely it was that his father and Huw's companions were outnumbered. Huw was near to panic at the thought—but he'd learned something since finding his father, and that included a healthy respect for the sharp edge of a blade and a dose of caution when facing the sword of an enemy.

Knife in hand and moving a little more slowly and warily, Huw struggled to the top of a rocky outcrop. Trees grew out of the rock in places, and their leaves would have hidden him from view had it been summer. As it was, nobody was looking for him or up at him, and he crouched above the fight. His father and the others had squared off against a dozen of Modred's men.

Huw took in the whole of the battle as a single scene, as if it were a tapestry on the wall of a castle, and then he launched himself from the top of the rock onto the back of the man King Arthur was fighting. The man went down in a heap beneath Huw, who recovered enough an instant later to thrust his bared knife into the unprotected area at the back of the man's neck. It was just as well that Huw didn't have a sword to use, since it was all but useless for fighting in such close quarters.

On his feet a moment later, hardly stopping even to breathe, he spun around and drove the knife to the hilt into the back of another Saxon—and then had a moment of utter panic that he'd killed one of Godric's men by mistake. But no, the man he'd killed had been fighting one of Godric's men, a Saxon named Leofwine, who gave Huw a sharp nod and a relieved smile.

And just like that, the battle was over. Looking around at the dead men on the ground, Huw acknowledged that his friends had been facing stupid odds: seven men against twelve, and only one better after Huw had joined the fight. But the little Welsh band had been afforded the element of surprise—and they'd had one more fighter in Anwen with her bow. Half of the enemy dead had an arrow sticking out of them in one place or another. Most of her shots hadn't been fatal, but any arrow wound, whether to torso or limb, could slow a man—enough to have allowed one of Godric's warriors to finish the enemy soldier off.

Unfortunately, Godric had lost two of his company. Though these men hadn't been close friends with Huw, he'd known them from the time he'd joined Lord Cedric's forces, and it was a shock to see their blood mingling in the snow with that of the men

Modred had sent. Huw's little company was down to six fighting men: King Arthur, Myrddin, Huw, Godric, Leofwine, and Osgar. The latter two were strong fighters in their mid-twenties. But then, so had been the two who'd fallen. They also had Nell and Alan, of course, but he was wounded and had to be considered out of the fight.

Anwen swung down from her tree and landed in the snow a few feet from Huw. Her face was pale but impassive. He had to assume, however, that being young like him, she was struggling with what she'd just done. He stepped closer to her. "You did well. I wouldn't have known that you had never fought before if you hadn't told me."

She looked down at the ground, perhaps unused to praise or not thinking she deserved it for killing men, and didn't answer.

Meanwhile, Godric pulled off his helmet and dropped it to the ground, and King Arthur leaned against the rocky outcrop from which Huw had jumped. Arthur's blade dripped blood into the snow. "You saved my life, Huw."

Huw looked down at his naked blade, as bloody as the king's. He'd acted on instinct and without thought. "I suppose so, my lord."

"Knighting you appears to have been one of my better decisions."

Huw gazed wide-eyed at the king, unsure of how to take that comment, but then Myrddin put his arm around Huw's shoulders. "As opposed to when you knighted me, my lord."

King Arthur laughed. "Oh yes. I've come to regret that." The king held out his hand to Huw, who stepped forward to shake the king's forearm. It was only then that Huw recognized what the banter had been for: it was a way to dissipate the rage and fear that had come with battle. Godric's men, even as they were going through the belongings of the dead men, were making similar jests, though in English.

"Nell and Alan are well?" Myrddin drew Huw's attention back to him.

"Alan was bitten in the ankle," Huw said.

Myrddin tipped his head to indicate the barn. "Run back and tell Nell we're coming. We'll gather the horses and follow in a moment."

"He doesn't have to, Myrddin. We're here." Nell appeared in the pathway ahead, leading one of the dead Saxon's horses with Alan on its back. "How many more horses are there—" She stopped at the sight of the dead men on the ground, her face turning nearly as white as the snow falling around her.

"There should be twelve in total," Myrddin said. "Modred sent more men than I expected."

Huw looked at his father. That was one thing Myrddin might have to change about himself when he became king: he admitted fault or ignorance too easily. Then again, these men—Saxon men, no less—had followed him into battle without hesitation, and maybe Myrddin's ability to consult and to admit fault was part of the reason why they did. King Arthur had become a legend unto himself, which their escape from Wroxeter would do nothing to diminish. But Myrddin had lived as one of them, fought as one of them.

The question that Huw knew his father was asking every hour, because Huw was asking that question of himself, was if it would be enough. That which garnered him the respect of men-at-arms and foot soldiers was not what would gain him the allegiance of the other barons of Wales. King Arthur's heir Myrddin might be, but to become high king of Wales, crowned by the council, wasn't entirely a matter of heredity. Myrddin, and Huw by extension, would have to lead men into far larger battles than this—and win.

Chapter Four

14 December 537

Nell

SINCE CADOR HAD HELPED Arthur defeat the Saxons thirty years ago at Mt. Badon, he'd maintained the defenses at Caer Caradoc and held the fort as the first line of defense against the Saxon threat. Located ten miles southwest of Wroxeter, Caer Caradoc stood on the leading edge of a line of hills that tracked westward to Wales.

Northward, the fort overlooked the field of Camlann and the long stretch of farms and pastureland that the Saxons wanted for themselves. It was Britain's rich land that had encouraged the Saxons to take Britain from the Britons in the first place. The invaders had come from a barren country across the water, with land too poor to sustain their people, and they viewed the blood they'd shed in taking Britain as a consecration of sorts, even a covenant between them and the land. Now that they had it, they would fight to the death to keep it, just as the Welsh would do to keep what was left to them and prevent Wales from being overrun.

Cador had enlarged Caer Caradoc beyond its pre-Roman size until its palisades and ditches were a maze of defenseworks that even the ten thousand Saxons from Nell's dream would find hard to penetrate. That was all very well and good, but winning this war did not mean staying within the safety of the walls. King Arthur would have to come out and face Modred eventually.

"Brace yourself, Myrddin," King Arthur said as they approached the main gate into the fort. "This will be the first test."

"A test of what?" Huw said.

Myrddin turned to his son. "Of us." He lifted his chin. "Of me. I am King Arthur's heir, but nobody but we few know it. If Cador accepts me, then likely the other lords of Wales will too. If not—"

"If not, when I die, Wales's leaders will fall to bickering among themselves regarding who shall be High King," Arthur said, "and in so doing, they will allow themselves to be picked off one by one by the Saxons. I could defeat Modred here and still die from my wounds. In that instance, the battle will only delay our defeat for a time, rather than ending the threat."

Nell bent her head. What King Arthur described had been exactly the rationale behind her dream of Modred's camp. Thus, it was with real trepidation that she gazed up at the towers as they approached the entrance. For his part, Myrddin kept his back straight and his head high, as well he might. This was the first test of his new identity, and like every other test he'd ever faced, he intended to meet it head on.

Caer Caradoc, unlike Modred's stronghold at Wroxeter, or King Arthur's at Garth Celyn, had not been built on Roman ruins. It was to Caer Caradoc that Nell's ancestors had retreated during their war with the Romans. For ten years, Cador's ancestors, led by Caradoc himself, had held off the Roman legions, struggling to maintain the British way of life in the face of the invasion. They'd lost, of course, as the Britons always lost, up until King Arthur had stood on Mt. Badon and rallied his troops as no British general had managed since before even the time of Vortigern.

It wasn't until Modred decided that he couldn't wait for his inheritance and claimed supremacy over the Saxon kingdom of Mercia—promising the other Saxon lords lands in Wales if they gave him men—that the Saxons presented a significant threat. It was the first instance in over thirty years.

The master of the gate, a short red-bearded man in middle age, leaned over the top of the palisade to look at them. Anwen, who'd spent most of the journey riding at Huw's side, urged her horse forward so she could speak to him. "I am Anwen, Lord Cador's niece, and I request admittance." She gestured behind her. "I ride with King Arthur."

"Who rides with his cousin and heir, Myrddin ap Ambrosius!" King Arthur's voice echoed around the hill.

Nell hadn't expected such a grand announcement, and she gaped at the king in the same manner as the gatekeeper. Then he recovered, waving a hand to the men behind him. "Yes, my lord!"

The gate swung open, and as Nell entered, for the first time in days, she took a genuinely full breath and let it out, feeling her shoulders relax. If she wasn't careful, she could fall asleep right here on her horse. But that wouldn't do at all. She was Myrddin's wife and a lady now, so she took another breath and dismounted along with everyone else. Someone must have immediately run to fetch Lord Cador because he came out of the hall.

At the sight of him, King Arthur strode across the courtyard, his arms outstretched, and the two men embraced. It was a degree of affection Nell hadn't seen the king display to anyone before, and the sight of the two men grinning at each other had her grinning too.

"I apologize for not coming to Buellt, my friend." Cador was a few years older than Arthur, but still with the shoulders of an ox and full-bearded. "With Modred sitting at Wroxeter, I didn't dare leave these lands undefended."

"We didn't need you, as it turned out," Arthur said.

"The rider who brought word of the victory said that it was due in large part to Myrddin. They never said, however, that he was your cousin and Ambrosius's son." Cador looked past Arthur. "Where is he?"

Myrddin, who was standing with Nell a few feet away, took a step forward. Cador spied him and, advancing forward, gave him a low bow. "My lord. Welcome to Caer Caradoc."

Myrddin opened his mouth to reply, and Nell had a moment's intuition that he was going to make a self-deprecating comment, perhaps minimizing his role in the victory at Buellt. But then he seemed to stop himself and simply bowed his head. "It is an honor to meet you, sir." He straightened and held out a hand to Anwen, who had returned to Huw's side. "May I commend you for teaching your niece to shoot. There might not be so many of us standing here now if not for her."

Anwen flushed to the roots of her honey-colored hair and looked completely discomfited, but Nell gently urged her forward. "You did well. Go hug your uncle."

With a smile she failed to suppress, Anwen did as Nell bid and allowed her uncle to wrap her up in his arms.

They released each other, and Cador looked past her to everyone else. "Please come inside. If we are to conference, we'll be warmer doing it in my hall than on the stoop!"

"Thank you," King Arthur said. "We have much to talk about it and all of it is urgent."

Nell did not move forward with the others, however, and at Myrddin's inquiring look, she lifted one shoulder. "I need a moment alone."

Concern furrowed his brows, but Myrddin nodded and went with the others, while Nell climbed to the wall-walk at the top of the palisade that would allow her to overlook the valley below. Somewhere along the way, it had stopped snowing, and the low clouds had given way to patchy blue sky. Only a few hours ago they'd been fighting for their lives against Modred's dogs and hunters, and now here they were, momentarily safe. Nell almost couldn't encompass it. She was exhausted—from lack of sleep, certainly, but also from the near constant interchange between fear and hope.

Everything that had happened so far to the good could so easily have gone the other way. She knew from hard experience that things going badly was far more often the way of it, such that the string of successes was both comforting and terrifying. Their luck could turn at any moment. So much had been left to chance, up to and including the encounter with Anwen, which had brought them here instead of sending them to Caer Fawr as in the dream.

She closed her eyes and let her head drop, searching for grace to face what was to come, no matter how terrible.

BETWEEN ONE HEARTBEAT and the next, Modred attacked, leaping the distance between him and King Arthur and bringing his sword down with all his strength. He bore Caledfwlch, King Arthur's legendary sword, which they'd had to leave behind at Wroxeter.

King Arthur barely reacted in time, grasping his shield and bringing it up to block the blow. They were on the edge of the circle, and the people behind the king moved aside to give him room to stumble backwards as he twisted away from Modred. Then in a flurry of attacking blows, Modred's sword beat again and again on the king's shield, such that Arthur had no way to counter the assault and all he could do was retreat around the circle.

Then the king's wooden shield shattered. Instead of tossing it to the side, however, King Arthur threw it at Modred, who raised his own shield in time to knock it away. Then King Arthur leapt forward, hammering blows of his own, two fists on the hilt of his sword. Modred resisted, retreating as King Arthur had retreated. Just as the last blow fell, King Arthur unexpectedly feinted, and instead of swinging downward onto Modred's shield with his sword, he sliced under it with the knife that had appeared in his left hand.

But instead of opening a gash in Modred's belly, the knife rebounded off Modred's armor, leaving Modred himself undamaged.

Laughing, Modred pounced on Arthur again. This time, he was invincible, turning aside every thrust of Arthur's blade as if it were that of a gnat. Even the blows that did fall on him did not hurt him. With each useless blow that Arthur struck, Modred's men roared their approval, and whether worshipers of gods or the one God, they knew Modred to be protected. The rest of the fight was short and brutal and ended in Arthur's death.

"I WANT TO THANK YOU for your kindness to me."

Nell brought up her head and turned to look at Anwen, who'd come up silently behind her. Despite having achieved the safety of the fort, she still wore her breeches and quiver. She was taller than Nell by a few inches, and her bright eyes and earnestness reminded Nell of the novices she used to care for. "Have I been kind?"

"In my experience, other women can be—" Anwen raised one shoulder and let it drop without finishing her sentence.

"They can be mean. And unaccepting," Nell said. "I suspect you have been ill-treated as a Welshwoman among Saxons."

"My stepfather was not proud of me. He liked his women to be seen but not heard." She looked down at herself and gestured to her clothing. "I am not opposed to wearing dresses, but they do hinder one's legs when one is climbing trees."

Nell laughed, shaking off the last of the terrible vision. "I imagine they do. Fortunately, King Arthur does not share your stepfather's prejudices." Then she sobered and put a hand on Anwen's forearm. "We are grateful for all you've done for us. I don't know how much Huw has told you, but our need was great indeed."

"He told me that you were Modred's prisoners at Wroxeter, and you escaped. Those men chasing you—" She stopped again and swallowed hard.

"They would have killed us if we had not killed them first. You know this."

"That's what Huw said."

"Did he tell you also about the battle at Garth Celyn where King Arthur knighted him?" Nell said.

Anwen nodded. "His father almost died that day because Huw failed to act."

Nell bit her lip. Huw really did like this girl if he'd chosen to tell her the truth rather than encourage her admiration with a stirring tale of his bravery and nobility. "Then you know that what we do we do not do lightly."

Anwen turned her head to gaze at the countryside, as Nell had been doing before the *seeing* had overtaken her. "I didn't realize how easy it is to kill a man and how hard it is to live with afterwards, even knowing that we had no choice. There was so much blood." She shook her head and looked the other way, towards the great hall. Men were moving from it to the stable, readying their horses to ride.

"Who taught you to shoot?" Nell said.

"My uncle's captain, at my uncle's request. He has taught all the women in the household. With Saxons all around us, my uncle saw no reason for half of his family to be useless in a fight." She shrugged again. "We've been lucky that none of us have ever needed to defend Caer Caradoc."

"We'll need all of you now. You'll see too that your uncle is not alone in his beliefs. When the armies come, women will march among them, and not just as spearwomen or cavalry. There will be archers like you." Nell drew Anwen's attention back to the magnificent view before them. "When Caradoc stood on this very spot before his last battle with the Romans, the women painted their faces blue and fought alongside their men. I even heard that one of Britain's greatest generals was a woman."

Anwen smiled ruefully. "They lost though."

"They did." Nell gave a low laugh. "That wasn't, perhaps, the best example I could have used."

Anwen's gray eyes were grave as they looked at Nell. "Can you tell me what kind of man Huw is?"

"What kind of man do you think he is?"

The girl bit her lip. "Brave and kind. Honorable."

Nell smiled gently. "Never fear. What you have already learned of him is everything you need to know."

Chapter Five

SHOUTING IN THE COURTYARD distracted them both, and they turned to see Huw waving to them from below. "The king would speak to us."

Before Nell could answer, Anwen raised her hand in acknowledgement, another smile coming to her lips, this one genuine, and Huw waited for them to descend the steps. He held out one elbow to each woman and escorted them across the frozen courtyard, which would soon be muddy and churned by the feet and hooves of the army that was arriving to support them. It wasn't often that a churned up courtyard was something to look forward to.

Large, perhaps fifty feet on a side, Cador's hall was framed in wood. Upon entering, Nell found herself shivering, more than when she'd been outside, at her relief to suddenly find herself warm. The central fire was doing a passable job holding back the cold.

"I know what you're thinking." Myrddin's voice came softly from behind her.

"I really doubt that." She turned her head to look up at him.

His eyes twinkled down at her. "Then you should tell me, wife, so that I will know and don't have to guess."

Nell laughed to realize that her brief prayer for respite had already been answered. "You had the same dream I did."

"So it seems. You can be sure that I am not letting you enter Modred's camp today, tomorrow, or any day in a heroic act of self-sacrifice."

Nell's brow furrowed. "That's not—"

But she was interrupted by King Arthur, who, at the sight of Myrddin and Nell, tipped his head to indicate that they should approach. Huw and Anwen were already standing to one side of the central fire, not far from Cador. He regarded Huw and Anwen for a moment from underneath his bushy brows and then returned his attention to the king.

Silence fell, and it was only then that Nell became aware that the rest of the inhabitants of Caer Caradoc had filed inside too. Altogether, upwards of sixty people filled the hall. At least ten were women, and Nell hoped that Anwen was right and that they could shoot. A handful of children sat beside their parents or grandparents. Caer Caradoc was a home as well as a fortress, and Nell's stomach twisted in unease to know that she and her companions had brought war down upon them.

King Arthur spread his arms wide. "My people—" he turned to Cador, "my lord Cador, I give you my thanks for accepting me into Caer Caradoc. I have come because we—I—must make one last stand against Modred, just as our ancestors stood here against the invaders centuries ago."

Nell looked down at her feet, holding back an ironic smile. She was in no way surprised that King Arthur knew the history of this place, but she was surprised that he called upon it. As Anwen had pointed out, Caradoc had lost.

But Arthur wasn't finished. "In that last battle against the Romans, Caer Caradoc stood as an island, a last outpost of defiance against a far greater empire that stretched from Anglesey to Rome. We, however, stand not as an island but as the leading edge of a sword that is the people of Britain. Behind us lies all Wales, unconquered and unbowed. A few days ago, we defeated a Saxon army at Buellt. In a few days' time, we will defeat the rest of Modred's army on the field of Camlann before Caer Caradoc.

"And even should I fall in battle, able men will rise up to take my place. I have acknowledged my true heir and cousin, Myrddin ap Ambrosius," He held out a hand to Myrddin, "—and his son and heir, Huw."

The nods around the hall were almost universal—and some of the heavy weight, which had settled onto Nell's chest as a result of what she'd seen, lifted. Myrddin was accepted. In the coming days and weeks, if they survived this, he would spend much of his time in the public eye.

"The Saxons will come with an army unlike any we have ever seen. Thirty years ago I made a stand at Badon." King Arthur gestured to Cador. "Lord Cador was beside me then as he stands beside me now. That victory gave us peace for a generation. Although peace was lost to us the moment Modred decided that he wanted to rule Wales while I still lived and didn't want to wait for the honor, peace can be achieved again. All we have to do is fight—" Arthur paused, taking a moment to survey the people before him, "One. More. Battle."

A restlessness wafted over and around the onlookers. They had to know this was coming, but the clarity with which King Arthur was speaking made it real to them in a way his arrival had not. Nell had dreamed of Arthur's death her whole life, and the vision she'd had on the wall-walk was just one of a thousand instances where she'd seen it. She couldn't blame the people here for being unsettled by Arthur laying the possibility before them for the first time.

"Over the next hours and days, the armies of Wales will gather here, and then Modred himself will come. He will not be able to resist the chance to end this war with one great victory. He believes that if he strikes me down, all Wales will fall at his feet."

Myrddin leaned down to whisper in Nell's ear. "The king is right that Modred will come. King Arthur is too great a prize, and

Modred knows that as long as Arthur lives, he can never be the undisputed High King of the Britons."

Modred would have been far better off ignoring the army on the hilltop and instead driving his army straight into Wales to burn, pillage, and conquer. Fort after fort would fall to him, and King Arthur would be helpless to stop him. His army would disintegrate as lords hastened home to protect their people and lands. And then Modred could come and take Caer Caradoc last of all, just as the Romans had.

But as they'd discussed with Gareth and Edgar back at the barn, that course of action, though tactically sound, would take time. It was winter, and Modred had a huge army to feed. Her vision on the wall-walk had shown her that moving the battle from Caer Fawr to Caer Caradoc had changed nothing, or not enough. If they were to avert Arthur's death this time, they would have to do more.

Murmurs emanated again from the people in the hall, prompting King Arthur to raise a hand to silence his audience. "I did not say that we would fall—only that Modred believes it. I must warn you, however, that the odds are against us. He has the might of Mercia behind him and far more men than we can bring to bear. I understand if you wish to flee—"

The murmurs and calls grew louder, mostly in protest. Beside Nell, Myrddin stirred and seemed to want to speak, but then he subsided, settling back on his heels. King Arthur, however, had noticed him and now gave Myrddin a brief nod, indicating that the floor was his.

In response, Myrddin stepped forward and the hall quieted. The people didn't know this new son of Ambrosius and wanted to hear what he had to say. "There is no shame in fear, only in cowardice, which if you do flee you can turn into nobility. I ask that as you travel through Wales, you tell others of what we do here and urge them towards Caer Caradoc. Perhaps one will respond and fight in your stead. And then I ask that you find a place to be safe, if such a place exists—on the far end of the Lleyn Peninsula, perhaps, or in a cave in the mountains, as some of King Arthur's own counselors at one time urged on him. Survive, to ensure that the story of what we do here lives on among our people, even as we fall to Modred's force and the might of Mercia."

Myrddin raised a hand and clenched it into a fist in front him. "Or you could stay and fight with us."

NELL CLASPED HER HANDS behind her back, waiting for the people to disperse. The words that Arthur and Myrddin had spoken had been important, stirring even. Now that the speeches were over, she wasn't the only one who had tears in her eyes to think on what they said and what was coming. But King Arthur hadn't called her and Myrddin into the hall to listen to him prepare his people for battle. They were here to plan. For all Arthur's warning words of the dangers they faced, he had no intention of losing this fight.

Myrddin and Nell joined King Arthur by the fire, where a meal was being laid out on a round table that would allow them to confer equally with one another without having to shout from one end of the table to the other. The dais, with its long rectangular table, remained empty.

As Myrddin and Nell approached, Cador pulled out a chair beside Godric, and then he waved a hand to indicate that Huw and Anwen join the meal. "You don't mind, do you, my lord?" he said to Arthur, "I've found that the young sometimes have a perspective the old would do well to listen to."

"My usual counselors are spread far and wide." King Arthur's eyes were on Anwen as she sat down, her chair pulled out by Huw. "I think we can use all the help any man—or woman—has to give."

"Quite right," Cador said.

The variety and quantity of food before them was not far off from what Modred had fed the people in his hall at Wroxeter, but Nell hadn't been able to eat a thing that evening, since Gareth had arrived to inform Modred of Myrddin's death just as the meal was starting. That was the last real meal she'd been a party to. So, council of war or not, she fell to her food with enthusiasm.

They began by discussing the disposition of their men, few as they were now, and deliberating upon who might come to fight. Immediately upon arrival at the fort, King Arthur had sent out riders in every direction to call the lords of Wales to him, beyond what Gareth, Edgar, and Godric's men had already gone to do. They would need every man: Geraint and Gawain from Buellt; Cedric from Brecon; other lords from Powys, Morganwgg, and Deheubarth. Garth Celyn, King Arthur's stronghold in north Wales, was far away—seventy miles as the crow flies. Bedwyr, the steward, would lead men east the moment he heard the king's call, but first he had to know they were needed.

Cador leaned back in his chair, shaking his head. "We need more men, Arthur. My scouts have been watching Modred for weeks. Years." He laughed without humor. "He has more men than we do."

"Then we shall have to deploy the men we have more intelligently than he does." King Arthur looked to Myrddin, who was sitting next to Nell. "Begin with your dream, back at the barn. I need to know the whole of it. What did you *see?*"

"Myrddin is a seer?" Cador looked startled, but he was the only one. Nell assumed that Huw had said something of their visions to Anwen in their journey here, since it was the dream that had prompted them to come to Caer Caradoc instead of Caer Fawr in the first place. The others, even Godric, took the request in stride. Nell almost laughed to think they were more used to her and Myrddin's visions by now than she was.

Myrddin had been taking a sip of mead from his goblet, but he set it down. "Both Nell and I have the gift." He glanced at Nell, who nodded, and then he related their vision to the gathering. He gave Arthur the facts without emotion, for which Nell was grateful.

When he finished, however, she leaned forward and drew everyone's attention to her. "What Myrddin describes wasn't exactly what I saw."

King Arthur canted his head. "Is that good news? Because I'm with Myrddin that trading your life for Modred's is not a bargain I would make."

Nell patted Myrddin's thigh in what she hoped he would interpret as a reassuring way. "I submit that it might well be worth it, but in my dream, it is Myrddin who makes that sacrifice, not me."

Myrddin drew in a breath. "What?"

"That's what I saw. It wasn't I who went to the camp, but you pretending to be a Saxon man-at-arms."

King Arthur rubbed his chin. "Why would you two not see the same? Isn't that usually the way of it?"

Myrddin pushed back his stool and rose to his feet in order to pace away from the table. He stopped a dozen yards away and stared unseeing at the door.

His eyes on Myrddin, King Arthur eased back from the table too and clasped his hands before his lips as if in prayer. He looked over the top of his fingers at Nell. "Do you know why?"

"No," Nell said.

Myrddin swung around. "I do, my lord. It is what I have thought for some time, though I haven't said it. Nell and I dream in tandem. For most of our lives, we dreamed the same dream, but we were not together then. Since our marriage, we have had visions, some the same, some different, but they have, in a way, been paired. What I think now is that the dreams tell us of a possible future. They direct our steps—either away from what we see, as was the case at the church where your brother died, or towards what we see, as in the case of Wroxeter. If we are to interpret this most recent dream, as with the others, we must work in tandem. That was the message of the dream. While we were shown a possible future—one in which I risk my life, and another in which Nell does—we have much more to learn from it than not to do that."

"What might that be?" Cador said. "Did not Arthur just tell me that the battle was inevitable? Is that not what you told him?"

"It is inevitable—" Myrddin broke off, seemingly unable to find the words to explain, so Nell spoke for him.

"In the dream, Myrddin tries to kill Modred because he knows that the final battle where King Arthur dies by Modred's hand is coming."

Myrddin nodded. "We've both seen Modred's army on the march. Coming here has not been enough to change that." He looked at Nell. "Has it for you?"

She shook her head, thinking of the vision she'd just had on the wall-walk. "It's always in my mind's eye."

Cador stared at her for a moment and then transferred his gaze to Myrddin. "So what you're saying is that you had a vision of Nell trying to avert Arthur's death because your dreaming self had a vision of Modred killing him."

"Yes." Nell and Myrddin spoke together.

"So perhaps what is important is not what you immediately saw—" Anwen had listened to the whole conversation so far with calm eyes, "but what else it tells you. Perhaps the vision is a warning to you both not to try to avert the battle that is coming. Nell is warned against Myrddin's course of action, and Myrddin against Nell's."

429

Myrddin jerked his head in a sharp nod. "The battle itself will not be averted. What must still be, however, is its outcome."

"Or," King Arthur pushed to his feet and approached Myrddin, "you are being told that my death is inevitable, no matter what any of us try to do to stop it. And thus, we should not try."

"I refuse to believe that, my lord," Myrddin said.

Arthur gave a low laugh. "You are my heir, and I will not risk you. It is no longer your job to avert my death. If I fall, it is you who must stand in my stead. Only you can lead my people, and you can't do that if you are dead in a Saxon camp. Maybe the dream is telling you that you must put aside the seer to become king."

Myrddin shook his head. "My lord, I understand what you're saying, but I don't believe that either. Instead, I fear the dream is telling me quite the opposite. I fear, rather, that if I am not seer, none of us will be king."

Chapter Six

"I CAN'T SAY MUCH FOR the comfort," Myrddin said as he tucked the blankets around Nell, "but at least we are hidden from watching eyes."

Nell grinned. "Or listening ears."

Myrddin was the heir to the throne of Wales, and thus should have had a private room to sleep in. But while Cador had attempted to give up his own room to King Arthur, the king had refused, accepting a pallet and blankets among his warriors. That was all very well and good, but such nobility of action left no room for the intimacy Myrddin craved with Nell. Thus, he'd made a nest for them in one of the stalls in the stable. His horse, which still didn't have a name, peered at them over the gate that blocked the doorway, confused as to how he could be tethered in the aisle rather than in his own stall. He whickered his objections and nudged the stall door with his nose.

"Just give me an hour, old fellow," Myrddin said.

"An hour!" Nell poked Myrddin's belly. "That's all I get?"

Myrddin scooped her into his arms and kissed her thoroughly. "Two hours maybe, but I can't promise the stable boys won't come back early. I bribed them with a jug of mead."

"That was kind of you, but you didn't need to bribe them." She poked him again, this time on the breastbone. "You keep forgetting that you are Ambrosius's son."

"All the more reason not to do as I please when I please and expect everyone to fall all over themselves doing my bidding."

"I know you're right." Nell made a rueful face. "A dozen times just since the council meeting, people stopped before me and bowed as if I was already queen."

"We've both come a long way since the road to Denbigh." Myrddin started kissing her again, wishing they could hold onto this moment forever and never have to leave. But thinking about returning to their duties would only ruin the time they did have together—and that he refused to do. Nell was his wife, and so far in their short marriage his opportunities to be her husband had been few and far between.

Afterwards, he fingered his cross as it lay between her breasts. The blame for nearly all the good and bad that had happened to him in his life lay within its golden arms.

Nell held the cross up by its long chain. "Just think if Huw's mother hadn't kept it, or if she hadn't given it to him and told him to seek you out."

Myrddin pulled Nell close again, so that her head lay on his chest, and spoke the truth. "I have made many mistakes in my life, Nell. I'm sure I'll continue to make more than my share. I should have returned to Brecon to see how Huw's mother fared, but I can be grateful that he was raised well, even if I wasn't the one to do the fathering."

Nell stroked his upper arm with one finger. "What are we to do, Myrddin?"

He had no trouble following the change of subject and didn't have to ask what she meant. Despite their quiet interlude, the coming battle remained at the forefront of his mind too. This evening had been a brief respite—a diversion—but they could hold off what was coming for only so long, and their two hours were almost at an end.

"You are asking how we can avert what is to come?" he said. "Maybe King Arthur is right that we aren't supposed to."

She pushed up onto one elbow so she could look down at him. "I refuse to believe that. Why show us what is to come if we can't change it? What we are seeing now is too much like what we dreamed for all those years for me to agree with the king on this."

"I take your point. It is essentially what I said to the king."

"But you are not yet convinced yourself?" Nell said. "I admit I did wonder at our hubris to think we could change the future—especially once Gareth walked into the hall at Wroxeter and told Modred that you were dead. In that moment, I had to accept that everything we'd tried had come to nothing. But I was wrong about even that, so I'm thinking King Arthur is wrong about this too."

She *was* beautiful, bending over him in the half-darkness, their stall lit only by distant lanterns near the front of the stable. He took both of her hands in his. "We didn't go to Caer Fawr as we dreamed, so what we do now is already different, but Modred is still coming." He paused. "You see that too?"

"When I was on the wall-walk before we met with Arthur and Cador, I *saw* Arthur die again by Modred's hand. Even without that vision, I catch a flash every now and then of marching feet. It's so real sometimes I turn my head to get a better look, only to find myself still inside the hall."

Myrddin nodded. "We may not have changed anything."

"We will change the dream if we don't go to Modred's camp," Nell said.

"In which case, Arthur will die." Now he'd done it. He'd started her thinking about something besides him, which was clearly a huge mistake for him personally, but perhaps not for Wales.

Nell sat up and wrapped the blanket around her shoulders to sit cross-legged at his side, with her elbow on one knee and her chin in her hand. "Modred has a huge army. We know that."

"We do." He reclined on the bed, his hands clasped behind his head.

"We know that the other lords of Mercia have chosen Modred to lead them because Wales is rich in land and livestock, and they want that richness for themselves. They think he can get it for them."

"Yes."

A curious look crossed Nell's face. "But will they support him for the kingship after he wins?" Her eyes became fixed on Myrddin's face. "Why would they be any less prone to infighting than we are? How many of them truly want Modred as a leader in a time of peace?"

"I don't pretend to understand the Saxon mind, but leadership to them devolves on the man who brings the most riches."

"Yes," Nell said, "but everyone will want their share, won't they?"

"Modred isn't going to want to share." Myrddin's eyes narrowed. "Who among the Saxons might have thought that far ahead?"

"Any lord with any sense, which means that the enemy of my enemy—" She broke off.

"—might be a friend." Myrddin was on his feet in an instant. He snatched up his breeches and began to shove his feet into the legs. "We can get Arthur the men he needs."

Nell stretched across the blankets to where her clothing had been discarded. Grabbing her shift, she pulled it over her head. "Who are you thinking of?"

"True rivals of Modred. Men like Cynyr of Wessex or—" Myrddin stopped and grimaced. "I hate even to say it."

"You speak of Urien of Rheged?" Nell said. Rheged was a British kingdom far to the north. Chester, known in Roman times as Deva, was its seat.

Myrddin raised one shoulder. "At least he's a Briton."

"After the death of Ambrosius—I still struggle to think of him as your father!—he opposed Arthur's ascension to the high kingship and never pledged his fealty. He's hardly an ally, despite marrying King Arthur's cousin."

"He hates the Saxon advance as much as we do and has been fighting for his life against Bernicia and Deira, two of the more northern Saxon kingdoms. He might fight for us if it meant more land for him when we win." Myrddin wrinkled his chin. "He has many men at his disposal."

"That he does," Nell said, "but could we trust him not to betray Arthur at the last moment?"

"He might see King Arthur as the lesser of two evils, as I know he has no love for Modred either. Arthur might prefer an appeal to him over an alliance with another Saxon, who will not remain faithful once he has what he wants. That was the mistake Vortigern made. Besides, Urien is older than Arthur, and the son is not the father. Urien might realize that he has to make some concessions to ensure that Owain has something to inherit."

"You know Owain?" Nell said.

"He owes me money."

Nell laughed. "Will I ever cease to be surprised by you?"

Myrddin grinned. "God forbid."

"How did that come about?"

"Owain, like Arthur when he was younger, had a habit of moving among his men disguised as a man-at-arms. He joined a game my friends and I were playing. This must have been five or six years ago when we were fighting a Saxon incursion near Chester. That was before Modred began his rebellion, and Owain was only twenty. I'm sure he's smarter now."

"You won and then forgave the debt," Nell said, not as a question.

"I did so the moment one of his guards leaned in to whisper in my ear who he was," Myrddin said. "He had no money on him and swore he'd pay me in the morning, but I refused it. Of course I did. His father would have wanted to know what had become of those coins. On top of which, Urien is surrounded by priests, who forbid gambling."

"That would be because Roman soldiers gambled at the base of the cross during the Crucifixion," Nell said, reverting very briefly to the nun she'd once been. "Urien would not have looked favorably upon a son who gambles, not even in the cause of better knowing his men."

"For my purposes, the gratitude of a king's heir was worth far more to me than a few coins. What need had I of money when I could have that?"

"Clever."

Myrddin put his hand to Nell's jaw and pulled her in for a kiss. "Your new husband is not entirely without merit, is that it?"

She laughed, but then almost immediately sobered. "We should speak to the king."

Myrddin grimaced. "We have, at most, three days before Modred comes. I assume his spies have informed him by now where we went, but he has many men to move."

"Caer Caradoc is a stronger fortress than I had thought," Nell said. "As it turns out, King Arthur chose his refuge well."

Myrddin nodded. "You and I, meanwhile, can take the Roman road to Chester. Even from here, we can be there by morning."

"It's fifty miles!" Nell said.

"Then the sooner we ride, the sooner we'll be there." Myrddin narrowed his eyes at her. "You're not saying you want me to go without you?"

"No! Heaven forbid I leave you alone for a single hour. Who knows what mischief you might get into?"

Myrddin laughed. "I could easily say the same about you."

"The king isn't going to like you leaving," Nell said.

"We'll see."

A quarter of an hour later, having collected Huw from where he'd been sleeping with other young men, who had, without anyone saying anything as far Myrddin could tell, become his guards, they were admitted into the king's room in the barracks. He hadn't been asleep—Myrddin wasn't entirely sure Arthur ever slept—but he had at least been resting. He blinked at the sight of Myrddin and Nell dressed for traveling.

"I have a feeling I'm not going to like whatever you have to say," the king said.

Huw frowned. "I suspect I won't either. What are you doing, Father?"

"Nell and I have had an idea," Myrddin said.

"A seeing?" Arthur said.

"No, actually, not that," Nell said. "It is more that we have come to a conclusion based on all that we've seen and heard over the last few days."

Myrddin took up the explanation. "It occurs to us that other lords might view the coming battle with skepticism. We know that we have to commit everything to it, but the Saxons might be warier and find they don't trust Modred's motives as much as they once did."

"He has their men," Arthur said.

"Yes, but for how long?" Nell said. "Modred leads them now, and he hopes to claim all Wales for Mercia, but the lords of the other Saxon kingdoms—of Wessex, Kent, Deira—can't be happy with the amount of power doing so will gather to him."

"You want to reach out to those lords." King Arthur understood immediately. He hadn't become king by being slow of mind.

"We do. More, we were thinking specifically of Urien of Rheged," Myrddin said.

Arthur hesitated. "He is British."

"Thus he would be the most likely ally, don't you think?" Nell said. "I saw some of his men in Wroxeter, but not nearly as many as he has or could have sent. His commitment to Modred didn't extend so far as to come himself."

"I noticed that too." Arthur rubbed his chin.

"There's something else about Wroxeter that has occurred to me since we last talked." Huw didn't often participate in these free-wheeling conversations of his elders, so the fact that he was speaking at all pleased Myrddin, and he turned to him.

"Tell us."

"It has to do with what Modred is hiding," Huw said. "Are we convinced from what Archbishop Dafydd told us that he and Modred came to an agreement to the effect that Modred would spare the king's life if at all possible?"

"Yes." Arthur eyes were fixed on the young man.

"One of those promises seems to have been that he would open his court to you, my lord—his accounts, letters written to other warlords, and the like. Yes?"

"Yes," Arthur said again.

"But that wasn't to happen until the day after we arrived. Why the delay? Modred had come to the agreement before he knew that Beorhtsige had captured you, so at the time it was purely theoretical. Once you were actually at Wroxeter, however, Modred didn't just give you free reign over his affairs. He needed time to hide something."

"The boy may be on to something." Arthur paced to the window of his bedchamber and looked out, though in the darkness, there wasn't much to see.

"Could what he was hiding be what we've already guessed—letters, perhaps, from other Saxon lords saying that they are not coming or arguing against a particular course of action?" Nell said.

"I imagine it's worse than that," Myrddin said. "More likely he's out of money."

"And food, which is bought with money," Huw said. "Maintaining all those men at Wroxeter can't be cheap, but he doesn't want to allow his men to ravage the countryside when it's his own people he'd be stealing from."

King Arthur turned to look at the three of them. "That is why he's coming. That is why he has pressed his advantage through the winter when all sane men know that winter is when you send your men home to starve on their own lands. Another month or two at most and the spring planting will take precedence. If he doesn't move his army now, if he doesn't win this war soon, by spring he won't have an army."

"So what does that mean?" Huw said. "Do we stall?"

"No." Myrddin's brow furrowed. "But perhaps we're looking at this the wrong way round. We had to send out riders to call the men of Wales to us—of course, we did. But we should also be sending riders to the Saxon lords who ostensibly support Modred, arguing for why they shouldn't."

King Arthur shook his head. "No, that's where you're wrong, and where you were right to think that Urien of Rheged is our only option. I have nothing to offer the Saxons. I will not give up one more inch of British soil."

"I'm not suggesting that you do," Myrddin said. "It isn't our land that's for the taking—it's Modred's."

King Arthur stared at him with something approaching awe.

"We have retreated. We have given ground year after year after year," Myrddin said. "Maybe it really is time we stopped."

Chapter Seven

15 December 537

Huw

HUW ENTERED THE HALL for breakfast, intending to join some of his new friends—the wounded Alan among them, since he was immobile until his ankle healed—but it was the sight of Anwen standing against a far wall that drew him. The eve of battle was hardly a time to form a new friendship, but then ... perhaps it was the best time. Huw hadn't dallied much with women, nor befriended many in his life. Like many children born out of wedlock, he was reluctant to father a child into such a state himself.

"You changed your clothes." He looked her up and down. She had bathed and now wore a dress, deep green in color, which set off her hair and skin beautifully. He found himself hoping that she would consent to wear female clothing more often. She looked less fierce with her hair curling around her shoulders.

Anwen smiled. "I am a woman, my lord."

Huw coughed a laugh. "I did notice."

"My breeches are being laundered, and I had to restock my quiver. No point in wearing one that's empty. Besides, my uncle would prefer I go unarmed in the hall."

"Most lords prefer that. Even a knight doesn't wear his sword to the king's table." He gave her a little bow. "Thanks to your uncle, I now have one to leave at the door."

Anwen lifted her chin to indicate the people behind Huw. "They watch and judge."

He didn't turn around. "I know. I am not yet accustomed to it."

"I think that's for the best. Too many princes act as if they earned their station." She tipped her head to look at him. "You don't."

"That would be because up until a few days ago, I didn't know who I was."

"Yes, you did. That's my whole point. You know who you are without being a prince."

Huw looked down at the ground, humbled by her assessment of him. Before he could make some sort of reply, however, he found himself being nudged in the ribs by Osgar, one of the men with whom he'd fled Wroxeter. "The king wants you with him, my lord."

Ducking his head to Anwen in a half-embarrassed nod, Huw made his way across the hall to the dais. It wasn't as if he'd never sat at the high table before. He'd dined there yesterday evening after the meeting of the king's council, such as it was. But his parents had been with him and, since it was Myrddin who was the long-lost heir to the throne, it was to him that most of the attention had been given.

Myrddin and Nell were gone, however, riding to Chester to speak to Urien of Rheged about his choice of allegiance. Arthur had also sent an emissary to Cynric of Wessex, but that was a far longer journey than the one Myrddin and Nell were undertaking. If Urien marched at dawn, he would be hard pressed to reach Caer Caradoc in time to fight on Arthur's behalf. With twice that distance to go for Cynric, he wouldn't make it unless the battle lasted far longer than either Arthur or Modred could afford to fight it.

"Are you worried, son?" King Arthur tipped his head to indicate that Huw should take the seat next to him. "Your parents have experience taking care of themselves."

"What if my father is not received as the son of Ambrosius should be?" Huw said. "Urien did not support your claim to the throne, but to deny Myrddin's right to it would be tantamount to treason. Urien might prefer to simply kill him, and then he doesn't have to face his own iniquity."

"I am glad you speak plainly. I always need to hear the truth from you. You, as much as your father, are my heir. One day you will be high king," Arthur laughed under his breath, "if we can keep ourselves together beyond the next few days."

"Modred will never be King of the Britons," Huw said. "That was another lesson from Myrddin's and Nell's dream. Even if all three of us fall, the lords of Wales will never accept him. They might temporarily submit, but he will spend the rest of his life fighting them."

King Arthur pressed his lips together in a thin smile. "I never would have thought that our penchant for infighting would be an advantage. Modred is right to fear us." But then he really did smile. "When you first came to your father, I worried that your Saxon upbringing might have made you arrogant, and that you would disparage the British part of your heritage as Modred does. He doesn't want to rule Wales for its own sake because he loves it. He wants to rule it to make it Saxon, as most of the rest of Britain has been made Saxon."

"Believe me, my lord, I had all the arrogance beaten out of me in the first three months of my service to Lord Cedric," Huw said, remembering the long nights of watch, the humiliating jobs forced upon him, and the lack of opportunity to rest.

Arthur laughed. "Cedric doesn't suffer fools gladly, it is true. Before a man can be trusted, he must be tamed—" Arthur canted his head, his gaze again fixed on Huw, "or tame himself."

As the king spoke, Huw realized that the people in the hall weren't the only ones who were watching him. King Arthur, probably from the moment he had arrived at Garth Celyn, had been aware of everything Huw had been doing. Huw was glad that he hadn't known about the constant testing at the time, or he might have been unable to act at all. It also gave his knighting at the beach a new significance.

The door to the hall opened, and the steward of Caer Caradoc, a man named Aron, strode towards the dais. He came to a halt on the opposite side of the table from Cador. "Lord Tefyn of Caer Croesi has come!"

Cador stood. "He has brought men?"

"He has come himself with a dozen riders. More of his men follow on foot."

Cador looked to King Arthur, who stood now too and said, "Good. I will greet him."

Aron bowed. "Yes, my lord."

He strode back the way he'd come.

"The first of many, I hope," Cador said, "or this will be the shortest battle in our long history."

King Arthur glanced down at Huw. "Stay at my side. Watch and learn. Lord Tefyn is the younger son of Pedr, a man who died suddenly last year along with his eldest son."

Huw looked warily at the king. "Is there some significance to these deaths?"

"I am concerned about how they died."

Cador grunted. "The rumors about the sudden sickness that afflicted them are what has brought Tefyn and his men here so quickly. He will want to distinguish himself in battle, as proof that God loves him—and out of the hope that you will too."

"Have you questioned him about how they died?" Huw said.

"No, no." Cador wagged a finger at him. "His lands are only six miles from here and form part of the border with Mercia. Modred made overtures to Pedr, and Pedr withstood them. I have needed time to judge the capacity of this younger son."

Huw nodded his understanding. "You don't want to drive him into Modred's arms."

443

"I do not," Cador said. "As with the way the king observed you, it takes time to determine if we have a snake in our midst. A man can't kill his father and elder brother and remain unchanged."

"Listen to Cador. He has wisdom," King Arthur said.

Cador eyed Arthur for a moment, but then looked again to Huw, having more instruction to give him. "A lord wields power. He does not allow it to wield him."

"Yes, my lord," Huw said, even though he didn't really have any idea what Cador was talking about. He did understand that as lord of these lands, Cador had the power to depose Tefyn at any time were he to learn definitively that he was a murderer. The issue at hand wasn't just the way Tefyn's father and brother had died. It was the politics of the time.

Questions had been raised about Arthur himself upon the deaths of Ambrosius and Uther within six months of each other, since their deaths had opened the way for Arthur to take the throne. Urien of Rheged had been one of those doubters, and he had never fully come around to supporting Arthur. But because his lands were located to the north of Mercia, the Saxon kingdom that separated Rheged from the remaining British kingdoms in Wales, Arthur had never called Urien to account. For the most part, both men had been kept busy in their own lands fighting off the Saxon invaders. While Arthur had to contend with Mercia and Wessex, Urien had long been beset by the Saxon kingdoms of Deira and Bernicia. And like Arthur, almost daily, he lost ground.

Huw met the king's eyes. "Is it your intent, if Urien helps you defeat Modred, that you will send men to the north to aid in his fight against Deira and Bernicia?"

"The Saxons drive us farther west with every year that passes. They have been able to do so because they have taken so much land already, and they outnumber us. One Saxon army attacks us in the south, another in the west, and a third in the north. If we can defeat

Modred here, then I will have men to spare to aid Urien. He is backed up against the Irish Sea as we are."

"And if we cannot defeat Modred?" Huw said.

"Then Urien will be on his own. Now—" Arthur put out a hand to Huw. "Watch carefully. Later I will want to hear your impression of Tefyn."

"Yes, my lord."

Tefyn came through the door and made his way on long legs towards the high table. To Huw's eyes, he and Tefyn were similar in age, though Tefyn was taller. It seemed he'd taken a moment to wash before entering the king's presence, because his hair was wet and smoothed back from his face, which was also clean. He really did want to make a good impression.

"My king." Tefyn put his feet together and bowed. "I have come."

Arthur put his hands flat on the table. "Thank you, Tefyn. You are the first. How many men do you bring me?"

"A hundred men, my lord. Ten horse, who are with me now, twenty archers, and seventy spears, though many of the spearmen carry bows as well."

Arthur left his seat to come around the table, and he surprised Huw—and seemingly Tefyn too—by embracing the young lord. "You are most welcome. How did you hear of our need?"

"A rider passed through yesterday, my lord," Tefyn said. "I came as soon as I could. The men coming on foot will be arriving later today."

Huw had stood when the king had stood, as was required, but now the king gestured him around the table too. "This is Huw ap Myrddin. His father is my cousin and heir. Huw is overseeing the disposition of all of the men who come. Anything you need, you ask him."

Tefyn's eyes had widened to look at Huw, and Huw hoped he'd managed to hide his surprise a little better—not so much to be mentioned in the same breath as his father, but that Arthur had effectively just made him steward of all the Welsh forces, for now at least.

"Where shall we set up camp, my lord?" Tefyn said to Huw.

Huw cleared his throat, hoping that when he spoke his words wouldn't come out a squeak. "We will cover the Lawley and the Long Mynd with men. Modred, when he comes, will find himself surrounded on three sides and confined to the field of Camlann that lies before Caer Caradoc."

Huw spoke as if he knew what he was talking about, but everything he'd just said he'd learned by listening to Arthur, Myrddin, and Cador yesterday. They'd outlined the defenses, where they would ideally position the spearman and the archers, from what lords they could draw for food and mead if the battle was extended, and strategy for defeating Modred's forces themselves.

Tefyn put his heels together, bowed first to Huw and then to King Arthur, and departed.

Hiding a smile, King Arthur put a hand on Huw's shoulder and shook him slightly. "Good. You were listening. And better, you remembered what you heard."

"I don't know that I am ready for this, my lord."

"This is our last stand, Huw. We all have no choice but to be ready."

Chapter Eight
15 December 537
Nell

MYRDDIN AND NELL WERE going to have to sleep eventually. With a twinge, Nell ran over the last few days in her head, calculating that she'd slept fitfully the night of the eleventh of December at Edgar's lodge, after she and Myrddin had parted. The night of the twelfth had been spent on the road to Wroxeter, and then she, Arthur, and Huw had slept through most of the following day, a blessing that had saved them for the night of the thirteenth, in which sleep had been aborted entirely by their flight west to Caer Caradoc. She'd slept yesterday after the council of war with King Arthur, though she did not know that Myrddin had done so, busy as he'd been with planning and preparations for the coming battle.

And then last night had again been spent in the saddle. No wonder they were both prone to visions. Their minds had become addled from lack of sleep.

Twelve hours after leaving Caer Caradoc, they were both still managing to stay upright, however, even after a fifty-mile journey. Side by side, they approached the main gate into the city of Chester, yet another abandoned Roman fort that had been refortified in recent years, this time by Urien of Rheged, who'd made it the southernmost outpost of his kingdom. Like Wroxeter, the entire city was a fort, laid out on a flat plain rather than on the heights like Caer Caradoc, though it did occupy a large sandstone bluff that overlooked the River Dee. Unlike at Wroxeter, however, the Roman stone had not given way to wooden defenses. Urien had rebuilt whatever had been damaged in the century since the Romans left, and the Saxons had yet to take it from him.

The River Dee looped around the city, protecting it from enemy advances on the south and west sides. A guarded stone bridge spanned the river to the south. To the west, the road from the city's west gate ended at a dock, which allowed the city to be fortified from the sea if necessary. Nell and Myrddin crossed the ditch and rampart that protected the approach to the walls, and with hardly more than a cursory glance, were admitted through the gatehouse. As Nell entered the city proper, it struck her that this was what Modred had hoped to make of Wroxeter: a monument to his power and wealth. Except that Urien had succeeded where Modred had failed.

Nell had never met King Urien before, but Myrddin knew him—and he certainly knew his son, who was just coming down the steps from Urien's hall, presumably once the headquarters of the Roman general who ruled here. Nell and Myrddin came to a halt in the street.

Owain stopped too, recognizing Myrddin immediately. His face lit with a mixture of surprise and amusement. "You sly dog, Myrddin! What are you doing here?"

"Much has happened since we last spoke, Prince Owain." Myrddin dismounted and helped Nell down too. She noted that Myrddin had carefully not called him *my lord*. The only person Myrddin was obligated to defer to these days was a king. "First, I would like to introduce you to my wife, Nell."

"Wife!" Owain looked like he was on the verge of calling Myrddin a dog again, but thought better of it now that he knew who Nell was. Instead, he canted his head and gave her a quick bow. "It is a pleasure, madam."

"To me too, my prince," Nell said.

Owain made a sweeping motion with his arm. "Come in where it's warm and tell me the rest of your news! We've had no riders from the south in days, and my father was beginning to wonder if Modred hadn't overtaken all Wales by now."

"Far from it." Myrddin escorted Nell up the steps and through the doors. "And we are here to see your father, if we may."

"Of course," Owain said. "Are you sent by Arthur?"

"Yes."

Nell turned her head to whisper to Myrddin. "You have to tell him who you really are!"

He gave a low laugh. "I don't know how. I can't."

"Someone had better, because it will be awkward later if we don't."

"Leave it for now. It isn't what's important," Myrddin said.

Myrddin was asked to leave his sword at the hall's entrance before they were allowed to enter. Though Roman in origin and built in stone, the hall functioned like any other in that it was filled with breakfasters. The sun was newly risen and shone weakly through the eastern windows. Despite the absence of a central fire or any visible means of heating the hall, it was amazingly warm. If they had time, Nell would have loved to learn the secret.

For now, however, their business was pressing. King Urien held court at the high table, and Owain led them directly there. Even though Myrddin was the son of Ambrosius, he put his feet together and bowed as if he wasn't. "My lord. I bring word from King Arthur."

"Finally." Urien dropped a piece of buttered bread to his bowl. "Last I heard, he'd gone south to meet with Edgar of Wigmore."

"You knew about that?" Nell was suddenly wary as to *how* he could have known about it, since Edgar's message wasn't something Arthur had shared with many people.

"Of course." Urien gestured to Myrddin. "Please continue."

Myrddin hesitated. "Some of the things I have to say might be better said in private."

King Urien narrowed his eyes for a moment, but then he jerked his head at his son, stood, and left the hall for a smaller room accessed through a doorway in the wall behind the high table. Nell, Myrddin, and Owain followed, and Nell was pleased to find that this room was even warmer than the hall. Owain took up a position against the wall, alongside several guards who seemed permanently posted to the room. Urien gestured for Nell to sit next to a brazier, and he took a second seat catty-corner to her.

Myrddin chose to stand, and again he put his heels together and dipped his head in a bow. Straightening, he said, "King Arthur's forces met the Mercians at Buellt and were victorious. Agravaine, Modred's foremost counselor, was killed. Now, King Arthur seeks a final confrontation with Modred, who is much weakened, on the field of Camlann."

"Before Caer Caradoc?" Urien said.

"Yes," Myrddin said. "King Arthur has fully committed all his men and resources and asks for your support for the endeavor."

Urien pursed his lips for a moment, and then he nodded to the guards behind Myrddin. "Take him."

"What?" Nell surged to her feet. "My lord—we are emissaries from King Arthur!"

"He is an enemy spy," Urien said.

"Nell, leave it." Myrddin himself seemed completely unsurprised at this turn of events.

She gritted her teeth to keep herself from speaking. Neither of them had *seen* this outcome. Or if Myrddin had, he hadn't said anything about it to her. One look at Urien told her that she would get nothing from him, so she turned in appeal to Owain. He, however, was looking on impassively without so much as a single shift in his shoulders, so she backed away. Meanwhile, Myrddin was bound, his hands behind his back and his arms held by Urien's soldiers.

Myrddin lifted his chin to Urien. "You intend to betray Arthur?"

Urien scoffed. "It is only a betrayal if I was ever loyal. Which I have not been, as you well know."

"You fought with Arthur a few years ago against the Mercians," Myrddin said.

"A temporary alliance."

"Without your men, there is a good chance that Arthur will fall. Wales will fall," Myrddin said.

"Such is my hope," Urien said.

"You hate him that much?"

"I am being pragmatic."

Myrddin laughed without humor. "Do you think that by supporting Modred against Arthur he will leave you be? That he will be so occupied with his new conquest that he will not turn his attention to you? Do you think he has some influence on the men of Deira or Bernicia who press you so hard? I assure you he does not. If you allow Arthur to fall, you will have no place to retreat to when the Saxons come for you."

Urien scoffed again. "I have long been deprived of what was rightfully mine. No longer."

Nell quailed inside, finally understanding what was happening. Urien had made a deal with Modred. If Urien supported him against Arthur, a portion of Wales would be his. She didn't speak what was in her mind, however, and Urien jerked his head to his men to indicate that they should remove Myrddin from the room.

Two soldiers tugged Myrddin towards an outside door, which lay behind Nell. But as they approached, Nell stepped forward to block their way. "May I have a moment?" She would have preferred to fade into the background and not call undue attention to herself, but she couldn't allow them to take Myrddin away without a word.

451

Owain moved to stand near Nell. At first she thought it was to stop her from speaking to Myrddin, but as the guard looked at him for permission, Owain flicked out one finger. "One moment only."

The guards didn't let go of Myrddin, but they looked away as Nell went up on her toes to kiss Myrddin's lips. "It will be all right."

"Nell." Her name came out a growl. "You will not do what is in your head. You will not."

"I told you I wouldn't."

His eyes narrowed, clearly not believing her. "As your husband, I forbid you to try."

Nell clenched the edges of his cloak with both fists and looked up into his face. "It might be the only way."

"It is not. Promise me that you will not leave Chester, that you will not go to Modred's camp. Say it!"

Nell let out a breath. "I will not leave. Not today. Not until we've tried everything else."

Myrddin still didn't look satisfied. "Say you promise, Nell. Give me your word."

"Yes, my lord. I promise."

Myrddin was right to be wary whenever she called him *lord*, but they had no more time to talk because the guards, who'd listened with interest to this cryptic conversation, prodded Myrddin's back and got him walking.

Owain stared after him. "What was that about?"

"Defeating Modred, whatever the cost."

Owain sneered in mimicry of his father. "There is nothing you can do to prevent Modred's ultimate victory. The Britons are few and the Saxons many. We decided long since that if we are to survive, it must be at their side."

Nell turned on him. "You do realize what legacy you will inherit, don't you? Your father will be known forevermore as Urien the Betrayer."

"Not if Arthur falls," Owain said.

"You fool. This is King Arthur we're talking about. If Arthur falls, Urien's name will be cursed, and he will be consigned to the farthest reaches of hell. And if Arthur wins, nobody will remember either Rheged or your father at all."

Chapter Nine
15 December 537 AD
Myrddin

MYRDDIN RAGED AROUND his cell, from the bars that made up one wall to the window and back again. The whole *point* of journeying with Nell was so they could work together. Back at Caer Caradoc, he hadn't questioned the idea of her riding to Chester. While on the surface it might seem ridiculous for just the two of them to go, he'd taken her with him to ensure that she didn't wander off on her own as was her wont. But now, he was stuck in a cell with no way out and no ability to keep an eye on her.

Myrddin kicked at the bucket in the corner. He hadn't used it yet, but the very fact that he had a bucket to use made him even angrier. She could be getting into all kinds of trouble. Worse, in here, he couldn't protect her. He had thought that Owain might ensure her safety in a town full of fighting men, but given Urien's disregard for Myrddin himself, he had no hope of it.

Never mind that Nell had managed to take care of herself without him for the first thirty years of her life; she hadn't been able to save herself on the road to Denbigh. He just prayed that she had taken refuge in the hall or, better yet, the chapel, which was a place, as a former nun, she would willingly seek out.

The sounds of Chester came through his window. Myrddin had never been in a settlement this large: the city was significantly grander and more populated than Wroxeter. In the journey to his prison, they had crossed four streets and passed a dozen large buildings. He hadn't been blindfolded, fortunately, so he'd been able to chart his passage and knew that he was on the eastern side of the city, near the east gate and adjacent to the barracks—a massive building at least two hundred feet long.

The noise from outside his cell grew louder, and he went to the window to look out. While Urien's hall had been built on risers, under which warm air flowed to heat the room (Myrddin knew this having seen the inner workings of Wroxeter), his cell had no such luxury. It was made of rough square blocks on three sides and on the floor, fitted securely to each other, and there had been no step up when he'd been hauled in here. The window in the eastern wall was at head height and only a foot square. It faced an alley which afforded little view of what was happening outside, but if he stood on tiptoe he could see men marching down the main street to the south.

From the number gathered, it looked to him as if Urien's army would march soon. Since it was getting close to noon, likely they would march day and night with short rests in order to reach Caer Caradoc in two days' time. The snow would delay them, especially as most of the soldiers wouldn't be on horseback, but Myrddin could see now that Urien had been ready to leave before he and Nell had arrived. All Urien had been waiting for was news that he was needed—by Modred, not Arthur—news which Myrddin had so kindly brought him.

Myrddin inspected the construction of the bars in the window, wondering how long it might take him to dig them out of the stone in which they'd been fitted. Cold air blew on him, and he put his hands to his lips to warm them. At least he still had his thick cloak, and while his captors had taken his sword and knives, they hadn't stripped him. He wouldn't freeze to death, but the brazier in the guard room on the other side of the door was too far away to feel, so he was mighty cold already.

Giving up on the window, Myrddin turned his attention to the iron bars that took up the whole of the western wall of his cell. His was one of three cells which the room enclosed. On the far side of the room, a narrow door led to the guard room and the exit.

Sadly, the iron bars were also well mortared and the door was kept in place by strong hinges and a lock. With the key far away in the guardroom, Urien knew the cell was impenetrable, and thus he had left only one man to watch Myrddin. The guard was tipped back in his chair with his feet up on the table, which Myrddin could see a sliver of through the open doorway.

Then the exit door, which aligned exactly with the door between the guardroom and the cells, opened, and Owain entered. "Give us a moment." He flicked a hand to the guard, who swung his feet off the table.

The guard probably bowed, though Myrddin couldn't see it from the angle he'd been afforded, and then the man left through the door Owain had just come through. Owain sauntered towards Myrddin's cell. Myrddin hadn't been entirely sure that the other cells were unoccupied, but from Owain's attitude, it was clear that Myrddin was now alone with the prince.

"You should sleep, while you can," Owain said.

"Should I?" Myrddin clenched his hands around the bars that separated him from Owain, wishing they were really around Owain's neck.

"Care to tell me what I could have done to prevent this, Myrddin?" Owain said. "You would have had me defy my father openly in the hall in front of a hundred of his men?"

As Owain's words sank in, Myrddin found his anger fading, to be replaced by calculation. He gave Owain a sharp nod. "You could do nothing, as I could have done nothing if you'd appeared in Arthur's hall and been tossed in a cell on Arthur's orders."

Owain scoffed. "You think you understand, but you don't. Urien is my father. Arthur is your liege lord. It makes a difference to know that I could defy him and be forgiven. I have chosen not to."

Myrddin decided that now was not the time to tell Owain that, in point of fact, their situations were exactly the same. "Where is Nell? What have you done with her?"

"I have done nothing with her. She is not a prisoner."

"Then why am I in here?"

"Why would my father lock up a woman when imprisoning you is surely sufficient?" But then Owain frowned. "Though—I looked for her in the hall a moment ago and did not see her. Perhaps she has abandoned you and departed to warn Arthur of my father's plans." He shrugged. "It is no matter."

"If it is no matter, why keep me here?"

"A precaution, to allow my father to act unimpeded. Whether or not your woman reaches Caer Caradoc in time to tell Arthur that my father sides with Modred won't change the outcome of the battle. It will merely let Arthur know sooner rather than later that his defeat is inevitable. That is, if she can make it all that way on her own."

"Then let me go too." Myrddin shook the bars, but they didn't budge. It would take more than the strength of ten men to bend them.

"I was thinking about it." Owain jerked his head to indicate the room behind him. "The key to your cell is hanging from a hook on the wall. You can wait until we return victorious, or—" he shot Myrddin a mischievous grin, "—you can figure out a way to get it. In the meantime, I'll make sure you're fed and watered."

And with that, he saluted Modred, turned on his heel, and departed.

Myrddin was torn between shouting something profane after him and the dawning realization that there was more here than first met the eye. While Owain was no longer the boy who'd gambled with his father's men five years ago, by leaving Myrddin unguarded and the key within hailing distance, even if currently out of reach, he proved that he hadn't quite left the boy behind. Still, Myrddin couldn't reach the key yet, and maybe that was a message for him too.

With a groan of aching muscles and exhaustion long deferred, he stretched out on his back near the wall. The blanket beneath him hardly protected him from the cold of the stones, but at least the cell had been swept clean recently, and it didn't stink.

He closed his eyes. A good soldier slept when he could. Of all the things Myrddin had ever resolved to be, it was a good soldier.

HACK! SLASH! THRUST!

The fight had gone on for far too long already, especially since Arthur was putting his entire strength into his blows, all of which Modred had absorbed with hardly a scratch. Modred had stung the king several times, however, and the wounds in king's arm and belly were bleeding freely. If the flow of blood in Arthur's side wasn't staunched, he would soon become too weak to stand.

Modred was quicker than Arthur and younger, and it had become clear to Myrddin by now that Modred's strategy all along had been a battle of attrition: to allow Arthur to expend his energy in fruitless assault while Modred merely parried and evaded. Even Arthur's blows that landed did no damage. Myrddin longed to wipe that perpetual smirk off Modred's face, but instead it deepened. "You cannot defeat me, uncle! I am the rightful king of Wales!"

This was truly the end of all—

MYRDDIN SAT UP WITH a start, cursing that despite what they'd tried so far, the outcome of the battle remained the same.

He didn't know what had woken him at first, so he listened hard and then listened again. There was nothing to hear but the *drip, drip, drip* of water somewhere above him. Unlike when he'd had the dream in the barn, which had passed in a few heartbeats, this time he'd slept for many hours. While his heart was heavier than when he'd gone to sleep, he had to admit that his eyes were not as tired.

He cupped a hand around his mouth and called into the oppressive silence, "Hello!"

A little light came through the window in his cell, but it was torchlight, not daylight. A single lantern on the wall in the guardroom lit the area beyond his cell, but he saw no sign of the man who earlier had been guarding him. The prison was deserted but for him, and from the lack of sounds outside, the entirety of the town that the walls enclosed might be empty too. Urien had committed everyone he had to this endeavor. Arthur and Myrddin weren't the only ones who were gambling everything on one last throw of the dice.

Cursing his complete isolation, Myrddin went to the door and studied the lock. It was as solid as ever, and he had no piece of metal with which to pick it. Owain was good as his word, in that someone had left a flask of water and a loaf of bread within arm's reach of the bars, but nobody was coming to free him. He tried not to think about where Nell was and how she might fare making her way south alone. She was going to Modred's tent. He knew it, and it was a stabbing pain in his heart that she had chosen not only to sacrifice herself, but to leave him. She didn't trust him enough to understand that they would find another way, just like they had every time before.

Then the door to the outside opened, and Nell entered. "I really doubt that shaking the bars is going to loosen them. Urien strikes me as a most thorough captor."

Myrddin clenched the bars tighter, drinking in the sight of her. "Owain told me you'd gone!"

Shaking her head at him, and with casual grace, she reached up for the key on the guardroom wall and came forward to unlock the door to his cell. He pushed it open and grabbed her up in a hug.

"You thought I'd gone to Modred." Nell's voice came out muffled by Myrddin's cloak.

He loosened his grip slightly so she could breathe. "I confess I did." He hung his head.

"I hid myself in the chapel. Urien is a traitor, but he would never send someone to harm me there. And honestly, harming me was the last thing on anyone's mind today." She released him and stepped back, frowning. "You actually believed Owain? How could you have so little faith in me? In us?"

"I'm sorry. I'm sorry. You know what it's like when you're alone in the dark. You fear the worst. You imagine scenarios involving people you love doing things that make you angry, and become angry at them even though they haven't done them."

Still shaking her head, Nell walked a little bit away, towards the guardroom door, paused, and then strode back to him. Taking the edges of his cloak in her fists, she tugged at him so he had to bend closer, his forehead to hers. "I forgive you this once."

A huge relief. "Did you dream again just now?"

She nodded. This time when she released him and paced away towards the door, it wasn't in anger. When she reached the outside door, she looked out, made sure nobody was close by enough to listen, and then shut the door again. It banged a little harder than it needed to. Her movements revealed frustration—this time not directed at Myrddin but at all they didn't know. "What is the dream telling us? What am I not seeing?"

Myrddin rested his hands on the top of his head and bent back his neck to look up at the ceiling. "Right now it's telling us that Arthur is going to die."

She wrinkled her nose in disgust. "What's the point of that? We dreamed for years about Arthur's death, but we changed it. The outcome wasn't what we feared because we acted. At Wroxeter we both dreamed of the future, and those dreams guided our actions and allowed us to free the king. What are we not culling from these dreams that will allow us to change the future?"

"Else why dream, is that what you're saying?"

"Exactly. Before we found each other and realized that we had a chance to change what we could *see*, we despaired. Now we know that what we see is one possible future that can be changed, and yet—" She raised her hands and dropped them.

"All we can do is try, Nell." Myrddin followed her into the guardroom and found his sword stashed in a trunk in the corner, but his armor and knives were gone. The soldiers must have known that even Urien wouldn't countenance the theft of a sword. He slammed down the lid of the trunk in frustration and turned to Nell. "My armor isn't the only thing that's missing."

But Nell stood with her hand to her mouth, her eyes wide and staring at him. "That's it, Myrddin! Your armor! Or rather, Modred's."

Myrddin's mind was still on the injustice of losing his possessions. "What are you talking about?"

Nell put out a hand to him. "Modred's armor. Do you remember in the dreams of his fight with Arthur how Modred's armor seemed impervious to Arthur's blade?"

"Yes. I dreamed of it again right before you came."

"So did I. How is it that Arthur's blows were so easily turned aside?"

Myrddin tsked through his teeth. "It isn't because Modred is anointed by God, I can tell you that."

"Think back to the dream where I enter Modred's tent on the night before the battle. Can you see the whole of the interior? Can you describe to me where his bed and table are?"

Myrddin's brow furrowed as he thought. "I'm afraid all I see is you. All I feel is fear for you."

"As I do for you, but in that dream, even as my conscious self is screaming at you not to enter his tent, you do anyway. Once inside, your eyes are on Modred's back as he faces the table, but to the left is an armor stand. Think. Can you see it too?"

Myrddin closed his eyes and cast his mind back to the dream where Nell had died by Modred's hand. It was true that his entire being had vibrated with fear for her, but as she looked at Modred's back, he caught a glimpse of what she was talking about. Off to one side stood an armor tree, holding a breastplate, shoulder guards, and solid metal thigh and shin guards. His first thought was that he'd never seen such solid armor in his life—except, now that he thought about it, on carvings and the remains of frescos found in Roman ruins. The house in which Arthur, Nell, and Huw had been kept at Wroxeter had been adorned with tilework showing warriors wearing very similar gear.

"We should go," Nell said.

"Go where?"

"To Modred's camp."

"A moment ago you were angry with me when I thought you'd gone there. How can you suggest that we go there together now?"

"I was angry because you thought I'd gone without you," Nell said. "There's the difference. What we do, whatever it is, we do together."

"To what end?" Myrddin said. "Any one of Arthur's men could scout the camp more easily than we can. We should ride to Caer Caradoc to tell Arthur that Urien marches to Modred."

"No. This battle begins and ends with our dream and what we see in that tent. Modred defeats Arthur because of his armor. We need to take it from him! If we allow the battle to go forward as we have dreamed, we know the outcome. Coming here appears to have only made the situation worse by sending Urien in on Modred's side. We *have* to think beyond the usual." She touched his arm. "On the battlefield, King Arthur was stronger and more skilled than Modred. We saw it. He should have won, but Modred's armor allowed him to outlast Arthur. Being older and wounded, Arthur tired more quickly."

"I agree that Modred's armor protected his body, and taking it from him could give Arthur back the advantage, but I don't think that will be enough to make the difference in this fight. We have to do more."

"It will do more. The loss of his armor will sow doubt in Modred's mind." She looked pleadingly at Myrddin. "I know it sounds mad."

Myrddin hesitated. He remained skeptical, but Nell's surety and enthusiasm, if not contagious, was something he wanted to support. Besides, motion was always better than no motion. "No. The more I think about it, the better this idea seems. Honestly, I think it's time for a little madness." He picked her up and swung her around, laughing. Then he sobered and set her back down. "If we do this right, Modred won't know who took it or where it has gone. He will be angry, and he will be uncertain."

"I like the idea of Modred uncertain," Nell said.

"I do too." Just making the decision increased Myrddin's confidence. "In fact, it could be that making him feel that way is essential to victory. Come on." He took her hand in his and headed towards the door. "The time has come to hurry."

Chapter Ten

16 December 537

Huw

"MODRED'S BANNERS, MY lord." Cador halted beside Huw, who was standing with Anwen on the wall-walk, looking through a gap in the palisade wall towards the field below the fort. Another day had passed in preparation for battle, and with evening coming on, it seemed that dawn would bring war, whether or not they were ready for it.

"I recognize them," Huw said. "This is really going to happen, isn't it?"

"Yes," Cador said. "At dawn tomorrow, King Arthur and Modred will meet briefly, they will talk, but there can be no peace because Modred will accept nothing less than our complete surrender."

"We could ride from the fort and attack now—surprise them like we did at Buellt," Huw said.

"That might have been a viable strategy at Buellt," Cador said, "but we are not ready, and after Buellt, the Saxons won't be as unprepared as we might like. They know how to fight, and we would find them organized against us by the time we reached the field."

"Now that Modred is here, we could stay inside the fort and make him take it from us." Anwen was back in her breeches. She held her bow in her right hand and wore her quiver, replenished with twenty arrows. Like most women, she had braided her hair to keep it contained and had again wound her braid around her head and pinned it. She didn't want any strands in her way when she reached to her quiver to pull out an arrow.

Cador looked past Huw to his niece. "You heard the captains' council with the king. Modred doesn't want the fort. He wants Wales. He outnumbers us, so he could simply surround us and starve us out while he sends the bulk of his men west. While we sat inside our walls, we would lose the country. Under such circumstances, our people would be right to beg Modred to be their king because we would have abdicated our responsibility to protect them."

Huw felt for Anwen's hand and squeezed once. "Besides, most of our men are not inside the fort. Exposed as they are, even if they maintain the high ground, they will have no choice but to fight." He let go, because even that sign of comfort was too much familiarity on such short acquaintance. But then she surprised him by reaching for his hand herself and entwining her fingers in his.

"Better that we choose the ground and the time." Cador kept his gaze outward, though Huw had no illusions that he didn't know what was going on between him and Anwen.

"Has there still been no word from my father and Nell?" Huw said.

"No word."

"How many men have come to fight for us?" Anwen said.

"Some two thousand," Cador said.

Huw shook his head. "Not enough."

"No," Cador said, "but more come every hour."

Huw shook his head. "Modred's men are here. We are all but out of time."

Thirty years ago when Arthur's force had defeated the great Saxon army, it was said that King Arthur carried the cross of Christ on his back for three days in the victory. Arthur himself had told Huw the true story of that battle as they sat up late the night before. It hadn't been a fight Arthur had been looking for, being the last of a dozen that he'd fought against the Saxons over the course of a spring and summer in the year before Myrddin had been born. Uther, Arthur's father, and Ambrosius, who'd been king at the time, had ordered Arthur to Mt. Badon to defend the pass into Wales while they had led a stronger force south and east, having heard rumors of a gathering of Saxon armies. Then, as now, they were hoping to end the Saxon threat in one go.

Unfortunately for Arthur, it had been at Mt. Badon where the Saxons had gathered, not Bath, where Ambrosius and Uther had gone. Though outnumbered, Arthur had used the men he had to great effect, particularly his archers, and what had started out as a sure Saxon victory had become a Welsh one and a rout for the Saxons. Underneath the covering fire of his archers, Arthur had led charge after charge. With the victory at Badon, the Saxons had been defeated for a generation, and they hadn't risen again until Modred had begun his rebellion.

Thinking of that long ago day, Huw looked towards the Lawley, the mountain that rose up to the northeast of Caer Caradoc. Now that the light was fading, here and there he could make out the flare of a campfire or a torch. "Lord Cador, how many men did the Saxons bring against Arthur when he defeated them at Badon?"

"We had perhaps a tenth of the numbers of the Saxon force. King Arthur has faced these odds before and won."

Anwen smiled. "As my Saxon stepfather tells it, it wasn't Arthur's skill that won the day, but a great trembling in the earth, which opened up and swallowed half the Saxon army whole. I wish that would happen here."

Cador laughed. "It didn't happen then. It won't happen tomorrow. We can't think to rely on miracles."

"Then we'll have to make our own," Huw said.

Cador had been nothing but steady and sure in his belief that they could win, but Huw's words had him swallowing another laugh. "How?"

"What if we light three times as many fires on the Lawley tonight as we have men to sit at them, and even more on the Long Mynd." Huw gestured to the mountain in front of them. "Never mind that we may never have the men to sit at them, we will sow doubt in the minds of Modred's men."

Anwen's eyes were bright as she looked at Huw, understanding instantly what he intended. "They will think we have more men than we have, and even tomorrow on the battlefield, even if they kill hundreds of us, they will be wondering how many more we have to send against them."

Cador fisted one hand and pounded it into his other palm, more light in his eyes than when he'd come up to the wall-walk to greet Huw. "You have a bit of your father in you, don't you?"

Huw gave a low laugh. "If what we believe about Modred's numbers is true, I pray to God that it turns out to be more than a bit."

Chapter Eleven

16 December 537 AD

Nell

NELL AND MYRDDIN CROUCHED in a ditch in the darkness, twenty feet from the nearest sentry posted on the outskirts of Modred's encampment. Their own army lay less than a mile to the southeast within the safety of Caer Caradoc or on the mountains beside it. As the darkness had overtaken the hills, cooking fires had sprung up, and Nell's spirits had lifted. Far more lights shone out in the darkness than she'd hoped she would see. The men of Wales had come to support Arthur in one last battle.

"If we get separated, meet me at that hollow tree we passed," Myrddin said.

"I remember it."

"You do realize that this is one of our crazier ideas." Myrddin's tone was casual.

She gave a low laugh. "Yes."

"This could be where we meet our deaths."

Nell took in a deep breath and let it out. If she lived to be eighty, she would never forget the sight of Modred driving a knife into Myrddin's throat. And she knew that it was the same for him, seeing her die by Modred's hand. It didn't matter that these were dreams. They were as real to each of them as the other's face.

But that fear didn't change what they had to do, or that this course was the right one. She'd had no visions at all since they'd left Chester, just as when they'd approached Buellt a few days ago. But while the dream of Arthur's death had haunted her for twenty years and this one of Myrddin had consumed her for only a few days, it was no less potent in its power—or potentially crippling.

"If we don't do this, we're dead anyway soon enough—if not on the battlefield tomorrow then later, in another battle before another mountain." She turned her head to look at him. "In all the long years of dreaming of Arthur's death at the church, we both found strength to do difficult things because to not do them would bring that future closer. We didn't care about our own deaths because we knew already they were inevitable. If that was true then, it is even more true now."

"When you put it that way—" Myrddin hefted the satchel they'd brought for carrying the armor and was up and running at a crouch towards the back of the closest tent. Nell stayed hard on his heels. They'd been waiting for the guard to face the other way, which he had done for just a moment when someone called to him from within the ring of torchlight.

She and Myrddin had been watching this tent for some time, so they knew that it was empty. Myrddin slashed at the fabric with Nell's knife, and they went through the hole he created almost without stopping. Light filtered through the half-closed front flap, but anyone outside looking in would see only darkness.

Myrddin shifted, the shape of him unfamiliar in his borrowed leather armor and Saxon helmet, which were the best that could be salvaged from Urien's depleted armory. As if Myrddin knew what Nell was thinking about, which wouldn't surprise her at this point, he said, "I think I'll keep these bracers. I like them."

"Pray you don't ever need them," she said.

He ducked his head. "Nell, you know I will. No matter what we achieve tonight, there will be a battle tomorrow, and I will fight in it."

Nell looked down at the grassy floor of the tent. She did know that. Huw would be fighting too. They were here only to make that battle more winnable, not to avert it. Even if they came upon Modred alone in his pavilion, the plan wasn't to kill him. Maybe that was something to consider again, since there were two of them now.

No. Better to accomplish what they came for—quick and easy and back to Caer Caradoc before midnight.

"Come on," Myrddin said. "The camp will never be busier than it is now."

As when she'd dreamed of infiltrating the camp, they were doing it in the evening when it was busy. That might seem counterintuitive, but if they were to steal Modred's armor, it had to be when he wasn't there—not when he was asleep and might wake to shout an alarm, or when almost no one was about and the few stray people who were would be looked at closely. In the bustle of the camp, with Myrddin dressed like a Saxon warrior and Nell in a hooded cloak, they could blend in among the Saxons. Coincidentally, they each looked just as the other had dreamed: she was attempting to pass for a camp follower, and he for a Saxon man-at-arms.

With darkness coming so early this time of year—Wales had hardly eight hours of daylight even including the murk before dawn and after sunset—the men of Modred's camp hadn't stopped working just because it was dark. Soon it would be mealtime. Here on the eastern side of the camp, they were close to the kitchen fires, and the smell of stew wafted towards them. The men would be fed stew and gruel—as much as they could eat—in preparation for the battle tomorrow. Sadly, from Nell and Myrddin's perspective, none of the soldiers would be given much in the way of beer or mead. Modred needed them sober for tomorrow.

The pair left the relative safety of the tent, Myrddin's arm draped casually across Nell's shoulders. Several people close by eyed them, assuming they knew what they'd been doing inside that tent. It was such a far cry from what they had actually been doing that

Nell almost laughed, which was probably to the good since it made her relax a little.

"Where's Modred's pavilion?" she said to Myrddin in an undertone. "It isn't in the exact center of the camp?"

"No—that's the command center. It's this way. I saw it from the hill before it grew dark."

"That's one way this camp is different from the one we dreamed." Nell started to feel a bit of hope.

And then there it was, located in the northeastern quadrant. Nell and Myrddin took a circuitous route, cutting through some other tenting areas and campfires, so as not to come directly at it. They also wanted to make sure that Modred wasn't inside. When they were fifty feet away in the shadow of another tent, they stopped. Modred *was* there, actually. But as they watched, he ducked out the opening and headed towards the command pavilion located fifty yards away. As he walked past them, men bowed in greeting, and many stood in order to follow after him. Clearly something was happening.

"I think he's going to speak to the men," Myrddin said.

"You get rid of the guard while I get the armor." Nell spoke in an undertone into his chest. He'd kept his arm around her, and they'd been nuzzling each other as if she was his woman. Which she was, of course, but never had she paid so little heed to his attentions.

Nell took a step towards the tent, but Myrddin pulled her back, handing her the satchel. "Let me go first." With sure strides he approached the sentry, who was standing three paces from the entrance, holding a pike and looking straight ahead. "You are relieved, soldier."

The man blinked. "But I just came on duty."

"Beorhtsige's orders. He wants you at the meeting with the others. I'm to take your place."

471

"The king has left, so the tent is empty."

"I will guard it with my life," Myrddin said.

The man handed him the pike and hastened away after Modred. A heartbeat later, Nell crossed to the tent and ducked through the doorway. Straightening, she took in Modred's quarters with a glance. They were orderly. Furs and blankets, empty of women (thankfully), were layered on the bed to one side. A table stacked with maps and papers, for when he brought his captains inside to consult more privately than in the command tent, stood in the center, and to Nell's left was a cross-shaped armor stand holding the armor of which she'd dreamed.

It had been King Arthur, in fact, who'd given the different pieces their Roman names when Huw had asked about the images on the walls of the manor house in which Modred had kept them at Wroxeter. These included a metal cuirass to protect the chest and back, manicas (levered shoulder armor that protected a man's arm from neck to wrist), thigh pads, and shin guards, all in a silver metal that had been polished until it gleamed. It wasn't iron, the metal from which everything British or Saxon was made. It was *steel*, the secret of which had been lost after the Romans had departed Britain.

She touched the cuirass and realized her mistake. It would be impossible for her and Myrddin to sneak this armor out of the tent—much less the camp—without calling attention to themselves. This wasn't normal mail or even leather armor, which could be bent, manipulated, or stuffed into a bag. The cuirass alone was too big and bulky for the satchel she'd brought to hide it in.

She crossed back to the doorway and whispered to Myrddin. "I need your help."

Myrddin spoke out of the side of his mouth. "I can't leave the tent unattended! Someone will notice."

"We have to risk it. The only way we're leaving here with that armor is if you are wearing it."

With a low groan, Myrddin took a step back and then turned and ducked through the doorway. He straightened and stopped, in an almost identical pose to what hers had been. "Oh."

"Exactly." She motioned with her hand to indicate that Myrddin should start stripping off his gear. "Hurry, before anyone comes."

While Myrddin unhooked his cloak and started unbuckling the bracers that he'd liked so much, Nell went to the door flap, intending to keep some kind of watch, but Myrddin snapped his fingers to gain her attention. "Never mind the door. I'll need your help to get it on." He shrugged out of his leather armor, leaving him in his shirt, overtunic, and breeches.

Nell turned back to him, looking between him and Modred's armor. She shook her head. "You'll need to hide that you're wearing it, so take off your shirt and tunic. You can wear the armor underneath everything, next to your skin."

Although the armor as a whole was unfamiliar, the Roman buckles weren't dissimilar from what she was used to. Her hands shook, but she tried to breathe easy to steady them. By the time she finished, however, both she and Myrddin were breathing hard—mostly from the panic that threatened to overwhelm them. They *had* to get out of here, and acquiring the armor had already taken far longer than they'd planned.

Myrddin swung his arms in a full circle. "The Romans knew what they were about. No wonder they conquered us so easily. This armor fits me like a glove and is much lighter than I expected—and more comfortable than that boiled leather I was wearing. I could turn a somersault."

"Let's hope King Arthur thinks so too." With some effort, she helped Myrddin get back into his shirt and tunic, both of which were stretched tight in places, since they weren't made to go over metal armor. His leather armor, which had been too large to begin with, went over the top of it all. It was ridiculous to attempt to wear it, but if he was approached by any Saxon without it on, they would know instantly that something was wrong. No Saxon spearman in his position—in the lead up to battle—would ever go about without it.

"Now I feel like I'm one of those statues we saw at Wroxeter," Myrddin said. "I can hardly move my arms, much less turn a somersault."

"Well, you don't look like a statue, which is the point." Nell fastened his cloak at the neck. "You simply look bulky."

Myrddin took a few steps. "I creak a little. Can you hear it?"

She shook her head. "No more than usual from a man in armor."

"All right." Myrddin walked stiffly to the exit. "I'll take up the sentry position again. Give me a count of five and then come out."

Myrddin ducked under the tent flap and immediately was accosted by an angry superior. "How dare you leave your post!"

"I'm sorry, sir. I needed to give the maid a hand."

Her breath in her throat, Nell crossed to the bed and lifted up the side of the mattress, thinking to hide Myrddin's bracers under the bed (she hadn't been able to buckle them over his armor) and at least delay their discovery. But as she did so, she kicked something hard that hurt her toe all the way through her boot. Bending, she flicked the furs aside and let out a gasp: Caledfwlch, King Arthur's legendary sword, lay on the ground in its sheath. Modred had brought it from Wroxeter and cared for it so much that he was sleeping with it next to his bed.

The captain outside was still talking to Myrddin. Despite rising panic that she was taking too long, Nell knew absolutely that she couldn't leave the sword behind, so she grabbed it up and ran around the table with it to the back of the pavilion. Lifting up the bottom edge where there were no stakes, she shoved it outside the tent to lie along the edge in the grass—hoping as she did so that there wasn't anyone outside to notice.

Then she bundled Myrddin's bracers into one of the blankets from the bed and bent forward so she could pass through the entryway as Myrddin had done—and ran headfirst into the superior officer. "Sorry! Sorry!" She rubbed at the top of her head with her free hand.

The officer grunted at the impact of Nell's head against his chest, though since he was wearing armor it had hurt her far more than him. "Watch where you're going!"

Nell ducked her head and groveled. "I'm so sorry. Please don't punish him. It was me, cleaning up for my lord Modred." She straightened in order to give the officer her sweetest smile, thankful from the bottom of her heart that this wasn't Beorhtsige, who would have recognized them both.

The man's eyes narrowed. "What do you have there?"

"I was to take this to be laundered." Nell held out the bundled blanket. She shouldn't have kept the bracers, but she hadn't wanted to leave any trace of their presence behind for Modred to find.

The man snorted and waved a hand. "Be off with you before the king returns."

Nell obeyed instantly, hustling around to the back side of the tent. The sword was still there, but she didn't bend to it yet. She wanted to wait to make sure Myrddin got away and she wasn't needed again, but then she heard the captain say. "Move from this spot and I will have you whipped!"

"Yes, sir!"

Nell peered around the corner in time to see the captain nod his approval of Myrddin's response before moving away. Unfortunately, he didn't move away far enough and seemed to be waiting for something—possibly for Modred's return. Nell couldn't believe the speeches were ongoing, but maybe Modred was more longwinded than Arthur. While Myrddin would want her to return to the woods to wait for him, she couldn't just run away when he was so close to being caught.

A roar went up from the center of the camp, and people began moving back towards their cooking fires. The meeting had ended. Dinner was next. It was possible that Modred would eat in the command tent with his captains, but it was equally likely that he would return to his own tent, a woman or two in tow.

Feeling like time was slipping away from her, Nell straightened her skirt, tucked the bundle more securely under her arm, and walked to where several soldiers had stopped to talk near the closest fire. One of them said, "It's just as well Arthur escaped. Now we can kill him and his army in one go!"

The others laughed. She'd wondered what kind of brave face Modred would put on their escape, and now she knew.

She chose to speak to the youngest of them. "That captain there? What's his name?"

The young man turned to look. "Leofric. Why?"

She ducked her head. "My lord Beorhtsige sent me to fetch him, but I feared to approach him, since I know he has a terrible temper and no patience with women."

One of the other men laughed. "You have the right of it." He looked her up and down. "You belong to Beorhtsige?"

"Yes, my lord."

He laughed. "I am no lord, but I don't mind helping Beorhtsige's woman. I'll tell Leofric. Where is Beorhtsige?"

Nell pointed with her chin to indicate the center of the camp. "Thank you so much!" And then to her horror, she really saw him. He was taller than most men and stood out even among Saxons, who tended to be taller than the British.

The man rose to his feet and sauntered over to Leofric, who looked sharply at him before glancing towards where Beorhtsige was conferring with some of the other captains. With a nod, Leofric marched away. As Nell's new friend turned back to the campfire, Nell put up a hand in thanks.

Myrddin must have been waiting for any chance to depart, because he moved the instant Leofric's back was turned and darted between two neighboring tents. Nell lost sight of him immediately.

Remembering the sword, Nell walked casually behind Modred's tent. She stood over the sword for a moment before bending to pick it up and tucking it inside her cloak, pressed against her side under her left arm, which still held the wadded up blanket. Then she headed towards the eastern edge of the camp. Once she was a hundred feet away, she picked up her pace, weaving in and around the tents and fire circles, praying nobody stopped her and hoping she had such a look of purpose on her face that they wouldn't.

Finally, she reached the edge of the camp and looked back. She didn't see Myrddin, but there were hundreds of men within hailing distance in Saxon helmets. Myrddin would think that she'd done the sensible thing and left. Nell took in a breath, telling herself that she'd done what she could, and it would be foolish to continue to search for Myrddin when he might have already reached the safety of the woods. It was time for her to do the same.

Chapter Twelve

16 December 537 AD

Myrddin

THE ENTIRE TIME THE captain had been watching, Myrddin's heart had been in his throat, fearful that he would be recognized or someone would notice his unusual bulk. Myrddin himself was on the tall side, but not freakishly so. Modred's armor actually fit him quite well, which perhaps shouldn't have been surprising since he and Modred were cousins. King Arthur was slightly broader around the waist than they were, being older, but Myrddin was confident that the armor would fit him too.

Then, in answer to Myrddin's prayers, the captain turned his back. It was just the moment Myrddin had been waiting for. The key was to get out of sight as quickly as possible, so he slipped between two neighboring tents and kept going at a run, his head down, as if someone had sent him on an urgent errand. Only after he was several fire circles away and on the perimeter of the camp did he pull up and look for Nell. He didn't see her.

Unfortunately, as he was gazing around, he caught the eye of another man who outranked him. "You there!"

Myrddin stiffened to attention. "Yes, sir!" Like Modred in the visions, Myrddin would have felt invincible if he wasn't terrified that at any moment someone would recognize him. If that happened, armor or no armor, his head would be removed from his body.

"Who are you and why are you not at your posting?"

Myrddin looked straight ahead, not into the man's face but at the space above his right shoulder. "My name is Cedric, sir. I am on watch on the perimeter." He sent a silent plea for forgiveness to

Lord Cedric for borrowing his name. It was the first Saxon name that had popped into his head.

"Then why are you not there?"

"I am headed there now, sir. Something I ate disagreed with me, but I'm better now."

The man grunted. Myrddin still hadn't gotten a good look at his face and didn't want to. He had finally realized what the problem was: he was wearing a helmet. Only men on duty wore their helmets, and any true soldier in Modred's army would know it. While his gear hid Myrddin's features, it also called attention to him. It was too late to correct that mistake now.

The officer made a dismissive gesture. "Be off with you then."

"Yes, sir." Myrddin turned smartly on one heel. Hastily attempting to formulate some kind of plan and knowing without turning around that the officer was watching him, he set off across the empty space that formed a no man's land around the camp. He was very close to the spot where he and Nell had come in. Unlike in Myrddin's dream, Modred had not thrown up a palisade around this camp.

Myrddin decided that his best option was to relieve the soldier he and Nell had snuck past earlier. He marched straightforwardly there, as if he knew what he was doing. It was only when he approached to within fifty feet or so, however, that he noticed that a second man guarded the perimeter, this one standing farther down the hill from the sentry, right on the edge of the trees.

Myrddin hesitated at the sight of him, but the first sentry had heard him coming. He turned, a finger to his lips, and whispered. "You're my relief?"

"Yes."

His brow furrowed. "I don't know you."

"Cedric."

"Aelfric."

They nodded at each other in the companionable way soldiers of equal rank do. Aelfric didn't leave, however, because at that moment the man who'd been relieving himself on the edge of the trees turned towards them. As he approached, his face showed clearly in the torchlight behind them.

It was Modred himself. The sick ball of fear that had been Myrddin's constant companion up until now solidified into a solid rock in Myrddin's gut. At any moment, Modred would recognize him, and he would die, and everything they'd done would be for naught. Still, like mummers in an Easter play, Myrddin resolved to see this through. As long as there was life, there was hope, and he refused to lose faith at the last pass—even if it was the last pass.

Myrddin and Aelfric bowed and said, "My lord."

Modred nodded. "As you were."

When the two men straightened, Modred pointed with his chin at Myrddin. "And you are?"

"Cedric, my lord." Myrddin choked out the words, and perhaps because he was so nervous, the name came out guttural with little relationship to his natural voice. Modred seemed to think nothing of it, and Myrddin allowed himself a thin, shuddering breath. He was intensely grateful that his back was to the light, so all Modred could see of his face were faint features and shadow.

Then Myrddin's heart started beating faster at the realization that not only had Modred not recognized him, but this could be an opportunity to drive his knife into Modred's heart. With only one other guard present, Myrddin could kill him too and be off into the wood before anyone was the wiser.

Unfortunately, Myrddin's arms were stuck straight down at his sides and refused to move. He could barely bend his arm at the elbow, never mind reach for his knife and pull it from its sheath.

Thankfully, Modred had no notion of the turmoil going on inside Myrddin. "Where are you from, soldier?"

With no alternative, Myrddin stood beside the Saxon guard like he was carved from wood and answered Modred's question. "Shrewsbury, my lord."

Modred bobbed his head in a nod, knowing the town since it was only a few miles from Wroxeter. "Keep an eye out, Cedric. We don't want any surprises tonight, do we?"

"No, my lord."

Modred lifted a hand but, terrified that the king was about to clap him on the shoulder, at which point he would feel Myrddin's all too solid underpinnings, Myrddin bowed again. Modred settled his hand on Aelfric's shoulder instead. "Time to eat, son."

"Yes, my lord. Thank you, my lord."

The pair began to walk across the grassy expanse between the edge of the woods and the first ring of torches. Myrddin stayed where he was until they'd passed the first of the tents, and then he started walking towards the woods. Just as he reached them, he looked back. Nobody was watching.

So he ran, thankful that even if his arms couldn't move, his legs weren't so constricted. Thirty yards into the woods, he crossed a trickle of a creek running along the bottom of a gully, and then Nell appeared from behind a tree so suddenly he almost ran her over.

She caught his arm and gave a slight squeak. "You're so solid."

"I could take offense that you think I'm soft and fat otherwise, but I won't." He looked down. "What are you carrying?"

"Your bracers wrapped in an old blanket I almost forgot I still had and—" she laughed under her breath, "—Caledfwlch!" She held up a sheathed sword. Even in the darkness the finely wrought adornments were evident.

"My God. You're a wonder."

She accepted the aid of his hand, and they scrambled up the hill out of the creek bed and out of the woods too—he far more awkwardly than she as it turned out. They'd left their horses across a field on higher ground a good two hundred yards from Modred's camp. Now that they were well away from the lights, Myrddin's night vision returned. The moon had risen, and they were able to run without need of a torch. Their feet crunched through the snow and frozen grass that made up the field, leaving footprints that a blind man, much less one of Modred's trackers, could easily follow. There was no help for it if they were to get away quickly.

Just as they reached their horses, a great shout came from the camp. Myrddin managed to raise his arms enough to grasp the horn of his saddle and pull himself up, sprawling awkwardly on his stomach before righting himself in the saddle. Side by side, he and Nell raced their horses for the road that skirted the Lawley to the west and then down it towards the safety of Caer Caradoc.

It was near midnight by now, but many men were still out and about, preparing for the battle tomorrow. A dozen wary guards greeted Myrddin and Nell at the first gate, the entrance to Caer Caradoc's extensive earthworks. One of them leaned down to look at them from the top of the gatehouse. "Who goes there?" The man had a bushy beard and eyebrows of an indeterminate color, which was all Myrddin could see of him in the torchlight.

"It is I, Myrddin ap Ambrosius, and my wife, Nell."

"Father!"

Myrddin twisted in his saddle, though any movement was difficult wearing so much armor. Huw rode at the head of a company of twenty men, descending the path from the Lawley.

"Son!" Myrddin moved his arm a few inches, which was fortunately enough to clasp Huw's forearm. "Many men have come!"

Huw gave a slight shake of his head, his brow furrowing—possibly at the size and solidity of Myrddin's arm. "Not enough."

"But the fires—" Nell said.

"They are a ruse to dismay Modred and his army, that is all. We are short of numbers."

"Geraint has not come?" Myrddin said.

"Not Geraint, Gawain, Gareth, Edgar, nor Cedric. Not yet."

Myrddin closed his eyes for a moment. He and Nell had been riding on joy and relief at their escape from Modred's camp, and now the reality of what they were facing settled over him again.

"We will face Modred with what we have," Nell said, staunchly faithful, "and that will have to be enough."

The gatekeeper had overheard. "More men come every hour, lords. We'll have enough by morning. You'll see."

"I'm sure you're right. The men of Wales know our need." Huw raised a hand to the guard, the lines around his mouth smoothing into something resembling a smile. Myrddin cursed at himself under his breath for allowing any sign of doubt to show. He could be doubtful to Nell or Huw, but not in front of the men who would be called in a few hours to lay down their lives for Arthur. But he was glad to see that his son was growing up.

Then Huw canted his head at Myrddin. "Father, why are you holding yourself so stiffly? Are you injured?"

"I am wearing armor purloined from Modred. I'll show you once we're inside," Myrddin said.

Caer Caradoc's ramparts wended their way back and forth across the face of the mountain, a distance that couldn't be traversed with any speed. Myrddin and Nell took the opportunity to update Huw on all that had happened, though Myrddin noted that Nell made no mention of Caledfwlch, tucked as it was along her horse's side by the saddle bag.

Huw returned the favor of information. "The king is prepared. I think he hopes that Modred calls him out, and the fate of the battle decided by single combat, to spare us the loss of many men, but I hope it won't come to that."

483

"It will come to that, Huw," Nell said. "We've *seen* it."

"You've seen other things too that have not come to pass, or not in their entirety," Huw said.

"That is true," Myrddin said, "and since neither of us has been visited by a vision in the last hour, we have no insight into what will happen now that we have absconded with Modred's armor."

Huw reached out a hand and knocked on Myrddin's chest. It resounded hollowly. "You are like a beetle."

"Hopefully, one not easily squashed," Myrddin said.

"Will armor be enough to turn the tide? To ensure the king can defeat Modred?" Huw said.

"In our visions, Modred hid his armor beneath garments, as I am. But King Arthur can wear it openly so Modred can see what we have done and what he has lost," Myrddin said.

"Battles are won by men, it's true, and Modred has more men than we do, especially with Urien's defection," Nell said. "But this is about fostering doubt and about men questioning Modred's right to lead. It's about Modred questioning himself. He felt invincible in that armor, and now his enemy will be wearing it."

They arrived at the fort itself and were admitted through the gate. Either King Arthur had seen them coming, or he'd been crossing the courtyard on business of his own, because he was there to greet them when they dismounted. He stood looking from Myrddin to Nell, shaking his head.

"What?" Myrddin said.

"Every time I lose hope along this path that God has led me, my faith is renewed—usually as the result of something unexpected. God has aided us time and again—by the turn of the tide, by the weather, by His own archbishop. And again, here you are, not unlooked for, but unexpected nonetheless. Several of my captains were skeptical that you would return since they believe Urien will betray me."

"Oh, he's doing that, my lord." Myrddin's faith had always had a fine vein of fatalism running through it, but with everything that had happened in the last month, he had to admit that the king had a point. Still, Myrddin wasn't convinced they wouldn't lose. Like every Welshman, he'd been raised on poetry and song. His blood hummed with the music of the bards. But almost every song, even as it celebrated the heroism of their leaders and their warriors, ended in defeat, sorrow, and loss. Other than the story of Arthur's victory at Badon, the glory was in the attempt and in the fight, not in the outcome.

"Perhaps this will help ease the pain of that betrayal." With a shy smile, Nell pulled the king's beloved Caledfwlch from where she'd secured it and held it out to Arthur. "Myrddin and I don't feel all is lost quite yet."

Rarely had Myrddin seen King Arthur undone, but there was awe in his face as he took the sword from Nell. Then he laughed.

They might be outnumbered and outmaneuvered, but as the king's laughter echoed around the courtyard, Myrddin felt his own hope renewed.

Chapter Thirteen

17 December 537 AD

Huw

DAWN WAS IMMINENT. Huw stood beside King Arthur, taking account of the numbers of men who had come and accepting their obeisance and pledges.

"Ten horse, twenty bow, and forty foot, my lord!"

"Ten archers and seventy spearmen, my lord!"

"Two hundred total, my lord, horse, bow, and spear!"

No matter their enthusiasm, the numbers were too few. As the captains and lords arrived, greeted King Arthur, and then went on to speak to Myrddin about the king's strategy and to be assigned their location in the battle, a grimness settled on everyone watching. Finally, Huw couldn't endure it any longer. He put a hand on King Arthur's shoulder, begging forgiveness for retreating for a moment, and departed for the battlement. The sight that greeted him, however, wasn't any more cheerful. Modred had brought an army unlike Wales had ever faced before. To say the Saxons outnumbered Arthur's force was to woefully understate the case.

Morosely, Huw turned his attention to the cooking fires that still blazed on the sides of the Long Mynd. It had been a good idea to light them—he didn't regret that—but in his heart of hearts he'd hoped in the end they'd be more than a charade. But then he squinted through the murky light of near dawn and frowned. Small figures moved around many of the fires—more men than could be explained by the need to tend them.

Confused, he looked back to where King Arthur was holding court and then at the mountain again. Deciding that he must be missing something, he trotted back down the steps and halted beside the king. "There's something I'd like you to see, my lord, if you will."

A lull had occurred in the line of oncoming captains, so King Arthur turned to him. "What is it?"

"My lord, please, just come look."

Smiling slightly at Huw's confusion and leaving Myrddin to accept the obeisance of the few more lords who'd reached the fort, King Arthur followed Huw up the steps to the west-facing battlement. As he reached the top step, the first rays of the sun cast their light on the mountain before them and reflected off row after row of shields, axes, spears, and helmets.

King Arthur took in a breath. "I've been keeping count of the men so far recorded and have reached some three thousand total."

Huw laughed and pointed. "There are more than three thousand men on that mountain."

King Arthur swung back to the courtyard. At that very moment, Gawain and Gareth rode underneath the gatehouse side by side with Geraint just behind them. King Arthur threw out a hand to point to the mountain as Huw had done. In so doing, he revealed the glory of the armor he wore underneath his cloak. Nell had suggested that the king leave off his tunic so the polished metal could shine for everyone to see—and shine it did as a ray of the newly risen sun struck his chest.

Throughout the last month, Huw had wanted with all his being to defeat Modred's armies, but in the back of his mind, he'd known it was impossible. He hadn't regretted throwing in his lot with his father, but even as he'd done it, he'd acknowledged that it was unwise.

But now ... now as King Arthur stood on the battlement, for the first time since Huw had come to Gwynedd and allied himself with his father, he allowed himself real hope that King Arthur could triumph against Modred.

"Take off your cloak, my lord," Huw said.

Arthur twisted at the toggle that held his cloak closed at the throat, and the fabric dropped to the wall-walk. Then the king pulled Caledfwlch from its sheath and held it above his head. The sunlight reflecting off it was blinding. Huw didn't think King Arthur had intended to make a speech at this hour, but circumstances required one, and the king obliged.

"There was a time before the Saxons came when our lands were bountiful. We had wealth and peace. We can look to that time and remember it, but we cannot wish the Saxons away. As spoke the bard, Taliesin, whose words have carried us through many victories: *To have lasting peace and true tranquility, we must have commotion first!* I aim to make a commotion the like of which the Saxons have never seen! Heroic men from every corner of Wales must stand together. For too long, we have retreated. For too many years, we have defended what was ours from those who would take it from us."

The king pointed to Myrddin. "We have long known that this morning would come. Myrddin foretold it years ago. He has seen us meet Modred's forces on the field of Camlann. He has seen us meet them sword for sword! No longer will we be outcasts in our own country. We will have victory, and we will drive the Saxons from this land forevermore!"

A great shout went up from the men assembled in the courtyard. Even if they couldn't hear King Arthur's words, the men on the mountain to the west could hear the cheering and they cheered too. The combined might of their voices rang from peak to peak and into the valley. Huw could only hope that Modred's men trembled at the sound.

With a nod at his men, King Arthur sheathed his sword and started down the stairs. Huw bent to scoop up his cloak and throw it over his arm, and then he followed. When they reached ground level, Myrddin approached, and he shook King Arthur's offered forearm. "That was a good speech," he lowered his voice, "except for the fact that I haven't seen our victory here."

"You haven't seen our defeat either, not since you returned from Modred's camp," King Arthur said. "Have you?"

"No."

"Then we will make our own fate. The men need courage, and I have given it to them."

"I don't object to that, just—"

"You don't like being singled out. You still aren't comfortable with either your visions or your birthright. I said once that you couldn't be both king and seer. I was wrong. You are Myrddin ap Ambrosius and thus, by definition, you are both. To deny one is to deny the other." King Arthur nodded sharply and then headed towards where his horse was being held, prepared to ride out of the fort.

Huw stopped at his father's side. "Is he right?"

"About most everything, in my experience. Who am I to doubt him in this?" Myrddin looked into Huw's face. "We will fight today, perhaps to the death. If the king falls, if I fall, are you prepared to be king? Are you prepared to carry on?"

"I—" Huw cleared his throat. "You know I'm not, but that doesn't mean I won't or that I don't understand that I have to."

Myrddin settled a hand on Huw's shoulder. "I have known you for all of a month, but you are my son, and I couldn't be more proud of who you are and what you have become."

Huw blinked, not wanting to be betrayed by tears.

Myrddin jerked his head towards the center of the courtyard where their own horses waited. "Come. The king needs his cloak before he rides. We must cover his finery until the time is right to unveil it." He started walking and his last words were thrown over his shoulder at Huw. "The king is right about what he said too. I haven't seen your death or mine. Whatever lies in store for us and however this ends, we will end it together."

Modred had come, and Arthur had come, and they would fight to the death in the full light of day on a field of King Arthur's choosing. It was the end that his father had spoken of, but still, Huw wasn't ready, even as he rode at the king's side, and they wended their way through the ramparts that protected Caer Caradoc to the valley below.

Whether because King Arthur planned it that way or because both leaders had an instinctual understanding of when the time was right, both armies arrived on the battlefield within moments of each other: long rows of men with shields, axes, pikes, and swords. Both sides had archers too, and King Arthur and Myrddin arrayed their men to take full advantage of the higher ground they'd claimed. The field was buttressed on the west by rising hills, on the south side by the Long Mynd and Caer Caradoc, and on the eastern side by the Lawley.

The banners the Welsh flew were many and varied. Often in the past when the Welsh faced a Saxon army (with the notable exception of King Arthur's victory at Mt. Badon), lords insisted on leading their own archers and spearmen, each lord's army fighting as a discrete unit. Today King Arthur had convinced his captains that they would need to fight as one—one army, one people. Men from Gwynedd rubbed shoulders with those from Powys or Ceredigion, though there were few enough of the latter.

Modred, by contrast, did not have a blended army. On the far left, Huw could see the banners of Urien. As promised, he had chosen Modred's side. Huw recognized other banners too, though Lord Cedric's were not among them. To Huw's great disappointment, he had not come at all.

The archers had been deployed to the two flanks of the main body of Arthur's spearmen, who stood shoulder to shoulder, shield to shield, as Britons had been taught to do by the Romans who ruled them for so long, facing Modred's force. Each archer had a bow, a quiver, and a sharpened staff, which he planted in front of him at an angle, pointing towards Modred's lines in case Modred ordered his men to charge. Any horse or man would balk at taking on such a forest of points.

The field was bowl-shaped, and Arthur's archers had claimed the east rim, which also happened to be wooded, though the trees provided little cover in December. It was some two hundred yards from the center of the field—easy shooting distance for an archer, even a less accomplished one. Anwen had taken up a position somewhere over there, a fact Huw was trying not to think about lest his fear for her distract him from his own fight.

Huw had expected Modred to want to talk before fighting, but the pause as the two armies looked at one another lasted only a few heartbeats before Modred raised his hand above his head. "Mercia!"

With a roar, the Saxons charged, as they were known to do—without order, without design, just with a wild-eyed madness that had driven the Welsh from the field time and again. This time, however, the Welsh lines held, and the Saxons had run only twenty yards before the first arrows struck them.

The front line went down, but those in the rear of the Saxon force had no idea what was happening in the front, and the second line of men ran straight over them, pushed by those behind them. Everyone was running forward, swords and axes high or spears at the ready. The Saxons had defeated the Welsh so many times in the past that they had no thought that this time should be any different.

But this time was different, if only because, for once, the Welsh knew they had nowhere to run, and if their lines broke, their way of life was ended.

"Brace yourselves!" Myrddin's voice rang out from somewhere in front of Huw and to his left.

Huw and Arthur were with the cavalry at the rear, as was the custom of kings. It wouldn't do for Arthur to go down in the first assault. If opportunity arose, they would fight on horseback, but if they tried to do so now, they would end up running over and through their own men, just as the Saxon foot soldiers were doing. The Saxons had men to spare, however, and even with the addition of the survivors of Buellt, whom Geraint and Gawain led, the Welsh couldn't afford huge losses today. Or any losses, for that matter.

Huw's head moved this way and that, trying to pay attention to everything at once. He and the king sat on a slight rise, so they could see above the bulk of the men. The archers on both sides of the field were firing at will now. Modred might be half-Briton, but his men were almost exclusively Saxon, and there were fewer archers among them. It wasn't that Saxons didn't know how to shoot a bow, but the common man didn't practice with the regularity of Britons, and thus the bow was less used as a weapon of war. Regardless of their numbers, however, the press of bodies on both sides was so close that the archers, of whatever allegiance, could hardly miss.

Initially, Arthur's archers shot in an orderly fashion, but now the opposing armies fought so close together that the archers had lost the advantage of their position. Many pulled their spears from the ground in preparation for the need to hold off the Saxons with them, were any to decide to flank the main body of the army by going through the archers.

King Arthur saw the problem. He pointed towards the line on the right, at the base of the Lawley. "Go, Huw! Tell the archers to head north. We need them to keep shooting! If they can flank the Saxon army, they can fire right into their backs."

"Yes, my lord!" Huw's horse leapt away. This was why he and the king had stayed out of the initial fight, since someone needed to be able to see the whole of the battlefield. It had been left to Myrddin, among others of King Arthur's captains, to lead the men—and to be seen leading them. Men found courage to fight in the face of terrible odds when their captains fought beside them.

Huw rode around the rear of his own force in order to reach the archers' lines, located three hundred yards to the north. He pulled up behind these lines and swung his sword around his head to get the attention of the captain, a man named Morgan. "Follow me! We must flank them to the northeast!"

Like King Arthur, Morgan had fought in enough battles to instantly understand what Huw wanted the archers to do. "Leave the stakes and come with me!"

As one, five hundred men and women drove their spears back into the ground and ran after Huw and Morgan. Anwen wasn't among them since she'd taken up a position on the other side of the valley, and he spared another thought for her and her party of archers, hoping that Urien's forces hadn't gone through them.

Huw leapt a stone wall and navigated through the woods alongside the column, his horse weaving in and among the trees. He glanced to his left, trying to pay attention both to where he was going and what was happening on the field. Regrettably, because Huw was moving the archers, the Saxons no longer had to fear their arrows, and the absence emboldened them. They surged forward with renewed effort, and as Huw gasped and reined in, the center of the Welsh line folded in on itself.

A river of Saxons poured through the gap and curved around to attack the rear of the Welsh force, much like Arthur had hoped his archers would do to the Saxons. Most of the Welsh fighters took a moment to notice that the Saxons were now behind them and still pressed forward, unaware that they'd been flanked. To make matters worse, with a roar, the vanguard of the Saxon force, which had been holding back just as Arthur's reinforcements had been holding back, raced forward, screaming their war cries to the sky.

Although Myrddin had set himself near the center of the line of spearmen, he hadn't fallen, and it was with huge relief that Huw heard his father's voice echo across the field. "Reform the line! To me! To me!"

At the same time, King Arthur himself gave a mighty cry: "Charge!"

His heart in his throat, Huw could only watch as the cavalry, which like the Saxon reserves had been held back behind the main force on the chance that this very opportunity presented itself, drove forward. At first Huw had eyes only for the king, but then the banners that flew above the heads of the men riding with him drew his attention. Geraint's wolf on a white background was clearly visible, but beside it flew Cedric's swans and the blue and white standard of Edgar. Huw didn't know how Edgar and Cedric had managed it, but they had come—and come just in time.

Side by side with King Arthur, they urged their horses towards the gaping hole in the Welsh line—and right over the Saxon foot soldiers who'd dared to fill it. The Saxon spearmen on the other side of the shield wall braced themselves to confront the oncoming horsemen. Horses whinnied and men screamed as they two armies collided. Many British horses went down on Saxon spears, and while many Saxons fell to the thundering hooves, it wasn't enough. More Saxons came on, including, finally, Modred himself, leading a cavalry charge of his own.

Huw couldn't bear to be so far from the action. With a wave at Morgan, who was perfectly capable of arranging his archers without Huw's help, Huw raced to join his father and the king. So desperate was he to reach the spot where his father was fighting that he hardly even noticed when he killed his first Saxon, slicing through the back of a spearman who was attempting to move around the outside of the Welsh line.

And then another great shout went up from the center of the field. Again it was King Arthur: "Hold! Hold, I say!"

Chapter Fourteen
17 December 537 AD
Nell

SOMEHOW MODRED AND King Arthur had found each other, and Nell had to believe that with fifteen thousand men on the field, their meeting was deliberate. They had sought each other out—Modred because he wanted to personally kill King Arthur, and Arthur because he believed that to take on Modred man-to-man was far nobler than losing thousands of men on both sides because of their personal disagreement.

Two kings meeting on the field of battle was an ancient means of settling a dispute over territory. That the two men hadn't chosen this route earlier testified to their mutual uncertainty that either one would survive it. This contest would not be to first blood, but to the death. The war had gone on too long for there to be any other outcome.

Once King Arthur had sent his command echoing across the field, Modred had ordered his men to hold as well. Slowly and with great deliberation, King Arthur dismounted from his horse and paced forward to stand across from where Modred had reined in, staring at him across sixty feet of cleared space. Nell's heart was in her throat as she watched from her vantage point on a small hill below the Lawley. Her view of what was going on before her was terrifyingly unimpeded.

Then Anwen reined beside her. "Come with me!"

Nell had left the safety of the fort itself because she couldn't see well enough from there. After thirty years of dreaming, if her husband and son were going to die today, she couldn't stand to be far away when it happened. Nell reached up to grasp Anwen's hand and scrambled onto the horse's back behind the girl.

Snorting at the smell of blood and fear, Anwen's horse picked its way across the field, which was littered with the dead and wounded, towards the great ring of men that had formed to observe the fight. Even if the horse had a mind to balk, Anwen wasn't taking no for an answer, and she clicked her tongue and prodded him with her heels to keep him moving.

"Stay back." Modred's voice carried all the way across the valley. He threw out a hand to reinforce his command to expand the circle. Dismounting too, he stepped away from his horse, his eyes fixed on Arthur. "So it comes to this, old man."

"As it should," Arthur said, "as we've always known it would."

The circle around the two kings widened. Nell had seen Huw racing into the middle of the battlefield towards the place Myrddin stood, ten paces away from the king, holding the reins of King Arthur's horse. Like Anwen and Nell, Huw dodged through the army of men, many of whom were too exhausted to do more than weave on their feet, though they made way for him.

Anwen had seen Myrddin too and urged the horse in that direction, circling around behind the front rows of onlookers. They reached Myrddin nearly at the same time Huw did.

Myrddin had put out a hand to his son to bring him into the circle of his arm, but then his eyes widened as he spied Nell and Anwen atop her horse. "You shouldn't be here."

"I could be nowhere else." Nell dropped from the horse's back. "As with everything we've done, we will see this through together."

Myrddin's attention returned to the king, but Nell inspected Huw up and down. He had blood on his surcoat. "You are hurt?"

"I'm not, but father is." Huw indicated the gash near Myrddin's left ear, which had bled profusely, covering his left shoulder with blood.

Myrddin made a dismissive motion with his fingers, his eyes still on the king. "It is numb only." He appeared to be talking about his left arm, which hung uselessly at his side. His fingers were all that he could move. "The bracer saved me from losing it below the elbow. I think the leather contains a hidden metal plate. I will have to thank Urien when I see him."

Nell didn't laugh. Neither did Huw nor Anwen, though all understood that Myrddin was making light of his injury as a way to counteract the tension in the air. While Nell had been talking to Myrddin and Huw, Modred and King Arthur had been circling the interior rim of the arena.

As always, Modred seemed to like the sound of his own voice. "Agravaine foresaw your death, old man."

"Since he did not see his own, I wouldn't necessarily believe everything he told you," King Arthur said. "His *sight* was obviously limited."

Modred pressed his lips together, irritated by the truth of Arthur's words, and Nell had a moment of silent pride that she followed a great man rather than the petty child Modred had grown to be. She had known what Modred was before she'd rescued Myrddin from Rhuddlan Castle, and everything that had happened since then had only reassured her of her choices. Modred had gained power by being more ruthless than any of his rivals, but that didn't make him fit to lead. The Welsh might lose. They might ultimately bow to him—but they wouldn't willingly follow.

"I hear that you sought to disinherit me, your rightful successor, by claiming a different heir. He is here?"

King Arthur actually laughed. "You heard that I have an heir but not his name?"

Modred made an impatient gesture with one hand.

King Arthur tipped his head in Myrddin's direction. "He's just there, Modred. You know him, though not by his full name. He is Myrddin ap Ambrosius."

By now the king had paced halfway around the circle and had reached a point directly opposite Myrddin and Nell. The men of Modred's army could have broken the contract with Arthur by attacking him from behind, but they didn't. It seemed Saxons had some honor, even if they fought for Modred. Then again, Gawain and Geraint, along with many of their men, had inserted themselves within the Saxon ranks, such that Saxon and British intermingled all around the circle. If the battle descended again into hand-to-hand, there would be no lines, no shield wall, only carnage.

Modred didn't look behind him to where Myrddin and Huw were standing, but simply kept moving around the edge of the circle until he was able to see them out of the corner of his eye to his right. He barked a laugh. "Ambrosius fathered Myrddin? You have proof?"

"I do." Cedric stepped to the edge of the circle just far enough to separate him from the ring of men.

"And I." Gareth lifted a hand.

"I am surrounded by traitors," Modred said.

"You are surrounded by men who defend their land and their lives against an invader. Mercia has no claim to Wales, nephew, and the moment you chose to lead an army of Saxons against your king, against your own people, you were lost."

The two kings had started out speaking in Welsh, but Arthur's last words had been in English, for the benefit of his Saxon listeners. A murmur of discontent swept among them, which King Arthur noticed.

He held up a hand, and Nell saw that he not only still wore his cloak to hide his armor, but also a surcoat. He couldn't disguise the levered metal on his arm, however, though Modred hadn't yet taken note of it. "Saxon friends, I never wanted this war, and if you fight for Modred because you believe him to be the rightful heir to the throne of Wales, then know that the true heir stands before you: he is Myrddin, son of King Ambrosius, who ruled before me. His claim to the throne is, in fact, greater than mine."

Here the king canted his head. "And if you care little for kingship or right of inheritance but fight because you want our land, I say that we will resist, and we will keep on resisting to the last breath of the last Briton, who would rather die than give up his language, his laws, or his land."

In the silence that followed, King Arthur set down his shield so it leaned against his thigh, reached up to his throat, and undid the toggles that bound his cloak closed at the throat and chest. As the cloak dropped to the ground, he also pulled off his surcoat, revealing the full glory of his armor. And then, just as it had on the battlement, the sun came out from behind a cloud and shone down on the scene. The fight had begun at dawn, and now it was noon, so the sun was as overhead as it could be on a winter day in Britain. Though stained with the blood of the men Arthur had killed, Caledfwlch shone with equal brilliance in his hand.

Modred bared his teeth. "You harbor a thief among your retinue, uncle. But it makes no difference—"

Between one heartbeat and the next, he attacked, leaping the distance that separated him from the king and bringing his sword down with all his strength. King Arthur barely reacted in time, grasping his shield and bringing it up to block the blow. They were on the edge of the circle, and the people behind King Arthur gave way to afford him room to stumble backwards as he twisted away from Modred. In a flurry of attacking blows, Modred's sword came down again and again on the king's shield, such that all he could do was retreat around the circle, very much on his heels.

King Arthur's shield was made of wood, and it shattered, but rather than toss it aside, Arthur threw it at Modred, who barely got his own shield up in time to knock it away. Then, a knife in his hand to replace the lost shield, King Arthur leapt forward in imitation of how Modred had sprung on him, hammering blows of his own. Modred resisted, retreating as King Arthur had retreated. And in the same moment that King Arthur landed a brutal blow with his sword on Modred's shield, he unexpectedly sliced under Modred's guard with the knife in his left hand, opening a gash in the middle of Modred's thigh.

Modred spun away with a grunt of pain. He'd thought himself the cat and Arthur the mouse. He'd been almost laughing beneath his shield as he'd retreated, thinking himself the superior swordsman. The wound wasn't mortal, of course, and he responded with a renewal of his earlier fury, delivering blow after blow, many of which Arthur only just managed to evade. Then Modred swept his own blade from right to left, intending to cut through Arthur's midsection as Arthur had cut through Modred's thigh. Rather than slicing through Arthur's chain mail to reach his skin, however, Modred's sword rebounded off the solid metal of King Arthur's cuirass.

King Arthur leapt backwards into the middle of the arena. Recovering quickly, Modred started after him, but both men were breathing hard, and Modred was limping from the gash in his thigh. At some point during the fight, Modred's shield had also cracked, so he tossed it towards where Arthur's shattered shield lay, after which he pulled a knife from a sheath at his waist to match Arthur. "You think your armor will save you? I say it's a cheat!"

Beside Nell, Myrddin scoffed, and he lifted his chin in order to call out across the ring. "What would it have been if you'd been wearing it, Modred?"

Modred's eyes narrowed, and Nell could see him wondering if it had been Myrddin himself who'd taken it.

King Arthur, however, straightened. "You think I cheat by wearing what you would have worn?" He canted his head. "So be it. I will remove my armor if you remove yours."

Nell, Huw, and Myrddin started forward at the exact same moment. "No, no, no—"

Modred threw out a hand. "Stay back! You will not aid him!"

Arthur held out his hand too, though much less menacingly. "Do as he says, Myrddin. Nell can help me."

Nell swallowed hard, but she crossed the thirty feet of trampled grass and mud that separated them. The snow was long gone here, and the day had warmed under the noon sun such that she was almost hot in her many layers of clothing and wool cloak. Gareth stepped forward to hold the king's sword and knife for him, and as Arthur took off his helmet, she saw that he was sweating. The king held his arms out at his sides in preparation for Nell's assistance in taking off his gear.

Nell spoke in an undertone. "My lord, this isn't a good idea. It's what we saw—"

"No, my dear, it isn't. Modred wore this armor in the dream. Now neither of us will have it, and it will be a test of true strength." Arthur smiled gently. "God is with me, Nell, in life and death. You must know by now that sometimes the only way out of peril is through it."

Shaking her head, though she did know his words for truth, Nell worked at the fastenings on the king's shoulder armor and chest plate.

Modred, meanwhile, with the help of a young Saxon squire, shed his mail and padding. Finally, both men stood in only shirt, breeches, and boots. Far less encumbered than before, they set themselves opposite one another. Nell retreated to Myrddin's side. She slipped her hand into his, and he squeezed it. "Do not fear, *cariad*."

And amazingly, Nell found that she did not. As he crouched in a fighting stance before Modred, the King Arthur who was the embodiment of every legend ever told about him was revealed. Here was the warrior who'd led the British in victory after victory. Here was the man who'd inspired an outnumbered and beleaguered army for three days at Mt. Badon. Here was the king who'd kept the Saxons at bay for thirty years. He was an old man now, but the spirit inside him that had inspired the victory over the Saxons at Mt. Badon—against all odds—was the same.

The two men attacked at the same time. In a flurry of movements, they countered sword with sword, blocking, slashing, and driving back and forth across the clearing. Unlike before, at no point did one man seem to have the upper hand. Even when King Arthur nicked Modred's upper arm with his knife, drawing more blood, Modred ignored it, instead swinging his sword downward for another slash at Arthur's belly. Arthur leapt out of the way, but as he landed, his heel sank into a hole in the uneven ground, and he sprawled flat on his back.

Modred pounced, bringing down his sword in a killing blow, except Arthur rolled away at the last instant. Nell acknowledged that if King Arthur had been wearing his armor, he might not have been as agile. Perhaps at Arthur's age, the loss of the armor's weight was more to his advantage than to Modred's.

Arthur came up from the ground in a crouch, sword and knife again in hand, but this time his sword was in his left hand and the knife in his right. As Modred brought down his sword as he'd done dozens of times so far in the fight, Arthur met the blow not with the knife blade, but with the sword, in a countering move so powerful and which swept upward with such force that Modred's sword was flung from his hand. The weapon flew through the air and landed fifteen feet away.

Shocked silence greeted the move. For a moment, Modred was off balance and as surprised as everyone else to find himself disarmed. Arthur used that instant of distraction to lash out with his right boot to Modred's left knee. The awful crunch of a broken kneecap could be heard across the field. Gasping in pain, Modred collapsed to the ground, though he still had the presence of mind to scrabble for his sword, dragging his useless left leg behind him. Arthur calmly strode over to the fallen sword and kicked it towards Gareth. It slid across the grass, and Gareth took one step out of the ring of onlookers in order to stand with his foot on the blade.

Modred spoke through gritted teeth: "Mercia will win in the end. One day there will be no more Wales."

"One day perhaps," King Arthur said, "but not today."

Modred's profile as he looked up at Arthur was all Nell could see, and that was fortunate because the angle allowed her to see the moment Modred flung his knife—not at Arthur, who would have been ready for it—but at Myrddin. The knife revolved end over end, its aim true, straight to Myrddin's heart.

Nell cried a warning, but Huw, who was standing on his father's right side, had already reacted. He brought up his shield, which he'd continued to hold in his left hand during the fight, and blocked the knife. The point stuck in the shield two inches from the rim, quivering.

Myrddin gripped Huw's shoulder tightly, in thanks and relief, but even with the gasps and cries from those surrounding them, the attention of both men never left the scene before them. King Arthur's eyes had followed the path of the knife, and the moment he saw that Myrddin was safe, he bent to relieve Modred of his last weapon, a knife in his boot. Then he circled the wounded Modred, who glared at him from the ground.

"You don't have the mettle to kill me, do you?"

Arthur pressed his lips together and almost seemed to sigh as he looked down at his wayward nephew. "You are right that I never wanted it to come to this, Modred. But you are wrong about how it ends." He put his boot into Modred's chest to force him completely flat onto his back. Then straddling Modred with a foot on either side of his torso, King Arthur raised his sword. "What you never understood was that for Wales, there's nothing I wouldn't do."

And he drove Caledfwlch straight down into Modred's heart.

Chapter Fifteen

17 December 537 AD
Myrddin

MYRDDIN WOULDN'T HAVE thought it possible for an entire battlefield to be completely silent, but for several heartbeats, this one was. Then, before the Saxons could coordinate themselves to renew the attack, if that was what they had in mind, Gawain, Gareth, and Geraint leapt into the clearing on either side of the king, followed by Cedric and Edgar, both again on horseback. Cedric stood in the stirrups, his sword swinging around above his head, and he shouted, "Stay back and lower your weapons. This battle is over!"

Perhaps it wasn't surprising that it was Cedric who had acted. One of the drawbacks to having a capricious and powerful ruler like Modred as lord was that he tended to slap down—or kill—anyone who was powerful in his own right, seeing him as a threat. Modred had allowed Agravaine to live, but Agravaine had enjoyed staying in the shadows and hadn't wanted the kind of power Modred craved. Even if Agravaine still lived, he wouldn't have stepped forward now. He would have gone around to Cedric and Edgar, after they'd taken charge, to attempt to manipulate them into doing what he wanted.

As it was, however, Agravaine was dead, and Modred's captains were shocked and angry. They would have fought—slaughtered everyone on the field out of mindless rage—but Cedric outranked every one of them, and even if he had fought on Arthur's side today, he had lived for all but the last day among them, as one of their lords.

Perhaps Urien of Rheged would have been the one to disobey, especially since he was British, not Saxon, but he was not of those who either defended the king or put himself forward to take charge of the Saxon army.

Nell stood on tiptoe beside Myrddin. "Did Urien withdraw?"

"He was here earlier. I saw his banners on Modred's right flank." Huw stood with his arm around Anwen's shoulders.

Myrddin glanced at his son, a small smile on his lips at how that might play out in future, and said, "I called him Urien the Betrayer. And so he will be known."

"No, he won't." Urien edged between two Welshmen just to Myrddin's right and stepped into the ring of men. He held his sword flat across his palms. Gawain and Gareth allowed him to within ten feet of the king, at which point, Urien went down on one knee and held out his sword. "Please know that my men did not kill a single Briton today. Although I came here to fight with Modred, my son convinced me of the error of my ways. Once the battle started I held my men back." He looked up into Arthur's face. "I am a stubborn old fool, Arthur. Please forgive me."

Myrddin might have made a comment about how Urien's behavior revealed him to be a double betrayer—of Arthur *and* Modred—but Arthur was more forgiving. He looked down at Urien for the space of a single breath, and then he stepped forward to grasp the hilt of Urien's sword. "You are forgiven, old friend." He reversed the sword and handed it hilt first back to Urien. "You and I are too old, and Britain in too great a need, to hold a grudge."

Myrddin held his breath, because this was the moment Urien could have driven his sword through Arthur's midsection, armorless as the king was, but Urien didn't. Owain appeared at Myrddin's side, nudging his shoulder with his own. "I see you reached the key."

"Nell did." Myrddin gave a low laugh. How many times in his life had help come from unexpected places? It seemed, here on the battlefield of Camlann, amidst the carnage and the bodies of the fallen, King Arthur truly had achieved peace.

Owain went to join his father in his obeisance to Arthur, but Myrddin turned away from the scene. His put his arm around Nell's shoulders, more exhausted than he'd ever been in his life, and pulled her to him. All he wanted was to sleep and not dream. With Nell tucked close to his side, he took a step towards where he remembered leaving his horse ... and came face-to-face with his old friend, Ifan, whom he hadn't seen since before the battle of Buellt.

He pulled up short, and it seemed that Ifan was feeling a similar uncertainty because he stared at Myrddin for a heartbeat. But then he bowed low. "My lord."

Something inside Myrddin broke loose at that. Releasing Nell, he strode forward and grasped his friend by the shoulders to raise him up. "Don't do that."

Ifan met his eyes. "You are Arthur's heir. You will be high king one day."

"I am Myrddin, your friend for twenty years."

"You are Ambrosius's *son*."

"I didn't know."

Ifan ducked his head in acknowledgement of that truth. "Gareth told us."

The two men gazed at each other for a long moment, neither knowing what to say. Then Myrddin raised one shoulder in a rueful gesture. "I will find myself surrounded by new friends in the coming days and weeks. It would be nice to know that the man I fought beside my whole life, who knew me before all this—" Myrddin gestured to the battlefield, but he meant so much more, "—is still my friend."

Nell gave a low cry from behind him, but Myrddin refused to turn and look at her out of fear that he wouldn't be able to stop his own tears from falling.

Ifan hesitated, looking warier than ever. "Likely being your friend means I'll continue to be stuck with the tasks you don't want."

Relief flooded through Myrddin at the familiar banter. "What are you complaining about now?"

Ifan pointed with his chin to a point somewhere off to the left. "I've had to be nursemaid to your brother while you've been adventuring about the countryside without me."

"Foster brother," Myrddin said, unable to hold back a huge grin. "Come here."

Ifan more than obeyed, wrapping Myrddin up in a hug worthy of a bear and lifting him off his feet.

Once Ifan set him down again and Myrddin got his breath back, he said, "I'd have you as the captain of my *teulu*, if you are willing."

Ifan's eyes lit, and then he looked past Myrddin to Nell. "See that, my lady? All the tasks he doesn't want."

THE AFTERNOON HAD BEEN spent in the burying of the dead and the succoring of the wounded. Once night had fallen, however, grief had given way to feasting and song. As the last hastily arranged paean to Arthur ended, the king nudged Myrddin's elbow. "Come with me."

Huw and Anwen were deep in conversation with Cador, and an exhausted Nell had retired to a tent, one pitched not far from the pavilion in which they were feasting. There wasn't enough room on the dais in Cador's hall to accommodate the many lords present—and certainly not enough space in the hall for their men. Thus, because all the men who'd come to Camlann needed the opportunity to celebrate with their king, Cador had ordered the pantries of Caer Caradoc emptied and the feast established at the base of the mountain.

As Myrddin and Arthur stepped outside the pavilion, though it didn't feel terribly cold and there was no wind, snow began to fall in thick flakes. Both already had their hoods up, and Arthur turned towards one of the fire pits. Thinking Arthur's plan was to walk among the men, as he used to do long ago, Myrddin pulled his cloak closer around himself and went with him.

But this time there was no fooling the men among whom they passed. Each group they reached stood in turn, bowed, and called out "My lords!" or "Arthur!" A few even said Myrddin's name, which prompted a low laugh from both Myrddin and Arthur.

When they reached the margins of the camp, Arthur kept going away from the light and towards the ruins of the battlefield. They walked some ways through the churned and muddy sod, now hardening with ice in the cold. After a hundred yards, Myrddin realized where they were going. He hesitated in mid-stride, wanting to protest, but King Arthur kept walking. Finally, another fifty yards on, the king stopped. "This is it. This is where I killed him." The king looked down at the ground and dug his boot into the earth.

Slowly, Myrddin approached. The snow that was falling had started to stick, covering the ground with white. It was only because the light from the camp reflected off the snow and the low clouds that they could see anything at all, but Myrddin didn't need to see Modred's blood to know that he'd lost his life there.

"Do you regret his death?" Myrddin said.

"I regret his life," Arthur said. "I never wanted to kill him."

"I know."

Turning together, they surveyed the huge and sprawling camp, Saxon mixing with British on Arthur's orders.

With Modred dead, the fight had gone out of the Saxons. It wasn't even as if Arthur had conquered a huge swath of Saxon territory. The boundaries between Saxon lands and British ones would remain much the same as before. The Saxons had lost their leader. That was all. The Welsh hadn't been fighting to evict the Saxons from their homes. They had simply not wanted to lose their own.

Still, while the Britons remained wary to have so many Saxons among them this night, refraining even from excessive mead on the off-chance that the peace was merely a ruse, what lay before Myrddin and Arthur was a dream come true—and not a sight Myrddin had ever seen in any dream or vision.

"Have you decided what you're going to do?" Arthur said.

Myrddin turned his head to look at the king. "Do?"

"You and Nell. Earlier you struggled with the idea that you could be both king and seer. Will you not take the throne when I am dead?"

"Must we speak of this now? Can't we enjoy the victory?"

"This was my last battle, Myrddin. You and I both know that age is upon me. Whatever conflict lies ahead, it will be for you and Huw to lead our people."

Myrddin licked his lips, trying to put into words the understanding he and Nell had come to at the end of the battle—almost without knowing it. "I will serve you as long as you live, and I will stand in your place when you no longer wear the crown, but—" he shook his head, "—I was not born to be a king."

"You were, even if you didn't know it."

Myrddin smiled ruefully. "When Huw is ready to take my place, I will step down." He met Arthur's gaze. "Whether I serve Britain as king or seer is of no matter. I swear to you that I will be a caretaker of our people to my last breath."

"There could be no greater legacy of my reign than that." King Arthur put his hand on Myrddin's shoulder, and there were tears in his voice as he spoke. "It was a blessed day when you came to me."

And as the two men gazed across the battlefield towards the festivities, a vision swept across Myrddin's eyes, this one fleeting and not one that brought him to his knees.

HE STOOD IN A CORRIDOR beside a closed door, his head pressed against the planks that made up the wall. Huw sat on a low stool nearby, leaning against the same wall with his legs stretched out in front of him and crossed at the ankles. "She'll be fine, Father. You've seen it."

"The future doesn't always happen the way it appears in my visions. That's the whole point of having them."

"This one will."

And then, for once proving Huw's words true almost as soon as he'd spoken them, a newborn's cry rose up from behind the closed door. Without waiting for the midwife to welcome him inside, Myrddin opened the door and bounded into the room. He stopped cold five paces away from Nell, drinking in the sight of her with a swaddled baby in her arms.

At his entrance, she looked up. Tears tracked down her cheeks and the smile she gave him was tremulous. But the child at her breast was alive and whole, and he found all of a sudden that he could breathe again.

"We have a daughter, my love."

AND AS THE VISION FADED, Myrddin finally understood what the king had meant about living without regard to possible futures. Every man, in the end, had only one.

The End

Thank you for journeying into medieval Wales with me. It's readers like you who make my job the best in the world!
To be notified whenever I have a new release, please see the sidebar of my web page:
www.sarahwoodbury.com[1]
Find me on Facebook:
https://www.facebook.com/sarahwoodburybooks

Continue reading for the opening of *The Good Knight*, the first *Gareth & Gwen Medieval Mystery*, available for *free* at all retailers!
https://www.books2read.com/thegoodknight

Sample: The Good Knight
August, 1143 AD
Gwynedd (North Wales)

"LOOK AT YOU, GIRL."

Gwen's father, Meilyr, tsked under his breath and brought his borrowed horse closer to her side of the path. He'd been out of sorts since early morning when he'd found his horse lame and King Anarawd and his company of soldiers had left the castle without them, refusing to wait for Meilyr to find a replacement mount. Anarawd's men-at-arms would have provided Meilyr with the fine escort he coveted.

"You'll have no cause for complaint once we reach Owain Gwynedd's court." A breeze wafted over Gwen's face, and she closed her eyes, letting her pony find his own way for a moment. "I won't embarrass you at the wedding."

1. http://www.sarahwoodbury.com/

"If you cared more for your appearance, you would have been married yourself years ago and given me grandchildren long since."

Gwen opened her eyes, her forehead wrinkling in annoyance. "And whose fault is it that I'm unmarried?" Her fingers flexed about the reins, but she forced herself to relax. Her present appearance was her own doing, even if her father found it intolerable. In her bag, she had fine clothes and ribbons to weave through her hair, but saw no point in sullying any of them on the long journey to Aber Castle.

King Owain Gwynedd's daughter was due to marry King Anarawd in three days' time. Owain Gwynedd had invited Gwen, her father, and her almost twelve-year old brother, Gwalchmai, to furnish the entertainment for the event, provided King Owain and her father could bridge the six years of animosity and silence that separated them. Meilyr had sung for King Owain's father, Gruffydd; he'd practically raised King Owain's son, Hywel. But six years was six years. No wonder her father's temper was short.

Even so, she couldn't let her father's comments go. Responsibility for the fact that she had no husband rested firmly on his shoulders. "Who refused the contract?"

"Rhys was a rapscallion and a laze-about," Meilyr said.

And you weren't about to give up your housekeeper, maidservant, cook, and child-minder to just anyone, were you?

But instead of speaking, Gwen bit her tongue and kept her thoughts to herself. She'd said it once and received a slap to her face. Many nights she'd lain quiet beside her younger brother, regretting that she hadn't defied her father and stayed with Rhys. They could have eloped; in seven years, their marriage would have been as legal as any other. But her father was right, and Gwen wasn't too proud to admit it: Rhys *had* been a laze-about. She wouldn't have been happy with him. Rhys's father had almost cried when Meilyr had refused Rhys's offer. It wasn't only daughters who were sometimes hard to sell.

"Father!" Gwalchmai brought their cart to a halt. "Come look at this!"

"What now?" Meilyr said. "We'll have to spend the night at Caerhun at present rate. You know how important it is not to keep King Owain waiting."

"But Father!" Gwalchmai leapt from the cart and ran forward.

"He's serious." Gwen urged her pony after him, passing the cart, and then abruptly reined in beside her brother. "*Mary, Mother of God...*"

A slight rise and sudden dip in the path ahead had hidden the carnage until they were upon it. Twenty men and an equal number of horses lay dead in the road, their bodies contorted and their blood soaking the brown earth. Gwalchmai bent forward and retched into the grass beside the road. Gwen's stomach threatened to undo her too, but she fought the bile down and dismounted to wrap her arms around her brother.

Meilyr reined in beside his children. "Stay back."

Gwen glanced at her father and then back to the scene, noticing for the first time a man kneeling among the wreckage, one hand to a dead man's chest and the other resting on the hilt of his sheathed sword. The man straightened and Gwen's breath caught in her throat.

Gareth.

He'd cropped his dark brown hair shorter than when she'd known him, but his blue eyes still reached into the core of her. Her heart beat a little faster as she drank him in. Five years ago, Gareth had been a man-at-arms in the service of Prince Cadwaladr, King Owain Gwynedd's brother. Gareth and Gwen had become friends, and then more than friends, but before he could ask her father for her hand, Gareth had a falling out with Prince Cadwaladr. In the end, Gareth hadn't been able to persuade Meilyr that he could support her despite his lack of station.

Gwen was so focused on Gareth that she wasn't aware of the other men among them—live ones—until they approached her family. A half dozen converged on them at the same time. One caught her upper arm in a tight grip. Another grabbed Meilyr's bridle. "Who are you?" the soldier said.

Meilyr stood in the stirrups and pointed a finger at Gareth. "Tell them who I am!"

Gareth came forward, his eyes flicking from Meilyr to Gwalchmai to Gwen. He was broader in the shoulders too, than she remembered.

"They are friends," Gareth said. "Release them."

And to Gwen's astonishment, the man-at-arms who held her obeyed Gareth. Could it be that in the years since she'd last seen him, Gareth had regained something of what he'd lost?

Gareth halted by Meilyr's horse. "I was sent from Aber to meet King Anarawd and escort him through Gwynedd. He wasn't even due to arrive at Dolwyddelan Castle until today, but—" He gestured to the men on the ground. "Clearly, we were too late."

Gwen looked past Gareth to the murdered men in the road.

"Turn away, Gwen," Gareth said.

But Gwen couldn't. The blood—on the dead men, on the ground, on the knees of Gareth's breeches—mesmerized her. The men here had been *slaughtered*. Her skin twitched at the hate in the air. "You mean King Anarawd is—is—is among them?"

"The King is dead," Gareth said.

The Good Knight is available for *free* at all retailers.
https://www.books2read.com/thegoodknight

Also by Sarah Woodbury

Après Cilmeri
Une Fille du Temps
Premiers Pas dans le Temps
Le Tourbillon du Temps
Le Prince du Temps

Godfrid the Dane Medieval Mysteries
Godfrid the Dane Medieval Mysteries Boxed Set

The After Cilmeri Series
Daughter of Time
Footsteps in Time
Winds of Time
Prince of Time
Crossroads in Time
Children of Time
Exiles in Time
Castaways in Time
Ashes of Time
Warden of Time

Guardians of Time
Masters of Time
Outpost in Time
Shades of Time
Champions of Time
This Small Corner of Time
Refuge in Time
Unbroken in Time
Outcasts in Time
The After Cilmeri Series Duo: Footsteps in Time & Prince of Time
The After Cilmeri Series Boxed Set

The Gareth & Gwen Medieval Mysteries
The Bard's Daughter
The Good Knight
The Uninvited Guest
The Fourth Horseman
The Fallen Princess
The Unlikely Spy
The Lost Brother
The Renegade Merchant
The Unexpected Ally
The Worthy Soldier
The Favored Son
The Viking Prince
The Irish Bride
The Prince's Man
The Gareth & Gwen Medieval Mysteries Boxed Set
The Gareth & Gwen Medieval Mysteries Books 1-7

The Last Pendragon Saga
The Last Pendragon
The Pendragon's Blade
Song of the Pendragon
The Pendragon's Quest
The Pendragon's Champions
Rise of the Pendragon
The Pendragon's Challenge
Legend of the Pendragon
The Last Pendragon Saga: The Complete Series (Books 1-8)

The Last Pendragon Saga Boxed Set
The Last Pendragon Saga Volume 1
The Last Pendragon Saga Volume 2
The Last Pendragon Saga Volume 3

The Lion of Wales
Cold My Heart
The Oaken Door
Of Men and Dragons
A Long Cloud
Frost Against the Hilt
The Lion of Wales: The Complete Series (Books 1-5)

The Paradisi Chronicles
Erase Me Not

The Welsh Guard Mysteries
Crouchback

Was nach Cilmeri geschah
Tochter der Zeit
Spuren in der Zeit

Standalone
Heroes of Medieval Wales
From Many Cultures, One Nation: Ethnicity and Nationalism in Belizean Children
Medieval to Modern: An Anthology of Historical Mystery Stories
Legends of Wales
Guardians of Medieval Wales (Four First-in-Series Historical Romances)

Watch for more at www.sarahwoodbury.com.

Lightning Source UK Ltd.
Milton Keynes UK
UKHW040740010223
416301UK00004B/292